'The kind of classic that rings with beauty and conviction and heart-stopping emotion' Amanda Craig

'This is McKay at her finest, all the heart and warmth of the Casson family books – with a touch of the Cazalets. It's both a thrilling family adventure and a truthful, heart-breaking examination of the impact of war . . . [an] exceptional historical novel' Fiona Noble, *The Bookseller*, Children's Book of the Month

'Wise and kind and utterly heart-wrenching and full of characters you will give your whole heart to' Anna James, author of *Pages & Co*

'Hilary McKay is surely the heir to Mary Wesley. *The Skylarks' War* is just lovely' Charlotte Eyre, *The Bookseller*

'The best children's book I've read this year' Katherine Rundell

Also by Hilary McKay
from Macmillan Children's Books

The Skylarks' War
Winner of the Costa Children's Book Award

THE CASSON FAMILY
(suggested reading order)
Saffy's Angel
Indigo's Star
Permanent Rose
Caddy Ever After
Forever Rose
Caddy's World

THE EXILES SERIES
The Exiles
The Exiles at Home
The Exiles in Love

The Time of Green Magic

Straw into Gold: Fairy Tales Re-spun

HILARY MCKAY

the Swallows' Flight

MACMILLAN CHILDREN'S BOOKS

First published 2021 by Macmillan Children's Books
an imprint of Pan Macmillan
The Smithson, 6 Briset Street, London EC1M 5NR
EU representative: Macmillan Publishers Ireland Limited,
Mallard Lodge, Lansdowne Village, Dublin 4
Associated companies throughout the world
www.panmacmillan.com

ISBN 978-1-5290-3333-5

1 3 5 7 9 8 6 4 2

A CIP catalogue record for this book is available from the British Library.

Printed and bound by CPI Group (UK) Ltd, Croydon CR0 4YY

For Venetia Gosling, who started this
story with a memory from her own family,
and for Molly Ker Hawn, my very lovely agent

You have both been utterly wonderful.

Contents

ONE
Erik and Hans
Berlin, 1931

One summer, when he was ten years old, Erik became famous for buying dead flies.

'Really!' said Hans, who was in the same class at school and had just moved into the apartment below. 'You're always becoming famous for something embarrassing!'

'I know,' admitted Erik, because it did seem a bit that way. The falling off the bridge on the school expedition to the river; his hospital for dolls – he'd fixed one small girl's doll and the news had got round, 'Erik can mend dolls!' and suddenly he'd found himself with a bedroom full of prim china faces not necessarily attached to their bodies.

And now he was buying dead flies.

The reason Erik needed flies was a family of little birds. Their nest had fallen; the fragile shell of dry mud had crumbled and split from the wall and two fledglings had been lost, but three had survived. Erik's *kleine Schwalben,* his little swallows.

He'd tried finding enough flies for them alone, but without having wings himself it seemed impossible. He'd taken a teaspoon to every rose bush within walking distance, scraping

1

off greenfly. Both the baker and the butcher had asked him very forcefully to get out and mind his manners when he'd offered, as politely as he could, to remove the wildlife buzzing in their windows. He'd haunted the rubbish bins at the back of the apartment building. Even so, he couldn't manage to keep up with the swallows' demand, and so he'd recruited his classmates. They naturally said they were not going to spend their spare time collecting flies for nothing, and demanded to be paid.

Erik had paid first in fruit drops, from the box he'd had for his birthday, and next with an assortment of rather chipped marbles, and after that with cigarette cards: scenes of old Berlin, Flags of the World, and his precious Exotic Birds and Animals. He had a few French cards too, mostly pictures of famous film-star girls.

'Girls!' said Hans, scornfully, when he came with his flies to trade. Hans had a sister named Lisa. She was one year younger than Hans, but she was taller than he was, and she bossed him about. Lisa had a hundred friends, or so it seemed to Hans. 'I've enough girls at home.'

'Well then, choose a flag,' suggested Erik, 'or an armadillo or a camel or something.'

Hans said he didn't care about flags, and that the camel and the armadillo had unfriendly faces. In the end he chose a girl after all, one with great waves of hair, and a very small top hat tilted over one eye, not at all like his sister or any of her friends. In return he gave Erik an envelope full of bluebottles, mosquitoes and other small flies. The mosquitoes were squashed and so no use, but the rest were all right. Erik, for about the tenth time that day, explained why squashed were no good, with all the juice wasted.

'You do know everybody is talking about you, don't you?' said Hans.

'Are they?'

'Saying you are crazy!'

'Oh, well, yes.'

'What other cards do you have to trade?'

'I don't really, Hans,' said Erik.

He did have an album of fairy tales cards, collected for him by his mother, long before. He couldn't trade them, because she was still fond of them. Now and then, on winter evenings, she would turn the pages and murmur, 'Yes, I remember,' when she came to the seven swans, or the tin soldier, or whatever. Erik also hoped that he might keep his five Dogs of the World: the German shepherd, the husky, the St Bernard with the little barrel on its collar, the English sheepdog with the smiling face, and the small French poodle. He had owned them for as long as he could remember, given them names and dreamed them stories. They were old friends, and yet . . .

He'd known these swallows since they were eggs: every summer a nest was built above his bedroom window; already the parent birds were building there again. And now Erik had these three.

He kept them in his bedroom, in a box by the open window, snuggled together in his winter hat, which would never be the same again. Hans came to watch his latest delivery of flies disappear.

'More than an hour's work gone in seconds,' he remarked. 'However do these ridiculous birds manage in the wild?'

'Easy,' said Erik. 'They can fly. What I really need is a butterfly net and a very small plane.'

'What you need is my Uncle Karl,' said Hans.

'Why?'

'He can fly. And he's mad, like you. I'll tell him about you, next time I see him. Have you given them names?'

Erik laughed and shook his head, so Hans named them on the spot: Cirrus, Nimbus and Cumulus.

'Cumulus is the fat one,' he said. 'He's my favourite. I shall go and catch his supper right now.'

After that, Hans stopped charging for his flies, and he was a great help to Erik because the little birds were constantly hungry. They were growing so fast that every few hours they seemed to change. Real colours replacing the down. Their pin feathers coming through on their wings. All three of them stronger every day, stretching out a wing, jostling for the next beak-full of food.

'How did you learn to care for them?' asked Hans, and Erik explained that two years before, it had happened just the same, a nest had fallen and he had scooped up a nestling and fed it on baby food. Bread and milk. And it had died. He wouldn't make that mistake again though, he said. Flies, that's what his swallows needed, from four in the morning until darkness at night, flies by the dozen, flies by the hundred, not caught in airy swoops around the rooftops like the parent swallows did, but delivered by a train of helpers

4

with matchboxes, cocoa tins, or sometimes just clenched fists. Up and down the building stairs, driving the occupants mad.

'Wash your hands!' his mother ordered the children, with every new delivery, and sent them to the kitchen sink and made sure they did it properly. The soap wore out and people got so tired of washing they stood under the windows and yelled instead, 'Erik! I brought more flies!'

'How much longer?' asked his mother, and Erik said perhaps a week or a little more.

'A week or a little more!' she groaned and suggested egg yolk, minced sausage and canary seed soaked in water. Erik shook his head. He dared not risk it.

'Well, well,' said his mother. 'I suppose you must do what you can.'

Erik did, although it wasn't easy. To part with the German shepherd, who he'd named Otto after his father who had died before he was born. With dear brave Brandy, hero of so many imaginary snowbound adventures. Comet, the blue-eyed, curly tailed, moonlight-coloured husky. Tessa, the smiling sheepdog. 'Take care of her,' said Erik, as he handed Tessa to her new owner, and there was an aching beneath his ribs that was beginning to feel familiar even though he still had Belle, the little French poodle.

'She's pretty,' said Lisa, who had come to see what all the fuss was about. 'One day I will have a dog like that, with a pom-pom tail and a pink ribbon in her hair.'

Lisa, although nearly always indignant or angry, was also

pretty in a furious kind of way, and Erik gave her Belle, even though Hans disapproved.

'She got exactly what she wanted, then,' he grumbled, when Lisa, clutching Belle, had run away downstairs again.

'Good,' said Erik.

On the fourteenth day after Erik found them, his three swallows flew from his open window, straight from his hand into a bird-filled apricot evening sky, joining dozens of others circling the roofs and eaves and skyways of the city.

Never, ever had Erik known such illuminated joy, such a lift of bliss that it felt as if he could have flown with them.

'Well,' said Hans, who had come to say goodbye to Cumulus and the others. 'That's three more birds in the sky.'

'Yes,' agreed Erik, hanging out of the window to watch. 'Imagine being a swallow. Racing about like that!'

'You'd have to eat flies, though,' pointed out Hans. 'What do you think they taste like?

'Pretzels and lobsters,' said Erik, so matter-of-factly that Hans started shouting and flinging his arms about and exclaiming, 'Erik? You didn't! Hey, tell me you didn't! You can't have! Are you crazy? Are you joking?' Then he stopped jumping about and came up close to look into Erik's face. 'You are joking,' he said. 'Aren't you?'

'Yes.'

Hans pushed his shoulder affectionately. Erik pushed him back. They both, at the same moment, realized how much they liked each other. Hans remembered how Erik had leaned over the bridge and leaned over the bridge and leaned over the bridge, and said, 'Oh, dear,' and vanished with hardly a splash. Erik remembered how quickly Hans had pulled off his jacket to wrap him up when they fished him out again.

'Nutter,' said Hans, catching Erik in a casual headlock.

'Nutter yourself,' said Erik, wriggling out backwards and dumping Hans flat on the floor.

'I wouldn't be surprised if they *did* taste like pretzels and lobsters,' said Hans, thinking about it, stretched out on his back. 'Perhaps you're not so crazy after all. Perhaps one day you will be head keeper at Berlin Zoo.'

'Perhaps,' said Erik, hopefully, once more gazing out of the window. 'Do you know, Hans, those little birds will go to Africa.'

'Oh, here you go again!' said Hans. 'Africa! I was wrong, you really are a nut . . . Hey! Erik!'

Erik's brown curly head was suddenly nodding. He wobbled where he stood, leaning against the comfortable wooden window frame. Only four hours sleep for two weeks and three insatiable babies all day, and now night was coming in over the rooftops.

Hans leaped and grabbed him just before he toppled out of the open window.

'Thank you, Hans,' said Erik.

Two
Ruby
Plymouth, Devon, 1927

R uby was her name, and even that caused trouble. All the girls in the family had flower names – there were Lilies and Daisies and Roses, an Iris and a Violet, once a Marigold. It was a family tradition, unbroken since goodness knew when, until Violet, who was Ruby's mother, said, 'Ruby.'

'Ruby?' asked a whole bunch of flowery relations, gathered in the room above the newsagent's shop. 'Ruby?'

'I like rubies,' said Violet, 'better than diamonds or pearls. I always wanted a ruby.'

'You can't pretend Ruby's a flower name,' said bossy Aunt Rose.

'I wasn't,' said Violet, in a mind-your-own-business voice.

'It's flashy,' said Aunt Lily, who had no tact. 'It'll draw attention.'

'Attention?' repeated Violet, in a tone of such unexploded fury that Aunt Lily took a step back. Even as she retreated though, she couldn't help glancing towards the baby sleeping in the wicker basket, and then, one after another, everyone else in the room glanced too.

Ruby's face was splattered with what looked like dark brown paint. Birthmarks; a large one like a paintbrush had swiped below her left eye, and showers of smaller ones patterning both sides of her face. They were the first thing anyone saw and nobody could say a word to Violet about them that didn't make her angry.

The family discussed it in murmurs when Violet was out of the room. There had been, according to Violet's mother, other babies born in the family with marks just the same. A boy was recalled, fifty years before.

'They said his might fade,' Ruby's grandmother remembered.

'And did they?' demanded Rose.

'He died when he was six or seven, they hadn't faded then.'

'Better not tell Violet,' whispered Iris.

'You can't tell Violet anything,' said Rose.

'I know,' agreed Lily, nodding. 'Ruby! What kind of a—'

'Shush!' hissed everyone, but too late.

'What are you shushing?' demanded Violet, appearing suddenly in the doorway.

A twitching silence followed while people tried to remember what they'd said.

'It's about the baby, isn't it?'

'We were just talking about her name,' said Iris, soothingly. 'I was thinking that there's Clover, and I once heard of a Lavender.'

'Clover is a cow's name and Lavender's for bath salts,' said Violet, witheringly. 'Anyway,' she added, picking up the sleeping baby and rocking her on her shoulder, 'you can all stop fussing because she's going to have a flower name too. Her dad picked it out.'

Violet paused.

'Go on, then,' said Rose.

'Amaryllis.'

'Amaryllis?' repeated the whole bunch, Iris, Rose and Lily. '*Amaryllis?* What in heaven's an amaryllis?'

'I've never *heard* of an amaryllis,' said Ruby's grandmother.

Neither had Violet. The name had been in a library book about gardening. There hadn't been a picture, just a list of 'Rewarding rarities' at the end of a chapter and the lovely word among them: *Amaryllis*, that rang like a chime and a charm. Ruby's father had read it aloud and it had caught Violet's heart.

'Ruby Amaryllis,' she said proudly. 'Her dad's looked it up and everything. He says it's a flower like a lily, but better.'

'It's even fancier than Ruby!' said all the horrified relations.

'Good,' said Violet.

It hadn't stopped there. The christening had been as extravagant as the new baby's name. Violet had sewn white silk into a christening gown and her best friend Clarry had brought from Oxford a shawl of snowflakes in soft white lace. Clarry was to be Ruby's godmother, and she arrived for the christening with other presents too: a rattle with silver bells, and a whole collection of parcels for Ruby's eight-year-old brother, Will.

Will was already sick of the whole business, the fuss, the new clothes he was required to wear, and the bone-deep knowledge that he would never again be loved as exclusively and completely as he had been loved before the arrival of the ugly, wailing baby. Therefore he unwrapped his torch, his book called *The Pirate's Parrot*, his jar of sweets and his box of coloured marbles with very bad grace and when prompted to say thank you, said, 'They're just to shut me up.'

To Will's disappointment, Clarry didn't immediately turn on him in indignation. Instead, she said cheerfully that maybe he would like them later, and nodded in agreement when he said he supposed they'd do for swaps.

All the grown-ups seemed to be amused by him. They talked to him about trains and school and football, as if he cared. He longed to ask if the brown marks made it more likely that the baby would die soon, but he didn't dare in case they guessed his darkest thoughts. His life was ruined, and no one understood. He tried to make himself sick in church but failed.

Ruby Amaryllis grew up in the three little rooms over the newsagent's shop, with her mother and father and Will, who she always treated warily, half ready to run. Plymouth was a naval town, with huge dockyards on the river that had their own train station. Ruby's father was a porter there, riding backwards and forwards on his bicycle every day. He said when Will was old enough he should get a job there, too.

'Catch me!' Will used to exclaim scornfully, whenever this boring idea was suggested. 'I'm going to do something a lot more exciting than that!'

Will was like his mother; tall, with creamy skin and grey-green eyes. There was no understanding between him and

Ruby. She still caused trouble. She was a pest. At school they said, 'What's the matter with your sister's face?' and he said, 'I don't know. It's horrible.'

'You're going red,' they said, and he would set about them with his fists and get in trouble with the teachers.

Ruby thought Will was much worse than a pest. Ruby thought Will was awful, and had done ever since she was five. There was a scullery behind the shop, and that's where she'd been the day that she'd heard his voice, husky and solemn, asking, 'Can I help?'

He had been busy in the backyard with the boy from the house next door. She heard him again. 'Can I do one, too?'

The scullery door was nearly always a little open, in order to let out the perpetual damp. Ruby had pushed it wider, to look.

They were drowning kittens in a bucket.

'Stop it! Stop it!' Ruby had screeched, exploding out and launching herself at Will. 'Stop it!' and she'd kicked his shins, headbutted his stomach, grabbed his hair and done her absolute best to drag him to the bucket and drown him too.

Will had not fought back. Instead, he'd held her off at arm's length, shouted to his friend, 'Save the black and I'll make our mum have it,' then carted her indoors and did his best to explain.

'You have to drown them,' he said. 'There'd be millions of kittens, else. They don't know nothing. They just go to sleep in the water. I promise.'

'I hate you and I'm telling Mum!' wailed Ruby.

'Telling Mum what?' demanded Violet from behind.

'She found me and Danny sorting out them kittens,' explained Will.

'They were DROWNING them in a BUCKET,' roared Ruby, and Violet said, 'Well, it's a shame you had to see that.' (*Taking Ruby's side as usual*, thought her brother.) 'You and Danny should have been more careful, Will.'

'We were being careful,' said Will indignantly. 'We shut their cat Sukey in Dan's house with the kitten that they're keeping for themselves, and then we did the other five in our yard so Sukey couldn't see. We couldn't have been more careful. We warmed the water, and everything. And I've told Danny to save the black for us . . .'

'Will!'

'. . . because Ruby's so upset.'

'He asked,' exploded Ruby, 'if he could help! "Can I do one?" he said. I heard him! He's a murderer!'

'Only to learn how,' said Will.

'Learn how!' shouted Ruby.

'I've had enough of this!' said Will resentfully. 'Are we having the black or had I better go back and tell Danny—'

'NO NO NO!' screamed Ruby, and Violet groaned and said it had better be a boy kitten, that was all, and it was, and when it was old enough it came to live with them and was Ruby's cat, Sooty. For weeks after that Ruby didn't know if she was grateful to Will, for saving Sooty, or hated him for what had happened to the rest. She couldn't forget his voice asking, 'Can I do one, too?'

Ruby's dad was not told anything about the whole awful

event. Violet ordered that. 'It would just make him miserable,' she said. 'He's a good dad to the pair of you, and he hates how you quarrel.'

Will and Ruby didn't argue about that. They knew it was true. And they knew he was a good dad, hard-working and generous, handing over all his earnings to Violet except for a few shillings every Friday. The shillings were usually spent on presents to bring home. Oranges, or a flower in a pot for Violet, another small bell to hang on Sooty's collar, sometimes a book for them all to share. He was never, ever cross. He was a gentle man.

Violet was the opposite. She was the boss in the family. The three rooms over the shop were rent free because Violet worked there. She was a hard worker and because of her the money stretched like magic so that there were warm suppers every night, schoolbooks and birthday cakes, Christmas stockings and days at the fair, coal for the fire in the living room and the copper in the scullery, where they had their baths on Saturdays and Wednesdays.

Violet made the three rooms into a comfortable home. The living room had a table in the window and a sofa made of boxes and cushions. There was a shelf of books, a little range for cooking and a dresser for the plates and saucepans. Will had the box room to sleep in, and Ruby had a curtained-off corner of her parents' room. When she was six and went to school and could be trusted with a candle, her parents promised they would whitewash the attic and she could sleep up there, with a view over the rooftops and across to the dockyards.

Ruby turned six, and this happened. Also, she went to school.

For those first years of her life, Ruby hadn't known there was anything different about her face. The three rooms above the shop were mirror free, and no one ever mentioned it. Not any of the flowery-named relations, nor even Will. Somehow, Violet stopped them all.

That was why, on the first day that Ruby started school, when fifty children, maybe more, looked at her face and demanded, 'What's those marks?' she honestly didn't know what they were talking about.

She didn't find out till she got home.

Sooty, now a half-grown cat, came with Ruby to the dark little scullery and watched as she climbed on to the copper to reach down the small speckled mirror that her father used for shaving.

That was when she saw her reflection; saw it properly, for the first time. In truth, the marks were not as shocking as they once had been. They had not grown larger as Ruby grew; they no longer entirely dominated her face. But still, they were bad enough.

Ruby stared and stared.

At school the next day a girl asked, 'What would happen to your face if you washed it?'

'I do wash it,' Ruby said bleakly, still stunned from the scullery mirror.

'Washed it hard?' persisted the girl.

It was true, Ruby didn't wash it hard, and neither did her

mother. They didn't work at it, like her dad did with the nail brush, grinding the station grime out of the cracks in his hands until the water in the basin went scummy and grey. That was hard washing, the way he would scrub and scrub.

And in the end, his hands would be clean.

After school on that second day, Ruby got the bar of soap from its soap dish by the copper, and the family washcloth from its hook, and she scrubbed her face very hard indeed. Her cheeks became hot, and very clean, but her reflection in the mirror didn't change. Will came in while she was busy, with Danny trailing behind.

Will burst out laughing and said she might as well scrub Sooty white while she was at it, but Danny said solemnly, 'It's the water.'

'What?' demanded Ruby, spinning round.

'You need special water.'

'What special water?'

'We have special white water at our house,' said Danny. 'If you use the right brush it scrubs anything clean.'

'There's no such thing as special white water,' said Ruby stubbornly, and Danny said, 'Want me to prove it?'

'How?'

'Give us Sooty!' said Danny and suddenly bent and scooped him up and shoved him under his jacket. Then he was gone, with Will running after him, and Ruby shrieking, 'You dare scrub Sooty! You dare!'

'I'll only do one foot,' called Danny, over his shoulder, and

16

in an incredibly short time was back, with a brown earthenware jug, and Will, clutching a small scrubbing brush and exploding with mirth in the background.

Danny had something squirming under his jacket.

'Look!' he said, unfastening his buttons, and out tumbled Sooty, furious and fighting.

With one wet paw, snow-white.

'Special water,' said Danny, showing Ruby the jug.

'And the right brush,' added Will.

'You painted him!' said Ruby and she picked up Sooty (still indignant from the jacket) and looked carefully at his paw.

It wasn't painted, though. It was truly white, wet but white. Pure white fur with pink skin underneath.

'See,' said Danny.

Ruby looked at him, and at Will. She squinted at her reflection in the little speckled mirror. She looked at Sooty.

'Give me the special water,' she said at last.

'Give you?'

'Yes.'

'Manners.'

'Please,' conceded Ruby. 'Give me, please.'

'It costs,' said Danny. 'Shilling a jug.'

'I haven't got a shilling,' said Ruby, looking at them both with hate.

'You've got threepence,' said Will.

It was true. Ruby had got threepence. Every Saturday she had one, shiny silver from her dad.

'Hmm,' said Danny. 'Perhaps.' Then he made Ruby fetch

her threepence and say please, and also pretty-please-with-sugar-on-top, but at last he nodded to Will to hand over the scrubbing brush and gave Ruby the jug and she looked inside at the white water and said, 'It's milk.'

'Milk!' scoffed Danny. 'Taste it and you'll drop dead.'

'Dead as dead,' said Will.

Then they took Ruby's silver threepence and went away and they left her with the jug and Sooty.

Sooty sniffed the jug.

'No, no,' said Ruby urgently, just in case, and she poured the special white water carefully into the enamel wash basin, where it looked more than ever like milk and Sooty sniffed even harder and patted with his white paw.

Ruby stuck in the tip of a finger and licked it. It was very salty and unpleasant but she didn't drop dead.

Sooty asked for a taste again.

'It's not for drinking,' Ruby told him and she picked up the scrubbing brush and dipped it in the wash basin. Then she gritted her teeth and began to scrub.

On the other side of the scullery door Will and Danny laughed and laughed in silent, doubled-over agony.

Ruby scrubbed until she bled red blood into the white water and she couldn't see in the little mirror for the tears of pain in her eyes. Sooty, meanwhile, turned into two cats.

Two cats.

At first Ruby didn't notice, and then she did, because they were both sitting on their haunches watching her. Two sooty dark cats, one with a white paw, one entirely black.

Two of them.

Two.

'Two cats?' said Ruby, and called, 'Sooty, Sooty,' and both Sooties came and rubbed their heads on her hands and she was entirely bewildered and cried, 'How?'

On the other side of the scullery door, Will and Danny gasped in pain, beset with laughter, and Ruby heard them.

Then Ruby's mother arrived. She saw the boys, staggering around, still howling with mirth. She saw the jug and brush, which had both been hurled. She saw smashed brown pottery on the floor.

'Ruby AMARYLLIS!' shouted Violet, and grabbed her so she had to stop kicking the boys with her new school shoes, all stained with salty milk.

Ruby's face was so swollen, her left eye wouldn't open. It burned like fire. It was a week before she went back to school. First she couldn't, because her face was so sore, and then she wouldn't because her heart was so sore. By the time she did, everyone knew the story.

'My beautiful Ruby,' said Ruby's father, and he polished her school shoes until they were as bright as conkers and gave her a pink balloon, a green hair ribbon and a sherbet dab. Even so, every day of that week she was sent to bed early, not for kicking and fighting, but for being so silly.

Said Violet.

Also, every day of that week Will had dry bread and milk

for supper and dry bread and milk for breakfast and dry bread and milk to take to school for his dinner and nothing else, not even butter. His father could hardly bear it. He said, 'Your little sister, Will.'

'Little tiger,' said Will.

His father put a sherbet dab behind the clock for him, and said, 'That's for when you're friends again.'

'It can stay there then,' said Will, and it did.

One interesting thing happened, which was that the white-pawed cat never went back home. It wouldn't. It refused to stay there. It went to live with Ruby and Sooty.

It wouldn't answer to its name. Ruby had to pick a new one for it: Paddle.

'You can tell them at school about Paddle and Sooty,' said her mother, encouragingly, but Ruby never told anyone at school anything.

Around her grew legends. The legend of the scrubbing of the dark marks on her face. Of the stolen cat. Of her strange name. There wasn't another Ruby in the school, never mind an Amaryllis. The marks on her face would not paint out, not with Violet's face cream and powder, nor with flour mixed up to paste.

Once Ruby found a fallen bunch of cherry blossom, tumbled in the street. Carefully, she licked the pale pink petals, stuck them on, and peered into the little speckled mirror. It almost worked: there, for a few moments, was a girl she had never seen. Green eyes, astonished. Dark curls and dark eyebrows. A missing front tooth.

'Look!' cried Ruby to her mother, but the cherry petals would not stay. They curled with the warmth of her skin and fell.

'Are they still saying things at school?' demanded Violet fiercely, and Ruby, equally fiercely said, 'I don't care if they do.'

Violet cared, though. She marched to school and through the gates which parents hardly ever passed and gave out orders in the playground: 'You leave my Ruby alone!'

So they did.

THREE
Kate
Oxford, 1928–1936

Kate was the youngest and her name was Katherine Clarissa, after Clarry, who was her aunt and her godmother too.

'Say you'll do it, please say you will,' Vanessa, Kate's mother, had pleaded. 'It'll be easy. You only have to adore her.'

'Only,' remarked Kate's father gloomily, looking down at his newest daughter, half lost in the shabby billows of the family christening dress, and he joggled her a little, to see if she would smile.

She didn't. She was a skinny, purplish person with an ancient unhappy frown. Nevertheless, Clarry laughed at her brother and said, 'Don't be silly, Peter. I'll have no trouble adoring her at all.'

'As if anybody could!' exclaimed Vanessa, and added that Kate could be a friend to Clarry's other god-daughter, Ruby, in Plymouth.

'They can write to each other,' agreed Clarry.

'I don't know about the one in Plymouth,' said Kate's father, 'but this one here doesn't strike me as the literary type.'

'You're wrong, you know,' said Clarry. 'She has a very intelligent face.'

Peter said that it was a common mistake to confuse baldness with brains, but good old Clarry anyway, and Vanessa said, 'Yes, definitely, it's awful trying to find godparents for six, Clarry, you've no idea, people just run. We'd have nobbled you ages ago but you were always off gallivanting with Rupert at the critical moment.'

'Oh, well, you've nobbled me now,' said Clarry cheerfully.

Kate was the last of the Penrose children, who had begun with Janey, who was brainy, swiftly followed by untidy, merry Bea. Bea wore glasses that she lost so often she tied them on a string, and ran a farm on her bedroom windowsill: carrot tops growing in saucers, two mice in a box and a flowerpot of earth where she planted apple pips.

Janey and Bea were a team, and Simon and Tod (whose real name was Rupert), the good-looking musical twins, were another. After Simon and Tod came noisy, impulsive Charlie. And then there was Kate, who was not brainy or untidy or merry or good-looking or musical or noisy or impulsive. Kate was shy and breathless and had to be looked after and have orange juice with cod liver oil because she caught illnesses so easily. This meant she missed a lot of school and in winter was wrapped in extra warm layers, in foggy weather kept indoors, and on rainy days was steered around puddles and had umbrellas held over her head. Even in summer, Kate sneezed and sneezed with hay fever, although she lived on a street in

Oxford where there wasn't any hay for miles.

Kate's parents kept her carefully close, within arms' reach if they were out and about, beside them in the car if they were driving. They did this so as to be handy if she needed help. People always did help Kate. 'Pass it over,' they would say, if she dried knives and forks too slowly in the kitchen, or struggled to undo a knot, or turn a key, or sharpen a pencil. In the mornings someone (usually Bea) would plait her hair into two mouse-coloured tails, in the evenings someone else (usually Janey) would whizz her through her homework. Her shoes were always magically polished and her bed magically made.

Except for her illnesses, Kate's life was entirely safe. Bea fell flat on her face roller-skating, smashing her glasses and chipping a large corner off a new front tooth. Janey broke her arm when her bike skidded sideways racing Tod and Simon across the market street cobbles. Charlie, practising being a burglar, climbed a long way up a drainpipe before it detached slowly from the wall. Simon and Tod found and repaired an ancient leaky punt, which frequently disintegrated mid river and sent them home dripping and shivering.

But nothing ever happened to Kate except kindness and illness.

'Is she like Beth in *Little Women*?' Bea once worried to Janey, but Janey said, no, Beth only got ill because she visited sick people to take them muffins and firewood and other useful things. Completely the opposite to Kate, who was ill naturally, without helping anyone. Janey explained this, and Bea nodded, reassured.

Although it did make Kate sound a little bit useless.

'I expect she's brilliant at something we haven't discovered yet,' said Bea, and Janey said probably, yes.

Kate was actually very good at being nearly invisible. A number of people hardly noticed she existed and one of these was Rupert, the Rupert after whom Tod was named. To everyone except Kate, Rupert was a sort of unofficial uncle.

'Why aren't you a real uncle?' Charlie asked him.

'Because I'm not a relation.'

'Not even a bit?'

'Not at all.'

'But did you used to be?'

'I used to think I was,' admitted Rupert. 'But then I went to India and found out that I wasn't.'

'How?'

'Oh,' said Rupert, 'it's hard to explain. No, it's not. It's easy. I found out that my father wasn't the person I thought he was. And that meant my grandparents weren't the people I thought they were. No one was who I thought they were. It explained a lot.'

'What?'

'Like why my parents dumped me on my not-really grandparents in Cornwall when I was three. And why the not-really grandparents dumped me at boarding school when I was seven. That sort of thing.'

'Were you very sad?' asked Bea, and she touched his sleeve sympathetically.

'Not at all. I'd guessed already. I just needed to know the truth.'

'We would never dump you,' said Bea, and Charlie agreed, 'You're safe now, promise.'

'Stuck,' said Janey.

'Trapped,' said Tod.

'You don't dump us, we won't dump you,' agreed Simon, and Rupert solemnly shook hands with all of them, except Kate, who was as usual, invisible, and said, 'Deal.'

But none of this was really necessary, because Rupert was part of the family anyway, mobbed every time he came through the door, hauled off to look at the drainpipe, taken for trips in the leaky punt, and advised, for the hundredth time, that he'd better marry Clarry.

'True,' said Rupert. 'But easier said than done.'

'Why?'

'Bit busy, both of us.'

'It would only take an afternoon!'

Rupert laughed, and said, 'Look at the time, I must be off. Bye, you Penroses. Be good.'

'You're always going!' Charlie complained, and it was true, he was. Rupert doubled their pocket money, made them laugh, provided boxes of fireworks on November the fifth, but more than anything, he vanished.

'Where are you going this time?' demanded Janey.

'London, of course,' said Rupert. 'Work in the morning.'

'What sort of work?'

'I'm a servant,' Rupert told her, solemnly. 'Civil. And

uncivil, sometimes. In Westminster and Whitehall. I listen to people. I listen and say, "Do you think so?" and they pay me.'

'Just for that?' demanded Bea incredulously.

'Yes,' he said.

'They can't pay you much,' said Janey. 'Not for that and nothing else.'

'True,' agreed Rupert, 'but every little helps. One day I'll take you with me, and show you.'

After he'd gone they looked at each and said, 'He won't,' but they were wrong.

He began with Janey and Bea, taking them on the train to London, showing them the long corridors and dusty courtyards of Westminster, the cupboards in walls with mousetraps inside and what it was in the middle of the clock tower of Big Ben.

'Stairs,' reported Janey.

'Stairs and a cat,' said Bea.

'I didn't see a cat,' said Janey. 'Are you sure that you did, Bea? You do see things that aren't there sometimes.'

'I saw the cat,' said Clarry, who happened to be visiting. 'I stroked it too. It followed us right to the top of the staircase.'

'You and Rupert?'

'Yes. Very early one morning. An inky-black cat, like a shadow with golden eyes.'

'That was the one,' agreed Bea, who had loved the whole adventure, but the cat most of all.

After that, Rupert would often swoop over to Oxford for a handful of Penroses and cart them away to see the sights. In

Westminster he would park them on the green leather seats of the Commons or the red leather seats of the Lords, where Janey and Bea roosted like swallows, listening intently. In contrast to their brothers, who read comics, wrote unparliamentary poetry in their heads, exploded into painful silent giggles, and in Charlie's case, bounced with indignation and had to be carted away like a bundle. Quite often on those trips, a Penrose would hear, 'Ah, Rupert, if you have a minute . . .' and then, after much more than a minute, fidgeting hours it seemed sometimes, 'Do you think so? Oh.'

At school, no one believed Janey when she told them where she'd been and what she'd seen. 'Mousetraps?' they asked, and those who had imagined Big Ben to be like a giant grandfather clock, 'Steps inside? Cats?'

'One cat, anyway,' said Janey, but even one cat was too much for most of them, so Janey stopped talking about their trips to London with Rupert, although it was hard to keep quiet when he gave her and Bea one of the Trafalgar Square lions for their own, to share.

When the twins heard of this, they demanded a lion too.

'The rest belong to other people,' said baffling Rupert, and took Tod and Simon to South Kensington and gave them the Minerals Gallery in the Natural History Museum instead. 'Just you two,' he said. 'Not Charlie. It's not a place for Charlie to be charging about. All that glass. And meteors. Asking for trouble.'

The twins agreed, and they didn't tell Charlie, but he found out anyway and was outraged and demanded to be given the polar bear instead. It was an enormous yellow beast with a narrow, furious gaze and shoulders like monuments, and Charlie admired it very much. But Rupert was unhelpful. He said the bear was not his to give away, and if he was, he'd keep him for himself. However, to cheer Charlie up he took him swimming in the Serpentine, which was excitingly full of ducks and paper bags and other things, floating and submerged. One of these caught Charlie by his foot and he screeched and screeched, remembering too clearly underwater monsters he had seen in the museum and assumed to be extinct.

'There are no ichthyosaurs in the Serpentine,' said Rupert sternly, and dived and retrieved an old umbrella and clambered out with it on to the bank showing all his awful purple scars as if he didn't care. It was a black umbrella and Rupert opened it and closed it and said, 'I wonder if I knew the man who owned it,' in such a thoughtful, alarming way that even unquenchable Charlie was silent.

'Well,' said Rupert, shooting out the umbrella's slimy folds and examining the pointy bit. 'You have to admit, it's odd.'

'Why?'

'No concealed sword. No hidden camera. No wind damage, so it's not been used for parachuting.'

'*Parachuting?*'

'Didn't you hear? Nothing like that. Perfectly good umbrella.'

'Can I keep it?'

'No, of course not,' said Rupert, and hung it by its greenish-yellow handle from the back of a bench and then he made

Charlie trot about to warm up and afterwards they went to tea in a Lyons' tea shop. There they had Welsh rarebit which wasn't even on the menu and only appeared because Rupert said, 'Oh, do you think so?' to the waitress girl when she said it wasn't possible. These must have been magic words, because seconds later she was taking down instructions about grated cheese and a little mustard (French, of course) and a beaten egg and beer. It was so good that Charlie ate three platefuls and turned down ice cream in favour of a fourth.

'How old are you?' demanded Rupert, who was drinking tea with lemon slices and not eating anything at all.

'Eleven,' said Charlie, 'nearly.'

'Not just you. All of you.'

'Janey's seventeen, nearly. Bea's sixteen, nearly. Simon and Tod are twelve but it's nearly their birthday—'

'We'd better get a move on,' said Rupert. 'Come on!'

'But . . .' protested Charlie, who still hadn't finished.

'You can bring that last piece with you!' said Rupert, as he left an enormous tip, half a crown, and hurried him home.

Charlie was the last Penrose that Rupert took to London. Kate, with her nearly invisibleness, never got to go. After Charlie, Rupert disappeared.

'Where's he gone this time?' Charlie wondered. Clarry, who was spending the evening getting on with her school marking and keeping an eye on him and Kate while the rest of the family were out, looked up from her work and said vaguely, 'Travelling.'

'Travelling,' murmured Kate. She was being unwell again, wrapped up in a blanket of patchwork roses, writing in her diary.

The fact that Kate kept a diary always amused her family. What could she possibly find to put in it, they wondered. If they'd been the sort of people who read diaries uninvited, they'd soon have discovered the answer. Kate's diary was all about other people. All the trips to London had been noted: the black cat inside Big Ben, and the lion in Trafalgar Square, with miniature drawings of both. A recipe for Welsh rarebit was carefully recorded. Other things too. The mystery of Bea's missing mice. A new patch on the punt.

Now Kate wrote, *Clarry's here but Rupert's travelling.*

'Travelling,' said Charlie enviously. 'Lucky, lucky Rupert.'

Charlie's homework was going very slowly that evening. He'd eaten a handful of biscuits, two apples and a lump of cheese, doodled his name in red and blue ink, drawn round his eraser and turned the outline into an elephant, decided how he'd spend a hundred pounds if he had a hundred pounds, and still it wasn't done. Kate was useless. She'd tested him on his Latin, checked the words in the dictionary, and marked every answer wrong.

'I asked you to test my Latin, not my spelling,' Charlie said. 'Spelling didn't matter in Latin days. Ancient Romers hardly ever wrote things down.'

'Absolutely untrue,' remarked Clarry.

'I wish Rupert had taken me with him. Where's he gone?'

'All sorts of places: Germany, France, Russia.'

'Russia?' repeated Kate, and thought of Russian tales of bears, and witches with iron teeth, and great frozen rivers that creaked and shattered into icy torrents and swept travellers away. She shivered, and Clarry noticed.

'Don't worry,' she said, smiling at her. 'Rupert has nine lives, like a cat.'

Charlie, remembering the banks of the Serpentine, said, 'Yes, but he's probably used most of them. You should see his scars! His back looks like someone tried to chop him up, and one of his legs has a hole in it.'

'A hole?' asked Kate, in a frightened voice.

'As big as . . . as big as an apple. Half an apple, anyway! It's not red or bloody or anything. It's just a hole. It's great. I bet he'd show you if you wanted.'

Kate asked, because she couldn't help it, 'How did he get a hole in his leg?'

'In the war, of course,' said Charlie.

'I didn't know he was in a war.'

'Course he was,' said Charlie. 'Same as Mum's brother Simon who was killed.'

'Killed? Killed?'

'How can you not know anything, Kate?'

'I knew he died, but I didn't know he was killed. I thought it was when he was a boy.'

'He was seventeen, not quite eighteen,' said Clarry. 'So you're right, he was a boy.'

'Oh,' said Kate, and she didn't say any more, just wrote unhappily and coughed a bit, until Charlie flung away his homework books and said he wished there was a war now, so he could have some fun.

Then Kate shouted, 'CHARLIE!'

It was the first time she had ever shouted in her life. It made her cough a lot more, but it shut Charlie up.

FOUR
Dog
Scrapyard, East London, exact date unknown

There was a dog who lived in a scrapyard. It had lived there so long that it had become part of the landscape, like the rust stains on the ground, the lace edge of broken bottles that topped the scrapyard walls, and the rattle of the gates in the wind.

All the good things about dogs were not true of this dog. It loved no one, and trusted no one. It wasn't loyal or merry. It didn't have wise brown eyes, or a hopefully wagging tail, in fact half of its tail was missing. Also its fur was coarse and greyish and matted behind its ears. Its legs were long and knobbly at the joints and they ended in paws with thick black nails, chewed down to iron stumps.

The dog made its living by its bark, which was harsh, like stone dragged on stone. Also by its lunge at the end of its chain. The chain was the dog's home.

By day the chain held the dog, but at night its ears fluttered, and its paws flexed and twitched.

By night the dog ran in its dreams.

FIVE
Erik and Hans
Berlin, 1936

Ever since the three swallows, Erik and Hans had been best friends. They had very much in common: the same school, and the same apartment block (although Hans's home was much bigger). Both their fathers had fought in the 1914–1918 war. The consequences to their families were with them still. Erik's father had been gassed and had never properly recovered. He had died when he was still quite young, two months before Erik was born. Hans's father was never really healthy either, and his left leg was missing below his knee. Now he walked stiffly on his wooden half leg, and worked in the post office, which was good because he could sit down nearly all day. Hans's mother didn't work, but Erik's mother did.

Erik's mother worked all the time. Every morning she swept and scrubbed the hall and staircases of their building, and of the one next door as well. In the late afternoons she cleaned the local elementary school. When Erik was little, too young to be left alone, she used to take him with her. Erik had played in the empty classrooms, and helped dust the chalkboards, and every day he'd climbed with his mother the shadowy narrow staircase that opened from their own landing to the two miniature attic rooms belonging to his mother's old lady: Fraulein Trisk. Fraulein Trisk lived all alone, tiny, white-haired, and permanently annoyed. Her movements were annoyed, and her eyes were annoyed, and every now and then, she would burst into miniature eruptions of spluttering annoyedness, like the sound of cold water drops in a hot frying pan.

'Tck! Tck! Tck!' scolded Fraulein Trisk. It took nothing to set her off: a bird shadow passing the window, a call in the street far below, the smallest noise from Erik, one little sniff, and she would explode, like a dolls' house firecracker.

No person ever visited Fraulein Trisk. No letter with her name on ever arrived in the wire letterbox behind the door. No one, not even from Hans's family, ever asked, 'How is Fraulein Trisk these days?' Very probably Hans's family never knew she was there. By the time they moved into their apartment, she had long since stopped going out. It was Erik's mother who fetched her shopping, cooked her soups, and apple tarts, and on Saturday mornings in wintertime, went early to light her very small fire. While his mother was busy, Erik would sit on a wooden chair by the window where Fraulein Trisk had her green fern. It was the only bright thing in the room; everything else was faded with age, just as Fraulein Trisk herself was faded. Time went very slowly on those visits for five-year-old Erik, trying not to fidget, wishing he dared stroke a fern leaf, secretly huffing on his chilblained fingers when he thought Fraulein Trisk might not notice.

She didn't seem to notice, but she must have done, because one day she handed him a parcel, wrapped in crinkled brown paper, with a green woollen bow, and when Erik untied the bow and opened it he found to his utter astonishment that she had knitted him some mittens. Green woollen mittens.

Erik was so pleased that he hugged her.

'Tck! Tck! Tck!' exclaimed Fraulein Trisk, like a horrified small wren. 'Make sure you don't lose them!'

'I never will,' promised Erik, who was young enough still to believe in never.

All that winter Erik had worn his green mittens, every time he visited. Then something awful happened. Somewhere, between the school and the streets and sweeping stairs, the mittens were lost.

'Lost!' exclaimed Fraulein Trisk, when honest Erik had made the mistake of telling her, and she walked to the window and stood looking out over the green fern and made many, many furious firecracker sounds.

It was disastrous. After that she always mentioned the mittens in a way that made Erik feel bad. Sometimes the whole visit would pass and he would think this time she had forgotten at last and then she would say, 'Those mittens, you are still searching?' or 'I used very good wool for your green mittens,' or, worst of all, 'I could knit some more, but what would be the use?' Always something like that, and the firework scolding more fierce than ever. Erik would feel terrible and sit even more carefully and worriedly on the chair by the fern, and afterwards go home and search yet another time. But at last he was old enough to go to school, and after that he hardly saw Fraulein Trisk, unless he craned his head back very far to look up at the window from the street. Sometimes she would be there, gazing out.

Erik's mother still helped her though, and every June she would make her a very small birthday cake. 'Poor old lady, with no one to make a cake for her,' she would say to Erik.

One year she sent him to the confectioner's to buy a sugar rose to decorate the top. Erik carried it carefully, so as not to break a fragile petal, and it occurred to him as he walked that his mother never had a birthday cake with roses on herself.

'I have you,' she said, when he pointed this out. 'Better than a sugar rose.'

For years afterwards, now and then, she would call him her sugar rose to make him laugh. 'Goodnight, sleep tight, my sugar rose,' she would say. After he and Hans became friends Erik begged, 'Never let Hans hear you say that, please!'

'Never let Hans hear me call you my sugar rose?' asked Erik's mother, not in a whisper, and the window open too.

'No,' said Erik.

'Hans's mother told me that when he was little she used to call him Dumpling Boy,' said Erik's mother. 'Because of his soft round dumpling cheeks.'

'Not any more,' said Erik.

'Not any more,' agreed his mother, and although she was usually a very cheerful person, she sounded sad and Erik was worried and asked, 'What's the matter?'

'You're growing up,' she said.

'Isn't that good?' asked Erik.

'Of course,' she said, and added, 'and you are probably right. No more sugar roses.'

'Well,' said Erik, who was absolutely incapable of making anyone miserable on purpose, even for the very good reason of not being called a sugar rose. 'Well, think how Hans and the boys at school would laugh if they heard you call me that! But, perhaps, in private, you could do it in an emergency. How about that?'

It made her smile, as he had hoped it would, and she hugged him and said, 'Thank you. Well then, I will only call you a sugar rose in times of great emergency.'

And so it was agreed.

Erik's mother was right. He and Hans were growing up. The seasons raced by. Every summer there were swallows. Every winter there was snow. In between there was school, where Erik worked hard because he liked it, and Hans worked hard because he wasn't going to let Erik beat him.

One spring, in 1935, there was a great surprise. A new baby in the family for Lisa and Hans.

'Another girl,' said Hans, rolling his eyes in pretend dismay.

Baby Frieda reminded Erik of his little birds: constantly needing to be fed, exhausting and astonishing. He mentioned this to Hans.

'Oh, good,' said Hans. 'Maybe in a few weeks she'll stop squawking and fly out of the window.'

'She doesn't squawk much,' said Erik.

'Not as much as Lisa,' agreed Hans. Lisa, now thirteen,

had lately become even more of a nuisance than before. Not only was she bossier than ever, but she had taken to marching to music and doing gymnastics at inconvenient times on the sitting-room floor. When her family complained, she argued that they were unpatriotic.

'I am doing it for Herr Hitler, our Chancellor,' she said.

'Herr Hitler, our Chancellor, doesn't have to step over your legs,' said her mother. 'Nor does he have a baby to get to sleep, and I am sure he would have more sense than to roll up the rugs and dump them in the hall where your poor father might fall over them.'

'If we had a proper balcony I could do my exercises outside,' said Lisa.

'Not half dressed like that you couldn't!' said her mother. 'The poor Chancellor might come by and see you prancing about in your underwear and have a heart attack.'

Then Lisa became indignant and rude, and her mother became angry and shouting, and Frieda woke up and howled louder than either of them and Hans escaped upstairs to have a good, long, disgruntled grumble about his family.

'It's all Lisa's fault,' he said. 'That stupid club of hers has taken over her senses. "The League of German Maidens",' he quoted, mimicking Lisa's voice. 'The Plague of German Maidens, more like. They're supposed to be going camping. The sooner the better, I say. What are you doing?'

'Show you in a minute,' said Erik, busy at the kitchen table with ink and writing paper. 'Lisa can't help it. Everyone is joining those clubs.'

'I know,' said Hans. 'Marching with flags, and singing songs about the Fatherland that don't rhyme properly. Half our school, I should think.'

'More,' said Erik. 'I suppose we should too. If you don't they say you're useless and unpatriotic. Anyway, I wouldn't mind camping.'

'Camping is one thing. Being told what to think, I don't like.'

'No one can tell you what to think, Hans,' said Erik cheerfully.

'All my family tell me what to think all the time, except the baby, and that's only because she can't talk.'

'Mmm,' said Erik, drawing a tiger.

'You're not listening properly!'

'I am,' said Erik. 'Lisa is going camping. Frieda can't talk. Now look at this! What do you think?'

He sat back so that Hans could look at his work. He had designed a poster. A tiger leaped across the top, a toucan decorated the bottom, and the words said:

Free!

Guided Tours of Berlin Zoo
with Expert and Knowledgeable Students
Erik and Hans!
Stay as long as you like!
Ask a thousand questions!
All you pay is the entrance fee of your
expert and knowledgeable guides!

Berlin had a wonderful zoo. Erik had loved it ever since he could remember. He went whenever he had a chance and it was always his birthday treat. Every year it got better: every year there were fewer bars, more outdoor spaces for the animals. There was a place where you could walk round a corner and come face to face with a lion. Whatever else was happening, you could go to the zoo and think that things were all right. Better than all right, wonderful.

But it cost money to visit, and that was the difficulty. Money was hard to come by. Erik sometimes earned it by delivering groceries, and sometimes waiting at the station, and running to carry bags or call cabs for travellers. In winter there was snow to shovel. However, most of what he earned went to help his mother; there was not much left for Erik.

Nevertheless, now he'd had this wonderful idea. All he had to do was find somewhere to fix his poster, and then he and Hans would stand beside it, ready for the queues of people needing their help.

'Ask a thousand questions?' said Hans. 'Expert and knowledgeable? Us?'

'We'll need to study a little first,' admitted Erik, 'but that's no problem. There are two shelves of animal books in school.'

'All right,' said Hans. 'When I've read the two shelves of animal books, I'll do it, and meanwhile we should put on our oldest clothes, and borrow your mother's brushes that she uses for cleaning the stairs and hall, and I will bring our snow shovel, and we'll turn up early on Saturday morning and tell them we've come to sweep the paths.'

Erik said it was a very good idea except that his mother needed her brushes on Saturday mornings, so they tried it on Sunday instead. It worked, and they got in, and for two hours or so swept industriously and happily near all their favourite animals, until a zoo official in uniform came and demanded to know what they were doing. He had just reached the point of taking down their names when who should come along but their schoolteacher, Herr Schmidt.

'Names, names, you do not need their names!' said Herr Schmidt. 'These are my students. I will take charge of them now.' Then together with Frau Schmidt, and grandmother Schmidt and a whole tribe of little Schmidts, he escorted Erik and Hans to the turnstiles and requested a thousand-word essay from each of them. He gave them the title, right there, at the zoo:

How I spent my Sunday morning and why I will never do it again.

'For tomorrow morning!' said Herr Schmidt. 'And be thankful I came along!'

Erik and Hans were groaning over this task, late on Sunday afternoon, working in Hans's bedroom because Erik would rather his mother didn't know anything about the matter. Erik had finished and was helping Hans by dictating long sentences about flamingos. He had learned a lot about these birds in preparation for being an expert and knowledgeable zoo guide and it seemed a pity to waste it.

'The flamingo's nest is cone-shaped, made of mud and fine gravel which the birds gather with their curved beaks. Male and female birds take turns sitting on their eggs. We saw these birds this morning at Berlin Zoo, as we swept the path near their enclosure.'

'More, more!' begged Hans, counting words. 'I need at least another hundred.'

'We also noticed swallows,' dictated Erik, counting words on his fingers as he spoke.

'I didn't,' interrupted Hans.

'They were everywhere, you must have done,' said Erik. 'Come on, hurry up! Swallows build in colonies, many nests close together. Their nests are also made of mud, collected by the birds from the edges of puddles and pools. For example, the otters had swallows visiting their pool. These beautiful black-and-white birds arrive in Europe in the spring, after spending the winter in South Africa. They feed on insects caught on the wing and are among the many interesting creatures I saw as I worked without permission at Berlin Zoo this morning, which I will never do again, on the instructions of my teacher, Herr Schmidt. Nine hundred and ninety-nine words . . . my esteemed teacher . . . One thousand! Done it!'

'This is very interesting, tell me more,' said a voice from the doorway, and they looked up and there was Hans's Uncle Karl, grinning down at them. 'Sweeping the zoo without permission, eh? Both of you, am I right?'

'We were doing a good job,' said Hans.

'We can hardly ever get in because of the cost,' explained Erik. 'And we really did sweep, and pick up paper bags and orange peel and all sorts of rubbish.'

'Very enterprising,' agreed Uncle Karl. 'I didn't know you were so fond of animals, Hans.'

'That's Erik,' said Hans. 'I just wanted to see if we could do it. It was my idea. Erik thought of something completely different. Look!'

He had kept Erik's poster. Now he passed it to his uncle, who read it carefully, started laughing and said, 'Expert and knowledgeable, eh?'

'Well, Erik really is an expert,' said Hans. 'Especially about birds.'

'I remember you telling me about Erik and birds, and how he wished he could fly. Tell me about your swallows, Erik.'

So Erik did, starting with the fallen nest, and ending with the flight from the window. 'You should have seen them,' he said. 'One moment in my hand and the next, like . . . like little darts, like ribbons in the air, like arrows, can you imagine?'

'Yes,' said Uncle Karl. 'And what do your family think of all this cleaning-at-the-zoo affair?'

'My mother needn't know,' said Erik. 'She worries about things.'

'And your father?'

'Oh,' said Erik, rather uncomfortably because he guessed he was going to make Uncle Karl feel bad. 'You perhaps don't know, but my father died before I knew him, a few years after the war.'

'I'm sorry,' said Uncle Karl.

'He'd breathed gas in the trenches and he caught flu. So . . .'

'Hans's father, my brother, still suffers from that war,' said

Uncle Karl, 'and now he worries about Hans.'

'Well, he needn't,' said Hans. 'I'm no soldier, and neither is Erik. Erik is going to take charge of the zoo when he finishes school. And I shall have a very expensive pastry stall, just outside the gates. With little tables, and hot chocolate and lemonade and things. But then the problem will be, who will wash the cups and glasses? I'll have to think about that. Perhaps Erik could train some monkeys.'

'Certainly not,' said Erik. 'My monkeys will be far too busy in the jungle I will make for them. I'll come and help you, though, after the visitors go home. You can pay me in hazelnut creams and iced gingerbread.'

'You see,' said Hans to Uncle Karl. 'Our futures are secure!'

Uncle Karl looked at him as if he had a hundred unspoken thoughts in his head, but all he said was, 'Meanwhile, however, I suppose the zoo is closed to you next weekend?'

'Maybe something will turn up,' said Hans.

'Maybe it will,' said Uncle Karl.

Erik and his mother were poor. No pretending otherwise.

Hans and his family were just-getting-by.

Uncle Karl was different. He was younger, he never seemed to worry about money, he had fun. He worked for the motor works, and with his job travelled all over Germany, and he owned a car.

It was bright red, beautifully polished, with black mudguards and a black roof that folded back for hot weather. Hans's father, who was terribly jealous, said, 'That car is wife and family to you, Karl!'

'Better!' said Uncle Karl. 'Four-cylinder engine and over seventy miles an hour. No wife or family could compete!'

'And you are an old woman about it!'

'Certainly am,' agreed Uncle Karl, and he produced two folded dusters from a clean linen bag, gave one each to Hans and Erik and said, 'Wipe your shoes and jump in, since the zoo is not possible just now.'

It was Erik's first time in a car, and for a few minutes he sat stiff and silent, too overawed to move. Beside him, Hans was equally speechless and when Uncle Karl asked, 'Didn't you agree that maybe something would turn up today?' he could only nod and smile.

Then they turned a corner, and slowed down, because a whole lot of people were crossing the road and at that moment everything changed. A miracle happened.

'The Schmidts!' cried Erik, and so it was, Herr Schmidt, and Frau Schmidt, and the grandmother Schmidt, and a whole line of little Schmidts, all staring at the wonderful car with Erik and Hans inside. All the little Schmidts waved very cheerfully, and Erik and Hans laughed and waved back at them, and Herr Schmidt raised his hat and nodded in a definitely friendly way. So Erik and Hans forgave him and their faces melted into huge grins, and Uncle Karl tooted the wonderful horn that belonged to the superb red car, and they went on their way across the city.

Afterwards, Erik remembered that day as being one of golden sunshine from start to finish.

Uncle Karl drove through the long streets of Berlin as if he owned them. 'We are following part of the route that the Olympic torch will travel,' he told them. 'Less than a month now! You will need to turn out early if you want to see it pass. The whole city will be there.'

'We thought we might camp out,' said Hans. 'So as to get a good place. If the parents will agree.'

'That's the spirit,' said Uncle Karl. 'Of course they will agree. I will have a word or two. Three thousand runners in relay, all the way from Greece to Berlin! How could you miss it! You know how they will light the torch? Straight from the rays of the sun!'

'With a lens?' asked Erik.

'With a mirror. A great parabolic mirror. Now then, we come to the Lustgarten. See the banners!'

There had been Nazi flags all the way, red and white, with black swastikas in the centre. Now, there were also great white banners displaying the many-coloured Olympic rings.

'Glorious Olympic flags,' said Uncle Karl, smiling up at them. 'Here the torch will arrive, and the next day out to the stadium.'

'Lisa is going to the stadium,' Erik told him.

'She is?'

'Her Plague of German Nuisances got tickets,' said Hans. 'I can't imagine how, since everyone says they are like gold dust to find.'

Uncle Karl's eyes twinkled across at him, but all he said was, 'Is she pleased?'

'Very. Will you be going too, Uncle Karl?'

'I will. No patriotic German would miss such a spectacle if they could possibly manage otherwise. I am hoping to see the track events. I was a sprinter too, you know.'

Hans spluttered, and even Erik had to turn his head away.

'Ha!' said Uncle Karl. 'You may smile, but I know about these things. There's a young athlete going to be competing that I am very anxious to see.'

'German?'

'American.'

'American?'

'African American.'

'*African* American?'

'Jesse Owens. You remember that name and one day, many years from now, you can tell me . . .' He paused to look round at them. His grin was wicked.

'Tell you what?' asked Hans.

'Oh,' said Uncle Karl. 'That I was absolutely right. Now then, we'll do a little sprinting ourselves . . . Hold tight.'

Neither Hans nor Erik had ever known such speed. Out of the city, past the end of the tramlines, and suddenly green countryside was flying by in a blur of white dust. The engine sounded like a thousand bees. Uncle Karl tooted his horn at every bend and Hans and Erik waved and called to every plodding cart and cyclist and pedestrian they passed.

'This is wonderful!' shouted Hans. 'Where are we going?'

'Airfield,' said Uncle Karl. 'Got a friend who says he'll show you his glider.'

There was a long wooden hut. You could get beer or coffee and sausage and bread. Uncle Karl introduced them to friends all talking of aircraft and engines and little airstrips. Erik knew already that Uncle Karl could fly a plane, but now he came to realize what Hans already understood, which was that Uncle Karl had been an airman when their fathers had been soldiers. Also, that whereas their fathers' memories had been of bad times, Uncle Karl's were mostly the opposite.

'But it was a terrible war,' exclaimed Erik, in astonishment.

'Yes, yes,' said Uncle Karl, guiltily, 'but also, you know, it was fun . . . I flew an Albatross, there's a bird for you! They used to flip very easily . . . We have a picture somewhere here . . .' He called across the hut, 'Is there still that old album?' and then somebody began opening drawers in an ancient bureau, and after a while they called, 'Here!'

Erik and Hans found themselves looking at an old photograph, an aeroplane on its back with its wheels in the air, and the pilot, who was Uncle Karl, hanging upside down from his straps, and unable to free himself for laughing. Looking at it, Uncle Karl began laughing again.

'It happened at the very last second,' he said, mopping tears from his eyes. 'Never a sweeter descent and then the wind underneath and whoops! That day! If I could pick one day to live over, one hour, it would be that one! Who'll give the boys a ride?'

Hans went first. He had second seat in a glider: it went ten times faster than he'd thought it would and the view made his stomach clutch his spine in fear. He was so cold he became rigid. The last fifteen minutes he spent concentrating all his willpower on not being sick. He staggered back to Erik as pale as paper.

'What went wrong?' asked Erik.

'You wait, that's all,' said Hans.

Perhaps because Erik had watched so many birds – the scythe-cuts of swifts, the kestrels on their sky hooks, the ribbon trails of his beloved swallows – perhaps because of these, the air seemed to him a natural place to be, from that very first flight. Coming back to ground level did not seem sensible at all. So many obstacles down there to be dodged, and the speed suddenly gone, and then clambering out on to the airfield, and the shock of discovering the way that gravity clung to your legs.

Back on the green grass, Erik took a step, then a few more, then stood uncertainly. He found himself staring at a tree and thinking vaguely how you only saw them properly from above. Then Hans came running and asked, 'Are you feeling sick?'

Erik shook his head.

People were collecting round him, laughing. One of them was Uncle Karl. 'Well, Erik,' said Uncle Karl. 'What's the verdict? Do you think you can get used to it?'

'Oh yes,' said Erik, looking at the grass, and he nodded solemnly and rubbed his eyes and said, 'Oh yes, of course, I was before.'

'He means the flying, you dope, not the coming back to earth,' said Hans, and there was more laughter and when

Erik understood he joined in too.

'We'll make airmen of them yet,' Erik overheard Uncle Karl say to the friend who had found the album, and as he and Hans walked back to the hut with their arms across each other's shoulders, he heard the friend reply.

'I think we already have.'

Six
Ruby
Plymouth, 1936

The sherbet dab stayed behind the clock for weeks, and months and years. Violet moved it when she dusted, but she always put it back. The writing on the paper packet faded a little, but it was still there when Will left school, got cider drunk, was sick in the yard, joined the army and went away. For good, Ruby assumed, and was confounded when she came home from school only a couple of months later and found him sprawled on the sofa.

'Does Mum know you're here?' she asked.

'Yep.'

'Where is she?'

'Rushed out to the shops for kippers for tea.'

Kippers were his favourite, Ruby remembered. Will's favourite; her worst.

'I'd forgotten how dead this place is,' he continued. 'What time does Dad get back?'

'Not for ages. He's on late shift.'

'I was going to drag him out to the pub with me.'

'It'll be too late. He'll be tired.'

'You in charge now, are you?'

'No.'

'You don't seem very pleased to see me.'

'I thought you'd gone to the army,' she said.

'*Gone to the army*,' he mimicked. 'Do you know what you sound like?'

'What?'

'Stupid.'

Ruby digested this. Perhaps she did. Even so, she persisted. 'When Dad was in the army he had to fight. He fought in a war.'

'Well, double-stupid, I can't do that because there isn't a war.'

'What, not anywhere?'

'Nope.'

'Why did you join, then?'

'To get away from you,' said Will. 'Have you pinched my sherbet dab yet?'

'Of course not,' said Ruby indignantly.

All the same Will got up to check behind the clock, and when he saw the paper packet still there, said, 'That's a surprise.'

'I wouldn't take it.'

'You've taken everything else,' said Will. 'Have you been sleeping in my room?'

'No!'

'Touched my stuff?'

'No.'

'I bet you looked inside the door, though.'

Ruby flushed red with guilt. She had looked inside the

door. She'd looked and gloated: he's really gone. Will saw her face, and knew she had.

'Other people's families are sorry when they go away,' he said.

'I was sorry,' lied Ruby.

'You don't know what that camp's like.'

'Is there a camp?'

'You don't know anything,' said Will. 'I wish I'd never come back.'

Will had come back though, and he came again, one bitter January day with the sherbet dab still behind the clock, and the clock stopped and the fire out, and his mother sobbing, 'Oh, Will, oh, Will, oh, Will,' because he was too late. His father had been knocked off his bike and hours later died in hospital, very quickly, like something already arranged.

'What was he thinking of?' cried Violet. 'Straight under a bus. They said he turned right in front of it. Oh, Will, I'm so angry! And Ruby ill too, she's not half over measles. Mrs Morgan took her yesterday so I could be at the hospital. What else could I do?'

'You couldn't do nothing else,' Will said staunchly.

'I hope she's not thinking I've sent her away.'

'Course she's not,' said Will, and built up the fire, and made tea and toast and answered the door with equal good manners to well-wishers and nosy parkers alike. He stayed for a week and was everything a son should be, said Violet. She was glad of him at the funeral, solemn and handsome in his uniform, giving her his arm. Everyone said he looked a credit to the family and his dad would be so proud.

Ruby, still not well enough to go out, spent that long sodden day with Mrs Morgan. She knew her well; she was an old friend of her mother's.

Mrs Morgan was strong and practical and kind. She said, 'I mind the day your parents married and your mum wore your Aunt Clarry's pink velvet beret.'

'I don't call her aunt because she's not my proper aunt,' said Ruby, much too miserable to be nice. 'My proper aunts hate me because of the birthmarks on my face.'

'Oh, Ruby Amaryllis, what nonsense.'

'They hate my name too.'

'Absolute rubbish.'

'I still don't know what an amaryllis is.'

'It's a flower like a lily but better,' said Mrs Morgan and Ruby could hear her dad's voice in those words so clearly that she doubled up and sobbed.

'Their wedding was a happy day,' said Mrs Morgan, gathering Ruby in her arms and holding tight. 'I gave them a horseshoe I made myself. I had five. Your mum and dad had one. Our Christopher had one. Peter, Clarry's brother, he had one when he married that Vanessa who always made me laugh. Miss Vane, their neighbour, who married the rag and bone man, had one. And there's one left I'm keeping for special.'

'What happens at a funeral, Mrs Morgan?'

'There'll be flowers. I sent roses. White. There'll be a lot of flowers because he was a highly thought-of man. They'll have readings and hymns. They'll say how happy he was, which he was, and how he loved you all, which he did. And he will be laid to rest in the good earth. With the flowers over him. I'll make us a cup of tea and then we'll have a look at the hens. I've not collected the eggs.'

Mrs Morgan lived out of the city, in a cottage that you had to go to in a taxi if you were in a hurry, or on a slow bus if you weren't, because it was nine miles. Or you could ride a bicycle, like Mrs Morgan often did, into town and back again, to do her housekeeping for Clarry's father, old Mr Penrose. Mrs Morgan was tough. She'd known hard times and survived them. She got Ruby through that day with words and hot soup, wood chopping for kindling, *Children's Hour* on the wireless, and sit-down-at-the-table-and-write-this-shopping-list-for-me. It was such a long list that Ruby fell asleep over it and when she woke up Clarry was there to collect her, saying, 'Will has had to go back this afternoon, Ruby, but I've borrowed my brother's car and I'm staying for a few days to give your mum a hand. There's a lovely fire at home, and a cottage pie in the oven for supper.'

'Is Mum all right?' asked Ruby.

'Yes, she is, but she'll be much better for seeing you. And I've brought you a letter from my other god-daughter, Kate.'

Halfway home Ruby demanded fiercely, 'Is he in heaven now?'

Clarry stopped the car, and put her fists under her chin to help her concentrate while she thought about this. Ruby watched her with great care.

'Yes,' said Clarry, nodding. 'Yes, I think he must be,' and started the engine and drove on again.

SEVEN
Kate
Oxford, Christmas 1936

Kate's grandfather lived in Plymouth, in the narrow stone house where her father Peter and Clarry had grown up. He was as firmly fixed in it as a tortoise in its shell. He would never come to visit them, and when they made the journey to go and see him he would ask, 'How long is this for? Is it necessary?'

Every year Kate's parents invited him for Christmas, and each time he wouldn't come, until one year, instead of saying, 'Er . . . perhaps not,' he said, 'Oh, very well. If I must.'

'Hurray!' said Kate's mother, Vanessa, 'He'll be happy and looked after and do all the proper Christmas things.'

'All the Christmas things in Christendom wouldn't melt that heart of stone,' said Kate's father. 'And I bet he'll change his mind.'

'We won't let him,' said Vanessa, and when a postcard arrived from Plymouth, just as she was about to set off to fetch him, she put it writing-side down on the mantelpiece and arranged a spray of holly on the top. Then she rushed away and the next day returned triumphant, with Grandfather beside her looking exactly like someone who had written to say that on second thoughts they would very much prefer to stay at home.

Which he had.

'I'm completely unprepared for all this,' he complained, as they helped him out of the car and he looked with distaste at the holly wreath on the door and murmured damningly, 'Quaint.'

Kate got behind Janey for safety.

'In we go, in we go!' said her mother, her arms full of luggage that Grandfather made no attempt to carry. 'Boys, bring the rest for us. Charlie, be careful!'

Charlie had picked up his grandfather's briefcase and staggered at the weight. 'It feels like it's full of rocks!' he exclaimed. 'What's it got in it?'

His grandfather turned and looked at him.

'Sorry,' said Charlie meekly.

Vanessa remained cheerful. 'Now,' she said, 'you must make yourself at home with us and not worry about a thing.'

'Hmm,' said Grandfather, doubtfully, and he looked around the little hall, with the Christmas cards on the table and the banisters twisted with ivy and red paper and said, as if to himself, 'Gifts, I imagine, will be expected.'

'Oh no, no!' protested everyone, Janey, Bea, the boys and their mother, even Kate shook her head. 'No, you mustn't think . . .'

Grandfather ignored them all, looked down at Kate with his cold pale gaze, and said, 'Perhaps this child can advise me.'

'Me?' squeaked Kate, and began her panicky coughing. 'Me? I don't think . . . I don't know . . . I . . .'

'Of course Kate and I will take you Christmas shopping, if that's what you'd like,' said Vanessa, while behind her back Janey dabbed eucalyptus drops on to a handkerchief and held it out to Kate. 'We can visit the lovely bookshop, and afterwards get chocolates and things, almost next door.'

'I suppose that would suffice,' said Grandfather, and Kate stopped coughing and gave him a glance of startled interest because *suffice* was a word she had never heard outside of *The Tailor of Gloucester*. It gave her hope to hear Grandfather use it. Did he care for mice in satins and taffeta? Would he buy, with his last pennies, milk for a cat? The Tailor of Gloucester had been very, very poor. Was it fair to take Grandfather unexpectedly Christmas shopping?

As soon as she could, Kate dragged her mother aside and whispered these worries.

'Kate, he has dragon hoards of cash!' said Vanessa. 'And he can't spend it all on booze. It isn't good for him. Besides, it was his idea.'

'Perhaps he'll forget,' said Kate, but he didn't. The next day at breakfast he asked peevishly, 'What about this bookshop? Has the child remembered?'

So they went with him to Blackwell's, and although he glanced around the Christmas displays and asked, 'Who buys this stuff?' he did allow them to pile on to the counter *Sweet William* for Charlie, *Cold Comfort Farm* for Bea, Arthur Ransome for Simon (who liked stories), an atlas for Tod (who didn't), a lovely blue diary with silver-edged pages for Janey and *The Box of Delights* for Kate (which she pretended not to see).

After this, Kate's mother led the way to the sweet shop, where they found chocolate cherries for Clarry, and Kate managed to secretly buy her grandfather a gold chocolate pocket watch with her own private money. Then they took him home, Vanessa pointing out the beauties of Oxford on the way.

'Dank,' said Grandfather. 'It gathers the fog. It was dank in my day, and it's dank yet and the pavements are still a disgrace.'

'Did you . . . did you used to live here?' asked Kate, surprised into speech.

'Classics,' Grandfather said.

'He studied here,' translated her mother. 'Like Daddy.'

'Not like your father at all,' said Grandfather. 'He was a damned medic. Mind you, that cuckoo in the nest was worse. Had my doubts about him all along. Not the slightest family resemblance. No brains at all.'

'He means Rupert and he loves him really,' whispered Kate's mother.

Grandfather snorted.

'And it's *Christmas*!' said Vanessa. 'Christmas Eve! The carol service tonight, and all the boys in the choir.'

'Must be a relief to get them out of the house,' grunted Grandfather.

'That's not . . .' began Vanessa. 'I meant . . . Oh, never mind. Poor Peter can't make it, he's at the hospital till ten, but the rest of us have been looking forward to it for ages, haven't we, Kate?'

Kate nodded.

'The children are going to get on with decorating the tree this afternoon,' continued Vanessa brightly, 'and Clarry will be with us for supper.'

Grandfather said he'd had a headache ever since the unspeakable coffee at breakfast time, that he must have lunch exactly at one, and that he couldn't miss his afternoon rest.

'It was terrible coffee; it was out of a bottle,' Vanessa agreed. 'You shall never have it again.'

'I'd like to think not,' said Grandfather in a voice of such melancholy that Kate looked up into his face. For one swift moment his eyes gleamed back at her with such intensity that she was astonished. Was he angry? Or was he, possibly, laughing at them?

'Poison,' he said.

'What?' asked Kate, startled.

'Bottled coffee.'

'Oh.'

They took him home and cosseted him with soup and smoked salmon and scrambled eggs. Also tea and hot-water bottles up in his bedroom, and his briefcase left handily by his bed. Kate noticed it clinked very gently, and Charlie, loitering outside the door, heard it too.

'Like bottles,' he said. 'Bottles snuggling up to bottles. Hurry up, Kate! Dad bought electric lights for the Christmas tree.'

Always before they'd had candles – beautiful, fragile, extraordinarily unsafe. These lights were an extravagance and Charlie unpacked them solemnly. 'They cost nearly a pound,' he said. 'Nineteen and six. More than the turkey.'

'Charlie, you be careful with them,' warned Janey.

'I am being careful,' said Charlie, and wound them round his neck like a necklace and plugged them into the wall, so that his face glowed green and yellow and red and blue, all at once.

'Take them OFF,' ordered Bea, and unwound him while Simon and Tod fetched battered boxes from the cupboard under the stairs. They were filled with homemade snowflakes, glass balls, pipe-cleaner reindeer, fat felt robins, and a china angel for the top of the tree. There was an argument about what was junk (most of it, said Simon), and what was family heirloom (most of it, said Bea), but in the end it all went on, and so did the coloured lights. The room became a chaos of empty boxes, pine needles, moulting strands of tinsel, and crumpled tissue paper. Grandfather looked round the door and said, 'Good Lord,' and disappeared.

'It does look awful,' admitted Janey. 'Let's tidy and then have a proper lights switch-on with everybody here.'

So the floor was cleared, the adults rounded up – Clarry with them, just in time – the room darkened and Janey said, 'Now, Kate.'

'Me?'

'You can be switcher-oner,' said Janey. 'Get down behind the tree.'

'Not me,' said Kate, shaking her head.

63

'Of course you,' said Janey, hardly impatiently at all. 'Scrooch down on the floor and be ready when we all say *Now*.'

'I don't think I know how.'

'You just shove,' Charlie told her.

'Shove what?'

'The plug into the plug socket,' said Janey. 'Now then, *Three . . .*'

'Does it matter which way up?' asked Kate, groping around in the dark.

'It only fits one way. You can't get it wrong.'

'I trust you have checked that they are properly earthed?' enquired Grandfather.

'They worked when Charlie put them round his neck,' said Simon cheerfully, 'and necks don't come much earthier than Charlie's.'

'Is this a countdown or not?' demanded Tod. '*Three, two . . .*'

'Gaudy gimcrack rubbish,' remarked Grandfather. 'Don't say I didn't warn you if the whole house goes up in smoke.'

'We won't, darling,' said Vanessa cheerfully, taking his arm and hugging him. 'Ready, Kate? *Three, two, one . . .*'

Kate fumbled madly, found the plug, located the socket, discovered she was sitting on the lead, tugged in desperation, and cried, 'Wait, wait!'

'*NOW!*' chorused all her relations except Grandfather.

Kate yanked at the lead and to her relief it came suddenly loose. 'Got it!' she panted, and plunged the plug into the socket.

64

Sharp blue fire flickered between the newly wrenched wires. The room lit up in a rainbow flash of colour. *Bang!* went every coloured light bulb, all of them blowing at once, and Kate leaped screaming to her feet and became terribly tangled in fir branches.

The tree toppled sideways and thudded to the floor.

Tinkle, tinkle went the thin broken glass of the fragile coloured balls, and the branches seemed to sigh.

It was no use telling Kate that it wasn't her fault, because it was. Her last desperate pull on the lead had been disastrous. Even after two hours doctoring by Clarry, the tree was not the same. The branches were bent, the nicest decorations shattered, the angel with her silver wings had landed in several pieces. Early supper in the kitchen with chicken pie and devilled eggs was supposed to be a treat, but Kate couldn't eat. She coughed miserably over her pink jelly, spilled her lemonade and drooped.

'Kate, you're a bit dampening,' complained Tod. 'Nobody liked that angel anyway.'

'I expect she'll glue back together,' said Bea. 'Did anyone save the bits?'

Clarry said guiltily that she knew where most of them were and everyone tried to look as if this was good news, as if they didn't know perfectly well that the angel would spend the rest of her Christmas sifting slowly down to the bottom of the dustbin.

'Whole thing was inevitable from the start,' said Grandfather, and pulled out a silver flask and gave himself some whisky as a reward for being right.

'One day I'm going to have a flask like that,' said Charlie admiringly. 'I know something that'll cheer you up, Kate, only I can't tell you.'

All day, Charlie had been bursting with a secret. He, the second smallest choirboy, was to be the opening soloist in 'Once in Royal David's City' at the carol service that night. This honour, known as being 'Once In', was a privilege that no choirboy was ever given twice. Usually, people were only told at the last minute, but Charlie, who was so often late, had been given a hint about being on time and had understood at once. No one else was to know though, and to put his family off guessing his secret, he said, 'If it's me being Once In, no one's to look at me in case I laugh.'

'You won't laugh,' said Tod, who was safe because he'd done it the year before. 'You'll be dying of fright.'

'It might be any of the other boys,' said Janey. 'Or Simon. He's never done it.'

'Not me,' said Simon sadly. 'Too old.'

'And too dozy,' said Tod.

Their mother took charge then, and demanded help with the clearing up, and in the rushing about that followed, Charlie dropped a dish of trifle much too close to Grandfather, who immediately trod in it.

'Whoops!' said Charlie and vanished, and didn't reappear until much later, when all the work was done.

'Hello,' he said, sticking his head round the kitchen door,

'you've washed up supper. Good!'

'You've got a flipping cheek,' said Tod. 'And you'd better get moving. The choir's supposed to be there half an hour before the rest.'

'Quickly, then,' said Vanessa. 'Off you go. Scoot! The rest of us will be along soon. Oh, Kate . . .'

Kate was coughing again. It was awful. She'd ruined the Christmas tree and now she was going to cough all through the carol service. She said, 'Could I not?'

'Not go?'

'I don't mind staying on my own.'

'Of course you can't stay on your own, Kate darling,' said her mother, and a chorus of people chimed in to say of course not, of course not, but they would love to stop behind too.

'Er . . .' said Grandfather. 'I haven't the slightest intention of singing carols.'

They paused, the whole room.

'And I trust you don't think me incapable of supervising er . . . er . . .' He looked at Kate.

'Kate,' she said faintly.

'Kate,' he repeated. 'Yes.'

'Oh,' said Kate, and gazed around at her family who were all suddenly watching her very intently indeed.

'Would you be all right?' asked Clarry, so hopefully, that despite her alarm, Kate had to say of course she would. The next thing she knew, she was abandoned. The front door had slammed and the house was suddenly very silent.

'Fuss,' said Grandfather, and then he looked at Kate, now

blinking back tears, and demanded, 'What? You wanted to go with them?'

'Yes, but I cough.'

'Control it. Are you coughing now?'

'No, but—'

'Well then. For heaven's sake!'

'What?'

'Get your coat! Wait in the hall. Hurry up.'

'I—'

'Before I lose patience,' said her grandfather.

That was how Kate found herself scurrying after him, out of the house, and down the street and into a seat far back in a chilly corner of the lamplit church. The organ was playing. There was no sign of her family, she guessed they were near the front, but two bundled-up people came to their pew and asked, 'Do you mind if we join you?'

'It would be quite intolerable,' said Grandfather coldly.

Kate blushed in shame as they backed away. She wished she'd never come, yet here she was, Grandfather on one side, a large cracked tomb on the other. She began to cough.

Grandfather took from his pocket his silver flask, with its cap that unscrewed to make a cup, half filled it, and handed it to Kate. She smelled it instantly. Whisky.

'Calm down,' he hissed. 'Sip.'

Kate shook her head and gasped desperately.

'Sip the water.'

It was water. It smelled of whisky, but it was cold water. It was a miracle liquid. It saved her. She could hold up her head and wipe her streaming eyes, and there were the candles, dazzling bright, and the choir in white surplices, and the most tremendous feeling of happiness all about, because it was nearly Christmas.

The service began, and it was Simon after all who was Once In and sang the opening verse, neither too old, nor too dozy, nor dying of fright, his voice dropping the notes like the chimes of a clear bell into the golden light.

It's perfect, Kate thought.

Grandfather's eyes were half closed with boredom and his thin lips folded shut. The stone statues in their alcoves looked more alive than he did, yet three times he saved Kate, filling and passing the silver cup.

His eyes snapped open when the final blessing began. He sat tense until, at the words 'now and forever more', he nudged Kate with a very sharp elbow.

'Amen,' finished the minister, and echoed the congregation, all except Grandfather who ordered, 'Now!' and under cover of the general shuffling and collecting of dropped bags and service sheets, got sharply to his feet.

'Out!' snapped Grandfather, and as the organ began flinging 'In Dulci Jubilo' up to the roof arches and all along the nave, he hustled Kate into the night. 'And you keep quiet about this, or they'll be bleating even more.'

'Who . . .?'

'Wretched family, flock of sheep, never a moment's peace.'

'But—'

'Don't you start bleating too!'

'Aren't we going to tell them?'

'Are you an absolute fool? Faster, please.'

'I thought your flask had whisky in it. Did you pour it away?'

'Pour away good whisky? Of course not, I drank it. Filled it in the kitchen while you were dithering about.'

They were almost home, and they were unpursued. There was time to pause under a streetlamp and catch their breath. The lamplight pooled around them. A few snowflakes fell. Somewhere a bell chimed.

'It was lovely, wasn't it?' asked Kate timidly.

'It was absolute bilge,' said Grandfather. 'Supposedly intelligent adults wallowing in ridiculous fairy tales. Come on!'

They'd accidentally left the door unlocked, but they hadn't been burgled. They were back in the living room when the rest of the family appeared, marvelling at the snow, teasing Simon, and most of all, congratulating Kate and Grandfather, who'd survived so well without them that everyone was too kind to mention that they'd let the fire go out.

'I saw you!' said Charlie, as soon as he and Kate had a moment together. 'No one else did, though.'

'Don't tell!'

Charlie held up a finger, licked it, and drew it across his throat.

'Did you mind not being Once In?'

'No,' said Charlie, who'd seen Simon's face when he'd said 'Too old', and left as soon as he could, to sprint all the way to church, blurt out, 'Simon wants it more than anything,' and run all the way back home.

'Stockings!' said Clarry, coming in with a bundle of red and green and blue ones, made long ago by Vanessa. 'And bedtime, Kate, or you'll be too tired for Christmas in the morning.'

(Over by the fire Grandfather raised a sardonic eyebrow.)

'You as well, Charlie boy,' agreed Peter, just home from the hospital.

'Will you come up, Clarry, when we're ready?' asked Charlie. He had a camp bed in with Kate that night, while Clarry had his room. 'And stay and talk to us?'

'Perhaps,' said Clarry, but she sat down quite willingly when she arrived and admired their dangling stockings.

'Tell us your best Christmas present ever,' said Kate.

'That's easy,' said Clarry. 'One Christmas just before the war, Grandfather bought me a little silver watch. I have it still. I'll show you.'

'What else?'

'Another year we had a Christmas party, with presents for everyone on the Christmas tree. And we danced and played games and sang carols.'

'Once In?' asked Charlie.

'All the old carols.'

'Who was there?'

'Oh, our neighbours, and Vanessa and her lovely brother Simon, and your father and me and Rupert.'

'And did you have stockings?' asked Kate, but Clarry was lost in memories and didn't reply until Charlie said, 'I wish Rupert was here now.'

'Much too busy,' said Clarry bravely. 'Stockings? No. No one thought of stockings.'

'You'll have one this year,' said Charlie, who'd helped with the preparations and added a necklace of red glass beads as his own contribution. 'Everyone will, except I don't know about Grandfather.'

'Of course he will, I made him one.'

Kate sat up with delight.

'Are you going to put it on the end of his bed?'

'No, no! He wouldn't like that. I'm going to leave it by his door.'

'What's it got in it?' asked Charlie, so Clarry took a deep breath and recited: 'A-green-scarf-with-tassels, a-pen-with-his-old-college-crest-on, anchovy-spread-for-toast, peppermint-cremes, cedar-wood-shaving-soap, a cigar, the-Christmas-*Punch*-rolled-up-with-a-ribbon, and a cracker.'

Kate went to sleep reciting this list, and woke to find it was Christmas morning. There were sugar mice and chocolate pennies and Charlie had indoor fireworks. Kate found a glass globe with a reindeer inside, and falling snow when she turned it upside down. Then Clarry came in with her chocolate cherries and a tiny model of the Eiffel Tower. It had a label underneath that read, *This time next week.*

'From Rupert,' guessed Charlie at once.

'Clever boy!'

'And you must be going to Paris. Have you been before?'

'Not for ages, but Rupert has, lots. He lived there for a long while.'

'It's a good present,' said Charlie, carving coconut ice with a new pocket knife. 'I've got a sort of rubbish torch thing. Look.'

'It's not a torch, it's a bike lamp,' said Clarry, inspecting it.

'What good's a bike lamp without a . . .' began Charlie, and then leaped out of bed. They heard him jump the stairs in three bumps, the back door flung open, and jubilant shrieks.

Then it was breakfast time and Grandfather appeared holding his stocking and saying in a very complaining voice, 'I fell over this. Can somebody please reclaim.'

'It's for you!' said Charlie. 'Open it! Open it!'

'Oh, really,' said Grandfather wearily. 'I don't think so.' Nevertheless, he picked out the red cracker, looked at it solemnly, said, 'Very droll,' laid it aside and unpacked the rest with such withering remarks that Charlie became crimson with suffocated laughter. The twins picked him up, carted him to the kitchen, and dosed him with cold water poured over his head.

'Help!' squealed Charlie, and reached for the cooking brandy, put ready for the pudding, and took a great swig, just as his mother arrived.

'Charlie!'

'It's all burny and lovely!' said Charlie, and took another gulp.

'Charlie Penrose,' protested his mother, grabbing the bottle. 'You will end up an old soak just like . . . just . . . just . . . Goodness, there's the telephone! Who would telephone at this hour on Christmas morning?'

'Bea says to tell you it's the hospital for Daddy,' said Kate, appearing in the doorway.

'No, no, it can't be!' moaned Vanessa, but it was, and two minutes later Peter was gone, and no sooner had the door closed than there was a loud bang, which was Grandfather dropping his cracker on to the newly stoked fire. Vanessa put down the brandy bottle and ran and Charlie, who was suffering a very strong reaction after his extreme unselfishness the night before, had a few more fatal swigs, marched into the dining room, and sang with very great clarity:

'Wild shepherds washed their socks at night
And piled them on the grasses
Don't do your pants, the angel cried
Cos then I'll see your—'

Clarry, who was nearest, seized Charlie by his shoulders and hurried him out of the door. From the other side they heard:

'Good King Wenceslas went out
To the pub on Monday
Tuesday, Wednesday, Thursday too
Friday through to Sunday
All that day he said his prayers –
(That was not a fun day)
Never mind, King Wenceslas!
You'll be back on Mo-hon-day!'

'Everyone, breakfast!' called Kate's mother, who had rushed back to the kitchen and returned with an enormous tray piled high. 'Fresh tea and proper coffee! Eggs, hot sausage rolls, orange fruit salad. Clarry's dealing with Charlie. What a morning!'

'I think I would like to go home,' said Grandfather.

Kate's mother let go of the breakfast tray so suddenly that it hit the table with a crash. 'Go home?' she repeated.

'You did say that if I should decide not to stay, either you, or Clarry or Peter . . .'

'But it's Christmas Day,' said Janey.

'Does that make a difference?' asked Grandfather, sounding so genuinely surprised that for a moment Vanessa's patience slipped and she said, 'There are all these children in the house, a turkey in the oven that's been there since six this morning, presents under the Christmas tree, two elderly neighbours coming to dinner and Peter's at the hospital because there was an accident at the railway crossing . . .'

'Coffee, Grandfather?' asked Janey. 'Kate, I've taken the top off an egg for you . . .'

'*We three kings of Oxford St Giles,*' Charlie's voice, choirboy bright, came floating down the stairs.

'*One with pimples, another with—*'

'Not that one!' exclaimed Tod and Simon, and went racing out of the room together.

'They learn them in the choir,' explained Bea placidly to her grandfather. 'They can't help it. It's traditional.'

'All sorts of lovely traditions,' said Kate's mother, who was recovering with hot coffee. 'Of course I'll take you back, Grandfather darling, if you absolutely insist, but . . . Kate!'

Kate was awash, silent tears pouring down her face at the

75

thought of Christmas over before it had hardly started.

'Look at Kate!' said Janey, and Grandfather looked and said, 'Really. Not again. Control yourself! Here!'

In the surprised silence that followed he splashed water into a tumbler and pushed it towards Kate, who gulped it down and said, 'Thank you, Grandfather. Please don't go.'

'One damned drama after another,' said Grandfather. 'I suppose I can wait another day. What's going on upstairs?'

'Charlie's being put to bed to sleep it off,' said Vanessa, and as she spoke they heard Clarry's voice as she left him. 'Sleep tight, sweet Charlie. May flights of angels sober you up in time for dinner . . . Hello, everyone, sorry I'm late. Yes, please, coffee!'

'Family life,' said Grandfather, getting out his flask, which plainly wasn't filled with water any more. 'No, thank you!'

Then he poured himself a whisky, picked up the whole plate of sausage rolls, said, 'If you can spare me,' and stalked out of the room.

Only Kate saw, but as he passed, he glanced at her and winked.

A great rush of affection swept over Kate. She ran after Grandfather calling, 'Wait!' and when he turned to look at her, she very carefully, her face solemn with concentration, winked back.

EIGHT
Dog
Scrapyard, East London, 1937

The scrapyard dog belonged to the family that lived in the crumbly brick building, half warehouse, half dwelling place, at the back of the yard. There was a girl and a shrill-voiced old woman, and three or four loud-laughing, rough-booted men, who came and went. The girl was mostly invisible, but sometimes the door would open quietly and narrowly, and she would seep out of the gap to lose herself in the chaotic misery of the yard. There was a huge, broken winch that had once unloaded cargoes from the holds of ships. The girl would hunch down there, so near to the dog that he could smell her old clothes smell. Mostly she was motionless, glaring at the house, blank-faced and snivelling. Other times she would look around, at the broken-glass-topped walls, and the sky that hung just above the chimney pots, and the iridescent colours that spilled oil made in the puddles. Now and then she stirred a puddle with her toe, gazing as the patterns broke. All the time the dog watched her, in case she should suddenly lash out. Every time she moved, he flinched, although she never brought the yard broom, his greatest enemy of all.

'*Hello, dog.*'

She was looking at him.

'*Dog?*'

It was absolutely terrifying, being watched like that.

'*Hello, dog.*'

The door was pulled open then, and the old woman screeched down the yard, 'Don't you make a pet of that dog!'

'Shut up,' muttered the girl.

'You make a pet of that dog and it'll go soft!'

'Old bat,' the girl said quietly.

'What did you say?'

'Wash your ears!' yelled the girl, so loudly she tumbled off the winch, and the old woman grabbed the broom and came scurrying down the yard.

'*Waah! Waah! Waah!*' barked the dog, over and over, flinging himself forward, choking on his chain, hysterical with fear. '*Waah! Waah! Waah! Waah!*'

Not gone soft at all.

NINE
Erik and Hans
Berlin, 1937

The war that Hans's father and Uncle Karl had fought in, the war that had ruined Erik's father's health so he died before Erik ever knew him, had ended with defeat for Germany, late in 1918. The next year, a treaty had been drawn up by the winning nations. It was called the Treaty of Versailles. Germany had been blamed more than any other country, and made to pay for the damage the war had caused. They had to pay with land, and with gold, and they had to agree to having a smaller army, and a much smaller navy and no air force at all.

Erik and Hans grew up hearing opinions of the Treaty of Versailles. It was a sort of national ache that nobody could forget. Hans's father, once started on the subject, could go on for hours and hours. He said the youth of Germany should rise up in indignation about the Treaty of Versailles. He especially said this on Sundays when Lisa and her mother were in the kitchen and Hans was the only youth of Germany about. Hans used to groan because he had heard it so many times before. One Sunday, Hans's father was saying it yet again, and Hans was groaning, yet again, when Uncle Karl arrived.

'The youth of Germany,' said Uncle Karl, clapping Hans on his shoulder, 'should fetch their friend and come with me to the airfield . . .'

'Oh, thank goodness!' shouted Hans and bolted for the door.

'. . . if their father will allow,' finished Uncle Karl, laughing.

'Yes, yes, take him along!' said Hans's father. 'Better up in the sky than down in the mud.' He was thinking – he never forgot – of the war he'd fought himself.

Quite regularly now, Uncle Karl took the boys to the airfield, and they also often went on their own. They made the journey by bike; Hans on his and Erik on Lisa's, swapping on the way back because Lisa's bike was slower and Hans was always fair.

'Everyone starts with learning to make the coffee,' Uncle Karl had warned them, but neither of them minded making the coffee, nor washing up the mugs. The teasing was good natured: 'Poor boys. They have to do something now they're blacklisted by the zoo.'

They didn't just learn to make the coffee. They learned map-reading, and planning a route, which seemed like it should be simple and turned out to be anything but. They polished windscreens, rubbed down old paint and added new, and lubricated wheels. They hauled on ropes and ran down hills to launch the little one-man sailplanes. They argued over altimeters and compasses. They found out that propellers must be balanced, and cables checked and winches greased. They went on flights with dual controls and men who sat back with folded arms and said, 'You take her for a bit.'

That was how it began. It was an adventure and a sort of escape. Now in Berlin, *Heil Hitler* salutes were everywhere and huge red-and-white flags with black swastikas were appearing all over the city.

At school, Herr Schmidt had a new responsibility and a new organization to run. It was called the Hitler Youth.

'Everyone enrolled now?' he asked his students, and everyone had, even Erik and Hans, but when it came to the long, tedious, after-school meetings, they were seldom there. This had been easy enough to get away with when they first signed up, but now things were changing.

'Boys,' Herr Schmidt told them privately. 'Come on. No more excuses. Gets you fit. Outside in summer. Lots to learn. Besides, bright boys like you might want to go on to university. Completely impossible if you don't join in. Even a decent apprenticeship, for that matter, would be ruled out.'

Ever since the day in Uncle Karl's car when he had smiled at them and raised his hat, Herr Schmidt had been a friend, so Erik and Hans told him very cheerfully about the pastry stall and the zoo.

'This is the new Germany,' said Herr Schmidt. 'Open your eyes. The fairy tales are over.'

He suddenly sounded terribly sad.

'Please don't worry, Herr Schmidt,' said Erik.

'Don't worry!' repeated Herr Schmidt, no longer sad, but indignant. 'It's you who should worry! You should have been much more involved long ago. You'll be leaving school soon.

It looks very bad. Reflects on your families too. Your father will want to keep that job at the post office, Hans. I am telling you this for your own good.'

They looked at him and believed him.

'For your own good, Hans. For your own good, Erik. Heil Hitler,' said Herr Schmidt.

When someone said that to you, you were supposed to say it back.

'Heil Hitler,' said Hans.

'Heil Hitler,' said Erik.

And that was that, but it could have been worse because now the airfield was doubly wonderful. And doubly patriotic. Helping at an airfield unquestionably trumped marching about with the Hitler Youth. Even Herr Schmidt agreed.

Erik was first to take the controls and land a glider. Hans did it a week later. They went to the zoo to celebrate, and the zoo was looking magnificent. Recently Germany had passed the strictest animal protection laws in the world. Lion cubs were hoped for.

Yet even the zoo was not free from the swastika flags. Paper ones made for children could be bought at the kiosk near the entrance. Erik saw a small boy poke one through the bars of a monkey cage. A very tiny monkey reached out a miniature hand and took it, and then, with thoughtful round eyes, and nimble brown fingers, shredded the flag into wisps and fragments and let them fall to the ground.

Erik looked at the monkey with love, and murmured, 'Good monkey.'

Hans said, 'We need more monkeys like that.'

Both of them spoke carefully, making sure nobody was about who could hear. They did this hardly realizing they were doing it. Their world had changed, and they had changed with it.

One day Erik suddenly remembered Fraulein Trisk, who he hadn't thought of or seen for years.

'Poor old lady,' said his mother. 'Well, I always thought she would be better off staying with her niece in the country.'

'Oh,' said Erik guiltily, thinking that he really ought to have said goodbye, but still, it was all a long time ago and anyway she would probably have got annoyed and spluttered her firecracker splutters. 'You used to bake her a birthday cake and light her stove on Saturdays,' he remembered.

'Sundays,' said his mother, not looking at him.

Erik opened his mouth, and then shut it without speaking. He thought, *Fraulein Trisk*, and realized for the first time that it was a Jewish surname. He didn't say anything to his mother because she was plumping cushions. They had six cushions. Erik's mother picked them up in pairs, one in each hand, and clapped them together, leaning out of the window.

Smack! went the cushions.

The rug was already hanging over the windowsill, shaken clean and upside down. The furniture was all pushed into a corner. Erik's mother flung the cushions in a heap, swept the floor like a whirlwind, dusted the shelf, swiped the table, rubbed the photograph of Erik's father with a corner of her apron, put her hands on her hips, and looked at Erik. He was taller than her now.

'Sundays,' she said.

'Are you sure?' asked Erik.

'Of course I'm sure! I should know! Who else could know but me?' she cried.

'Only me,' said Erik.

There were no Jewish students left in school. Often you saw signs on shops: NO JEWS. The signs had disappeared for a few months when the Olympic Games had been held in the city, but soon after they were back. Hans said that people were divided into three groups about the signs. There were those who were glad to see them. Those who were not glad to see them. And those who pretended they didn't see them at all.

Erik repeated this to his mother.

'Yes, yes, Hans is probably right,' she said. 'Such a fuss about nothing, though. There are plenty of good shops the Jewish people can use. It's not so important.'

'Not important!' exclaimed Erik.

'Listen, Erik. Men have shops that women would never go to, right? And women have shops where men would blush to enter the door. And children have toyshops and book readers have bookshops and there are rich people's shops in Charlottenburg where I would never dare show my nose! Never! Not a chance! The looks I would get if I did! They really might as well write "Apartment Cleaners Not Welcome" on the door.'

'What are you saying?' asked Erik. 'Are you saying it's just the same?'

'Of course it's the same!' she cried, beginning to bang cushions about again. 'Of course it is. So stop always asking questions.'

There were grades of glider pilot licence : A1 ('One loop and three landings,' Erik told Hans. 'Easy.'), A2 ('Two loops, six landings, circle a church tower upside down. Easier still!' Hans told Erik). 'What next?'

'Next is just the same as before but you do it with your eyes shut,' said Erik. 'The only problem is, you have to flip pancakes on the loops.'

'Flipping pancakes is all wrong,' said Hans. 'You should fold them over gently, with spiced apple in the middle. I shall serve them in the mornings at my stall outside the zoo.'

'With cream?' asked Erik.

'Naturally.'

'You're going to be very busy,' observed Erik.

'I know,' said Hans. 'I shall probably need staff.'

'Don't look at me,' said Erik. 'No one can manage a whole zoo and pancakes too.'

'My dear Erik,' said Hans. 'I plan to recruit pretty girls in white aprons, not shambling zookeepers with birds' nests in their hats.'

'After National service,' said Erik.

'After National service,' said Hans.

They were both sixteen. National service was compulsory in Germany now, as soon as you left school.

Whenever it could be managed, Erik and Hans still visited the zoo. Their blacklisting was long forgotten, even by Herr Schmidt. And the zoo was more fascinating than ever. An Indian elephant had given birth, and a new gorilla had arrived. He looked much smaller than Bobby, the gorilla Erik remembered from his childhood, but then, sometimes, the whole zoo looked smaller.

But no less beloved.

The new Siberian tiger was the latest exotic arrival. Unusually for Berlin Zoo, the Siberian tiger had a cage – there was no attempt to contain it with moats and ditches and glass. Once Erik saw it charge, from stillness to a terrifying anger, shoulder first at the bars of its prison.

It was an astonishing, shocking animal, not only because it was twice the size of the other big cats, but also because it would meet a human gaze. The Siberian tiger hated people. It would lock gaze, eye to eye, in a glare of such menace and power that it would be hard to move away.

Hard to move at all, Erik found. When he first went to see it, he stayed all afternoon. Hans found him there, looking miserable, and they didn't leave till closing. They had been in a fight with some other boys that morning, and the marks were very visible, even though they'd won. Hans was still smouldering.

'We should have dropped them in the river,' he said. 'Nazi bullies.'

Erik felt the bridge of his nose, very gently, between thumb and fingertip. 'I think it might be broken,' he said. 'What are we going to tell them at home?'

'We'll say we had an argument!' said Hans.

'You and me?'

'Yes.'

Erik laughed so much the tiger was startled. It was good to laugh again.

It was not long afterwards, on the last day of school, that Erik noticed something in the attic window, high above the street. It was a fern, bright green. He was so surprised he stood still for a moment, and Hans asked, 'What is it?' and followed his gaze.

'Absolutely nothing,' said Erik, but when he got in he mentioned the fern to his mother. She gave him a glance that not only shut him up, but made him decide he'd never look up at that window again. All the same, he couldn't help saying, 'I thought . . .'

'Erik,' said his mother. 'What did I say to you when you came back here a few weeks ago, your jacket all ripped and your face like a half-fried frankfurter, trying to tell me you'd been fighting Hans?'

'Nothing,' said Erik.

TEN
Ruby
Plymouth, 1937–1938

For as long as Ruby could remember, every time Clarry came to Plymouth to visit her father, old Mr Penrose, she would hurry across town afterwards to see Ruby and her mother. Then, no matter how dismal the day, everything would be transformed. If the shop was busy, Clarry would take over the till, or the shelves, or the sorting and numbering of the newspapers for the delivery boy. However, when things were quiet, Ruby's mother would turn the OPEN sign on the door to CLOSED. 'Shopping?' she would ask hopefully and all three would rush into town.

Violet was a great shopper. She and Clarry especially liked looking at hats. Ruby loved the pet shop with its perpetual supply of kittens in the window, but it didn't really matter what they did. They could be perfectly happy in Woolworths choosing hairslides for Ruby, or buying a cake at the bakers, or a bunch of blue cornflowers from a market stall. It was the being together that they loved. Violet and Clarry would chatter and laugh, and Ruby would hop along beside them, her splattered, vivacious face sparkling with brightness. Afterwards, always a little late, they would scurry to the train station, and she and

Violet would wave *Goodbye, Goodbye* and Clarry would call back, 'Next time! Soon!'

'When did you first know her?' Ruby asked once, and her mother replied, 'We've been friends since we were girls.'

After Ruby's father died, things changed a little. Violet didn't seem as interested in shopping any more. But Clarry came just the same, sometimes to eat toast and help tidy the shop, now and then to say, 'Let's get a tram down to the seafront, I should like to sniff the sea.' All the time, they chatted. Will's most recent letter would be shared, and the latest news about Kate, Clarry's other god-daughter, who still coughed too much and wheezed too much and missed too much school, but was getting better. Ruby always liked to hear about Kate. They'd never met, but she felt there was a sort of connection between them. Kate had written when Ruby's father died, and sometimes after that she would send a message via Clarry.

'You should reply,' said Violet.

'I do reply,' said Ruby. 'I always say to Clarry to tell her thank you.'

'Not the same as writing.'

'Kate doesn't write much,' pointed out Ruby. 'Mostly she draws.'

That was true.

Dear Ruby,

Clarry said you like cats.

Here are some cats.

Love Kate

The rest of the page, and all round the edges, was covered in little pictures of cats, stretching, sleeping, twisting round to lick their shoulders, sharing a saucer of milk, prowling a rooftop under the moon.

Each little sketch was carefully detailed. The cats had whiskers and silky shadows, there were tiles on the roof and stars in the sky. Ruby was so clearly pleased that when her mother hugged Clarry goodbye she whispered urgently in her ear, 'Try and bring Kate one day,' and the next time Clarry visited, she did.

They arrived one rainy teatime. Ruby opened the door to find Clarry smiling underneath a dripping umbrella with a skinny, coughing girl lurking just behind.

'What a lovely surprise!' called Violet, hurrying to meet them, but she didn't deceive Ruby, who with her usual fear of strangers hissed, 'If I'd known she was coming, I'd have run.'

'Behave!' hissed her mother back. 'Don't spoil it!' and to give her a chance to get over her indignation, sent her out for raspberry jam to go with the bag of teacakes that Clarry had produced. By the time Ruby returned, Kate had already begun toasting, obviously left to get on with it while Clarry and Violet sat at the table by the window and said, 'Tell me everything, tell me truly how you are,' and 'Oh, I've missed you,' and things like that.

Kate looked relieved when Ruby appeared, and offered the toasting fork.

'I fetched the jam,' said Ruby mutinously.

'I only thought you might be able to do it better,' said Kate. 'We brought butter too, but I don't know whether to put it on.'

'Why'd you bring butter? Did you think we were poor?'

'I think it was supposed to be a treat,' Kate murmured, blushing so nervously that all at once Ruby was ashamed of her bad temper and said, 'It is a treat. I love teacakes. You toast, I'll butter. Mum made gingerbread this morning, too. Now I know why.'

Tea was cheerful. Sooty and Paddle were included. They had cat biscuits and milk and were endearingly polite, crunching with blissful half-closed eyes, or gazing longingly at the milk jug and gently patting Ruby with a wistful, asking paw. Afterwards Ruby took Kate on a tour of the newspaper shop downstairs, Will's blessedly empty bedroom, and her own snow-white attic with the patchwork quilt and the window on to the rooftops. Both cats followed after them, and when they arrived in Ruby's attic, Kate produced a pencil and a notebook from her pocket and drew them, very small.

'Draw them big,' said Ruby.

'I can only draw small,' said Kate. 'I put pictures in my diary to help me remember things.'

'Is that your diary?'

'No. It's just a book I practise in.'

'Will you draw being here when you get home?' asked Ruby.

Kate looked startled, but replied hesitantly, 'I might try.'

'The raspberry jam? The cats having tea?'

'Oh, yes.' Kate nodded, smiling.

'Clarry's umbrella when it wouldn't close?'

'That might be really hard.'

'Me?' Ruby turned her face away as she asked. What if Kate said yes? What if Kate said no?

'I don't know,' said Kate.

'Don't know?'

'I'm not very good at faces. I never get the noses right.'

This answer was so unexpected that Ruby's eyes opened wide, but she couldn't help smiling as Kate tried to explain about noses; so sausage-shaped and yet so triangular, and the problem of the two holes in them, all right on animals but awful on humans.

'You have to be careful with noses,' said Kate, 'because they're not like eyes and hands and mouths. They never change shape.'

'You've thought about it a lot,' said Ruby, and Kate said yes she had, so seriously that Ruby started laughing.

'Noses matter,' said Kate and Ruby laughed even more and then quite suddenly found herself being handed the notebook. There she was. Hair tangled, eyes crinkled, her laughing three-cornered mouth, and her nose a triumph, recognizably her own and not sausagey at all.

But no birthmarks. No dark, destroying birthmarks.

Only shaded shadows where her birthmarks should be.

Over the years, Ruby's mirror-avoiding had become complete. Even so, she had often wondered what she looked like to strangers. Now she was outraged.

'Are you sorry for me or something?' she demanded.

'Why?' asked Kate, astonished.

'You can't trick me!'

All at once Ruby grabbed Kate's pencil, and bent double over the notebook, scribbling over the shadowed marks until they became dark and huge and dominating.

'There!' she said.

Kate was so dismayed, she protested, 'They're not a bit like that.'

'I know what my face is.'

'But—'

'I'm not stupid.'

Kate spoke all in a breathless rush, before Ruby interrupted again. 'You've made that mark on your cheek as big as your ear and it's really smaller than . . . than . . .' she looked around for help and spotted Paddle, 'than a paw print! And those others are quite little—'

'Little!' exclaimed Ruby.

'Compared . . .'

'You wouldn't say that if they were on your face!'

'I wou . . . wou . . .' Kate was halted by coughing, but when she began again continued doggedly, 'wouldn't mind.'

'What a lie!'

'I think—'

'You think you're so clever, that's what you think,' said Ruby furiously.

'No, I don't,' said Kate and subsided, concentrating on breathing. When she spoke again she said, 'That was the best nose I ever did and you've spoiled it.'

'I'll get rid of it then,' said Ruby, and spoiled it completely by tearing the drawing out of the notebook, screwing it up, running down the attic stairs and throwing it in the fire.

'What was that?' demanded Violet suspiciously.

'Nothing.'

Violet gave her a very that-isn't-true-and-I-know-it look as Kate trailed in, avoiding eye contact with everyone but the cats, and Clarry became very brisk, saying, 'We must absolutely rush or we'll miss the train. Loveliest afternoon for weeks, Violet! Thank you. Bye-bye, Ruby! Come on, Kate!' and vanished.

After Clarry and Kate had gone, there was an emptiness.

There was often an emptiness. In the past, the three rooms above the shop had made a home, but however hard Ruby's mother tried, without Ruby's father, it wasn't a home any more. It was a place where Violet and Ruby waited.

Will came back quite often. He would arrive without warning, and (thought Ruby) take over everything. Her mother would rush into an orgy of cooking. Puddings and buns would appear that were never seen on ordinary days. Bananas too, and eggs at breakfast, and delicious baked beans in tins. Meals would suddenly last twice as long, with extra talk as well as extra food, and Violet jumping up and down to the stove, and Will in their father's chair feeding Sooty and Paddle with cheese and fragments of bacon rind. Both cats seemed to have forgotten Will's kitten-drowning past; to Ruby's dismay they welcomed him and jumped on to his knee.

Then, as suddenly as he'd appeared, Will would vanish. Violet and Ruby would return to bread and jam breakfasts and bread and soup suppers and there would be no spare cheese for the cats.

'He'll be here again before we know it,' Violet would say, to comfort herself, and Ruby would hope that she was wrong, then they would both go back to waiting.

They waited for the sadness to fade. For time to pass. For aunts with flowery names to arrive (and then, as soon as they had done, for them to hurry up and go). They waited for customers and cashing-up time, and night, when at least you could be miserable in peace, and morning, when you could get up again at last.

One day, when Ruby's loneliness had reached an unendurable level, she wrote a two-word message to Kate:

Sorry,

Ruby.

And immediately Kate replied:

It doesn't matter,

Kate.

These notes went in with Clarry and Violet's letters to each other, carefully sealed from adult eyes.

Draw a picture of yourself, wrote Ruby next.

Kate sent back a picture of herself with a towel over her head, inhaling eucalyptus from a jug of hot water.

To help me breathe, she wrote.

There was nothing to be seen of Kate in the picture, just the jug and the towel and a whiff of steam. It made Ruby laugh and she took it down to the shop to show her mother, and she laughed too.

'What's the joke?' asked a customer, coming in at that moment, and Violet answered carelessly, 'Ruby was just showing me a picture of her friend.'

Somewhere inside Ruby then, a little glow began, like a candle flame, wavering into life

'She's not my friend,' she protested, argumentative and defensive as usual, but the candle flame didn't go out.

Will noticed it when he came home.

On school days, Ruby was always back before her mother was free from the shop. She'd spend the time doing what she could to help, especially the things her father would once have done: shoe polishing and coal-bucket filling, and chopping broken greengrocer pallets into kindling for the fire.

One evening Ruby was on her hands and knees in the kitchen, laying a fire with her newly chopped wood, when a voice behind her said, 'That's my job,' and it was Will.

Ruby jumped so hard she dropped her match and wasted it. When she reached for another, Will got the box first.

'Out the way!' he said.

'No, thank you.'

'You've got it built too far forward. You'll fill the room with smoke.'

'No, I won't.'

'Budge!'

'No.'

'You'd better!' said Will, who still had the matches, and then, in a completely different voice, 'Hey, what's the matter with that cat?'

He had moved to the window, and was staring out as if alarmed. Ruby hurried to look as well, and of course it was a trick. Will was down at the fire in a moment, dismantling her arrangement of rolled paper, wood and coal, and rebuilding it his own way. It lit with one match, flaring into brightness as if it was on his side, and he said, 'That's how to do it. Who chopped the wood?'

'I did.'

'Too thick. You want to make it thinner. Lights faster and wastes less. Anyway, hello.'

'Hello,' said Ruby, crossly.

'How you doing, then?'

'All right.'

'Managing without me?'

'Of course.'

'I've been thinking. Soon as I can, I'm going to chuck in the army. Oh, thanks. I see. Great.'

What he had seen was Ruby's eyes open wide with dismay.

'Charming,' said Will.

'I didn't say anything,' protested Ruby.

'You didn't need to,' said Will, and continued to stare at her curiously.

'Stop it,' she said, and turned her face away.

'Mum would be pleased if I came home for good,' said

Will, now beginning to feed his fire with a very extravagant amount of Ruby's carefully chopped kindling. 'Someone else earning. I could get work easy, share the cost of keeping you.'

'I don't cost hardly anything,' said Ruby, very hurt. 'And I help with the newspapers and mind the shop often. And when I finish school I can get a job too.'

'How do you get on at school?' Will asked.

'Good,' lied Ruby.

'Top of the class, like I was?'

Ruby didn't reply.

'You've got friends and that, too?'

'Of course,' said Ruby through gritted teeth. 'I've got hundreds.'

'Hundreds,' repeated Will, solemnly, nodding.

Ruby ignored him, stepped over his legs, tipped potatoes out of a brown paper bag on to the draining board and began rinsing them under the tap.

'I'm starting supper,' she said.

'Hundreds,' said Will again. 'Are you going to peel those spuds?'

'No, I'm doing them in the oven. In their jackets. Mum said earlier.'

'Before she knew I was coming?'

'I've put an extra one for you.'

'One?'

'Two, then,' said Ruby, splashing another potato under the tap, and then pushing past Will to put them in the little iron oven at the side of the kitchen range.

'I like mash,' said Will, and took them out again. 'Mash, with sausages. I'll peel them.'

'You don't know how! And we haven't any sausages.'

Will smirked at her and nodded towards the table, where she saw not only a paper-wrapped parcel of sausages, but also a tin of beans and a very small box of chocolates. 'Remembered you liked beans,' he said. 'The chocolates are for Mum.' And he began peeling potatoes very deftly, much faster than Ruby could have done, having had practice in the army where he did it by the bucketful, spud-bashing being a punishment for minor crimes like messy kit, turning out late, and cheeking the sergeant major.

'You're doing all my things,' complained Ruby.

'*You're* doing all *my* things,' he retorted. 'Tell me about these hundred friends.'

'No.'

'A few names? Where they live? So's I can get to know them when I move back home?'

'Mind your own!'

'Oh?' said Will, chopping potatoes at lightning speed and sliding them into a saucepan. 'Can't remember?'

'Shut up.'

'Not even one?'

'Kate,' snapped Ruby. 'That's one. Kate.'

'Never heard of her,' said Will, swishing down the draining board, bundling the potato peelings on to the back of his blazing fire, drying his hands and grinning so annoyingly that Ruby, against her better judgement, pulled a book from her school bag and pushed it into his hands.

'What's this, then?' he asked.

'Look!' commanded Ruby. 'Look inside!'

Will obediently opened the book.

'See!' said Ruby, pointing, and he read the words written there, *To Ruby, with love from Kate.*

'I told you so,' said Ruby. 'Kate. She sent it for my birthday.'

Will turned the book in his hand and looked at the title: *Wild Animals I Have Known.* 'Bet you haven't read it,' he said.

'I have,' said Ruby. 'As soon as I got it.'

'I'll borrow it, then,' said Will, standing up as if to leave. 'That all right?'

'No!'

'No?'

'No. Give it back!' said Ruby, grabbing.

'Give it back?' asked Will mockingly, with the book held high above Ruby's head. 'Why? You've read it. You told me so, just a minute ago.'

'Not all of it.'

'Not what you said! Shouldn't tell lies, Ruby. Ruby *Amaryllis.* Whatever that even means.'

'It's a—' began Ruby, but he interrupted.

'I don't want to know. There's your book, then. Have it.'

It was spoiled. Somehow he'd spoiled it. And he was angry, and what would he do next?

He looked behind the clock.

'Why do you *do* that?' she cried, suddenly as hurt as if he'd slapped her. 'Why do you always do that? Why don't you just take it? Dad meant it for you!'

'You've forgotten what he said when he put it there,' said Will. 'I haven't.'

He slammed furiously out of the door. Ruby also fled, up to her attic, through the window and on to the slippery sloping tiles, where she sat hugging her knees until the cold and the salt wind drove her back inside again.

After this latest visit of Will's, Ruby wrote to Kate:

Dear Kate,
My brother Will has gone back to the army.
Good.
But the war hasn't started yet.
So he keeps coming home.
Bad. Bad. Bad. Bad. Bad.

ELEVEN
Kate
Oxford, Autumn 1938

A ll that year the threat of war had been grumbling like the distant rumble of a thunderstorm far away. Even Kate heard the echoes.

At school people talked, sometimes not very sensibly.

'My mum's started saving things,' said her friend Hatty, who was often confused.

'What things?'

'Light bulbs and baby wool.'

'Light bulbs and baby wool?'

'For in case there's a war,' said Hatty.

'Your mum,' said someone, 'just doesn't want to have a baby in the dark.'

'But she isn't having a baby.'

'That's all you know!'

Hatty went home and demanded the truth and came back not confused at all. 'I'm going to be a sister!' she announced. 'A sister! What's it like?'

'Depends on the baby,' said everyone-who-was-already-a-sister, but Kate said, 'It's nice.'

'Yes, but you're not a big sister.'

'I think it's still all right,' said Kate. She was very relieved to hear it was a baby that was being prepared for instead of a war, and for a few days she forgot to worry and concentrated instead on helping Hatty choose baby names, even though Hatty said, 'Oh, *no*, Kate,' to every suggestion.

But then had come Ruby's latest letter, with its alarming fourth line:

But the war hasn't started yet.

Yet.

That *yet* made Kate's heart bump with fear. It sounded so certain. Ruby's brother was in the army. Ruby lived in a newspaper shop; she must hear all the news. Ruby was clever. Who could tell what Ruby knew?

At home the adults were also worrying.

Vanessa said, 'Peter, we'll have to try to talk to your father. If the worst comes to the worst, he shouldn't be on his own. I know after that Christmas he said never again, and so did you, but was it really so bad?'

'You have a wonderful tolerance for people who are drunk by lunchtime and set fire to their beds,' said Kate's father.

'He wasn't very drunk and the bed only smouldered. It could have been much worse.'

'Mad woman.' Peter got up and limped round the table to hug her. He was back in time for supper for once. For weeks he had been getting home later and later.

'We hardly see you,' Kate's mother complained.

'I'm sorry.'

'Are lots of people poorly?' Kate asked him.

'Not at all, don't you worry, Kate.'

'It was Kate's birthday yesterday,' said Vanessa. 'You entirely forgot it. She's allowed to wonder why.'

'Gosh, oh, gosh, Kate!' exclaimed Peter. 'I'm sorry. Did we remember presents? Did you have a cake?'

'I had lovely presents. You bought me a bracelet. Silver beads. It was a chocolate cake with pink candles and I blew them out in one go.'

'All ten? Well done. Have you made a wish?'

'I'm saving it for in case.'

'Very prudent.'

'Why are you so busy at the hospital if there aren't lots of people being ill?'

'I've been doing extra teaching, new tricks to very old dogs. Or very old doctors. There's lots of new stuff in the hospital world that the older staff haven't bothered to learn.'

'Why haven't they?'

'I suppose they thought it wasn't worth it if they were going to be retiring.'

'Aren't they now?'

'They probably are, but just in case we need them . . .'

Peter suddenly noticed that behind Kate's back, Vanessa was making *Shut up* signs. He hastily changed the subject. 'Can I see the bracelet I bought you?'

'I'm wearing it. Dad, now I'm ten, would you tell me if something awful was going to happen?'

'If you are thinking of your grandfather coming to stay,

your mum's the one to talk to,' said Peter, laughing. 'But as far as I know, that idea's not going well.'

'I thought I was getting somewhere a couple of days ago,' said Vanessa, and it was Kate's turn to laugh, because she'd been there when her mother had telephoned Grandfather and said, 'Darling, we must make some sensible plans for the future, and I thought it might be good to talk now.'

Afterwards, Kate had written about what had happened in her diary.

Grandfather said, 'Quite right,' in such a pleased voice that Mum turned round and gave a thumbs-up sign to all of us. Because we were all listening. Then Grandfather said, 'The only logical thing to do at this moment in time is to cash in all your shares and long-term bonds. Put aside enough to cover household expenses for the next five years. Invest the rest in gold.'

'Gold?' said Mum, in a voice like she might faint.

'Let me know if you have any problems,' Grandfather said and put down the telephone.

Kate had enjoyed writing that diary entry, and beneath it she'd drawn three bulging sacks, with gold spilling out of their tops. For weeks afterwards, in frightened moments, she turned back the pages to look at those sacks.

Magically, they quietened the distant thunder of war. Not long afterwards, Mr Chamberlain, the Prime Minister, told them on the wireless about his agreement with Hitler. *Peace with honour*, he reassured them. *Peace for our time.*

Kate found the sacks of gold worked better.

Twelve
Dog
Scrapyard, East London, 1938

Everything in the dog's world had its own strong smell. Traffic smells rolled in from the road, sometimes engines, sometimes horses. There was the food smell of the fish shop in the evenings, and the cold fog smell from the nearby River Thames. There was the smell of the scrapyard girl.

'*Hello, dog*,' said the scrapyard girl, hoarse with winter, as she swept away the puddles that flooded his tea-chest kennel.

In summer, when he panted on his patch of sun-baked concrete, he heard it again.

'*Hello, dog*,' she whispered, and found a square of old tarpaulin and rigged him up some shade.

Not without consequences, of course.

'You make a pet of that dog and it'll get what-for.'

What-for was the yard broom raised high and brought down. What-for was screeching. What-for was boots. A pet dog wasn't needed. A burglar alarm was.

The dog was still quite a good burglar alarm. Footsteps in the yard, a rattle at the gate in the night, and he would be yammering and snarling and lunging on his chain.

Only not quite so swiftly as in the past. Nowadays the dog would hesitate for a moment. He would check for the smell of old clothes. He would listen for, '*Hello, dog.*'

This was noticed at the scrapyard.

'Gone soft,' they said with disappointment.

They raised the broom more often, and shouted louder, and although he was not the same savage animal he once had been, it worked enough to tide things over, more or less.

THIRTEEN
Erik and Hans
Berlin, 1938

The January evening before Erik and Hans were to go off for National Service, their families, Erik's mother and Hans's parents and Frieda and Lisa, all went out for supper together. Lisa nearly didn't come because she couldn't get her plaits right. She tried and tried to look like the girls in the posters for the League of German Maidens, but when she parted her hair on one side like they did, one plait became very much thinner than the other, and yet when she parted it in the middle, she looked (she said) like a frumpy old witch.

'Never mind, we are used to you looking like a frumpy old witch,' said Hans, which made things worse. Even after her hair was arranged, she was cross because she had lost her red-and-black swastika badge and when it was found, it had been trodden on and was impossible to wear. But supper cheered her up, and she got powdered sugar all down her front and her hair came loose and on the way home it started snowing. Lisa had always loved snow, and she quite suddenly gave Erik her coat to hold and did a cartwheel there in the street, with the snowflakes swarming in the light of the street lamps and the boys laughing and Frieda trying to copy, and her parents saying, 'Well!'

'Well, what?' asked Lisa, and did two more, very quickly, and came up red-faced and panting, saying, 'At least I learned something useful at that boring stupid League.'

'I thought you liked it,' said Erik.

'I'm tired of it now,' said Lisa. Then she went and did more cartwheels until her father sternly ordered her to stop.

'Next year you will be doing National Service too,' Erik reminded her when she flounced back to snatch her coat.

'More people bossing me around!' said Lisa.

'If they can,' said Erik, laughing, and much later he remembered Lisa that evening, with hair all over her face and her eyes very bright, and the first snow of winter swirling down like white feathers.

The night ended back at Hans's family's apartment, in a panic. Erik had already packed for their early start the next morning. All his things were ready in a huge grey kitbag with a drawstring top that had once been his father's. He'd left it in the shared hall, to be out of the way, and Frieda had spotted it.

'Hans doesn't have a great big bag like that,' she observed.

'Hans has a new one,' explained Erik. 'Mine is very old.'

'Older than me?'

'How old are you?' asked Erik.

'Nearly three,' said Frieda.

'Much older than you,' said Erik solemnly.

'And much bigger than me,' said Frieda, measuring herself beside it, and it was.

'Hans's bag is full of important things,' said Frieda. 'He told me. So I mustn't touch it. Is yours full of important things?'

'No,' said Erik, laughing, so when nobody was looking Frieda turfed out all the unimportant things from Erik's bag: his clothes, his rolled-up blankets, his canteen and his book of European birds. She pushed them all under the dresser, climbed inside and closed the top.

They found her by the giggling, after they had ransacked every room and rushed up and down the street outside, calling in the snow. Erik had to pack everything all over again.

'Get used to packing kitbags,' Hans's father advised.

National service was almost a joke. Erik and Hans hardly had time to unpack their bags and remember how much they detested marching round a parade ground, before their flying record was discovered. As soon as it was known, they found themselves accepted into flight training. Next they were adding up their flying distances, until they reached three thousand kilometres in the air.

Three thousand kilometres was the turning point, the difference between students and potential Luftwaffe pilots. It came easily to Erik.

When Erik was flying, his senses filled with the sound of engines, the smell of the plane, the speed and height. Often, immersed in sky, he forgot there was an earth beneath him.

For those few months of hard, intense training, Erik was so absorbed he hardly remembered the outside world at all. When he wasn't flying he was studying navigation, photography, mechanics. He hung over aerial photographs, and plans and maps. He developed a wonderful sense of direction; he never got lost.

Hans did.

They had to pass a solo flight. It was set out in a triangle, six hundred kilometres wide, with a precision landing on a target at the end. It would be a milestone in their training; afterwards they would move on to a new airfield and larger planes, and in between they would have forty-eight hours' leave.

Erik managed without problems, landing on target several minutes early with fuel still in his tank and hardly a bounce. Hans was ten minutes late, half an hour late, seventy minutes late.

At first Erik stood alone, watching for his friend. As time went on he was joined by more and more people. Hans was popular, and now long overdue. It wasn't just fellow students. The mechanics started looking up. The cooks peered out from the canteen. The old soldier who kept the grass short with two ancient donkeys and a clattering mower hobbled over to join the crowd. There were at least twenty people waiting when Hans came in at last, battling the evening wind to land like a log dropped out of a window.

Hans climbed out very shakily and bowed to the applause and said to Erik, who was the first to reach him, 'I was hoping no one would notice.'

'I'm sure nobody did,' said Erik, who was so pleased to see Hans safe that he couldn't stop grinning. 'These people staring at the sky, I think they were just admiring the clouds.'

'You think so, do you?' asked Hans. 'I tell you what, Erik, I hated that. It was scary. And I bet I've lost my leave.'

Hans was right. His leave was cancelled, and he had to do it over again. Erik went home without him. It was late November 1938, the first time for nearly a year that he'd been back in Berlin. He stepped out of the train at the station and noticed the difference at once.

When he'd left, there'd been a simmering tension in the city. The red-and-black flags. The 'Jews Forbidden'. It had been uncomfortable, militant, shaming. But in a strange way it had also been possible to avert your eyes because things had changed so gradually, for so many years. They'd been part of his growing up.

This time, it was different. Now Berlin was alarming. There was violence loose in the city squares and menace prowled the streets. In the air was the sour smell that comes after burning. Everywhere, there was broken glass, swept into heaps like dirty snow. Erik looked in disbelief at great piles of it outside the shattered shops and businesses of the Jewish people who had once believed the city to be their home.

'Last week,' said his mother, 'you must have heard. They're calling it Kristallnacht.'

She had met him at the station, pale-faced, clutching his arm. She said, 'All over Germany, but they say Berlin was the worst. Keep walking. Don't stop and look. Your face shows too much. How can you not have known?'

'I knew. Of course, we all did. I didn't understand.'

'They have disappeared. All but gone. Probably for the best, of course . . .' She looked around uneasily, and Erik realized that she was talking to protect them both from any passing stranger that might be listening to their conversation. 'Look at you in your uniform!' she exclaimed. 'Taller each time I see you! How is Hans?'

'Very well. A new girl every week. I have thousands of messages, and tobacco for his father, and chocolate for his mother and Lisa, and a sugar pig for Frieda. This is an outrage.'

'Yes, perhaps. Lisa is away.'

'No!' exclaimed Erik, so loudly that people turned to look. 'Hans doesn't know that. Lisa was at school when we saw her last.'

'Don't be so loud, Erik! Of course she has to do her National Service, like all the rest of them. Hans must have forgotten. It's better for her parents that she's occupied. She always was a difficult girl. Come inside, it will be better inside. Did you need to bring that big bag for just a few hours?'

'It's full of presents,' said Erik, a little blankly. 'And Hans said to pack Frieda and bring her back for a visit . . . for a joke.'

'Oh, yes, a joke,' said his mother and smiled as if she had forgotten until then about jokes, and looked uncertainly at him, and quickly away again.

'What is it?' Erik asked, and when she didn't reply, to cover the awkwardness he felt, he said, 'Shall I you show you what we found for Frieda?' and pulled out a package, wrapped in brown paper. Inside was a bright red blanket, with brown felt bears stitched in the corners. The bears had bells around their necks, on green ribbons. At any other time it would have delighted his mother. She would have examined the bears and shaken the tiny bells and said how perfect for a little girl, and how clever they had been to find it. Now she hardly looked.

'Yes,' she said. 'Very nice. It will be warm.'

'Every bear is different,' said Erik, watching her with increasing alarm.

'Erik,' burst out his mother. 'I do what I can, but she's so frightened of you. She is so terribly, terribly frightened of you.'

'Frieda?' asked Erik, in absolute astonishment.

'Not Frieda.'

It's easy to forget about someone, when you don't see them for years, nor hear them. When nobody mentions them, and you have travelled on to a different world.

The fern in the window was dried to a grey ghost of a fern. Cobwebs laced its fronds, and laced the window too, as they would in a room where nobody lived. The wooden chair was dim with dust. Erik kneeled down in front of it, a Luftwaffe pilot in full uniform.

Shrunken against the cushions, her hands pressed against her mouth, her eyes wide with fear, Fraulein Trisk shook and shook.

'No, no,' begged Erik. No one had ever been frightened of him before. No person. No creature. Not even his swallows when he first picked them up. The feeling was terrible. He said, 'It's Erik, Fraulein Trisk. It's me.' He couldn't help crying, although he knew it was no way to behave, and never had been either. He had been brought up by a brave woman, to be brave. So he rubbed the tears away on his hands and said, 'It's still only me, Fraulein Trisk. Only Erik.'

Fraulein Trisk took her hands from her face.

'You knitted me mittens.'

She nodded a very small nod. She was altogether small.

'I loved them. I am sorry that I—'

'Phut!' said Fraulein Trisk. She gave a quivering smile and reached out a hand as light as a bird and touched his hair.

Then Erik's mother, who was watching from the door, gave a great sigh, and laughed out loud with relief and looked with pride at Erik and said, 'Didn't I tell you he was still my little sugar rose?'

Before he left, Erik said, 'When all these troubles are over I will buy you a new fern. I promise. Green as a forest.'

FOURTEEN
Ruby
Plymouth, November 1938

All sorts of people came to the newsagent's shop, and one of them was Mrs Cohen. The Cohens' shop was just a few doors down the street from Ruby's home.

COHEN & CO. CLOCKMAKERS AND GOLDSMITHS

Those were the words written in small gold letters across the front. The letters had to be small, because the whole shop was small, right down to the half-sized doormat that customers stepped on to when they ducked through the very small door. From the door to the counter was one medium-sized step, and from the counter to the workroom was another. Very few clocks were made in that workroom, but very many battered overwound watches were mended and clockwork toys set running again. There wasn't much goldsmithing done either, but for a few pennies Mr Cohen could repair a chain, or fix a broken locket, or reset a stone in a treasured ring. He did this work invisibly. It was Mrs Cohen who stood behind the counter, and dusted the shelves, and arranged the display in the small, curved window. Ruby always paused to look at the cuckoo clock, the silver candlesticks, and the tray of rings. She and her mother often inspected that tray, in the hope of new and extra-bright rubies.

The Cohens were a Jewish family. They went to the synagogue on Catherine Street, and it was for them that Ruby's mother ordered the *Jewish Chronicle* once a week. Ruby liked Mrs Cohen, who actually had a ruby ring of her own. Sometimes she would take it off and let Ruby hold it. Ruby would turn it until it caught the light and blossomed into a speck of crimson fire.

'It's a pity it's not bigger,' Ruby had once remarked, and Mrs Cohen had laughed and agreed that it was indeed a pity. She and Ruby had talked about rubies and decided together that one the size of half a cherry would be perfect for a ring. Big enough to really shine, but not so large as to be knobbly, said Ruby, and Mrs Cohen agreed, and said that anything bigger, say the size of a whole cherry, would be better used for earrings.

'Only then you would need two rubies,' Ruby had pointed out.

'Or four,' said Mrs Cohen. 'Cherries are best when they hang in pairs.'

'How much would that cost?' Ruby wondered, thinking what a nice present such earrings would make for her mother, and Mrs Cohen said thoughtfully that she couldn't be sure, but she imagined perhaps between ten and twenty thousand pounds if the rubies were properly matched.

This conversation made a pleasant friendliness between the two of them, and Ruby was always pleased when Mrs Cohen came in. She never had the feeling she had with other customers that Mrs Cohen was secretly looking at the marks on her face.

So Ruby was dismayed on the November day when Mrs Cohen arrived, distracted and unhappy, and hurried past, ignoring her completely.

'What . . .?' began Ruby, and then saw that Mrs Cohen was pushing into her mother's hands the *Jewish Chronicle* that she had bought from them less than an hour before.

'Terrible things are happening!' exclaimed Mrs Cohen. 'Terrible things! You should know!'

'Mrs Cohen!' exclaimed Violet.

'Yes,' said Mrs Cohen. 'Look! Look what I just saw!' and she flattened the newspaper out on the counter for Violet to read. 'We Jewish people have already heard so much bad news,' she said. 'So many things, but this!'

'Show me too,' said Ruby, pushing forward to look.

'No, Ruby, you go upstairs and leave me to talk to Mrs Cohen,' said Violet, but Mrs Cohen shook her head and said, 'Ruby should see too. She should know! Everyone should know!'

Violet was reading even while Mrs Cohen spoke.

'Nobody knows and nobody cares,' continued Mrs Cohen. 'I don't think anyone in this country is paying any attention at all. I had to come. I have nobody to talk to that could possibly understand. You know Mr Cohen. He just shakes his head, shakes his head . . .'

Violet didn't look up from her reading, but she reached out a hand towards Mrs Cohen.

'I felt so alone,' said Mrs Cohen, and took the hand and held it tight.

This was how Ruby first heard the word *Kristallnacht*.

Kristallnacht: the night of broken glass. The bitter night of terror and persecution that Mrs Cohen had discovered in the *Jewish Chronicle*.

'Nobody cares,' she repeated. 'No one is interested. Are the other papers reporting it, have you seen?'

'I don't know, Mrs Cohen,' admitted Ruby's mother. 'I can't say I've noticed, but . . .'

At this Mrs Cohen broke down and sobbed, and Violet took her other hand and held that too, while Ruby, suddenly inspired, rushed upstairs and returned with cups of tea so floating with too many tea leaves that they had to be fished out with a spoon. Most surprisingly, the fishing out helped, and so did walking Mrs Cohen home afterwards, but even so Ruby only partly understood her distress. This changed when Violet, with her usual resourcefulness, set about comforting Mrs Cohen in the most practical way she could devise.

'She needs to know people are paying attention,' she told Ruby. 'That, at least, we can show her. You can help.'

They began at once. Every night, all that week, Violet spread out newspapers on the kitchen table. Then she and Ruby would scrutinize them, and very soon they found what they needed. People in Britain *were* paying attention. Carefully they cut out columns from the *Manchester Guardian*, *The Times* and *The Daily Mail*, and other papers as well. Even their own local paper, the *Devon and Exeter Gazette*, had an article.

'Right on the front page too,' said Ruby when she found it, and read out loud, '*Friday, November 11th. Germany and Jews. Outrages Throughout Country . . .*'

'It's not nice to read,' said her mother, 'but what's happening isn't nice. It's wicked. But it hasn't gone ignored. Snip it out carefully, Ruby, and don't drop bits on the floor.'

They found a report with a photograph: an image of shop fronts, knee-deep in broken glass, daubed with rough letters: *JUDE JUDE JUDE*. There were people in the picture. One of them caught Ruby's attention: a slim woman, hurrying forward and holding very tightly the hand of a small, scurrying girl.

'That woman has a coat just like yours,' said Ruby to her mother, and so she had; double-breasted with turned-back lapels and big buttons down the front. 'It must be her good coat,' said Ruby, because that was what Violet called her own winter coat. 'Her good coat, but no hat.'

Blond curls escaped from under the child's woolly hat, but the woman was bareheaded, her hair smoothed back from her face and gathered in a knot at the nape of her neck. Her eyes were dark and intense, looking down at the little girl.

She's pretending, thought Ruby suddenly, *pretending she hasn't noticed the broken glass.* She's pretending she only cares about the girl, and she's thinking, thinking, thinking. What is she thinking?

(She was thinking, *Hurry. I should never have offered to take care of Frieda today. I should never have come out here. I must smile. Am I smiling? Do I look like I don't care? I must persuade her to come down to us. Let the rooms grow abandoned, like no one is ever there. In case . . . No. No. Please no. I forgot, smile. Oh, God, I used to buy his school shirts from that shop. Good flannel for winter, it washed and washed. Hurry, Frieda. Smile.*)

There were other people in the picture too, standing in small groups, looking about with sidelong glances. A round-shouldered fellow, half in profile, ashamed at what he saw. A girl laughing. She wore a little cape of snuggly dark fur. *She thinks she's pretty*, thought Ruby, and unconsciously raised her hand to her face. *She is pretty*, admitted Ruby.

The broken glass had been very neatly swept.

'Will it really help Mrs Cohen to see these things?' Ruby asked. 'I don't see how.'

'There's knowing bad things on your own,' said Violet briskly, 'and there's knowing them with other people. And there's a difference.'

Ruby nodded, accepting that.

At the end of the week they packed up their collection of clippings and took them to the Cohens' shop. Violet handed them over, together with a reminder that her Will was in the army and was not the sort to stand for such things as were going on over there. She nodded in the direction of the sea.

'Isn't he?' asked Mrs Cohen, her eyes angry and unhappy. 'Good.'

'And nor am I, Mrs Cohen,' said Violet. 'For what it's worth.'

'A lot,' said Mrs Cohen, nodding. 'Thank you.'

'And I'm not either,' said Ruby, and added belligerently that if anyone smashed Mrs Cohen's shop window and stole her rings and candlesticks, she, Ruby, would find out who they were and kill them.

'Ruby!' said her mother, but not very angrily because, miraculously, Mrs Cohen was laughing.

'I'd be good at it,' said Ruby. 'I'd be perfect, because the police would say, "It can't be her, she's just a kid."'

'Well, you won't be called upon to do any such thing,' said Ruby's mother. 'Besides, anyone who interferes with our shops round here will get what-for from me!'

'And what-for also from me,' said Mrs Cohen, now a woman transformed.

Then she and Ruby's mother talked about how things would be if they were in charge of the country and Ruby, listening, thought it was a pity that they weren't, they would get so much done, and so quickly. Before they left, Violet gave Mrs Cohen a present she'd brought, a special sort of tea in a red-and-gold tin with an elephant on the lid to show it was from India. This was also a great triumph.

Ruby and Violet walked home together, feeling warm with success.

'Will there really be a war?' asked Ruby, all fired up with the thought, and her mother replied, 'We've fought wars over less.'

'Have we?'

'When I was a girl we did. You know that, Ruby. Your dad fought all through the last war.'

'I only know it happened. I don't know anything about it much. Was it terrible?'

Violet paused.

'For some, yes, it was,' she said, at last. 'Yes, it was. It really was. But . . .' She hesitated again, and this time for so long that Ruby asked, 'But what?'

'I worked in those days for your Aunty Rose. She kept a shop that was as dead as a doornail, and I'd been stuck in it ever since I was twelve. It wasn't until Clarry walked in that I started to wake up. We bought her pink beret that day!'

The pink beret was a family wonder. Ruby's mother had worn it on her wedding day. Clarry had worn it at Ruby's christening. When Janey, aged eleven, had run away to Cornwall because she'd seen a ghost in her bedroom, she'd stolen it and taken it with her. Ruby herself had been lent it the time that Sooty had gone missing for two whole weeks.

'It cost twelve shillings!' remembered Ruby's mother now. 'Twelve shillings! I was shocked. I couldn't get it out of my head at first. I lay awake and I thought, *Well, if a girl like her can get herself a hat like that, then what about me? There's more I can do than this shop!*'

'So what did you do?' asked Ruby.

'I got a job on the trams, because with the men at war there was work for girls like we'd never had before. And suddenly I was free. Out in the town all day, half the night too, as often as not. And earning good money as well, three times what I'd had.'

'It sounds fun,' said Ruby.

'It was,' admitted her mother. 'But don't you go repeating that, because it makes me sound heartless. Which I'm not. Poor Mrs Cohen! That Hitler wants giving something to worry about. Our Will could keep him busy. What's the use of us having an army if we don't stand up for what's right?'

'Germany has an army too,' pointed out Ruby.

'Well, I know they do, of course they do,' said Violet rather crossly. She became silent, thinking perhaps of the German army, who might very well be able to keep Will busy too. Ruby was quiet as well, but every now and then, all the way home, her steps broke into a very small skip.

FIFTEEN

Kate

Oxford, 1939

In the spring of 1939, Charlie came home from school with streaming eyes and a feverish cold that his father said wasn't a cold at all.

'Measles,' said Peter.

'Measles!' Vanessa groaned. 'And Kate's only just got over her winter coughs.'

So Kate was banished to Clarry's, where she was given the only bedroom for herself. 'But where will you sleep?' she asked Clarry, slightly dismayed, and was shown how the sofa made into a bed, with its own pillow and bedclothes in a drawer underneath.

'How perfect is that?' demanded Clarry proudly, and Kate agreed it was very good indeed.

'But I could sleep here just as well,' she suggested.

'You'll be much less trouble in the bedroom,' said her mother, who had come to help move her in. 'Then all your clutter can be out of the way.'

It was true that in the rush to hurry Kate out of the house, they'd packed a tremendous amount of stuff. Far more than Clarry seemed to own. Clarry's clothes all fitted into one smallish cupboard, and her books on to one long shelf, which also held her paintbox, a brown china pot of pens and pencils, a box of shells from Cornwall, and a pink pottery jug for flowers. The whole flat was so perfect that Kate thought she'd better unpack very carefully, and she was doing this when Clarry stuck her head round the door and said, 'Come on, Kate! Let's do something good, since I've got you here to myself. Let's go to the cinema.'

'The cinema?

'Mm.'

'What to see?'

'Whatever there is,' said Clarry.

It was a film about Robin Hood. It was magnificent. It made Clarry say, 'I should have learned fencing,' and Kate reply, 'Janey and Bea do at a club after school, but it doesn't look like that.'

'Not at all?' asked Clarry.

'Much slower,' said Kate. 'And lots of arguing in between stabs and not the right clothes.'

'No doublet and hose for Janey and Bea?'

'Vests and navy-blue gym knickers,' said Kate, so gravely that Clarry laughed out loud.

For the next two weeks, Kate went to school from Clarry's, and toiled over her homework there in the evenings. It was strange to be in a two-person home, instead of the youngest of eight. It made Kate feel surprisingly grown up. One evening they went out for supper and had spaghetti, which she'd never eaten before. Several times, after it was discovered that none of Kate's family had ever taught her to ride a bike, they had cycling lessons, round and round the empty tennis courts of the school where Clarry taught. In between, Kate discovered that she could cook. It seemed she had learned without noticing, watching her mother. Kate cooked mushrooms on toast, tomato omelettes and cheese sandwiches fried until they melted in the middle and the outsides turned golden brown.

'I was always quite careful not to learn to cook,' said Clarry, 'in case I ended up doing it instead of everything else I wanted to do more.'

'You'd probably be safe to learn now,' said Kate, seriously.

'I probably would,' agreed Clarry, and Kate said she'd write her out the recipes for making the omelettes and things. She was busy with this one rainy Saturday afternoon when suddenly there were running footsteps on the stairs and a voice calling, 'Clarry, Clarry, Clarry.'

A moment later Rupert appeared in the doorway, carrying an armload of wet carnations, pink, deep red and cream, in a cloud of misty ferns. Their scent poured from them, sweet as a rain-damp garden, and Rupert said 'Clarry' one last time and looked over his flowers and saw Kate.

'Oh, hello,' he said, in a not-very-pleased voice. 'Is it . . .?' He paused, and Kate could see him hunting to remember her name.

'It's Kate,' said Clarry, putting an arm round her. 'Vanessa's Kate, you know it is. She's staying with me and being an absolute darling while Charlie's having measles. How wonderful to see you, Rupert. Why didn't you let me know you were back?'

'Then I wouldn't be a surprise,' said Rupert. 'Would I, Kate?'

Kate smiled speechlessly.

'Kate understands,' said Rupert, kissing Clarry, ladening her with flowers and shrugging off his dark, heavy coat. Then he looked down at Kate and asked thoughtfully, 'Can you sew on buttons?'

'No, she can't,' said Clarry. 'Sew on your own buttons, Rupert.'

'Yes, I can,' said Kate, deeply honoured, so he handed her a large black button that had come off his coat so suddenly that the threads were still hanging loose in the holes and said, 'Needle?' to Clarry.

'Not me,' said Clarry unhelpfully. 'I go and visit Vanessa when my buttons come off.'

'Clarry,' said Rupert.

'Vanessa sews them on beautifully,' said Clarry, sniffing her carnations.

Kate looked from face to face.

'Come with me,' said Rupert to Kate, and took her down the stairs to the front door, and along the road to a shop where they bought needles, black thread, white thread, blue, green and purple too, a thimble, a bundle of bright silks like a soft slice of rainbow, some thin pointed scissors with gold handles, a tape measure that pulled out of a round, ladybird-shaped case, and a Scotty-dog pincushion. There was a strawberry-shaped pincushion too that Kate might have had, and another like a fat little cottage, but she unhesitatingly chose the dog.

'Pins,' said Rupert. 'No good having a pincushion without pins.'

'Oh, no!' exclaimed Kate, and she held the Scotty dog protectively, as if Rupert might stick pins in him right there.

'Ah,' said Rupert. 'I see. No pins in the dog. Now, what else do we need?'

Kate shook her head. She couldn't imagine needing anything else for years. It seemed an astonishing amount for the repair of one black button.

'Nothing,' she said.

'Wrong,' said Rupert. 'We need something to put it all in.'

He found a basket of woven wicker with a quilted green lining. 'Perfect,' he said, and added it to the pile of things already on the counter. 'Isn't it?'

'I don't know,' said Kate uncomfortably, because the basket was plainly labelled twenty-five shillings, which seemed a tremendous amount of money – twenty-five weeks' pocket money, in fact.

Rupert looked at her through half-closed eyes and said, 'You SAID you could sew on buttons.'

'I can!' said Kate. 'I'm sure I can!' And when they got back to Clarry's she did, although it took her all afternoon alone in the bedroom, with the enormous coat spread out over the bed because it was so big that was the only way to manage it. As well as the original lost button, two more had come off on the way back from the shop.

'I don't know what's the matter with my buttons today,' Rupert had remarked shamelessly, when the second one fell to the ground.

The thimble was very useful. Kate used it like a hammer to force the needle through the heavy cloth. The Scotty dog wasn't useful, but he was company. He wore a red tartan jacket and had shining bead eyes. Kate looked at him lovingly as she worked. She felt wonderfully happy. Through the half-open door she could hear Clarry and Rupert's voices, catching up on all the months of news that had happened while they'd been apart. After about half an hour Rupert appeared at the doorway and said, 'Are you all right there, Kate?'

Kate nodded.

'I have to tell Clarry something quite private and important now,' he said. 'And I know it might sound very rude to you, Kate, but I'm going to speak in French.'

'It's all right,' said Kate.

'You don't speak French?'

'*Seulement un peu,*' said Kate and he burst out laughing and said, 'You sound like your mum.'

'Mum said the only thing she ever learned at school was French,' said Kate, 'and we do French together when I'm at home with my cough.'

'What sort of French?'

'Fairy tales mostly.'

'And are you often at home with your cough?'

'Not as much as I used to be. And you could close the door. I wouldn't mind.'

'I wouldn't dream of it,' said Rupert.

The conversation in French wasn't like the one in English. It was more of an argument. When Kate heard Clarry exclaim, 'Rupert, *non, pas encore, non!*' she closed the door herself.

Clarry opened it a minute later and said, 'I'm going out

for crumpets. Or muffins or buns or whatever I can find.' Her cheeks were red and her eyes unhappy and she vanished before Kate could ask, 'Do you want me to come with you?'

Rupert appeared again.

'Ça *va?*' he asked.

'Ça *va bien,*' said Kate. 'I didn't listen.'

'I know. Well, what's the news, Kate? How's your wicked old grandfather? I heard about that Christmas! Getting you drunk in church!'

'It was only water,' said Kate. 'And it was supposed to be a secret.'

'I won't say another word, then,' said Rupert, solemnly. 'Nor about when he set fire to his bed.'

'It was Janey's bed really. She and Bea moved out into the twins' attic.'

'Does that make it any better?'

'It was only a bit smoky. It was the cigar he got in his stocking. I wish there wasn't going to be a war.'

'Kate?'

'If there is.'

'If there is, so do I.'

'Might there have to be, Rupert?'

Rupert hesitated, and then sat down on the end of the bed and said, 'Perhaps there might have to be. We'll have to make the best of it, Kate.'

'I don't know how.'

'It's a problem,' he said, nodding.

'Don't you either?'

'As a matter of fact,' said Rupert, sounding suddenly very cheerful, 'I've recently made up my mind that the easiest thing to do is . . . is . . .' He paused, and looked down. Kate's hand was suddenly clutching his arm.

'. . . is to be extraordinarily brave,' said Rupert gently.

'Extraordinarily brave?' repeated Kate.

'It seemed obvious, once I'd thought of it.'

'Yes!' said Kate. 'Oh, yes!'

'I'm glad you agree.'

'I do, I do!' said Kate, her face suddenly illuminated with relief to have such a simple answer. 'That's what I'll do too.'

'Oh, Kate.'

'You'd better put the kettle on for Clarry. I've got another button to finish.'

'Leave it.'

Kate shook her head. Nor would she stop for tea and muffins. 'Later,' she said, when they told her to come, because this button-sewing was the hardest thing she'd ever done. The cloth was so thick, it made her hands stiff. Her fingers were sore and terribly pricked. It took extraordinary bravery to unpick the last button that she'd fixed out of line and put it on again straight. Even so, she persisted.

'I am wracked with guilt,' said Rupert, when at last she staggered in to them, the coat an armload that half extinguished her, smiling in triumph, blinking with exhaustion. 'Wracked,' he repeated. 'Clarry is right. You really are a darling.'

He put on the coat, and enveloped them, first Kate, then Clarry.

'I love you,' said Clarry.

'I love you,' echoed Kate.

'I should hope so too,' said Rupert, and vanished down the stairs.

That spring and summer were full of rumours. Rumours and preparations. In factories all over the country, everything from aircraft to gas masks were hurriedly being made. People stopped wondering 'What if?' and began asking 'When?'

Kate, passing the kitchen door where her parents were talking together, heard her father say that the hospital was stockpiling anaesthetics, ether and chloroform, as many other drugs as possible, surgical instruments, disinfectants and dressings. They were buying a new X-ray machine. They were running out of space to store things.

Kate's mother said bleakly, not in her usual voice at all, 'We never had enough rubber sheets the last time. They cracked, with all the scrubbing and then the mattresses got smelly.'

Kate knew her mother had nursed soldiers all through the last war. That wasn't what shocked her so much. It was the practical bluntness of the rubber sheets that cracked with scrubbing. The smelly mattresses.

For days, for weeks afterwards, Kate would replay that conversation in her head. Every time she heard it, it was just as bad.

Meanwhile, the news from Europe became steadily worse.

In September, Germany invaded Poland.

'That's it, then,' said Kate's father, and it was.

SIXTEEN
Dog
Scrapyard, East London, September 1939

When the war came the dog was quite old, six or seven, or eight or nine. No one knew exactly, because no one had kept count, but he was a very large, full-grown dog, not as much use as he once had been, because of going soft.

The war brought new worries to the scrapyard, such as air raids and food rationing. The scrapyard people looked at the large, not very useful dog.

'How are we going to feed that?' they asked. 'Big dog like that, with a war on?'

All over the country, people were asking the same sort of question: what was to be done with the pets? How could they be kept safe when bombs were falling? How in the world were they to be fed?

The wartime government had an answer. 'Visit your vet. Before they get hungry. Before the air raids start. Do the kindest thing.'

Thousands and thousands of people, tens of thousands of people, gave their pets last walks and last brushes and last favourite meals and last hugs. Then they queued outside their vets and they had them put to sleep. Going home afterwards, some of them wondered.

Going home afterwards was bleak.

The scrapyard people didn't have these problems. They weren't the sort to waste money on vets. They'd never troubled themselves much with kindness either. Nevertheless, one autumn morning they came out to look at the dog.

The dog saw them looking.

'He'll have to take his chance,' they said.

The dog heard the words, but they meant nothing to him. He didn't know any words in the world.

Well, two.

He knew two.

'*Hello, dog.*'

It was not quite dawn.

The scrapyard girl was transformed. She smelled of soap. She walked lightly, as if her boots had secret wings. She carried, hugged under her arm, a small case with a paper label. Another label, just the same, was pinned on to her coat.

The scrapyard girl didn't sound the same either. Her voice was bubbling with excitement.

'*Hello, dog,*' she said again, and she came closer to him than any person had ever done without a yard broom in their hand. She touched him.

It didn't hurt.

She crouched down beside him and held something out.

An hour or two earlier, if the dog's chain had been long enough for him to look, and if he'd known to look, he might have seen the scrapyard girl in the kitchen, heating an old knife over a gas ring. He could have watched as she burned letters on to the back of a leather luggage tag. The letters spelt the truce word that they used at school when times were difficult. They were her gift to him: a name.

The luggage tag was threaded on to a piece of cord. The girl kneeled beside the dog and slid it over his head. Now he had a label too.

It was over. The girl was standing. She was looking around in the pale dawn dimness, at the oil-stained puddles, the piles of scrap, the broken-glass-topped wall.

She looked upwards at the lightening sky.

'*Goodbye, dog,*' she said.

Seventeen
Erik and Hans
Germany, Autumn 1939

After the abomination of Kristallnacht, Erik did not get home for many months. He and Hans trained in airfields far away from Berlin. Also, for the first time since they were ten years old, they were separated. It was nearly a year later, and only with much contriving and swapping of favours with friends, that they managed to arrange a short leave home together.

'Luftwaffe officers,' said Hans.

Erik and Hans could say things to each other that they could say to no one else.

'I am not,' said Erik, who in forty-eight hours would climb into a fighter plane to escort German bombers raiding Poland, 'planning to do any damage to anyone.'

'I wouldn't mind doing damage to someone,' said Hans, and he pressed two fingers against his top lip in the shape of a narrow moustache.

'Stop it!' said Erik.

'Why?'

'Frieda. Lisa. Your parents.'

Hans snorted with frustration, like a horse.

Frieda was the first to greet them, racing into the hall and flinging herself into their arms, a squealing small girl pendulum swinging between them: Hans, Erik, Hans, Erik, until Hans picked her up and held her high and swooped her through the air making Messerschmitt noises.

'Erik has brought his kitbag,' she shouted, spotting it from that height, and insisted on climbing inside again and being raced up and down the stairs on Erik's back.

'She is too heavy!' exclaimed Hans's mother, but Frieda shrieked, 'I'm not, I'm not, I won't ever be too heavy.'

'And much too noisy. They will hear her on the street!'

Hans's mother's protests were only out of habit. No one really minded, the excitement and brightness were so welcome. 'As if we had the old days back,' said Hans's father, 'and children on the stairs all day.'

'With cocoa tins full of flies!' added Erik's mother.

'Were the swallows back this summer?' Erik asked her, and she said, 'Yes, oh, yes, of course they were and all of them asking questions about you. How is Erik and where is his hat?'

'Or did he fall out of the window?' finished Hans. 'What did you tell them?'

'I told them the sugar rose had learned to fly, and so had Dumpling Boy.'

Erik and Hans groaned in dismay, while everybody laughed.

In the hall, with the familiar black-and-white tiles on the floor, and the dark corner where the mop bucket lived, and the yellow light from the lamp that had never hung quite straight, and still wasn't straight, and the old smell of scrubbed stairs and polish and coffee, in that enclosed space it was hard to believe that outside the door the world had changed forever.

Later they knew.

That evening the street was full of a different noise: hammering on doors, furniture being shoved aside, orders bawled, heavy feet clattering on the tiled floors. Armed police were searching the houses, banging on shutters, pushing into homes. Hans's father had answered the door to them, with Hans's mother and Erik's mother behind him. Erik, at the first sound of alarm, had touched his mother on her shoulder, and headed up the stairs.

Frieda took one terrified look at the strangers and began to screech.

'Quiet that child!' snapped one of them, but Frieda would not be quiet.

'Where's Hans?' she howled. 'Where's Erik? What are the horrible, horrible men doing here?'

'Hush, Frieda, hush!' said Hans's mother, but Erik's mother said, 'They are not horrible men, Frieda. They are the police looking for hidden people.'

'But we haven't got any hidden people!' wailed Frieda.

'No. But they have to look.'

Erik and Hans seemed, unbelievably, not to have heard the noise, not even when Frieda screamed indignantly, '*Vati! Vati!* They are stealing our things!'

One of them had opened the ancient black dresser and

pulled out the hoarded bottle of brandy kept for emergencies.

'Take it, take it,' said Hans's father wearily. 'It doesn't matter, Frieda.'

Then one of the men noticed, 'There's a door behind that dresser!' and the whole heavy piece of furniture was heaved aside. All Hans's mother's china rattled and slid and a small hand mirror with a daisy-painted back fell to the floor and shattered.

'My mirror!' shrieked Frieda, and before anyone could stop her she had hurled herself at the nearest of the intruders, hammering with her fists. Exactly at that moment, Hans came running down the stairs, followed, a minute or two later by Erik, carrying his kitbag.

That caused a pause. Hans, tall, blond, furious, in full Luftwaffe uniform, peaked cap, polished boots, outrage on every feature. Erik behind him with his pilot's silver eagle on his breast. The sight halted the searchers, until the leader recovered and began, 'Our orders—'

'Your orders?' roared Hans. 'You are frightening a little child in the home of two officers of the Reich! I'll report the lot of you!'

'We were informed—'

'Names!' snapped Erik, stepping forward and pulling a notebook from his pocket. 'I'll have your names and numbers . . . Frieda! No!'

'Be very careful, my little sugar rose,' said Erik's mother, urgently. She glanced at Erik, but she spoke to Frieda, who had stooped for the broken glass, and immediately cut herself.

Bright blood ran from her palm, her face contorted, and she took an enormous, about-to-bellow breath. Her mother pounced on her at once, clucking and exclaiming.

'I am holding you responsible,' said Hans, now no longer roaring but calm and cold and furious. 'Your names! One of you, clear up that glass. Then my colleague and I will supervise your search. Myself down here. Erik, would you take these gentlemen to the rooms above. Frieda, very soon they will be gone, let *Mutti* bathe your hand. Now!'

In a few minutes it was over, the three apartments searched, Fraulein Trisk's, clearly long abandoned, empty as a shell. Erik and his mother's, Hans's family's.

'Look under the beds!' Erik had ordered, his kitbag still on his back. 'Behind the curtains. Get this done properly. The cupboard under the second staircase. That chest!'

Downstairs, Hans was saying much the same. 'Roll up the rug. Check the floor is sound. The water closet. Frieda, lift the tablecloth!'

'That's my secret house!' protested Frieda, but Erik's mother said, 'We must do what we can, Frieda,' and the tablecloth was lifted to show Frieda's cushion and her doll and her china mug with the robin painted on it.

Erik came down to join them again, shepherding the searchers in front of him. The broken glass had been cleared away, he noticed, and the brandy bottle stood in the middle of the dresser. 'Now,' he said, 'if you are satisfied, gentlemen . . .' He snapped open his notebook, read their names and numbers aloud, pocketed it, and looked pointedly at Frieda.

'We apologize for any distress caused to the child. We were following orders and it was not our intention to disturb her,' said the leader. 'She is not hurt.'

'She is hurt and frightened,' said Erik. 'Her parents are distressed. Her friends are angry. Is your duty here done? If so, please leave.'

Even when they were gone, the rooms still felt invaded. Frieda sobbed with temper. Erik put down his kitbag at last and sighed with weariness. Hans growled, 'So this is what it's come to,' and his mother looked at him with fear and said in a loud, clear voice, 'They were good men obeying orders,' and glanced at the door, as if they might be in the street listening even now. Hans's father said nothing, but set up a line of five glasses, opened the brandy bottle, and divided it between them.

'I'll take mine upstairs, if you will excuse me,' said Erik's mother.

'I'll come with you,' said Erik.

'Don't forget this,' Hans reminded him, and very gently he lifted the kitbag and held it steady while Erik looped it over his shoulder.

'Thanks,' said Erik, and hurried away.

Before the night was finished, there was another happening. Erik answered the door to a gentle knock and found Hans standing outside.

'Uncle Karl has arrived,' he said. 'In all the trouble earlier we forgot he might be coming. My father told him a few days ago that you and I would be here, and he said he would try to see us both. Will you come down and say hello?'

'Yes, yes of course,' said Erik. 'Right now?'

'Just when you can.'

'Five minutes then,' said Erik, and five minutes later he was there.

Then Erik blinked in surprise, because it was as if the frantic hours of the early evening had been utterly wiped away. A transformation had taken place. Hans's mother was pouring coffee, his father was puffing his pipe, Hans was teaching Frieda to wriggle her eyebrows and Uncle Karl, undoubtably the one responsible for all this magic, was smiling benevolently across from the window.

'Well, well, here is the second of our young fledglings!' he exclaimed, coming forward to greet Erik, and Erik found to his absolute astonishment that he was now taller than Uncle Karl. It felt so strange and wrong that for a moment he was entirely lost for words.

Uncle Karl was the same Uncle Karl as ever. Confident, cheerful, at ease with himself and the world, dismissing problems with a wave of a hand.

'Pooh, pooh,' he said, when he heard about the searching of the apartments. 'Don't tell me they actually worried you! They were only doing their job.'

'I cut my hand,' said Frieda, holding up her bandage.

'Very interesting,' said Uncle Karl. 'And what's that behind your left ear? Oh, a Reichsmark. That's so nice. And behind the other one? Come, come, stand still. Another, and another

143

and is that one in your pocket? Wonderful. You are rich.'

Frieda's face was pure delight. Her mother clapped, and Hans said, 'You never found money behind my ears.'

'Didn't I?' asked Uncle Karl. 'Well then, let me look now,' but there was nothing behind Hans's ears except two matches in a box and a stump of pencil.

'Not all people have the right sort of ears,' said Uncle Karl, shaking his head sadly, and everybody laughed, Frieda most of all.

Under cover of the laughter Uncle Karl nodded to Erik and mouthed, 'A word?' and motioned him over.

'What is it?' asked Erik, too startled to hide it in his voice.

'Nothing at all to worry you. Perhaps a little drive with me when I leave? You'll come?'

Erik nodded, because whoever said no to Uncle Karl?

'Good,' said Uncle Karl, and picked the empty brandy bottle from the table, tipped the last few drops on to the back of his hand, and dabbed them up carefully, one by one, with his finger.

'They finished the bottle without me,' he explained to Frieda, who was watching.

'Without me too,' said Frieda.

Uncle Karl passed her the empty bottle and said, 'I was planning to enjoy it later, but you may have first sniff.'

Frieda inhaled long and deep.

'Is it nice?' asked Uncle Karl.

'Very nice,' said Frieda. 'Thank you.'

'I do what I can,' said Uncle Karl, and Erik recognized

his mother's phrase and felt cold fear run down his spine. He never knew quite what to think of Uncle Karl, who was everyone's friend, who a much younger Erik had once hoped might marry his mother, so that she would no longer have to scrub staircases and could ride around in the wonderful red automobile instead.

Frieda offered Uncle Karl the brandy bottle. He sniffed, and said, 'Wonderful,' and passed it to Erik, who held it uncertainly.

Uncle Karl gave him one of his amused, blank looks and said, 'It's a game, Erik.'

It was very late before Uncle Karl left, nodding to Erik, who waited until the goodbyes were all said, and the doors all closed, and then followed him into the street.

The red automobile smelled as exotic as ever, and there was still a duster for passengers' shoes. Uncle Karl laughed out loud when Erik picked it up. 'Those days are long gone, I'm sorry to say,' he told him. 'Now then, I wanted to talk to you. I've been thinking about this since it all began. Berlin will soon be a target. I must get the family out of the city. Your mother too, of course.'

Erik said nothing. Berlin could well become a target. Their friends might leave. But his mother would stay. She would do what she could.

Then Uncle Karl said calmly, 'And your grandmother.'

Silence hung like a heavy curtain between them.

They were driving though the city, the buildings tall,

shuttered against the night, the long streets that led to the centre all empty, the great squares and monuments hung with flags, motionless, huge. If ever a city looked invincible, thought Erik, it was this one, his Berlin.

'The city will be a target,' said Uncle Karl, reading his thoughts, 'from the west and from the east. She will need papers which I can arrange.'

'Where could they go?' asked Erik at last.

'The Munich factory needs workers, with so many young people gone to fight. I know a place where they could live.'

Erik, with the help of his father's kitbag, had now saved his first life. He could fly a plane, a fighter plane, with heavy machine guns attached. He had twice saluted the Führer, and once momentarily looked into his eyes (pale blue. Mad). But he had not yet got over the feeling that when he was grown up he would go and work in Berlin Zoo, with Hans and his pastry stall handily stationed at the gates.

'Munich's a long way,' he said.

'I'm dropping you here,' said Uncle Karl, pulling up a mile or so away from his street. 'Enjoy the walk. I think it will be a bright morning. Do what you can.'

'Thank—'

'Don't mention it,' said Uncle Karl. He started off, stopped, reversed back to Erik, and leaned across to speak.

Erik looked into his eyes (Hans's eyes; grey-green, not mad).

'*Don't* mention it!' Uncle Karl repeated, and Erik nodded, tried to smile, couldn't, nodded again, and walked away.

146

EIGHTEEN

Ruby

Plymouth, Autumn 1939

Once they had begun, Ruby and her mother continued searching the newspapers for information about what was happening in the outside world. They quickly discovered that the more they read, the less they seemed to know. 'Where's Poland?' Ruby asked. 'What's it got to do with Germany? How can there be battles in Russia? I thought it was all snow.'

'Russia's east,' said Violet. 'Poland's . . . I don't know one thing about Poland,' she admitted. 'We'd better go to the library.'

The library was a great help, and so was the librarian. All that spring and summer she'd found answers to their questions. Nothing ever dismayed her. When Ruby read from her latest list of things she didn't understand: 'Why do Americans speak English? Why did my dad fight Germany in France? How do ships not sink when they're made of metal? What's the Treaty of Versailles and is Russia all snow?' the librarian said calmly, 'I'll show you where to look.'

A film called *The Wizard of Oz* came out. Ruby and Violet went to see it. It was shown with a newsreel. Hitler, making a speech to thousands of people.

'How can anybody listen to him?' asked Ruby. 'He's madder than the Tin Man. He's madder than the Scarecrow. He's madder than the Wicked Witch, he's madder than that tornado. If he behaved like that round here they'd chuck him in the docks to calm him down.'

'That's just what we'll do if he turns up on our street,' said Violet cheerfully.

'The librarian said he needs someone to stand up to him,' said Ruby.

'The sooner the better,' agreed Violet. 'Poor Will's bored stiff.'

Ruby knew that all too well. They had just had another visit. Will had stayed two days, checked behind the clock, ridiculed the library books, said of course he knew where Poland was, the Treaty of Versailles was boring, ships didn't sink because their engines kept them up, stupid, just the same as aeroplanes, and everyone knew that Russia was all snow.

'It isn't!' Ruby had exclaimed. 'You should look at this library book, and what about sailing ships that don't have engines?'

Will had replied that she should stop trying to be so clever, sailing ships were made of wood, and had she realized that when the war came all the kids would be sent away from Plymouth, including her.

'Good riddance,' Will had finished.

Then September had arrived, Britain was at war with Germany, and to Ruby's surprise her mother and Mrs Cohen, instead of saying, 'Good, just what we wanted,' had looked at each other with sober faces.

'Sooner it's begun, sooner it's done,' said Violet, at last.

'I think your Will will be too young to be sent overseas,' said Mrs Cohen hopefully, but she was wrong. Suddenly Will was on his way to France. He sailed as part of the BEF, the British Expeditionary Force in Europe, laden with baggage which included an emergency kit provided by his anxious mother. Violet had put so much thought and effort into this, that by the time it was all collected together it seemed that he truly was equipped for anything.

It held:

Winter socks and gloves (with his name in).

Horlicks tablets. ('It's food and a nice hot drink.')

Four ten-shilling notes in an envelope for just-in-case.

A first-aid kit containing aspirin tablets, a remedy for
    seasickness (supplied by Mrs Cohen, who had never
    once been on a boat), some sticking plasters and a little
    bottle of iodine for cuts.

Ginger biscuits.

A large pork pie.

It also included a notebook full of helpful things Violet had written down, such as *Gran's birthday, Dec 2nd, if you have time to drop a line*, and useful reminders about foreign dogs and rabies, drinking water and boiling it, and not to forget that over there they drove on the wrong side of the road. In the back of the notebook she had listed some French words copied from the library dictionary (*Please, Thank you, I am an English boy, I have lost my way, I need a good doctor, I am hungry* and *No, thank you, I do not drink wine*).

Very shortly after they sailed, Will ate the pork pie and the ginger biscuits, spent the ten-shilling notes on a second-hand watch, and read the notebook in horror before dropping it safely overboard in case anyone else should see it.

He came to regret all these things; the pork pie almost immediately, the money very soon afterwards, and the notebook last and most painfully, when homesickness hit him like an illness and if he could have magicked one thing into his life it would have been his mum.

Meanwhile at home, life was changing. Will, although wrong about Russia and snow, and engines and aeroplanes, was right about one thing: the kids were sent away. Ruby's school was evacuated, every pupil labelled and put on a train with their belongings in a case and a teacher in charge. They were going to Cornwall, they were told, where there wouldn't be bombs.

Or cinemas or indoor toilets, added the rumours, and there would be seagulls' eggs for breakfast, and fish bones in the beds, and the locals would call you a foreigner and the kids would beat you up.

There were a lot of tears shed on that chaotic train journey to Cornwall, but not by Ruby, who had prudently borrowed the train fare home from the shop till before she left. At Exeter, where they had to change, she found the ladies' waiting room, located the cleaners' cupboard and perched herself on an upturned bucket until the brief panicking search was over and they were forced to leave her behind. Then she removed her cardboard label, tucked her school hat under her arm, and caught the afternoon train back home.

'I might have known,' said Violet, but she didn't send her back.

There followed a blissful few months with no school and no bombs and no Will either. In town they built air-raid shelters, criss-crossed the windowpanes with paper tape to stop broken glass flying, and began taking the road signs down. Ruby spent a lot of time at the library and Violet trained to be an air-raid warden.

'I thought you'd have to be a man,' said Ruby, very impressed.

Now at night, the streets were very quiet, and the houses all dark, not a chink of light that might guide a bomber to the city.

Ruby thought sometimes that the blackout worked too well. Week after week passed, and then month after month, but no bombers came. Will wrote from France that he had nothing to do, so they sent him another emergency kit: a puzzle book, a large bag of humbugs, a woolly hat (with his name in) and his old, but nearly new, football boots.

'They'll keep him going for a bit,' said Violet, and she was right, they did.

NINETEEN
Kate
Oxford, 1939

By the autumn of 1939 the world had changed, and Kate's family had changed with it.

Bea was the first to take flight from the nest. She was eighteen, and had just finished school. She said, 'Would you believe it! There's a Land Army and I can join! Think of lambs in the spring! And I'll get paid! Paid! I'm going to save up for a motorbike!' Then, before her family had time to say, 'Are you mad and what about us?' she was gone. They had a postcard from a hostel where she was sent for six weeks' training:

> *They let us drive tractors! Someone teach Kate to*
> *plait her hair. I forgot.*
> *Love Bea*

Janey was next. Janey was nineteen and had done a year at university. There was no reason why she shouldn't carry on studying except that she had a letter from the Foreign Office. They wanted her to come for an interview in London.

'You!' exclaimed her family. 'They must have got mixed up.'

'I expect they've heard she's brainy,' said her father gloomily, and they had.

'It's sort of office work,' said brainy Janey. 'I think it might be fun.'

Very soon she too was sending postcards:

I see squirrels in the park every morning. That's all I'm allowed to tell you. Someone help Kate with her homework. I forgot. Love Janey

Simon and Tod joined the Sea Cadets. They said it was the quickest way into the navy.

'We can enlist properly when we're sixteen,' said Simon.

'With parental consent,' said their mother. 'Meanwhile you are just horrible little boys, so go and get on with your homework!'

'Poor old Mum,' said Tod. 'She doesn't understand there's a war on. She thinks we can carry on doing homework and messing about in a leaky punt.'

'She wishes we were still choirboys,' said Simon. 'She can't help it. Poor old mum.'

The Sea Cadets swallowed them up. They left their punt to sink back into the Cherwell, gave up homework, grew lean and starving, and became intensely interested in first aid. For a while their conversation was full of drowning and choking, broken bones and splints. They practised on whoever they could catch, which was usually Charlie.

'Charlie, you've just been dragged out of the sea, stop kicking, you're unconscious . . .'

'No, I'm not,' said Charlie, somewhat indistinctly.

'Yes, you are. Shut up. You've been two hours in the water and there's something blocking your airways.'

'It's a gobstopper,' said Charlie, shifting a large bulge from his left cheek to his right and slurping a little.

'Spit it out, so's I can check your breathing.'

'I only just put it in!' said Charlie indignantly.

'Tod, I have a non-cooperative patient here with worsening conditions,' reported Simon.

'No, you haven't,' said Charlie, and in proof he jumped to his feet and escaped by way of the living-room window.

'Let him drown,' said Tod. 'Right, Kate, have you still got a pulse?'

'I don't really want . . .' began Kate, who didn't always remember that she was now extraordinarily brave.

'Make a note, Simon, patient waterlogged, but responsive.'

'Noted,' said Simon. 'Pulse irregular and feeble. Turn her so she doesn't choke if she vomits.'

'I don't feel a bit sick,' said Kate indignantly.

'Conversation irrational,' commented Tod, rolling her on to her side. 'Shock and hypothermia. Pass me something to cover her up. The hearthrug will do.'

'Too dusty, it'll start her off coughing.'

'True.'

'Any bones broken?' asked Simon. 'What have we got? Both legs? Both arms? Any bleeding requiring compression?'

'What's compression?' Kate squeaked in alarm.

'You'll see. Tod, fetch a tea towel and fold it into a pad and hold it tight against the wound. Kate, don't wriggle.'

'The tea towel tickles.'

'Put up with it. Don't move till we find some splints.'

'Why'd you need splints?' demanded Charlie, reappearing at the window. 'How did she get broken bones in the sea? Why didn't she just get wet?'

'She was hit by flying wreckage when the ship was torpedoed, of course.'

Kate sat up very quickly and asked, 'Might that really happen?'

'Obviously,' said Tod.

'But you say you're going into the navy!'

'And?'

'What if your ships are torpedoed?'

'Kate, how many times did that punt tip us into the Cherwell?'

'I don't know.'

'Think!'

'About once a week in the summer.'

'Correct. And did we ever drown?'

'No, but . . .' protested Kate and then their mother came in and asked, 'What are you horrible sailors doing to my daughter?'

'They're saving her,' said Charlie, still perched on the windowsill.

'What from?'

'Drowning and broken bones and concussion and being torpedoed and shark attack.'

'Not sharks,' said Simon. 'There were never any sharks.'

'Well, there soon will be when they smell the blood,' said Charlie.

'There is no blood,' said Tod. 'Not any more. We applied compression until it stopped. You missed it, rushing out of the window.'

'I think we should change the subject,' said Tod. 'We're frightening poor old Mum.'

'Poor old thing,' said Simon, nodding sympathetically.

'You boys forget you're talking to a woman who has clamped more arteries than you've had sausages for supper,' snapped Vanessa.

'Mum!' wailed Kate, clapping her hands over her ears.

'Mum,' said Tod reproachfully. 'Now look what you've done. Poor old Kate.'

Then, as quickly as it had started, first aid stopped. Map-reading and marching and rifle skills took over. Soon training camps began, and after that the twins were hardly ever home.

Quite suddenly it seemed to Kate that there was only Charlie left. At breakfast one Saturday morning when it was just the two of them, she asked, 'You're not going to do war things too, are you, Charlie?'

'Of course I am,' said Charlie, with his mouth full of toast. 'I'm going to learn circus tricks. Juggling and stilt-walking and fire-eating and stuff.'

'What for?' asked Kate, astonished.

'So's I can be in shows to raise money. Everyone's wanting money, haven't you noticed? Aeroplanes and Red Cross and evacuees and ambulances. My class at school are saving up for a lifeboat. It was my idea.'

'Mum and Dad will never let you fire-eat and stilt-walk,' said Kate certainly.

'They will. I've got the stilts already,' said Charlie, successfully balancing a licked marmalade spoon on the end of his nose. 'A boy in choir was selling them and when I told Dad he said "excellent" and lent me the ten bob. I'm singing in a concert too. I've been joining everything at school. Yesterday I signed up with the drama club and they were really pleased because I ticked the box on the joining form to say I don't mind playing girls.'

'But what about me?'

'You're a girl already, and anyway, you don't go to my school. You couldn't. It's all boys.'

'You know I didn't mean that! What am I supposed to do?'

She sounded so anxious that Charlie put down the marmalade spoon and thought. What *could* Kate do? How had he known what to do? He hadn't at first, he'd been thinking and thinking, and then suddenly he'd heard of the stilts for sale and everything had fallen into place.

He tried to explain this to Kate.

'I suppose I was watching out for something useful,' he said.

'It will be useful,' Kate agreed. 'You'll make people laugh and cheer them up as well as getting money.'

Charlie was immensely pleased. So rarely did his family take him seriously. He said, 'You watch out like I did, Kate, and I bet something turns up for you. Do you want to come and see me on my stilts?'

'All right.'

'Will you write about them in your diary?'

'Yes.'

'Can I read it after?' asked Charlie. 'What else have you written about?'

'Oh.' Kate thought. 'Tod and Simon doing their first aid and you jumping out of the window. Bea. All the Brussels sprouts she has to pick and then having to eat them every day for dinner. Janey's squirrel that waits for her in the mornings. Ruby and her brother. Dad at the hospital so much. Clarry and Rupert. Mum when she talks about the twins being sixteen. Grandfather's gold.'

'I'd forgotten about that,' said Charlie, and later when he was reading Kate's diary, he found many other things he'd forgotten. 'Bea's lambs,' he said, as he turned pages backwards, 'and when Janey used to live with us. When it wasn't just me in the choir. When we didn't have to bother about gas masks. When I swam in the Serpentine . . . It's a good job you wrote it all down, Kate. Or else it would all have been wasted.'

Kate nodded.

'Bea's got her farm and Janey her squirrel place. Tod and Simon will be sailors soon. I'll be the money-getter with my stilts and everything, and you'll be the writer-downer.'

'But I'd do that anyway,' objected Kate. 'I was going . . . I was going to try and be, because Rupert said . . . it was his idea . . . extraordinarily . . .'

Charlie waited.

'. . . brave.'

'I expect you'll be that too,' said Charlie kindly.

158

TWENTY
Dog
London, late November 1939

The dog was lost. One evening an old van had rattled to the scrapyard and not without difficulty, he'd been loaded into the back. The journey that followed had been so painful and bewildering that he'd blanked it from his mind.

They'd travelled north and west into the city until, under the shadow of some monstrous shapes that he didn't know were trees, the van had stopped and the back had opened.

'Off you go,' a voice had ordered out of the darkness, and the dog had crawled out and stood sick and trembling beside the iron railings of a shabby London square.

Then the van had gone.

Now there was no scrapyard, no tea-chest kennel, no chain, no girl, no river smell. The streets were strange. Also, for all the miles the dog had run in his dreams, in real life he'd always been chained. His muscles were wasted and his movements were unbalanced and lurching. For the first few days, this clumsiness and unease kept him to the shadows, until hunger made him desperate. Then he became bolder. He grabbed and stole and scavenged. Day after day, he wandered, in search of dustbins and scraps and the leavings of street markets. There was nothing he wouldn't eat. Nothing.

Rupert encountered him late one night in cold December. There was no moon, and it had rained and the clouds were still low. The blackout had sealed the city into the sort of deep darkness where any moment you might step off a kerb, or knock into a stranger. The sort where you navigated by the smell of fallen leaves, pungent under the plane trees, the hot breath of an underground station, and the dank whiff of alleys.

Rupert had a thousand things on his mind, and he was thinking of them as he hurried along when he noticed a smell like old clothes and dustbins and ancient dead fish. A moment later something pushed him from behind. His hand touched coarse fur. He heard panting.

'Oi,' he said, pausing, and the reply was a long rumble, like the sound of a distant engine.

When he started walking again, the shove came once more. When he stopped, there came the rumble.

'Waylaid,' said Rupert, 'by a highway dog.' And he reached out his hand to the rumble and felt bones under the fur. It was weeks now, since the scrapyard.

'You poor chap,' said Rupert. 'You poor old chap. Wait there.'

There was a pub just ahead, still open, and the comforting sound of voices came from behind its shuttered windows. Rupert went in, bought a cheese roll with very little cheese in it and a pale-looking pie from under the glass dome on the counter, and hurried out again. The pie was seized from his hand in one hot invisible lunge and there was a choking gulp. The cheese roll went the same way.

'That's it, then,' said Rupert, giving the bony shoulders a rub. 'Best I can do. Good luck.'

He went back into the pub again, and half an hour later, when he reappeared, the dog was still there, waiting.

Rupert tried to lose him, but the dog followed. He followed all the way to the little basement flat that Rupert rented when he was in London. However, at the steep steps down to the entrance, he halted.

Just as well, thought Rupert, as he hurried to unlock the door and get inside, but the dog had not given up. In the darkness, he was very slowly negotiating his way down towards the door. Rupert heard grumbling growls come closer and closer, and then a heavy thud.

After the thud came silence, and after the silence, a long, sorry, sigh.

It was the sigh that made Rupert find a plate and get out all the things he had to eat, which wasn't much, because his basement was just his place to sleep, not a home. Nevertheless, he found some smelly cheese, some biscuits, a tin of sardines and a forgotten slice of bacon, which he toasted over the gas ring and then arranged like a garnish beside the other things. After this, he filled his largest dish with water, made himself a cup of tea without any milk, because he hadn't any milk, and opened the door.

The smell came in first, and then, very quickly after it, the dog.

The dog didn't look at Rupert. He went straight for the dishes on the floor. The food vanished in one swallow, the water in a few great slurping gulps.

'Excellent,' said Rupert cheerfully, and then a most un-excellent thing happened. There was an ominous silence, some terrible sounds, and very suddenly cheese, biscuits, sardines, bacon, water, together with the pub pie and a slightly chewed roll, all reappeared in a large and hateful pile in the middle of Rupert's floor.

'No!' he cried, leaping forward, but he was too late, and helpless to prevent the whole heap being hastily eaten up again, even faster than the first time.

'Never since boarding school have I seen such a meal,' said Rupert. 'What's that round your neck? Will you show me?'

He reached cautiously towards the dog so he could inspect the leather tag and the three burned letters.

PAX

(*It might help*, the girl had thought.)

Pax, read Rupert.

Peace.

For years Rupert had worked for peace, argued for peace, travelled backwards and forwards through Europe in a quest for peace, and now here it was, slumped on his kitchen floor.

'So,' said Rupert. 'Pax.'

The dog gave him a swift glance, like a person agreeing a bargain.

*

It had been a long day. Rupert went to bed, and the dog went to bed too, on the only bit of carpet in Rupert's flat: his quite nice bedside rug. The smell that came from him penetrated Rupert's dreams so strongly that for a moment, when he woke, he didn't know where he was and remembered the earthy, stale smell of the dugouts he had slept in during the First World War.

It was quite a relief to see Pax.

There was no hot water in Rupert's basement, but there was a bath. Rupert boiled kettles and poured in soap flakes and stirred it until it was warm and bubbly and then he rolled up his sleeves and grabbed Pax and lifted him in.

The grumbling sounds were awful, and so was the curled lip that showed a broken yellow tooth, but Rupert, remembering his dreams, said, 'I faced worse than you in the trenches,' and began to scrub.

The first lot of bath water was soon the colour of wartime coffee – a sort of earthy, greenish brown. The second lot was much paler. Different colours began to appear on the dog; white on his chest, and a sort of rust mixed in with the grey. Rupert rinsed him down, hauled him out, rubbed the worst of the wet out of his coat with his only bath towel and, not knowing what else he could do with him, took him into work and parked him in a corner of his office.

For a few days, this worked fairly well. Pax mostly slept, recovering from the weeks of hunger and exhaustion. However, as he recovered, he grew restless. If Rupert left him for a while he paced and whined, or tried to dig holes in the floor. When people came in, he growled and ducked away, even from friendly hands. It began to be that the moment he appeared in the morning, someone would say, 'You're not bringing that animal in here again, are you? This is no place for dogs.'

Rupert knew it was no place for dogs, that soon the whole of London would be no place for dogs. It was only a matter of time before the bombing raids would begin. The silver barrage balloons were ready (Pax hated them, as he hated all things in the sky), air-raid shelters were built, buildings piled with sandbags. Civilians had been recruited and trained: firefighters, air-raid wardens, ambulance drivers.

There were hardly any children about, and hardly any dogs, especially big dogs like Pax. Quite often people commented, 'Blimey, what do you feed that on?'

'Horse,' said Rupert. 'He's horse-powered.'

Now that food was rationed, horse meat was the only thing you could buy for cats and dogs. Even that wasn't easy. The queues at the butchers were getting longer every day, and every day Rupert had less time to wait in them. In a phone call to Clarry he mentioned that it felt like he spent every spare waking moment queueing up for dark green horse.

'Dark green?' asked Clarry.

'They've started splashing it with green dye. It's to stop people buying it to eat.'

'I'm so glad I'm vegetarian. Did you call me just to talk about horse meat, Rupert?'

'Not just about that.'

'I knew!' said Clarry, suddenly furious. 'I knew as soon as the telephone rang. It's—'

'Steady on, Clarry,' said Rupert hastily.

Telephone calls weren't secure. They went through a switchboard where anyone could listen. 'It's what you talked about in Oxford,' said Clarry. 'When?'

'Very soon. Don't worry.'

'Don't worry! Why can't someone else do it? There must be hundreds of people who would be ten times more use than you.'

'Thank you. Mathematically devastating as usual.'

'Stop it. You know you have a choice.'

'Not much. Prime suspect really. Know the routines. Unattached.'

'I should have married you years ago.'

'Told you so.'

There was a pause, while Clarry sniffed.

'Marry me when I come back.'

'Yes, all right. If.'

'Take back the if and I'll give you all my worldly goods.'

'No, Rupert, I couldn't!' exclaimed Clarry. 'Not if you mean the worldly goods that eats green horse. In this little flat, and I'm teaching all day. You'll have to give him to somebody else.'

'Not easy.'

'You must know someone who likes dogs.'

'You'd think so, but . . . Yes, I do. Of course I do! Genius, Clarry, well done! There's the pips! I was going to ask you . . .'

The pips were the warning that the three-minute phone call was about to end. Rupert had just time to say, 'a very small favour,' and Clarry to reply, 'Yes, anything,' when the line went dead.

'This is wonderfully good news for you and me,' said Rupert to Pax. 'Clarry is going to marry me. And – this is your bit – Kate, I just suddenly remembered Kate, who is a darling, is very fond of dogs.'

Kate wrote to Ruby: *I am looking after a dog called Pax till the end of the war.*

It had begun with a telephone call, overheard from the landing by Kate, answered by her father.

'What? What? Clarry, are you mad? Absolutely impractical. Typical Rupert!'

'What's typical Rupert?' asked Kate from the stairs, but Peter was still protesting down the phone.

'One daft enterprise after another!' he continued. 'Swimming in the Serpentine! Carting the girls round London! Carting them *all* round London. I never could see the sense in it!'

'Perhaps,' replied Clarry, 'he remembered how no one ever carted us around when we were growing up.'

There was silence in the hall for a moment.

'They always came back safe and joyful,' said Clarry.

When Peter spoke again, his voice had changed completely. 'You're right. You're absolutely right. But explain to me, why Kate?'

'Rupert seemed to think she liked dogs.'

At this, Kate's fingers had closed on the Scotty-dog pincushion in her pocket, and she'd come tumbling down the stairs to demand breathlessly, 'What are you talking about?'

Clarry brought him back from London on the train, wrote Kate.

The dog had hated that journey. He had been entirely distressed. If he had been free to choose, he would have been safe back in his yard on his chain.

Once again he was lost.

At the station Rupert had handed his lead to a strange woman, and, addressing her, ignoring him, said, 'I'll be back before you know it. Hold out your hand, Clarry. No tears . . . It's a pink sapphire to match your pink beret. Don't worry if you lose it, I'll buy you another.'

'Oh . . .'

'See? Perfect.'

'Can we write?'

'No, darling Clarry. Don't be daft.'

'I hate goodbyes.'

'Don't say it. He probably needs de-flea-ing. One kiss . . . There.'

Then he'd vanished.

The dog had been hauled on to a train and tied up on a stack of old newspapers in the guards' van. It had been lucky the newspapers were there because when the train lurched into movement he'd been sick with fright. And after that, at intervals for the whole nightmare event, he'd been sick again and again. It was true that the Clarry woman had spent the journey with him, but she, for some other reason, had seemed almost equally distressed. The dog avoided her with loathing because it was she who had taken him from Rupert.

The woman had to give the guard ten shillings because he was so ill. When she got him back to Oxford she'd washed him with rose geranium soap. The dog, who much preferred the smell of sick, had longed to bite her but he couldn't. The memory of the yard broom swung high to wallop him in his snapping puppy days held him back. He'd curled his lip and shown her his broken yellow tooth but she'd said, 'I don't believe you,' and continued with the soap.

He was damp and reeking of roses when more strangers came to stare at him. A man and a girl, who glanced and then looked away, backwards and forwards from the Clarry woman to his quivering self, with nowhere he could hide.

He was much bigger than I expected, Kate wrote to Ruby, and she had drawn two small sketches, a Scotty dog and Pax, for comparison.

'He's a big softy,' Clarry said, and then Dad reached his hands up into the air to tug at his hair like he does when he's going mad. We didn't know how frightened Pax was of being hit.

When Peter reached up it was more than the dog could bear. He ran.

Down the stairs, away across the streets, causing cars to hoot, cyclists to skid, and two buckets of chrysanthemums outside the flower shop to clatter to the ground. The flower shop woman came out and began to screech.

It wasn't a long escape. He was very soon surrounded. A semicircle of people blocked his way, and he was trapped. Then the girl arrived and grabbed his lead and the man came limping up behind. He said, 'I suppose we'd better take him home.'

The dog didn't want to go home with them. He wanted to stay where he was there in the road until either Rupert came and rescued him, or he miraculously remembered his way back to the scrapyard. Those were the only two futures he could imagine and so he dug in his paws and leaned backwards and raised all the fur in a line down his spine and snarled.

Traffic had to go around him. Bystanders suggested a good shove with a broom, a bucket of cold water to make him jump, and fetching the police. It went on and on until the dog, who was very tired, gave up all hope of any future, lay down on the cobbles, put his head between his paws and cried.

'Oh,' said the girl, and she kneeled in the road and gathered him into her arms. Her face was against his, and her hands were in his fur, rubbing behind his ragged ears. She told him over and over that he was a good dog.

The scrapyard girl had spoken kindly to him. Rupert had given him many friendly rubs and scratches. Neither could compare with this. For the first time in his life, the dog knew he had a heart. A proper, thudding heart, his own, to keep him warm and alive.

As soon as he had located it, he renounced all ownership, and gave it to Kate, for ever and ever.

Pax, wrote Kate to Ruby, *is another word for peace.*

TWENTY-ONE
Erik and Hans
Germany, Jan–Feb 1940

It was the best news for a very long time. Erik and Hans were together again, flying their planes from the same airbase. Perhaps it was good luck. Perhaps it was fate. Perhaps, perhaps, thought Erik, longing for a past world, it was Uncle Karl, murmuring a word to some old Luftwaffe friend from before the war, 'Do what you can for the boys.'

They flew little Messerschmitts, single-seater aircraft, and their task was nearly always the same: to escort the heavy bombers, to defend them from the fighter planes that rose up in fury from their invaded homelands.

Often in private, tired Erik rubbed his head, and tried to trace his journey from his *kleine Schwalben,* his little swallows, to being part of the planned attack on France. He could never quite manage it, and neither, when he consulted him, could Hans.

They were in the mess, drinking golden lager from tall glasses.

'It was probably because of the zoo that we ended up with wings,' Hans decided, after thinking for a while. 'Almost certainly, all our troubles began with your great need for elephants and monkeys and the like.'

'All Berlin went to the zoo,' said Erik. 'They didn't end up flying Messerschmitts.'

'True . . . Drink up! True, but we were different. Remember the time we swept the paths and met Herr Schmidt?'

'Your idea,' said Erik, smiling at the memory. 'We should have stuck to my expert and knowledgeable guided tours.'

'*How I spent my Sunday morning and why I will never do it again*,' said Hans. 'That was the title he set us.'

'I remember,' said Erik. 'A thousand words each, to be handed in the next day.'

'Yes. And we wrote them in my room so your mother wouldn't know you were in trouble. And Uncle Karl came in.'

'He did,' agreed Erik. 'And I told him about my swallows.'

'Those swallows!' exclaimed Hans. 'They were a bad lot! That Cumulus never stopped eating. By the time they flew away you were so exhausted that if I hadn't been there you would have toppled out of the window.'

'Well,' said Erik, clinking glasses. 'You were there. So.'

Now that they were together again, Erik and Hans often escaped into the old stories, the swallows and the zoo, and the pastry stall outside. Running out on to the airfield to climb into their cockpits, Erik would shout, 'Have you got fresh gingerbread? Is the coffee hot?' and Hans would call back, 'Of course, but are the bears all brushed and fed? Do the flamingos look pink enough and is that elephant happy?' Then, for a minute or two, they were boys back in Berlin, with no worse troubles than lost mittens, and bossy sisters and how to find the price of a ticket to the zoo. 'Two Reichmarks,' remembered Erik. 'Two Reichsmarks, to be happy all day.'

Uncle Karl had kept his word and their families had left Berlin. It had all been arranged very quickly, the goodbyes and the packing, and then, before anyone could think, Hans's parents and little Frieda were riding in a truck loaded with the furniture from both apartments, and Erik's mother was following by car with Uncle Karl.

'Ah!' Hans's mother had exclaimed, when she heard of this arrangement. 'I have thought for a long time, you and Karl—'

'I know you have,' said Erik's mother. 'But no.'

'No? It would have been nice for Erik when he was smaller.'

'Erik was happy enough.'

'He was,' her friend agreed. 'That smile! They were both happy boys, thank God. Hans was a rascal.'

'There was never a better boy than Hans,' said Erik's mother at once.

'All grown up now,' Han's mother sighed. 'I miss Lisa. Boys leave, I know they do, but girls should stay near their mothers.'

Lisa hadn't gone with them when they moved. She'd finished her National Service and was back in Berlin, living in a hostel and working long shifts in an office. Hans heard that she was miserable.

'It's her work,' he told Erik. 'She detests being stuck in a dreary office and she doesn't get on with the hostel people. She says she's lonely every day.'

'Surely she could find something else?' Erik asked, hating to think of Lisa so unhappy.

'Not that easy,' said Hans.

'Perhaps Uncle Karl . . .' suggested Erik, as the families had said for years, *Perhaps Uncle Karl*, but this time Hans shook his head.

'No.'

'No? Definitely no?'

'Definitely no. The family magician has disappeared.'

'Since when?'

'Since Berlin. My mother says he moved them across half Germany to work in Munich and then turned his back on them all. My father says he's up to no good.'

'What does Frieda say?'

'He forgot her birthday.'

'Disaster! How did they manage?'

'Luckily a random kitten turned up and saved the day.'

'A kitten?'

'Yes.'

'On her actual birthday?'

'Just walked through the door, my mother said.'

'A completely random kitten?'

'Must I continually repeat . . .' began Hans, and then finished, in quite a different voice, 'Oh, I see.'

'At last.'

'Perhaps, after all, the magician is not dead.'

'Dead?' asked Erik, startled.

'I have wondered.'

'What a terrible thought.'

'He is a terrible meddler,' said Hans. 'A magician and a meddler. Are such people welcome these wonderful days?'

Erik said nothing.

'He magicked us here,' said Hans. 'Where would we be without him?'

Erik thought wistfully and briefly of his beloved Berlin Zoo. Hans read his mind and laughed. 'No you wouldn't,' he said. 'You'd be conscripted into the infantry before you could say "mind the tiger".'

'So would you. Before you could say "apple strudel".'

'Certainly,' agreed Hans. 'He magicked us away from the fate of our fathers. Out of the mud. Into Luftwaffe pilots. So now, where shall we fall?'

'Stop it, Hans.'

'How is your mother?'

Erik glanced at him. He had never forgotten the evening of the police raid. He'd come out of their apartment with his kitbag on his back to find Hans stationed as if on guard at the top of the stairs. Later, when the police had gone, Hans had actually lifted his bag.

'*Don't forget this*,' he had said. He must have felt the weight.

They had never spoken about it. Erik had never known what Hans guessed, what Hans knew.

'Your mother?' repeated Hans. 'Does she miss Berlin?'

'She hasn't said so.'

'Is she happy?'

'I wouldn't know.'

'Be careful, Erik. Don't fall out of the window. I'll do what I can, but what if one day I'm not there to save you?'

'Hans. What is this?'

'I don't know. I don't know. I feel very mortal. Do you?'

'No. Not really.'

'Not when the searchlights catch you? Not when the guns on the ground won't stop? Not when the fuel's on zero and you can't find the way back down? It may have been a completely random kitten, you know. The magician may be gone. Then who will look after them? My complaining parents. Bossy Lisa? Little Frieda?'

'You shouldn't be thinking like this.'

'But I am,' said Hans. 'Would you look after them, Erik?''

'I . . .'

'Frieda? Someone has to take care of Frieda. Would you do what you could?'

'Yes,' said Erik. 'I would. I promise. I'd do what I could.'

Twenty-Two
Ruby
Plymouth, May 1940

Germany invaded France and Ruby's brother Will suddenly, shockingly, catastrophically, stopped being bored. Before the bewildered eyes of half the world, none more bewildered than those of Will, France fell in forty-six days. Denmark, Belgium, the Netherlands were also lost. In Paris, Rupert was soon behind enemy lines, with Hans and Erik in the air above. Day after day, the news grew worse.

The newsagent's shop in Plymouth had never been as popular. People might hear the latest happenings on their wirelesses, but they absorbed them best written down. Besides, they needed to talk. In the shop there was always someone to listen, even if it was only Ruby, with her atlas and her opinions.

Violet and Ruby were glad to be so busy. It helped to have people about because in France the British Army was in retreat, moving backwards to the coast as the German troops advanced. And for everyone in the newsagent's shop, the army had more or less become one particular soldier, and he was Will.

Will, who they had known since he was a screeching

toddler, who played knock-down-ginger all along the street when he should have been in bed, who chalked rude remarks on walls, who started his gang carol singing in November and tried it on again in January, who left his bicycle chucked down on the pavement for anyone to fall over. Will, who had been such a pest, until the army took him in hand and about time somebody did.

But now he was their own heroic Will.

Day by day, with Sooty and Paddle weaving anxious circles round their feet, the visitors to the shop read of how Will and the rest of them were being forced towards the coast, abandoning kit, sheltering in ditches, tuning and re-tuning their field radios to catch the latest static-crackling instructions.

They saw the pictures too. Dispatch riders, desperately trying to hold the lines of communication together. Frightened local people gathered in town squares. The refugee-filled roads that crossed the French countryside.

As the days passed, it became increasingly clear what would happen next. Will would be trapped. The army would be trapped. They would reach the coast, they would be herded on to the French beaches and there would be nowhere left to go.

When Ruby heard this she wrote a letter addressed to 'Mr Churchill, London'. She also wrote 'URGENT' on the envelope. She felt very virtuous as she did this, because she wasn't that fond of Will.

During all those days, Ruby's mother couldn't rest. When everything else was done, she polished. She polished the insides of drawers and the undersides of cupboards and every plate and saucepan that they owned. She polished the pennies and shillings in the till. Also, since she was the mother of a hero and standards must be upheld, she buffed her nails with lemon peel, powdered away the shadows beneath her eyes, and nearly wore her precious scarlet lipstick to a stump.

'I thought you were saving it for special,' said Ruby, at her bedroom door.

'And isn't Will special?' demanded Violet.

'They're sending boats,' said Ruby. 'That's what I came to tell you. Mrs Cohen's just run down to say she heard it on her wireless. A special announcement. They're sending boats across to France. Big ones are waiting out where the water's deep. Little ones are going right up to the beaches to get the soldiers off and carry them out to the big ones. It was my idea.'

'WHAT?' shouted Violet.

'It was my idea and I think they should say thank you,' said Ruby. 'I wrote a letter to Mr Churchill and I think he could have written back. Even if they're keeping it top secret.'

'What nonsense you do talk,' cried Violet, nevertheless hugging her, and then she put on even more lipstick and rushed down to the shop to exclaim about the big boats and little boats and how Will had swum like a fish from five years old, because his dad had taken him to the pool every summer.

Such was the kindness of the shop's customers that they paused their discussion of the evacuation at Dunkirk to say that they well remembered what a swimmer Will was and how proud his dad had been of him, and would be now, more than ever.

But then someone spoiled it. They said, 'It's going to take days to get them off.'

'Days?' asked Violet, in a voice so shocked that it was clear she had been thinking in hours, not days.

'There's tens of thousands. Hundreds of thousands. There's three hundred thousand and more.'

'Three hundred thousand and more?' exclaimed Violet.

'It's a lot to shift, under fire.'

'Under fire,' repeated Violet. 'Surely they wouldn't . . . not under fire . . . They're just boys, half of them. Our Will's not yet twenty. I'd have thought common decency . . .'

She looked helplessly around for someone to agree that of course no one would dream of firing at young boys, stranded on a beach. That they had driven them out of Europe, and what more could they want? It should be youngest rescued first and everybody home safe, the sooner the better, and after that talk about whatever should happen next.

Said Violet.

The shop had fallen silent, nobody having the heart to say, 'Violet, there's a war on.' Ruby scuffled her foot angrily behind the counter. Under fire hadn't occurred to her either. Perhaps her wonderful plan to save the British Army was not so wonderful after all.

'They've got guns,' she pointed out crossly. 'They can fire back, can't they? Anyway, isn't it past closing time? What about tea?'

'Tea?' said her mother, like it was a word she'd forgotten, and then she said, 'Yes,' and flipped the OPEN sign to CLOSED and held the door for people in a meaningful kind of way. 'Goodbye, goodbye, we'll see what the morning brings. Thank you . . . I'm sorry but we're just closing up. Ruby, get those cats off the counter and come into the scullery. I'm washing your hair.'

'Now?' asked Ruby, dismayed. Hair washing was an ordeal, involving green soap and vinegar rinsing and jugfuls of water poured over her head.

'Now,' said Violet, her eyes too bright and her lipstick gallant.

Ruby saw these things, and because of them she didn't put up her usual fight, understanding that this was all part of the polishing that was keeping her mother from despair. With hardly a sigh she kneeled on the wooden stool, hung her head over the scullery sink, and clutched a face flannel to her soap-stinging eyes. In silence she endured the deluges of water, until she emerged to the buffeting towel and the steel-toothed comb in her tangles.

'OUCH,' said Ruby, then.

Violet put down the comb, picked it up again, and said, 'We've got to carry on.'

'Yes,' agreed Ruby, 'but listen. Will will be all right. He'll be with his friends, lots of friends, all looking after each other. And I bet any day soon he'll come back and hug you and dump his stuff on the chairs and eat all the food in the cupboard and fuss the cats and say, "What's an amaryllis, anyway?"'

'Oh, Ruby Amaryllis!'

'You could do a welcome home party, with sausages and cider,' said Ruby.

Violet laughed a small laugh.

'We could borrow Mrs Cohen's gramophone and set it going in the shop! We'll get all the neighbours round!'

'We'll do that,' said Violet, and she took Ruby's hand and spun her under her arm and danced her round the scullery, round and round, until they were both breathless and neither of them crying any more.

On the beaches of Dunkirk, the soldiers waited on the sand. Now and then, German planes flew low, strafing the lines with machine-gun bullets. The tide rose and fell and Ruby's little boats scurried back and forth, all sorts of little boats from all along the south coast of England. They hauled on board men waist-deep in water, ferried them over to the bigger ships, and then scurried back again for more. It took three days and at the end of it, more than three-quarters of the army were rescued.

It was a miracle so great that it was hardly to be believed.

But not all of them made it.

Will did not come back.

TWENTY-THREE
Kate
Oxford, June 1940

Kate's diary, begun in peacetime in a pink notebook with white kittens on the front, had next moved to a purple journal with scented pages that her mother said she could do without, and then into a series of paper-covered school exercise books provided by Clarry. They were so ancient that their pages had buckled with damp, but the soft yellowed paper was perfect for both writing and drawing. Clarry had donated a boxful and Kate was working through them at a rate of about one a week.

The Christmas that hadn't worked was recorded; the one with neither Janey nor Bea at home, Clarry in Plymouth, and even Charlie's voice now too unreliable for the choir. The long January and February of cold and snow that followed were there too, with coal suddenly much harder to get and Bea freezing on a Lincolnshire farm with not a lamb in sight. Bea wrote that her glasses steamed up every time she breathed and she had chilblains on her fingers as well as her toes. They posted a rescue package, with bed-socks and a hot-water bottle, a knitted patchwork blanket, double-thickness mittens and an ancient sheepskin hat. Kate noted all this, together with Bea's opinions of winter greens, turnips, and sorting seed potatoes in a draughty open shed. When Bea said in her next letter that she wore everything they sent in bed, Kate immediately drew the picture. She also drew the snow in Oxford: the hero bicycles flung down and abandoned by college walls. They had turned overnight into great bumpy snowdrifts.

'Mine's there somewhere,' Clarry had said, and Kate helped her search, scooping pillows of snow from saddles and banging their shins on hidden pedals. 'It's black,' Clarry had added, but all colours were faded to black and grey that day. They abandoned their search when the cold got too much. Later that week the snow half melted and then froze in the night. Kate drew the bicycles all locked in ice, like tangled scaffolding, with every tyre flat.

Only Pax enjoyed that winter. His oily doormat coat was perfect for snow, and nobody had the stamina to bathe him. As Charlie said, it was a waste of time, anyway. No soap in the world smelled as strong as Pax. Once he was finally house-trained (an ordeal that took up many pages) he was allowed upstairs, where he slept across Kate's bedroom door and was an excellent draught excluder.

Spring filled more exercise books, and then in June, Janey came to visit. An unfamiliar-looking Janey with new short hair, rushing around Oxford meeting up with old friends. Nevertheless, she still found time to check Charlie's stilt-walking (*Fantastic, just what the country needs!*) and Kate's homework books (*Kate, I swear your maths is going backwards*).

Kate knew that perfectly well so she didn't argue, and it was nice having Janey again. Together they walked with Pax across Port Meadow, marvelling that there were chestnuts in flower, and chiffchaffs and white butterflies, just like any other year.

'I sort of expected it to stay always winter,' said Kate, and then, in a completely different voice, 'Quick! Ducks! Catch Pax!'

She was too late, and Pax was gone. He wasn't a dog with much self-control at the best of times, but what little he had, he lost with ducks. Ducks dismayed him. He hadn't minded them at all when he thought they could only swim, but the day he discovered they could fly he was absolutely horrified. Since then, whenever he encountered them, he went careering after them in yapping, outraged pursuit.

'Dreadful!' Janey scolded, when they finally caught up with him. Pax rolled humbly on his back and came up green with goose poo and Kate put that in her diary, too.

'Does everything go in?' asked Janey, and Kate let her look at the latest exercise book, which as well as Pax and ducks and Janey herself, had the news that had come from Ruby about her brother and Dunkirk.

'Poor Ruby,' commented Janey.

'I had to write it down.'

'Of course you did. It matters. Did you put in about the bells?'

'What bells?'

'They announced it last week. No bells to be rung, except for air raids. Imagine Oxford without bells.'

'Grandfather would be pleased,' observed Kate, thinking of how grumpily he had complained about the clamouring Christmas bells.

Janey laughed at the memory, but then said, 'Will you write about it in your diary, Kate? I know it's just a little thing . . .'

'I'll write it down,' said Kate, hugging Janey's arm. She was getting more and more requests like that. 'Tell Kate to put it in her diary' or 'Don't forget, will you, Kate?' Simon and Tod's turning sixteen and their mother's voice going ragged in the middle of 'Happy Birthday'. Pax's fear of the washing on the washing line. Mr Churchill's *We shall fight them on the beaches*, Clarry's sudden, tearful, 'What happened to my old pink beret?'

All these things Kate recorded, writing steadily evening after evening in the faded paper-covered notebooks, so they shouldn't be forgotten.

Twenty-Four
Erik and Hans
Germany, Summer 1940

'The aim,' Erik had said to Hans, 'is to destroy the French Air Force. Not the French. The planes.'

'And the airfields and hangars and landing strips and factories where more planes might still be built,' said Hans. 'And the supply lines to the factories. The rail tracks and the roads.'

Erik said unhappily that he supposed it had to be done, and that if only the French would surrender instead of fighting back it would be much less difficult for all of them.

'You talk like an old woman,' said Hans brutally. 'Or as if you were made of wood and rags. A stuffed puppet of the Third Reich.'

'Do I?' asked Erik. 'Is that how I sound?'

'I saw a plane hit from really close today,' said Hans. 'The first shots caught the wing, tipped it over. And the next bullets went through the fuel tank and it sprayed into the cockpit. Those French planes have no armouring round their tanks, like we all do. Still, the pilot could have bailed. Well, I admit, he tried. I saw him reach to try. But the fuel caught. It was

186

strange the way the fuel caught fire before the tank exploded. I swear I was so close I heard him scream. Maybe I didn't. Maybe I just heard the machine guns. They fired for a long time after it was over. I don't know why. Don't touch me.'

Erik, who had reached out a hand, stopped. He said, 'I'm sorry, Hans.'

'Who for?' asked Hans. 'Why do you think the machine guns kept on going?'

'Maybe something jammed.'

'No, it didn't,' shouted Hans. 'I just couldn't seem to stop. I must go! You come as well.'

'Where to?'

'To celebrate, of course,' cried Hans, his eyes full of horror.

One night, Erik dreamed of Berlin Zoo. It was a summer dream, the linden trees were in flower and he could smell them as he hurried towards the entrance. It was perfect, no queues, no kiosk selling paper flags. It was as it had been long ago and it was still early morning, so he had all day to spend exploring. When he'd come as a small boy he'd been so eager to reach the animals that he had hardly looked at the architecture. Remembering this, Erik paused at the Elephant Gate, the entrance he had scampered through so many times before. The carved elephants were magnificent, the bright arch full of welcome, but it was just like the old days, he couldn't wait to look properly, so he hurried through, half laughing at himself.

Inside, the baboons were hooting at some joke, and a patterned giraffe was reaching for a bundle of green leaves.

In the past, he and Hans had made mental maps of all the different ways around to take. The slow trail. The tiger trail. The wet-weather circuit and the rush-round. Erik set off on the rush-round for old times' sake, and then the slow trail, pausing as often as he liked. He wished his familiar zoo-wish for a camera.

To wake up and find himself a Luftwaffe officer was a sort of grief. He couldn't believe it at first. All day he was haunted by the smell of linden trees and all day he thought, *I'll go back. I'll go back. At the first chance I'll go back.* And he comforted himself thinking, *I could write to Herr Schmidt at school and ask for news of the zoo. I could do that,* thought Erik, *for an hour or two,* and then thought, *No, I couldn't.*

He had to be a stuffed puppet of the Third Reich, not in any way interesting enough to cause the briefest raised eyebrow. Nor could he renew any link with anyone who might suffer if it was discovered that he wasn't a stuffed puppet after all. That, far from being a stuffed puppet, he was Erik, who together with other people, had saved Fraulein Trisk; now, he hoped, safely with his mother. He wished he knew, but he couldn't write and ask, and of course, they couldn't tell him.

Erik's mother wrote him letters that said nothing at all. She would mention her factory work, or that she had bought a 'good loaf' and given half to Frieda to take back to her parents, or that the sun was welcome after the long cold winter, things like that. Once she told him she had washed three towels and they'd dried very nicely. Erik would search her letters for the slightest hint that she and Fraulein Trisk were safe, but there was never a word. Nor did she ever mention the old life in Berlin. She wrote to him as if he were someone she hardly knew.

The letters Hans received were no more helpful. They were all grumbles, mostly about illnesses and Frieda. His mother's aches. His father's sore stomach. Frieda wasn't ill, but she wouldn't have her hair combed. She had cut it off herself with Hans's mother's scissors and now it was too short to plait and she would undoubtably pick up *Kopfläuse* at kindergarten, but what was anyone to do? She was growing into a very stubborn girl, just like her sister. True, she was bright, but what was the use of that? Lisa had been bright, and where was she now? Not writing letters home, that was certain. Never mind, wrote Hans's mother glumly, the war was going well and the sooner it was over the better. It was all very tiring for someone of her age to deal with, and she hadn't been able to buy either butter or a piece of good cheese for weeks.

Erik and Hans often shared their letters. Hans passed this letter to Erik with a shrug that said, *There's nothing here.*

It was Frieda who sent the news. Hans had a birthday and she drew him a picture. *For Hans*, she wrote on the top.

It was a picture of her world, with every person labelled. Frieda in the centre, the tallest of them all, standing beside an equally tall animal, probably a cat.

Frieda, it said underneath, and, *Mitzi.*

On either side of Frieda stood a woman. They looked very much alike, except one had a heart shape over her head with the word *Erik* written in it, and the other had another, larger heart, with *Hans + Lisa*. Underneath the first woman it said *Tante Anna*, which was what Frieda had always called Erik's mother, and under the second it said, *Mutti*.

Mutti was propping up *Vati*, who was shown clearly with one leg. *Tante Anna* also had a companion. A small, small woman, half the height of the rest. *Kleine Oma*, it said underneath.

Little Grandma.

All the people that Frieda had drawn were smiling large smiles.

Hans showed the picture to Erik and asked, 'Happy now?'

'Yes, thank you, Hans,' said Erik. 'Yes. Much better.'

Twenty-Five
Ruby
Plymouth, July 1940

It took a while for Violet to admit that Will wasn't coming back. During that time no one, not even Ruby or Clarry or Mrs Cohen, could say a word that would help. This went on until Ruby could bear it no longer and went into Will's bedroom at two in the morning, where her mother was busy polishing a pair of old shoes he'd left under his bed.

'Stop it!' she said. 'Stop it, Mum! He hates having his stuff messed about with.'

Violet became quite still.

'You'll have to unpolish them in the morning,' continued Ruby. 'Or else he'll moan he can't leave anything safe. You know he always does.'

Her mother looked uncertainly down at the shoes in her lap.

'Don't worry, I'll help,' said Ruby. 'I'll scuffle them round the yard.'

'I don't think . . .'

'But now you should go to sleep.' Ruby took the shoes and put them down on the floor. 'I've checked the blackout and

I've set the alarm clock for a quarter to six. I'm taking it up to the attic with me, so I can wake up when they bring the papers in the morning.'

Violet gave a great weary sigh.

'Stand up,' ordered Ruby, heaving on her mother's arms. 'Come on, this way. Here's your room. Here's the bed. Give me your skirt and I'll sort it out. There . . .'

By the time the skirt was folded and laid on the bedroom chair, her mother was asleep.

Ruby crept away. She thought, *He's alive. I'm sure he's alive because he's still being a pest.* Then she tumbled so deeply asleep herself that it was like falling into the sky.

Five seconds later, or so it seemed to Ruby, the alarm clock was ringing and it was dawn. Any minute now the morning bundles of papers would be dumped on the doorstep. Unless the shop was open, the delivery man would ring the doorbell to let them know they'd arrived, and that would wake her mother. Ruby rolled out of bed, and tiptoed sleepily downstairs.

The postman must already have been.

On the doormat – the worn, so-old-it-had-become-invisible doormat – there was a postcard, lying like an unexploded heart.

Ruby froze, halfway across the floor.

Will. It was Will: she knew before she saw the printed heading, the unfamiliar stamp. It was Will, back in their lives again, and for one shameful moment, she was swept with dismay.

Then she shrieked.

'It's Will, it's Will!' she shrieked and Violet came flying down the stairs, grabbed her, hugged her, grabbed the card, stared, hugged it too, and cried, 'Oh, Will! Oh, Will!' hid her face in her hands and re-emerged, shining-eyed and radiant. Then, together, they bent over the card and read:

Kriegsgefangenenlager
Glad to say that this place is fine, great, etc. I hope you don't go worrying about me. Love from Will.
Address to follow. For parcels. If poss.

It was Will's handwriting, very carefully printed, every letter separate. Violet read it twice, then ran out to the street and cried, 'Look! Look!' Early rising neighbours collected around her. Mrs Cohen came hurrying, her face alight with joy. Everyone asked over and over, 'Is that your Will?' and each time Violet would reply, 'Yes, yes, it is. It's Will.' But she couldn't let go of the card so they could read for themselves. She just held it out so they could see, and laughed with relief, drew a finger under an eye to slide away a tear, blinked and laughed again.

All that day was bliss.

To go from Will, very possibly dead, to Will in a prisoner of war camp, hoping for parcels, all in a few hours.

Just before they went to bed, Ruby was allowed to hold the card at last. She looked carefully at the pencilled words. Very carefully. Ruby knew Will much better than their mother did. She knew his sharpness, and his subtle means of getting his own way, and she took the card and looked at how Will had written it:

Glad tO say ThAt this PLAce is fiNe, GrEaT, eTc.
I hope you doN't Go wOrrying aboUT me. Love from Will.
Address to follow. For parcels. If poss.

'He's got a plan. He's getting out,' she told Violet, and pointed to the letters where Will had written his message. 'It's the capitals,' she explained, and her mother suddenly saw the words, hidden in plain sight. Then it was all Violet could do not to run down the road in her dressing gown and slippers and wake up Mrs Cohen to tell her.

He wasn't just alive, and hoping for parcels. He was writing secret messages under the noses of the enemy. He was scheming to escape.

'Is your brother clever,' demanded his proud mother, 'or what?'

He was clever. He was remarkable. He could come walking through the door anytime. The whole street agreed.

'And we'll be here waiting,' said Violet, with shining eyes.

The photograph of him in uniform was now in a silver frame. Mrs Cohen had brought it. 'Not new,' she'd said, when she handed it to Violet. 'Old stock, but still, nice silver plate. Mr Cohen polished it for you.'

'Oh, I couldn't!' Violet had exclaimed. 'I couldn't take it, not silver!'

'For Will, of course you could,' said Mrs Cohen. 'Handsome

frame for a handsome boy.'

Now the photograph seemed to be the most precious thing in the house. It moved around, to the windowsill, or the kitchen dresser, and Violet's bedside shelf at night. Ruby was always encountering it. Will's skin was satin smooth, not even a freckle, and his smile was very pleased. Ruby wondered how long it would be before he managed to escape.

An address had arrived, and they'd packed their first parcel. Playing cards, toffees, cigarettes, a toothbrush and two white cotton handkerchiefs.

'In case he wants to surrender?' asked Ruby, not entirely as a joke, and was walloped on her behind with a copy of the *Devon and Exeter Gazette*. 'That's no way to talk!' said her mother. 'You heard Mr Churchill. You know what he said.'

Ruby knew. All the newspapers had reported that speech, and she and Violet had agreed with every word. Ruby herself had snipped out the last few lines, glued them on to cardboard and propped them up beside the cash register:

> *We shall fight on the beaches, we shall fight on the landing grounds, we shall fight in the fields and in the streets, we shall fight in the hills . . .*

'And, in case you've forgotten, my fine lady,' said Violet severely. 'We shan't ever surrender.'

'I never said I would,' said Ruby indignantly.

'No, and nor will none of us,' said Violet. 'Least of all our Will!'

*

So Will was a war hero now, plotting behind enemy lines, and Ruby knew she should be pleased about it, if only because it gave such courage to her mother, now putting on her air-raid warden helmet, ready for her evening patrol.

'It's about time we had a uniform,' said Violet.

'Perhaps you soon will,' said Ruby. 'If it goes on a bit.'

'It'll go on a bit,' said Violet.

It was July of 1940. All along the south coast, the Battle of Britain, in all its murderous beauty, was splintering the skies. Plymouth had had its first bomb. It had landed on a street of ordinary houses. People had been killed.

'There wasn't anything exciting to see, though,' said Ruby, who had been to have a look and was a little disappointed. 'There was just some tape around, and a lot of bricks and rubbish. Why d'you think they picked that house to bomb?'

'It would have been a mistake,' said Violet. 'They'd be aiming for the dockyards.'

'Well then, they're rubbish shots,' said Ruby. 'That street is ages from the docks.'

'Hmm,' said Violet, and gave her a look. It was a swift, appraising look, the sort that might precede a green-soap-and-hair-washing session.

'What?' asked Ruby.

'The thing is, Ruby, nowhere in Plymouth is ages from the dockyards. Not to a bomber. Don't give that sausage to the cats!'

They were eating their supper, a lot of mash and gravy and one sausage each, because sausages, although not rationed yet, had become much more expensive. Ruby was feeding Sooty and Paddle. They loved sausage. They wound in silky spirals, fluid with desire.

'They have to eat something,' said Ruby.

'There's no shortage of mice,' said her mother, absent-mindedly. 'Mrs Morgan's overrun with them, out there in the country. I spoke to her yesterday. They've eaten her peas.'

'What peas?'

'Peas that she planted. She said what's the use of digging for victory if the mice get the peas. Now, Ruby, listen, I've something to tell you and I want none of your arguments because it's just common sense.'

'I know what you're going to say already,' said Ruby.

'Oh, you do, do you?'

'You want to let Sooty and Paddle go and live with Mrs Morgan so as to catch her mice.'

'I had thought of that, yes.'

'Well then, let them go,' said Ruby bravely. 'It would be better. I can see it would. There might be more bombs here.'

'With a great naval shipyard on our doorstep, there'll be bombs for sure,' said Violet, and once again she gave Ruby the green soap look.

Ruby didn't see it because she had scooped up Sooty and buried her face in his furry shoulders. 'It'll be all right,' she said from that warm place, with hardly a wobble in her voice. 'Mrs Morgan is kind and anyway, it will only be a lend, until after the war. We can go on the bus to visit them, can't we?'

Violet said, 'Ruby, it's not just the cats that'll have to go away. It's you as well, this time we've got to face it. Mrs Morgan's got a spare room. She said she'll have you to stay any day we choose.'

'Me go to Mrs Morgan's?'

'For a few weeks, yes. I've lost your dad. Will's where he is. I'm not risking you.'

'But . . .'

'And after that,' continued Violet, 'it's time you were back at school.'

'BUT . . .' exploded Ruby, so loudly that Sooty leaped to the floor.

'I said, no arguing, remember?'

'But it's the holidays!' exclaimed Ruby. 'The school holidays! Anyway, there's no school except a village school where Mrs Morgan lives, and I'm too old for that.'

'There's Clarry's school in Oxford.'

'OXFORD!'

'Clarry tells me Kate will be starting there when the new term opens, sometime in September, and when it does, you'll be leaving Mrs Morgan's, staying at Kate's house, and going there too.'

'I can't, I can't,' screeched Ruby. 'You know I can't! What about my face?'

Violet said, as she had said so many times before, 'You have a lovely face, Ruby.'

'You have to say that because you're my mother.'

'No, I don't,' replied Violet, rather sharply. 'I have to keep you healthy and make sure you're not hungry and see you have clothes and are learning the right things and growing up proper because I'm your mother. But I don't have to tell you you've got a nice face. Although you have. Very nice indeed. Lovely. Bright.'

'No,' said Ruby.

'And,' said Violet, going one stage further than she ever had before, 'those marks, they add to the brightness. I can't explain how, but they do.'

'You can't explain how, because they don't,' shouted Ruby, and jumped to her feet and stormed out of the door and down the stairs and away along the street, slap bang into Mrs Cohen, who was putting up her shutters.

'Ruby,' said Mrs Cohen's gentle voice, and Ruby's panicking madness ran away from her, like water pouring into sand, and she turned round and went back home.

'Except for that one bad night, it's been quiet so far here in Plymouth,' said Violet, carrying on the conversation as if nothing had happened to interrupt it, as she always did at these times. 'It won't be for much longer, though. I'd like to know you were safe.'

'*I'd* like to know *you* were safe,' said Ruby. 'You come to Oxford too. We'll find somewhere to live together.'

'And what about the shop?' asked Violet, but as she spoke she glanced at Will's photograph, and Ruby knew she really meant, *And what about if Will comes back and finds that I'm not here?*

'Someone else could do the shop,' said Ruby, and shrugged. The shrug meant, *You're thinking about Will. You are always, always thinking about Will.*

There was a pause, full of unspeakable blackness.

'When can I come back?' asked Ruby eventually.

'When we've won this war.'

'I wish I could fight.'

'Oh, Ruby Amaryllis!' said Violet. 'I expect you'll find a way.'

Twenty-Six
Kate
Oxford, July 1940

M rs Morgan wrote to Kate's parents a long letter all in one sentence that said:

> *To let you know I have told old Mr P that what with the journey from the cottage into Plymouth and the blackout and me being the age I am (71) not to mention that when young Ruby comes to you for school as has been arranged there may be my Christopher's two little ones here come the autumn since word is it will be bad in Plymouth when they start aiming for the shipyards this is to give notice that after this summer I will not be able to do for Mr P as I have all these years and he has taken it very badly.*

'She deserves a medal for putting up with him for so long,' said Kate's father. 'I'd better get to Plymouth and see what can be done.'

He went on his next free day and came back in the evening to tell them that Grandfather had taken Mrs Morgan's perfectly reasonable announcement not just badly, but disgracefully, saying that he supposed he'd have to starve.

Mrs Morgan had been, as she ever was, more than a match for Grandfather.

'Of course you won't starve, you silly old man,' she'd replied. 'You can either take yourself off to your family as you've been asked a dozen times before . . .'

'That madhouse in Oxford,' Grandfather had commented.

'. . . or find yourself someone nearer to home to cook your blessed dinners and put up with your shocking ways.'

Then Mrs Morgan had left with, as was her habit, a good slam of the door.

'OH, YOUR GRANDFATHER!' wailed Vanessa to Charlie and Kate, and they understood, because how could Grandfather be left to take care of himself when the bombing raids began? And yet how could he be made to come to Oxford if he refused? Peter said that if the worst came to the worst, he'd drive down and kidnap him, and Vanessa said she'd help. Also, said Vanessa, when Grandfather came, kidnapped or of his own free will, he'd need a comfortable room.

This was the start of the great bedroom reshuffle, not only because of Grandfather, but to make space for Ruby too. It was decided that all the boys could go together in the attic, Ruby and Kate would share Janey and Bea's old room, Grandfather would have Kate's room, and the little box room left over could be used for whoever might turn up. A great many cobwebs and grimy corners appeared during this reorganizing. Scrubbing was done, and painting begun, all directed by Vanessa. 'War effort!' she cried when people rebelled or tried to slope off to be sailors and stilt-walkers.

'Very kind. No, thank you,' said Grandfather, when he was told of all this hard work.

'Kate's making you new curtains,' Vanessa told him. 'Lovely warm red ones, all by herself on the sewing machine. I'm only helping a bit.'

'Thoughtful, but I have curtains,' said Grandfather, and added that the sensible thing would be to have Clarry come and live with him for the duration of the war. It was no use explaining that this was impossible as Clarry had a job, since Grandfather thought it was all nonsense, women working, when they should really be at home. If Clarry wouldn't help him, he said, what about Janey or Bea?

'Or Kate?' asked Peter sarcastically, taking the telephone from Vanessa and causing Kate, too alarmed to realize he was joking, to whisper urgently, 'Dad!'

'Hold on a minute,' said Peter to Grandfather, and he looked solemnly down at Kate and asked, 'Problem?'

Kate nodded, speechless for a moment while she summoned the extraordinary bravery that had once seemed such a simple plan. Could she manage? Could she? She thought of Grandfather all alone, and remembered the silver flask in church.

They were waiting for her to speak.

'I could probably do the cooking,' she said at last, 'if he liked to eat the sort of things I cooked for Clarry . . .'

Peter nodded.

'And I'd have to take Pax.'

'Ah!' said Peter. 'Yes, of course you would. Kate's worrying about the dog,' he relayed to his father. 'Says she can manage the cooking, but she'd have to bring her dog . . .'

Grandfather said he couldn't see Kate being much use, what with the damage she'd done to that Christmas tree and the way she never stopped coughing, but he supposed he could put up with the dog.

'There'd be school too, after the holidays,' said Kate, 'and bombs.'

'She says school too, and bombs,' said Peter to Grandfather.

'Obstacle after obstacle,' said Grandfather, peevishly, but there was something in his voice that made Kate quite suddenly remember his wink to her as he left the room, another world ago. It made her abandon bravery in favour of common sense. She reached for the telephone herself and said breathlessly, 'Grandfather, by the end of summer the red curtains will be finished and the painting too, and we'll have enough petrol saved up to drive and fetch you in the car and it really would be MUCH better if you were here.'

There was a very long silence from Grandfather.

'Well,' he said at last. 'If you say so . . . er . . .'

'Kate.'

'Kate. I suppose I shall have to be resigned.'

Then the pips went that meant the telephone call was over and Kate and her father were left staring at each other and laughing with relief.

Twenty-Seven
Erik and Hans
French coast, July–Sept 1940

Erik's first ever sight of the sea was the English Channel, early one grey August morning. France was now under German occupation and so the squadron had been moved again. Now they were encamped in an apple orchard, very close to the French coast. The airstrips were newly made and spongy, they'd been told they could expect mail once a month at best, and the farmer who owned the land hated them. All the local people hated them. In the town they took their money, cheated them and hated them. There was a story told to new arrivals about another camp, further up the coast. The guard at the entrance there, although prudently armed with a machine gun, had been discovered in the morning with his throat cut from ear to ear.

'Not a sound was heard nor bullet fired,' was the last line of the story, 'and on the ground beside him, an open cut-throat razor.'

Erik and Hans glanced at each other with raised eyebrows. What might have alarmed them a year ago couldn't disturb them now. They were used to how quickly stories grew in camps, and the people who liked to tell them.

'Shaving in the dark is bound to be risky,' said Erik.

'What happened to his machine gun?' asked Hans.

'What d'you mean, what happened? Nothing happened.'

'It was still there in the morning?'

'Certainly it was. Clutched in his hands.'

'Nothing to worry about, then,' said Hans. 'Machine guns are expensive. Any sensible assassin would never have left it behind. It was, as my friend Erik realized from the start, a self-inflicted accident that could easily be avoided in the future by the allowance of shaving mirrors.'

'Or safety razors,' said Erik.

'Shaving mirrors and safety razors,' agreed Hans. 'Or simply encouraging a fashion in beards.'

'It's not so easy to grow a beard,' remarked Erik. 'They say to rub the chin with a raw onion.'

'Hard to find a raw onion,' agreed Hans. 'The poor things are relentlessly roasted.'

'Boiled,' said Erik.

'Battered.'

'Fried.'

'I had an onion omelette, last time I was in Berlin,' said Erik. 'It was very good.'

'I had potato pancakes,' said Hans. 'They were excellent.'

'My favourite,' said Erik, nodding, and Hans nodded too, and the cut-throat storyteller exploded with indignation.

'You find this funny?' he demanded. 'If so, you have entirely misunderstood the situation here in France.'

'Yes, you could be right,' said Erik. 'I speak very little French. Well, none, except *Joie de vivre*.'

'You probably won't need that,' remarked Hans.

'And *Je ne sais pas*.'

'You probably will need that,' said Hans. 'Quite a lot.'

'Hans is a linguist,' Erik explained. 'Not only French, but English too, for when we invade.'

'I am hoping for a kind and peaceful invasion,' said Hans, 'and so I have learned some useful phrases such as, *This is a pleasant place. I am sorry. I didn't mean to frighten you. Do not forget me. You are very beautiful. Please tell me your name. I admire your dogs and cats*.'

'The English are very fond of animals,' explained Erik. 'As am I, of course.'

'Erik has hopes to work in a zoo,' said Hans.

'Hans has hopes to sell pastries at the gate,' said Erik.

'Jokers,' growled the storyteller. 'And you can forget *You are very beautiful*. My brother spent a year in England just before the war. He said all the girls were terrible. Grey skin. Green hair. Scarlet lipstick. Bad teeth.'

'I'm sorry to hear that,' said Hans gravely.

'And don't try flattery either, because my brother did that too, and had his head chewed off.'

'Serve him right,' said Erik, at once. 'After all, there are other pleasant things one might say. Such as about the dogs and cats.'

'True,' agreed Hans. 'But I won't forget *You are very beautiful*. I may meet the only girl in England your brother didn't see, and imagine not having the right words.'

The storyteller growled with annoyance. He had the Iron Cross for shooting down four enemy planes. He also had a constant stomach ache, which he told them about. They were immediately very sympathetic and said he had done his share to contribute to the Third Reich's *joie de vivre*, and should now be allowed to rest and take care of his health. The Iron Cross hero grew more friendly and told them that when he was a boy he had dreamed of studying music. The great German composers. 'What am I doing here?' he asked, now entirely their friend. 'In this sodden tent. Beside this terrible sea.'

Je ne sais pas,' said Erik. He was feeling quite melancholy himself. His first sight of the sea had depressed him very much. Sunless, steel-coloured water, littered with shipping, churning and slapping and giving the complete appearance of being entirely on the side of the British. Among all the deaths he had been forced to consider since he became a Luftwaffe pilot, he had never included drowning. It now seemed to him much more likely than having his throat cut in silence while carrying a machine gun. He said so to Hans.

'You must be very careful,' said Hans, 'not to fall out of the window.'

It was in this camp that Erik and Hans met their first British pilot, face to face. Not only face to face, but also able to speak to them. His plane had been shot down, but he had managed, with great good luck, to parachute right on to their new bumpy airstrip. Everyone liked him very much; he became, for a few hours, the camp hero and comrade. They gave him cigarettes and chocolate and proper German beer. He spoke of Mr Churchill and Herr bloody Hitler and of how the British would never surrender.

'If only you would,' they told him, 'our countries could work together as friends.'

'Yes, but we won't,' said the British pilot, shaking his head. 'So there it is.' He was as stubborn as the rest of his nation. After a few hours, with many handshakes and good wishes, he was taken away to become a prisoner of war.

'A pity,' said Erik. 'Poor fellow.'

'He went off with a certain *joie de vivre*, don't you think?' asked Hans.

'*Je ne sais pas*,' said Erik.

Now the Luftwaffe were targeting the RAF, aiming at the airfields of the south of England. It was the job of the Messerschmitts to engage the Hurricanes and Spitfires that scrambled in defence. Dogfighting, they called it, when little plane sought to destroy little plane, spattering bullets, tangling and hunting in the blue summer skies. Sometimes a pilot would unravel the tangle and flee to safety. Other times, the loops would break, the sky would lurch, and there might be black smoke and orange fire where no fire should be. Often a parachute would appear, drifting down like a dandelion clock, its breathless slow motion stilling the watchers on the ground into silence. There was a chivalry between enemies about that: the man with the parachute was never a target. For those minutes, between sky and earth, he was safe.

*

The casualty lists at the camp in the apple orchard grew longer and longer, even though they were assured that very soon, in a matter of weeks, if not days, the RAF would be so utterly obliterated that the next stage, the invasion by land, could begin.

'About time the army did some work,' said the exhausted Luftwaffe pilots, flying day after day across the Channel, and coming back again with so little fuel that the only way to make it was to fly low, out of the strong upper winds, wave-hopping with the fuel gauge on red.

'How's the *joie de vivre*?' Hans asked Erik, late one night when the anti-aircraft guns, firing at the stubborn British fighters pestering overhead, put an end to all hope of sleep.

'*Je ne sais pas*,' said Erik.

Twenty-Eight
Ruby
Mrs Morgan's cottage, Devon, July–Sept 1940

Two years before, in 1938, the British government had begun making preparations for war, and so had Mrs Morgan. By the time Ruby came to stay, her cottage garden was stuffed with herbs and fruit and vegetables, she had eight hens and two ducks and was contemplating bees.

'We had bees at the forge when I was a girl,' she told Violet and Ruby. 'Growing up, we had bees and often a goat as well. I shouldn't mind a goat now.'

'For milk?' asked Ruby.

'Well, of course for milk, they don't lay eggs. I've thought of a pig, too. A pig or a goat. One or the other.'

'But,' began Ruby in alarm, 'you can't milk a . . . I've never heard of . . . What would you DO with a pig, Mrs Morgan?'

Mrs Morgan gave a big, noisy exasperated sigh and said, 'It's about time you spent a few weeks in the country. Sausages and bacon is what I would do with a pig, but perhaps I'll start with a goat.'

A week later this happened. A spotted goat, grandly named Victoria, appeared, and with her, to Ruby's entrancement, a snow-white kid that they immediately christened Plum. Plum was very pretty, but Victoria had horns which she did not hesitate to deploy. Milking time became a lively occasion.

'She'll quieten,' said Mrs Morgan, and as the days went by, she did. Also little Plum grew, and Sooty and Paddle hunted mice in the pea rows and rats in the henhouse, and Violet came on the bus now and then, and spent the night. Three times every week Mrs Morgan went into town to cook and clean for old Mr Penrose, and Ruby was left in charge of the hens and the goats and the garden.

'Will you be all right?' asked Mrs Morgan the first time.

'I'm thirteen,' said Ruby indignantly, and Mrs Morgan came back to find the kitchen scrubbed, hot scones just out of the oven, the eggs collected, the henhouse swept clean, and Ruby herself just setting off on a valiant mission to attempt to milk the goat.

'Your mum said you were handy,' said Mrs Morgan, 'and I see she was right.'

'Did she really?'

'She did, and more.'

'What more?'

'Never you mind or we'll have you big-headed. You need to wash Victoria down nicely before you try milking. Warm water and soap.'

'I know.'

'And have you the milk pail scalded ready?'

'Yes. I just did it.'

'Don't forget you'll need to have Plum tied up where

her mother can see she's not lost.'

'She already is,' said Ruby, nodding.

'Smart as paint, Violet told me,' said Mrs Morgan approvingly, and Ruby glowed and learned to milk the goat well enough to show Violet the next time she came.

'You're getting to know all sorts,' said Violet, laughing, and it was true, Ruby was.

Clarry sent a pile of books and a message. *You might like to read these before term begins.*

Between her ransacking of the library, and the newspapers in the shop, reading had become as natural to Ruby as breathing in and out. However, for Mrs Morgan it was not the same at all. For her, reading was a labour, like shifting furniture or heavy digging, and she looked distrustfully at Ruby, flat on her stomach with the book in front of her, turning the pages with no apparent effort.

'Are you sure you're taking it in?' she asked.

'Mmm,' said Ruby. 'I skip the boring bits.'

'I should think so too. Leave off and come and help me brush the goats.'

'In a minute. He's met Betsey Trotwood again.'

'And who is she? And who is he?'

'David Copperfield. She's a sort of aunt.'

Ruby absorbed *David Copperfield*, puzzled her way through a French storybook about a little girl named Madeline, and shared with Mrs Morgan a textbook called *The Microscope*. It fascinated Ruby, but it had colour illustrations of things Mrs

Morgan could hardly bear to contemplate. A book of maths arrived as well, questions in the front and answers in the back. *Times tables are useful,* wrote Clarry on a postcard. *Everyone stops at twelve times, but when I was little my brother made me learn up to twenty. I used to write them out and look for the patterns in the numbers.*

Ruby chanted as she weeded the onion bed, '. . . Seventeen seventeens are two hundred and eighty-nine. Seventeen eighteens are three hundred and six . . .' All her life, afterwards, the murmured chant of tables took her back to the sunlit, almost perfect summer of Mrs Morgan's garden.

Almost perfect, but not quite. August was passing, vanishing in a blink of bean rows and books and meeting the bus. September came blowing in and Ruby wrote to Kate:

> *I thought I was coming to your house by train, Mum and me together, and Mum staying a few days afterwards.*

That was what they'd planned, but now Clarry had written that she'd be borrowing her brother's car and driving to Plymouth early in September to collect Kate's grandfather. She could stop at Mrs Morgan's on her way back to Oxford and pick up Ruby too.

We'll be staying the night with Mrs M, she wrote to Violet, *because I don't think I could get my father packed and loaded and out of his house in time to reach Oxford before the blackout. It's such a long drive. At least six hours, plus stops. So instead of rushing him, we'll set off from Mrs Morgan's early the next day, with plenty of room for Ruby, if that would suit you too?*

Violet was delighted. She wouldn't have to find the train fares, nor leave the shop for days with Mrs Cohen, but Ruby heard the news in absolute dismay, all her fear of staring strangers suddenly once again alive.

'I don't know Kate's grandfather,' she wailed to Mrs Morgan. 'Will he look at my face?'

'Ruby Amaryllis, this has gone on too long!' Mrs Morgan declared. 'Will *you* look at your face?' She'd unhooked the kitchen mirror and handed it to Ruby, but Ruby hadn't looked.

Instead she wrote to Kate:

Now they've changed everything. Mum is glad but I'm not glad. The only thing I'm looking forward to is Pax.

TWENTY-NINE
Kate
Oxford, September 1940

Kate read her message from Ruby, and had an idea.

'Could I come with you when you go and fetch Grandfather?' she asked Clarry.

'I should have thought of it myself,' said Clarry. 'You can map-read for me on the way there and be company for Ruby on the way back. If you're allowed, of course you can. Is Ruby worrying?'

'Yes.'

'I know it'll be hard for her. She ran back home when they tried to evacuate her before. That's why Violet was coming with her on the train.'

'She says the only thing she's looking forward to is Pax. So, do you think we could take him?'

'Take Pax?' asked Clarry, startled. 'Gosh, Kate, I don't know. What if he's sick? He was awful on the journey from London.'

'I think that was just because he was frightened.'

'He was *dreadfully* sick,' said Clarry. 'I didn't know there was so much space inside a dog for so much stuff. It was like a terrible magic trick. Don't laugh!'

'Perhaps we could take him for a little drive and see if he's all right?'

Clarry shook her head. 'Since they started rationing petrol there's not a teaspoonful to spare. Your dad's been saving it for weeks for this trip.'

'Well, there's buses,' suggested Kate. 'There's one that goes right past our house. I could take him for rides to see how he manages. Very short rides first, one stop. And then a bit longer.'

'What if he's sick on the bus?'

'I could take some newspapers and my old seaside bucket.'

'Kate, you're wonderful,' said Clarry, solemnly. 'The bucket is heroic. Give it a try, and if it works we'll take him with us.'

For a several days Kate did this, very short rides, and then longer ones, and then all across the city. At the end of the week she reported to Clarry that there had been much tail wagging and tongue hanging and cheerfulness and no need of the bucket at all.

'Excellent,' said Clarry. 'Shall you tell Ruby you're coming, or keep it a secret?'

'I'll tell her that I'm coming, but I'll save Pax for a surprise,' said Kate, and wrote:

Dear Ruby,
When Clarry comes for you, I'm coming too. We can sit
in the back of the car together. As well, I am bringing a
secret surprise.

You needn't worry about Grandfather. He's only fierce because he's shy.

Even as she wrote it, Kate was startled. Grandfather? Shy? But it was true. Noticing him, thinking about him, writing about him, she'd discovered it.

He's quite a lot like Pax, wrote Kate.

Even more startling, and also true.

Another discovery.

Thirty
Erik and Hans
Sky, September 1940

It was the best sort of morning. Clear bright September. In Berlin there would be the first hint of autumn in the air. The swallow flocks would be gathering, limbering up for their great journey south. Under the trees there would be a primrose light, and the first yellow leaves coming down. It was football weather, new book weather, back to school weather.

It was no use being homesick. Erik said, 'This time five years ago . . .' and Hans said, 'Oh, shut up.'

Everyone was jittery. The destruction of the RAF that in early summer had seemed close enough to touch, now seemed more impossible every day. Losses were much higher than they'd ever expected, the English Channel a bigger obstacle, the opposition better armed than anyone had guessed.

That day they were trying yet again. Erik, Hans and eight others had flown out in formation over the Channel. They were aiming for the west of England, and the new airfields there. Six bombers, four fighters. Not enough.

They'd been waylaid by Hurricanes, diving in to attack with the sun behind them. They'd been outnumbered and outgunned. Planes had tumbled from the sky, commands had been fragmented, the static so bad that their radios were all but useless. Finally the squadron had split, each pilot turning to find their own way back. Fuel was getting low.

Erik's plane was staggering, bullet-bitten. The Perspex cover was holed and a pain like fire scorched down his back and into his left shoulder. The shock of it was brain-dazzling. His Messerschmitt flew heavily now, as if the air was thick and tangled. He thought he was alone, and then suddenly knew he wasn't. Hans came bursting through the radio static:

'BEHIND! BEHIND! BEHIND!'

Thirty-One
Ruby and Kate
Mrs Morgan's cottage, September 1940

The day before Ruby was to leave for Oxford, Violet came to stay at the cottage. As always in times of stress, she had comforted herself with present-buying. Cherry brandy for Mrs Morgan and a real leather satchel for Ruby with surprises inside. Ruby found a pencil case, a box of writing paper and stamps, and a bag of sherbet lemons.

'It's like being Will,' she said, very pleased indeed.

There was also a fountain pen, silver and crimson, with her name in curving letters on the side: *Ruby Amaryllis.*

'Mrs Cohen bought it for you, and Mr Cohen engraved it,' Violet told her.

Ruby was overwhelmed; she'd never owned anything like it. She borrowed Mrs Morgan's bottle of ink and tried to write her thanks.

*Dear Mrs Cohen and Mr Cohen, I didn't know
there were pens like this, shining like a jewel. I didn't
know Mr Cohen could write like that either. It is very
beautiful and I will keep it forever and I hope it didn't*

cost too much. I miss you, and I miss the street where
everyone is used to me. I will write to you as often as
I can . . .

Ruby looked up at her mother. 'I can put letters in for Mrs Cohen when I write to you, can't I?' she asked. 'To save stamps?'

'Of course you can.'

'And you won't read them?'

'The cheek,' said Violet. 'Did I ever read your letters to Kate?'

'No,' said Ruby, and she wrote:

Mrs Cohen, please, please look after Mum. Until I come back.
Love Ruby

She had hardly finished when Clarry drove up, together with not only her father and Kate, but also, to the absolute horror of Mrs Morgan, Pax.

'What is that animal?' exclaimed Mrs Morgan. 'Clarry Penrose, are you crazy?'

'He's mine,' said Kate, bravely. 'I thought he'd be a surprise.'

'And did we need a surprise?' demanded Mrs Morgan. 'And would you look at those cats!'

Sooty and Paddle, spitting their outraged feelings, were up on the cottage roof with ears laid flat and every hair on end. However, Violet was laughing, and Clarry too, and Mrs Morgan's face was not half as cross as her words.

'You should be warned, as I was not,' Kate's grandfather

remarked, 'that the animal isn't house-trained.' He was clearly enjoying the situation, his mouth turned down in a secret, smiling smirk.

'He's house-trained at home,' said Kate loyally. 'Mostly, anyway.'

'Mostly?' repeated Mrs Morgan, indignantly. 'Mostly!'

'You never said one word,' said Ruby, almost accusingly, to Kate.

'No, I know,' admitted Kate. 'Only I read your letter and I thought you . . . I thought he . . . I thought it might be more cheerful if I brought him. Do you mind?'

Ruby shook her head. She'd sent out a plea for help and Kate had answered. How could she mind?

'Tie him by the doormat while you come and see my arrangements,' said Mrs Morgan, resignedly. It had taken some planning to find a place for everyone to sleep, but she and Ruby had managed. Clarry and Violet were to have Ruby's room, with Ruby moved downstairs to share the sofa with Kate. 'Head to toe, you'll fit,' Mrs Morgan had said to Ruby. 'It's only one night. And I'm putting old Mr P in the box room, along where I keep the hen food, because it's nice and dry.'

The hen food smelled strong, nutty and earthy.

'I hope he likes it,' Ruby had said, doubtfully.

'He can like it or lump it,' Mrs Morgan had replied cheerfully. 'I doubt he'll notice with that pipe.'

All the same, Ruby had pushed open the window as wide as it would go, and by the time the visitors arrived the smell was so much fresher that all Kate's grandfather said was, 'Ah, melons. Am I right?'

'I daresay you might smell melons,' said Mrs Morgan, diplomatically. 'I've all sorts tucked away up here. Come and look at this.'

The landing was almost filled with an enormous, dark oak wardrobe. Mrs Morgan opened the doors to show rows and rows of stores. Stewed beef in cans, sardines in oil, raisins, blue-paper packets of sugar, tins of tea and cocoa and on a high shelf at the top, bright yellow Sunlight soap and long, paper-wrapped bars of red carbolic.

'The government can call it hoarding if they want,' she said. 'But I call it common sense. I remember the last war, not a bit of soap or a sausage to be bought without you stood in a queue for hours.'

'Really?' asked Kate's grandfather from the back of her audience. 'I don't recall that at all.'

'No, because me and Clarry did the queuing for you,' said Mrs Morgan. 'While you drifted around thinking lamb chops and socks floated down with the autumn leaves. Now just you come outside and see the rest.'

She led them past the overflowing vegetable beds, the flower patches, the chickens, the bees and the ever inquisitive goats, talking as she went.

'I've got paraffin and petrol in the old henhouse that we never got round to pulling down, and a new padlock on the outside convenience at the end of the garden.'

'Hardly a convenience,' remarked Kate's grandfather

sardonically. 'At the end of the garden.'

'It'll be very convenient indeed should anyone unwanted turn up,' said Mrs Morgan. 'Spies, or whatever. They're sending them over from Germany disguised as nuns and pedlars selling onions and I don't know what, but you can tell them in a minute because they can't say their "W"s. It's all in the papers about them.'

'It is,' agreed Violet.

'So my thought is, once I have them inside our convenience, I shall snap on the padlock and telephone the police.'

'Admirable,' exclaimed Kate's grandfather, nodding.

'Not very comfortable,' observed Clarry, laughing.

'Comfortable!' said Mrs Morgan. 'I wasn't planning on making them comfortable. Not that they couldn't perfectly well sit down if they lowered the lid. I was thinking of keeping them fast! They couldn't burrow out because we rat-proofed it two summers ago, and I think it couldn't be better.'

'But how,' broke in Kate, terribly bothered by this whole conversation, 'how would you get them in there in the beginning, Mrs Morgan?'

'I should prod 'em in with the potato fork,' said Mrs Morgan, triumphantly. 'I've got it sharpened up by the back door ready.'

'Very well thought out indeed,' said Kate's grandfather approvingly, and went off at once to test the sharpness of the prongs. Clarry and Violet headed inside with Mrs Morgan to get ready a picnic lunch, but when Ruby and Kate followed to help they were immediately shooed away.

'They want to talk without us,' said Kate.

'I know, they always do,' agreed Ruby, flopping down on the tiny, hearthrug-sized patch of grass. 'I hope Mrs Morgan catches someone. She'll be disappointed if she doesn't and she's going to have an awful time, eating up all that stew.'

'I thought that too,' agreed Kate, stretching out beside her with Pax for a pillow.

'If I was hoarding food,' said Ruby, 'which I wouldn't because everyone knows, whatever Mrs M says, that it's not patriotic, I'd hoard golden syrup and peaches and Mars bars. What would you?'

Kate pondered. A great sleepiness was overwhelming her, partly sunshine, partly getting up before dawn to help pack.

'Peppermint creams,' she said at last.

'They wouldn't be much use,' said Ruby critically. 'Not in a war.'

'It is a war.'

'I know.'

It didn't feel like a war, out in the warm garden, walled in by flowers and runner beans, with Mrs Morgan's hens crooning in their dust baths under the apple tree. From the cottage came sounds of laughter, and from towards the road another sound: the car engine firing and stopping.

'That's your grandad,' observed Ruby.

'Yes, don't tell on him.'

'Can he drive?'

'No. He'd like to, though. He tried to make Clarry let him, coming here.'

'Kate?'

'Mmm?'

'Is it posh at your house?'

'No. The landing carpet's worn right through and the plates never match because they get broken so often.'

'What else?'

'Shoes everywhere, and Pax.'

'That school we've got to go to?'

'It's posh,' admitted Kate. 'It's got ivy.'

'Ivy's not so special,' said Ruby, comforted, and they became quiet again.

THIRTY-TWO
Erik and Hans
Sky, September 1940

It was a Spitfire, fresh in the sky, newly fuelled, and hunting. Hans dipped his wings in mock salute, rolled, deliberately taunting it, and then, already much higher than Erik, went into a spiral climb.

'Get out of here!' bawled Erik into his radio, but if Hans heard he took no notice. He wheeled round again, firing now, and suddenly the Spitfire left Erik and turned after Hans. Bullets spat between them, high up in the shining blue.

Two minutes later there was no Hans, only a spurt of fire and a plunging black smoke trail. The Spitfire wheeled away and vanished into the sun. Then the pain in Erik's ruined arm overwhelmed him, and he slumped into a numbing blackness as his plane careered out of the sky.

THIRTY-THREE
Ruby and Kate
Mrs Morgan's cottage, September 1940

From the cottage came the sound of the wireless, mixed with the voices and laughter of Violet, Clarry and Mrs Morgan, three good friends making the most of their time together. Close by, the chickens murmured and squabbled. The loudest sound was the bees. There were many bees, fumbling through scarlet poppy flowers so freshly unfolded that their petals still showed creases. The bees moved between poppies, potatoes and a sowing of late summer peas, which thanks to Sooty and Paddle, were doing very well indeed.

'If Mrs Morgan is digging for victory,' observed Kate, 'I think she's going to win.'

'I do too,' said Ruby. 'If I was Hitler and saw Mrs Morgan's garden, I'd be frightened.'

They laughed together, but wedged between them, Pax suddenly stirred and growled.

'Don't, Pax,' said Kate and put her hand on him. 'Shush.'

Pax wouldn't shush because coming from high in the sky above his head, his least favourite place in the world, there was sound. It was a new sound, far away.

A mosquito perhaps.

'Kate,' said Ruby, squinting into the brightness. 'There's something way up in the sky. Moving. I can see it, then I can't.'

Kate turned on her back to look as well. The blueness seemed immense and empty, except for a high dappling of small white clouds, the sort that never rain.

Ruby spoke again. 'A plane. Two planes. Flying round each other. You're looking in the wrong place.'

Kate sat up to see better.

'I see one.'

'There's two.'

'Oh, yes! Pax . . .' Kate held him by his collar. 'No, Pax! Be quiet. Yes, I see them now.'

'What's the matter with Pax?'

'He always hates things in the sky. Anything, even the moon.'

The mosquito sounds came and went, as the hardly visible little planes left faint white trails like chalk dust, looping and spiralling in the clear September sky. There were other sounds too, like the tiny puffs of a very small, fast piston. Pax was tense with awareness.

'I think they're fighting,' said Ruby suddenly.

'Fighting?'

'That's one of our Spitfires. See the little rounded wings?'

'I can't . . . Pax, keep still . . . Oh, I do see! Oh, Ruby!'

'It's firing.'

Kate wrestled with Pax.

'There's bits coming off the other one!' exclaimed Ruby,

now on her feet with excitement. 'Gosh, how brilliant to see them! How lucky! Wow . . .'

'Ruby!' protested Kate.

'It's breaking up . . . there's a whole wing gone . . .'

'It's horrible!' said Kate. 'Oh no, oh no!'

The spurt of fire, clearly visible, halted Ruby's gloating.

'It's burning,' whispered Kate, and Ruby, suddenly quelled, said, 'Yes. But look . . .' and then, 'KATE! *KATE!*'

They had been so engrossed with the two little planes, that the third, much closer one, took them completely by surprise. It was suddenly roaring towards them, dreadfully big, dreadfully low . . .

'Lie FLAT!' screamed Kate, and as Pax wrestled free from her grip, Ruby flung herself down.

Overhead, so close it seemed it must take off the top of the apple tree, roared a German Messerschmitt fighter, grey-green, with a bright yellow nose cone, and black crosses on the underside of its wings.

Pax, barking madly, tore after it in frantic pursuit. Kate and Ruby raced after him, out of the garden and to the front of the cottage, where Grandfather, most luckily, had just managed to start the car.

'Drive! Drive! Drive!' screeched Kate and Ruby, tumbling in, and Grandfather hurried away for a moment, came back with the potato fork, said, 'I absolutely will,' and did.

Thirty-Four
Erik and Hans
Sky to Earth, September 1940

'*Wake up, you fool!*'
Two miles away, where Hans's plane had fallen, an ancient oak tree split and roared, briefly blossomed into crackling gold, ripened hot live bullets and flung them all around, and later dwindled into tangled blackness. Twisted shapes smouldered quietly under a reeking shroud of smoke.

Yet, in the cockpit of Erik's damaged Messerschmitt, very clearly, Erik heard Hans speak:

'*Erik! Wake up!*'

The voice came not from the radio, but from behind, as if Hans were standing just out of sight, at his shoulder.

With a great effort, Erik lifted his head. His swimming, floating, bubbling head, and found that he seemed to be ricocheting down an invisible giant stone staircase in an unfriendly sky.

'*Open your eyes,*' Hans told him calmly.

Erik blinked.

'*The rudder, if it still works.*'

It did still work, more or less. The plane regained some

balance, his descent on the giant staircase slowed, but not enough. There was a village, a church spire, scattered houses.

'*You must get higher,*' said Hans.

Molten pain flowed down from Erik's shoulder. His left arm was as immovable as a sodden sandbag.

'*Lift. LIFT NOW,*' ordered Hans.

Erik couldn't move the joystick with his right hand alone, so he unstrapped and used his stomach muscles and his chest and the weight of his dead arm. He took control, and the plane lifted. From behind he heard Hans sigh like someone who had held their breath too long.

Now he was flying much too fast and much too low over green countryside. He took the top off a haystack, leaving a trail of burning wisps.

'*Circle round again,*' said Hans. '*Get some height. Use some fuel.*'

It was true. The less fuel they hit the ground with, the less of it there was to explode into flame, and the better their chances would be. Erik hauled his wounded, flailing wings round another circuit, a little higher. The vibrations were so bad that he bit through his tongue. He was awash with pain and fear.

Hans said urgently at his shoulder, '*Try not to kill anyone. Miss that house.*'

Oh, God, he couldn't miss the house. He gasped, 'Help me, Hans,' and the house flew beneath them.

'*Still right behind you,*' said Hans, calmly. '*Nearly down. Nearly over.*'

How much fuel was left? Oh, for the long wings of a glider.

Hans again.

'*Miss . . .*'

Too late. The haystack.

'*MISS THE GIRLS!*' roared Hans.

There was no way to miss the girls. They were racing across a meadow. They cowered beneath him as he lurched overhead.

'*Miss the dog,*' said Hans.

It was easy to miss the dog. The dog dodged.

'*Down,*' said Hans, '*and get the top off!*'

Since the French plane, Hans had been terrified of fire, but at that moment moving the heavy cockpit cover seemed impossible.

'No time,' gasped Erik, and hit the ground so hard that the propeller ploughed a trench. Torn soil rained down in clods, but he was landed and, miraculously, the Perspex cover was flung back.

The strong raw smell of soil and the fumes of aviation fuel. The wave surge of returning pain. Hysterical barking. Sunlight.

'*Now, don't,*' said Hans, suddenly very far away, '*fall out of the window . . .* Erik . . . Erik?'

THIRTY-FIVE
Kate, Ruby, Pax, Erik
Sky to Earth, September 1940

Pax was out of sight, although not out of hearing, barking frantically in a hay meadow. Grandfather had driven grandly and quite slowly into a hawthorn hedge. Kate and Ruby left him there, safe, but swearing, to fling themselves over the gate and rush after Pax. As they ran, they realized that the plane must have veered away and was circling to return. Once again it was behind them, even louder, even slower, so low that for a second time they instinctively dropped flat.

It lurched and shuddered. The wheels looked enormous, the weight impossible.

It was on them. They lay braced in fear.

It passed.

'Pax!' screamed Kate, because it couldn't miss Pax.

It did.

It missed him.

It was down.

Unsteadily, they got to their feet and stared. Churned earth and the three propeller blades twisted like ribbons. The wings somehow pitiful, splayed out like a fallen bird. The Perspex cover open and the pilot clearly visible, his goggles gone and his helmet half off.

'We have to get him out,' shouted Kate and ran stumbling over the tussocky grass with Ruby and Pax behind.

'There's a step on the wing,' called Ruby, catching up. 'Look, there.'

It was the step that the pilots used to vault in. Kate climbed up and made room for Ruby, and together they looked down into the cockpit, and at the body of the airman slumped inside.

'He's dead,' said Ruby, but he groaned.

'His arm's all wrong,' said Kate. 'There's blood . . . there's a lot of blood, still coming out . . . Help me, Ruby, quick!'

'He'll be strapped in,' said Ruby, but he wasn't. By hauling on the collar of his heavy flying jacket they got him over the edge and then, using his own weight, they rolled him on to the wing and down. He moaned as he hit the grass, and his eyes stayed closed.

His jacket was so drenched in blood that they dragged him by his feet.

'Leave him now,' begged Ruby. 'Let's get help.'

'We have to stop the bleeding first.'

'How can we without bandages?' wailed Ruby. She was hating the whole thing, the blood, the touching, the weight of this alien stranger.

'Simon and Tod showed me,' panted Kate. She was peeling off the flying jacket, one sleeve at a time, first the good arm, then the bad. 'Compression, that's what they did . . . I think it's his shoulder . . . It is . . . There!'

Underneath the jacket was a shirt, soaked and torn.

Any bones broken? Simon had asked.

Yes.

But first there was the hole. Ruby saw it first and ran away in horror. When she came back Kate had pulled off her cardigan, folded it into a pad and was pressing down hard.

'Take off his helmet and turn his face sideways. Then if he's sick, he won't choke.'

'I can't.'

'Hold this then, and I will.'

'No. It's all right, I'll do it . . . There . . . Oh . . .'

'What?'

'I thought he'd be a grown-up.'

'He is.'

'He looks younger than Will. My brother, Will.'

'He's getting cold. There's a rug in the car. Could you fetch it, and maybe Grandfather's jacket?'

'How do you suddenly know what to do?'

'Hurry, Ruby.'

'All right,' said Ruby and left. She came back very soon, bringing the rug, but also the news that the car was stuck and Grandfather in it and his jacket with him.

'He said you're to come away at once and leave the dog on guard. And he made me bring the potato fork just in case.'

Kate groaned. She was still pressing hard against the pilot's shoulder, but she managed, one-handed, to tuck the car rug around the rest of him. 'I wish you'd put your jumper under his face,' she said. 'It would be a bit more comfortable than grass.'

'He's the enemy, Kate!'

'Not any more. He's not fighting now.'

'Oh, I wish someone would come,' moaned Ruby. 'What are we going to do?'

'If you come here and press where I tell you, I'll go and get the car out of the hedge and send Grandfather for help.'

'How could you get the car out of the hedge?'

'It's just reversing. I've seen them do it often. I could climb in from the back and make Grandfather move over.'

'I'll come with you.'

'Ruby, I can't let go here even for a second. I tried.'

'I hate blood,' said Ruby, who, with all her approval of war, had never considered actual bloodshed as one of the side effects.

'Shut your eyes, then. I won't take five minutes. Please, Ruby. Pax will stay with you. Look, press here.'

'All right.'

They changed places, Kate guiding Ruby's hands, Ruby's eyes tight shut. 'Pax, stay!' ordered Kate and ran. Commanding Grandfather into letting her reverse the car was difficult, but no harder than anything else she'd done that afternoon. She let him bark instructions, and although she ignored them, when the car was on the road they were both breathlessly triumphant.

'Now,' said Kate. 'It's pointing the right way. Could you drive it back to Mrs Morgan's and telephone for help?'

'Naturally. The steering went the first time. Nothing to do with me.'

'Yes. Could you drive very slowly, in case the steering goes again?'

'Only sensible. Of course.'

'I'm not quite sure which pedal is the brake,' said Kate, and Grandfather admitted that neither was he, so they worked it out together, and then Kate waved him off, calling untruthfully, 'No hurry . . .'

Back in the hay field, Ruby pressed on Kate's folded cardigan, with her eyes firmly closed. She told herself that she didn't care if he died, as long as it didn't happen while she was alone with him. Unscrewing her eyes to see how he was managing, she found he'd turned his head and his own eyes were now open. They were very young and frightened. When he saw that she was watching, he whispered, '*Danke.*'

Then he gasped and continued to gasp. Blood seeped up around Ruby's fingers. She'd forgotten to press. There was nothing else for it. She tugged off her jumper, folded it into a fresh dressing and started again. Despite Pax, whose worried eyes had never left the gate over which Kate had vanished, she felt so lonely that she started to talk.

'You'd better not die now you've ruined my jumper.'

He was silent.

'It's much worse for me than it is for you.'

A big lie.

'I don't mean to hurt you.'

That was true, anyway, and oh, thank goodness, here was Kate coming back to take her place.

Kate had not only got the car out of the hedge, taught Grandfather the rudiments of driving, issued him with instructions as to what to say when he arrived, but she had also grabbed his jacket. She draped it round Erik and he opened his eyes again, whispered another '*Danke*', noticed Pax, and smiled.

'Pax,' said Kate, seeing where he was looking, 'it's another word for peace.'

Ruby burst into tears and said, 'I hate this war, I hate it. He's going to die. Look at him,' and she scrambled to her feet and ran away, weeping. She ran in a big circle and when she came back she said, 'I can hear a car.'

It was help at last. Clarry and Violet, Mrs Morgan and Grandfather. Very quickly after them, an ambulance arrived.

'At last,' said Kate thankfully. 'People who know properly what to do.'

'If anyone knew properly what to do, I'd say it was you two girls,' said the ambulance driver.

'Not me,' said Ruby. 'It was Kate.'

'Who looked after him while Kate went off for help?' asked her mother, hugging her. 'And what's Mrs Morgan's potato fork doing up here?'

'It was for in case, but we didn't need it.'

'I should think not, poor young chap,' said Mrs Morgan, seeming to entirely forget that she had sharpened the prongs herself. 'You lift him in careful,' she told the ambulance people. 'He's been through enough for one day. And is anyone travelling with him?'

'I will,' said Clarry. 'I can manage a bit of German. It might help. And maybe Kate could come too so she can explain exactly what happened. But only if the ambulance can wait while I drive the rest of you back to the cottage.'

'I will drive back to the cottage,' said Grandfather firmly. 'As I did only an hour ago. And if anyone doesn't like it, they can walk.'

So Erik was taken away with Kate and Clarry, while the rest travelled back to the cottage with Grandfather driving and Mrs Morgan beside him making helpful remarks like, 'You've not hit anything so far,' and 'Go past the tree before you turn,' and 'Get ready with that brake.'

Despite this, they arrived safely, and found that the day had somehow vanished. They were all suddenly exhausted. Ruby realized that she was splattered with blood. Violet thought how young the airman had looked, and how out of reach was Will, and that soon Ruby would be far away in Oxford, and these thoughts made her sad. Sadness for Violet always turned to briskness and crossness, and so she ordered Ruby into a not very warm bath with Mrs Morgan's red carbolic soap, told her off for dripping on the floor, gave her boiled eggs and stewed gooseberries for supper, said she should be thankful, reminded her that there was a war on, bundled her off to the sofa in the front room and commanded her to sleep.

'Kids,' she said irritably, flumping down at the kitchen table with Grandfather and Mrs Morgan. Grandfather said, yes, vastly overrated, and Mrs Morgan agreed.

After a while they opened a bottle of last year's rhubarb and barley wine, and although Grandfather said it was raw poison, most of it got drunk. They staggered off to bed at last and were not impressed when Ruby woke them up with shrieks in the middle of the night.

'For goodness' SAKE, Ruby!' said Violet.

'Night terror,' said Mrs Morgan. 'Those gooseberries were too much.'

'Child,' said Grandfather. 'We cannot help if you will not control yourself.'

Ruby made no attempt to control herself. She blubbered that they must go and save the airman. She jumped out of bed and ran panicking to the door, and would have tugged it open and raced into the night if they hadn't held her back.

'Quickly, before he burns,' sobbed Ruby.

Then they thought they understood and gathered round to comfort her.

'Ruby, Ruby,' they said, all of them, even Grandfather. 'Ruby. Listen. Clarry telephoned from the hospital, not an hour ago, just before we went to bed. He's safe. He's being cared for. Kate's asleep, like you should be, but Clarry's sitting up with him. You did it. You and Kate. He's going to be all right.'

Ruby became furious at this stupidity, but it did no good. When they wouldn't let her out of the door she rushed to the window and tugged at the blackout.

'Ruby!' they said sternly, and pulled her away, and sat her down and told her all over again about the hospital and how wonderful she and Kate had been, and that this was only a nightmare, and that everyone was very, very tired and must now go back to bed.

'You don't understand,' said Ruby, blubbering, and they said she was in shock.

'Sugar for shock,' said Mrs Morgan. 'I'll go and put the kettle on and make something hot and sweet. And Violet, you telephone the hospital. You won't be popular, this time of night, but maybe it'll put her mind at rest.'

With this, they both went off and left Ruby with Grandfather.

'You've got to help,' she said to him, hiccupping with misery, and it was at this point that Grandfather produced his magic flask.

'Drink this,' he said to Ruby, pouring the silver cup half full, and Ruby, now very thirsty with all her shouting, drank it in one frightful burning swallow, gazed at Grandfather with astonished eyes, and became very woozy indeed.

'Drop more,' said Grandfather, administering another dose, and by the time Mrs Morgan and Violet came back, Ruby was fast asleep on the sofa, perfectly quiet and good.

'Did the trick!' said Grandfather, smugly. He was feeling very happy altogether, what with his heroic driving, and ambulance calling, and his own celebratory doses of whisky. 'Did the trick. It'll be all right in the morning, and now I'm going to bed.'

THIRTY-SIX
Kate
Plymouth, September 1940

While Ruby was keeping people awake at Mrs Morgan's cottage, in the hospital in Plymouth there were also dramas. Erik had been X-rayed and very quickly it had been decided that his arm was so badly hurt, and putting so much strain not only on his heart, but also on his equally damaged shoulder, that it couldn't possibly be saved. The news was told to Clarry at two o'clock in the morning by the elderly doctor who was on duty that night. He spoke as if he couldn't care less about his diagnosis, and was turning to go when Kate, who for hours had been dozing and waking and dozing again in the little, bare, green-painted waiting room, woke instantly and completely.

Kate jumped up, got to the door, leaned against it, and said, 'I won't let you cut off his arm.'

'I'm sorry. I'm afraid I must ask you not to make a nuisance of yourself,' said the doctor, staring. 'I need to return to my patient. I really don't know why you're here.'

'You've got to ask my dad,' said Kate, taking hold of the door handle in both hands. 'He's a . . . he's . . .' Her breath caught suddenly, and Clarry took over.

'It would be a good idea to speak to Kate's father,' she said, now also on her feet and standing in solidarity with Kate. 'He's a surgeon in Oxford. He specializes in reconstructive surgery. If you would give permission for him to come and see your patient, I could telephone right now.'

'I very much doubt that he would be able—'

'He would,' said Kate, wheezing furiously. 'And the airman's not just your patient; he's mine as well. I got him out of the plane.'

Something changed in the doctor's face, then. Perhaps, as Clarry said afterwards, he hadn't understood that Kate had been the one who'd pulled the German pilot from the plane. Perhaps it was Kate's sudden desperate coughing. Whatever it was, he transformed before their eyes from an elderly, impatient doctor into a tired but helpful friend.

'You're quite right,' he said, speaking directly to Kate. 'If you're the person who rescued him, then the young man is your patient too. I would be very glad of your father's advice. Shall we wake him now, or wait till morning?'

'Now,' said Kate. 'Thank you. Not in the morning. Now.'

THIRTY-SEVEN
Ruby
Mrs Morgan's cottage, September 1940

'Snoring,' said Ruby, in disgust.

It was dawn, pink dawn over the grey-green fields outside Mrs Morgan's cottage window. The whole house was snoring, and Ruby had woken in a state of rage. At first she couldn't remember why, and then she did.

Pax was looking at her.

'Come on,' she told him. 'We're going out.'

She found her shoes in the kitchen, and looked around for her clothes, but the only ones she could see were soaking in a bucket. The water was rusty-red. Ruby shuddered and turned away. Mrs Morgan's old garden coat was hanging from a hook in the porch, so she took that instead, pulled it on over her pyjamas and opened the door.

Pax streaked out at once, and then stood watching her, asking where to go.

'Back to where we saw them first,' said Ruby.

The garden was very silent, the chickens still shut up, the bees not yet awake. Every leaf was heavy with dew and the flowers hung like wet laundry. Ruby's feet left dark footprints on the hearthrug lawn.

'We were standing here,' she told Pax. 'There were two little planes. One turned away and the other fell into the wood. There was a line of black smoke. Then the big plane came over. But before that, there was something else . . .'

Ruby tried to picture again that split-second moment, between the little plane falling and the big plane so low overhead it had seemed they might reach up and touch it.

'There was something white,' she said, and began to run.

The whole of Ruby wanted to believe *parachute*, but she had seen parachutes on a cinema newsreel. They floated. They slid in airy zigzags down the sky. Whatever she had seen hadn't done that: it had tumbled and lurched.

Nevertheless, she carried on, leaving the road to climb gates, and cross meadows. Skirting round a field of red-and-white cows. Paddling carefully across the slippery hidden stones of a shallow stream, with Pax behind her, just as cautious.

Arriving at the wood.

The early light hadn't reached it yet. It crouched in its own shadows, greenish and thick with hidden shapes. There was no breeze, but from somewhere seeped a bitter smell, the smell of wet and recent burning. It frightened Ruby, and it frightened Pax too. He pressed against her legs.

There was no clear way into the wood. It was ringed with tangled brambles.

'We'll go round the edge,' said Ruby, leading the way, 'until we find an opening.'

Pax followed very slowly, pausing often to look mutinously

over his shoulder, back the way that they'd come. He'd had enough of wet fields and briars and ice-cold streams. He wasn't a country dog and this girl wasn't Kate. However, a few minutes later, when Ruby suddenly stopped and whispered, 'Pax, oh, Pax,' he nudged into her hand for comfort.

Even Pax, city dog that he was, could see that they had arrived at no ordinary tree.

It was enormous, standing right on the edge of the wood. A ravaged oak, laced in torn green ivy, decked with broken branches and garlanded with loops and swags of scorched white silk.

Nothing moved. No birds sang. But the tree spoke.

'You are very beautiful,' said the tree, and Ruby jumped and spun round in shock, her hands raised to cover her cheeks.

'There's only me here,' she said.

'I am sorry,' said the tree apologetically. 'I did not mean to frighten you.'

Slowly, Ruby lowered her hands. The leaves rustled, a green and silver sigh, 'You are very, *very* beautiful.'

'Where are you?' asked Ruby, trembling, and she clutched Pax hard as she spoke.

The tree didn't seem to notice Pax. It took some time to reply.

'This is a pleasant place,' it said eventually.

Ruby peered and peered into the great kaleidoscope pattern of greenness and ivy and oak and twisted silk. She retreated back into the field, hoping to see better from a distance.

'Do not forget me,' called the tree hoarsely.

'I was trying to work out where you were.'

'Please tell me your name.'

'Ruby Amaryllis. Wave your hand or something.'

'Pardon?' said the tree.

'Are you hurt?'

'Yes.'

'You're German,' said Ruby.

'Yes. From Berlin.'

'Kristallnacht,' said Ruby.

The tree became very quiet.

Thirty-Eight
Erik, Kate, Ruby
England, November 1940

Erik's arm stopped being a weight in a sling and he could move it, lift a cup, turn his hand. His shoulder (explored, cleaned, stitched and pinned by Peter) became a useful thing again. His fever cooled and his wounds closed and enough new blood flowed in his veins to keep him standing on his feet. He was lucky. He was well.

Well enough to be sent, along with nearly a hundred other German prisoners, on a late Atlantic sea crossing to a camp in Canada.

'Canada?' Kate had repeated, when the news arrived.

'A lot of captured German aircrew are being sent to camps over there,' her father told her, and his words startled Kate. Until that moment, she had thought of Erik as rescued, not captured.

But of course, he was both.

'Why Canada?' she asked, at last.

'I suppose it's so far away there's less chance of people escaping back to Germany, and joining up again. It won't be that bad. He should be pretty safe. Safer than flying a fighter plane, anyway.'

'Will his arm be all right?'

'It was a straightforward enough mend, once I got everything back in place. I did a nice job on his shoulder.'

'Good.'

Kate hadn't seen Erik since the day she and Ruby pulled him out of his plane. She knew nothing of him except the way he had whispered *Danke*, that his eyes had followed Pax. Her father hadn't seen him since the final of the surgeries that had fixed him back together. Yet both of them felt that he was still, somehow, in their care.

'He had a lot of damage in that shoulder,' said Peter. 'He'll need to build back his movement very carefully. I'm going to write him out a table of exercises to do.'

'In English?'

'I'll draw diagrams. You can help.'

'All right.'

Before Erik was sent away, Peter was able to get a parcel to him. He had to put in a special request to send it, and it had been passed as *Medical Advice and Supplies*. As well as Peter's exercises, they managed to add a German–English dictionary from Clarry, barley sugar from Kate, and yellow soap from Mrs Morgan, another person who felt that Erik was somehow in her care.

'Could we put in a letter?' asked Kate.

Peter shook his head. 'We did well to get permission

for the parcel. Barley sugar and soap can count as medical supplies, and the dictionary to help with understanding his exercises, but I think a letter would be pushing our luck too far. I'm pretty certain it would count as fraternizing with the enemy.'

'I keep forgetting Erik is supposed to be an enemy,' said Kate to Ruby, much later that day. 'And we're not meant to know he's going to Canada, either.'

It was night, pitch-dark in the room they shared, the blackouts down, the school day over, the streets of Oxford running like rivers under yet another deluge of ice-cold November rain. It was the time when they talked.

'Canada?' asked Ruby, who had not heard this before. 'Well, I hope he likes bears.'

'Why?'

'There's thousands of bears in Canada. I remember reading about them in that book you gave me and afterwards I looked them up. Grizzly bears, eight feet tall with paws as big as dinner plates. Black bears as well, and mountain lions.'

'Nowadays?'

'Think so. Packs of wolves too.'

'He'll be all right, then,' said Kate, with such certainty that Ruby laughed in the darkness.

'I think he likes animals,' said Kate. 'He liked Pax. I could tell. Isn't it cold? It feels like it might snow.'

'Haven't you got warm yet?' asked Ruby. They'd both gone to bed in woolly socks, with old cardigans over their pyjamas, but for the first time that winter, it didn't feel enough.

'Not properly.' Kate began tugging the cover from her hot-water bottle in case there was any heat left to be had from its bare rubber inside.

'You can have mine if you like,' offered Ruby. Her hot-water bottle was new, and it definitely lasted longer. Sometimes it was still warm in the morning. 'I was going to dump it on the floor soon, anyway,' she told Kate.

'No, you weren't,' said Kate. 'You're not that mad. Besides, I'm having Pax.' She slid out from under her blankets, groped across the floor for Pax, snoring in front of the door, lugged him up on to her bed, crawled into the narrow space he left for her, and covered them both with her eiderdown. The effects were immediate and wonderful, worth the venture into the cold. Pax radiated a fuggy warmth more enveloping than half a dozen hot-water bottles.

'I don't know how you bear it,' commented Ruby.

'I've got a lavender bag,' said Kate. She loved Pax, but she was under no illusions. In bed it was best to have your back to him, and your nose in a lavender bag.

'Oh, let me have a sniff of lavender,' begged Ruby, and Kate passed it over in the dark.

'Hmmm,' said Ruby, inhaling deeply. 'Mrs Morgan's.'

'Yes, she sent it.'

'Remember that last day we were there?'

'Yes. Oh, yes,' said Kate.

'I wish . . .' began Ruby, and then paused.

Kate waited, as she had waited so many nights already that

winter, understanding that Ruby had memories not easy to shape into words.

'No, it's nothing,' said Ruby at last, and then, in a completely different voice, 'I wrote to Will today.'

Kate nodded invisibly in the dark to show that she was listening.

'I asked Mum to post me that sherbet dab and she did and I sent it with my letter.'

Kate knew all about the sherbet dab. She knew about Sooty and the arrival of Paddle. She knew about the scrubbing brush and the white water, Mrs Cohen and the silver photo frame. She knew about the early morning postcard from the German prison camp. Little by little, night by night, Ruby had told her all these things, but she had never ever told her the story of exactly what had happened on that last day at Mrs Morgan's.

Kate remembered how she and Clarry had come back from the hospital in Plymouth to find Mrs Morgan making sandwiches in the kitchen, Grandfather snoring on the sofa, and Ruby nowhere to be seen.

'The boy's not too bad. Peter will be with him this afternoon,' Clarry had announced, rushing in, talking as she spoke. 'Kate's had a good sleep in the car . . .' Then she'd paused, noticing what was going on for the first time. 'Goodness, Mrs Morgan, what's all this?'

'Now, you stop with your questions, and I'll tell you everything,' Mrs Morgan had replied, shuffling great heaps of food around the kitchen table as she spoke. 'The egg and lettuce are for you to have in the car on your way, and there's half a sponge cake cut in slices and some gooseberries that want eating. So that's that. Those are sardine paste, and them's marrow and ginger and they're for the teams with the fire engines. There's two of them there now, and a police car as well and they're sending up a lad to collect—'

'FIRE?' burst out Clarry.

'There's no fire,' said Mrs Morgan. 'You'll hear if you listen! I've some apples for them too, and yesterday's scones that got forgotten—'

'PLEASE—'

'Stop!' Mrs Morgan raised a majestic hand, just like Britannia on the back of a penny only with a bread knife instead of a trident, and when Clarry had closed her mouth, continued, 'They're working over by Miller's Wood, past the stream through the bullocks' field and how Ruby knew it we haven't got out of her . . .'

'Knew what? Knew what?' asked Kate.

'There's one of them parachutists caught tangled in a tree,' announced Mrs Morgan solemnly. 'Been there all night and his plane burned out and goodness knows the state of him—'

'OH, NO!' exclaimed both Clarry and Kate.

Mrs Morgan pointed the bread knife very fiercely indeed at this latest interruption, and then shook her head and whispered hoarsely, 'Don't say nothing about that to Ruby, either of you. He was still alive when she came running back, and there's fair hope he'll stay that way. That's all we know for now.'

'BUT WHERE . . .?'

'Violet's had to go. She's said her goodbyes to Ruby and caught the bus back to Plymouth. She couldn't wait, she's on duty tonight. She said to tell you she would write.'

'I thought she might have to leave before we got back,' admitted Clarry mournfully.

'Now,' continued Mrs Morgan, counting off news items on her fingers. 'What else? Your dad's had that flask out, Clarry, I'm sorry to say, but he's caused no trouble and it might be worse. The goat's milked and the hens fed. That dog came back in such a state I've tied him up by the bin. Plastered in mud. He's had two buckets of water over him but I have to say it's not made a blind bit of difference.'

'SO . . .?'

'So now you know all,' Mrs Morgan had finished, putting down the bread knife and crossing her hands on her apron. 'And where are you off to, young Kate?'

'Ruby,' said Kate.

She'd discovered Ruby deep in the greenness of the garden, hunkered down behind the runner beans. Ruby had a very small mirror in her hand, and she was tilting her face from side to side. When Kate arrived she'd looked up.

'I've seen them now,' she'd said.

'Good.'

'I don't look awful.'

'The opposite of awful,' Kate had told her, and had hunched down beside her, hugging her knees.

'Kate, if you didn't see me for ages, and then you did,

would you remember who I was?'

'Yes.'

'For a long time, years maybe?'

'Probably forever,' said Kate.

'Oh,' said Ruby, 'they're useful, then.' And she'd looked in the mirror again and laughed, and jumped up and pulled Kate to her feet and hugged her.

'Guess what?' she said.

'What?'

'Nothing.'

'Oh, Ruby, what?'

'Tell you one day.'

Was it one day yet? wondered Kate, months later, in bed in the dark, with Pax behind her, twitching and snuffling in one of his enormous, animated dreams.

Across the room, Ruby was still silent. Presently she sighed and Kate guessed she was asleep. She still had the lavender bag; she'd forgotten to give it back. The smell of it drifted faintly across the room to Kate, clean and sweet, garden-scented.

Kate wriggled backwards into Pax's doggy warmth and remembered once more that September day.

Ruby's face had been shining. Dark-splattered, sun-dappled, bright as light on rippled water.

Very, very beautiful.

Shining.

THIRTY-NINE
Erik
Canada, December 1940–December 1941

anada.

C   As Kate's father had guessed, it wasn't that bad. If Erik's flying days were over, then so were his fighting days. Every time he remembered that, he was thankful.

'I was always on the point of falling out of the window,' he told an imaginary Hans.

Conversations in his head with Hans were a habit that had begun the September afternoon when he had been shot down over England, and his friend's voice had taken control of his shattered thoughts and talked him down to landing without killing anyone. That time it had happened unconsciously, but now Erik did it quite often. He laughed at himself, but he did it.

Before many months in camp, Erik had picked up English, as nearly everybody had. Soon he found that there were books he could read and courses he could study. In the Luftwaffe he had learned a good deal of engineering, and starting that first winter in Canada, he went on learning more. It quickly came in useful. When spring arrived, prisoners who could be trusted were sent out to work on the local farms. Erik was one of them, and his reputation soon grew. He had always liked mending things, and now he found himself fixing bikes and milking machines, generators and hay binders. He laughed out loud when a small girl arrived in the tractor shed, one hand clutching her father's jacket, a doll held tight in the other.

'Katy-Ann,' she said, presenting the doll to Erik like a baton in a relay race. 'Her eyes won't open.'

'Long ago I had a dolls' hospital,' Erik told her, in his new, careful English. 'Look away while I operate. I will tell you when it is done.'

She looked away, Erik removed Katy-Ann's head, re-attached the mechanism that opened and closed her eyes, put her together again, and said, 'There you are. I think she's well. If she has a little headache, give her tea with camomile flowers.'

This spectacular repair raised Erik's reputation even higher than fixing the milking machine had done. He was invited to a dolls' tea party.

'*You do know everybody is talking about you, don't you?*' said Hans the next day, and not for the first time either.

Erik nodded, and continued working on an ancient seized-up tractor engine that hadn't run for years.

'The great thing about tractors,' he explained to Hans, 'is that they don't drop twenty thousand feet out of the sky if you happen to get something wrong.'

'*Clearly we should have flown tractors all along,*' said Hans.

'It might have been wise.'

'*You think that thing will ever run again?*'

'Sure it will,' said Erik, and cranked the engine and the old tractor rattled and coughed and steadied into a regular *chud-chud-chud* of life. It was harvest time by then, nearly a year since the crash, and they were getting in the wheat and carting it by trailer down to the depot. Now the farm had an extra tractor, it could be shifted twice as fast.

'We're sending it overseas,' said the farmer, when Erik came to tell him the news of his success. 'Like to drive a few loads down for me? I'll go ahead, show you the route. You follow on behind.'

The old tractor blew out blue smoke and went at a top speed of about ten miles an hour. Its seat was bare steel, and its original colour lost in time, but Erik, bumping along the country roads, thought how much better he felt about feeding people than fighting them. A sudden jubilant happiness made him shout out, over the racketing of the engine, 'Look at this, Hans!'

'*You be careful. Miss that bear!*' the voice in his thoughts called back.

Sometimes, in the dusty harvests of summer, the giant snowfalls of winter, war seemed another world away. But then a rare letter would arrive, or a scrap of news would be heard in camp: London was burning, Berlin was a battleground. Rumours would spin the globe of war: Norway, North Africa, Japan, India, Greece and Malta. Pacts were broken. New weapons invented. Russia became a terror.

America was in.

It was a world war.

Forty
Will
Germany 1940–1946

British prisoners of war in Germany nearly all made plans to escape, and some of them managed it, and most of them didn't. The first time Will escaped was easy; he ran away from a work party sent out to help with timber felling. It all went very well. Will made his furtive, hurrying way across three or four miles of farmland at dusk, and was pleased to come across an open barn with a stack of clean hay at the back. He was discovered the next morning by two very small girls, who found him fast asleep there and woke him with their giggles. They were holding hands, standing just inside the open doorway with the dusty sunbeams flooding in around them. They looked like twins, with their brown boots and stubby brown plaits and identical blue-striped dresses. When they saw Will's eyes open they asked him very politely if he had slept well, and if he liked their grandfather's barn.

'*Ja, ja*,' said Will, the only word of German he knew. '*Ja, ja*,' he repeated, as if he had understood everything they said, when in fact he had grasped nothing at all.

'*Ja, ja*,' and he nodded his head and smiled.

The little girls smiled back and one of them held out a small bread roll and asked if he would like it.

'*Ja, ja,*' said Will gratefully, and ate it in three bites.

Nudging each other with anticipation as they spoke, the little girls next asked if he was an escaped prisoner from the camp beside the forest.

Will didn't disappoint them. '*Ja, ja,*' he said enthusiastically.

The little girls smiled more than ever, and said something else, which Will guessed was an offer to fetch more bread rolls.

'*Ja, ja, ja,*' he agreed, and they whirled round, and vanished into the morning sunlight, and Will stretched and thought how well he was getting on, happily unaware that what the little girls had actually told him was that they would now go and fetch their grandfather who had a big gun.

Afterwards, in his horrible, much more secure new camp, Will thought about that welcoming open barn with its tempting pile of hay, and he knew what a fool he'd been. It was more than a year before he tried escaping again. This time he had taken the precaution of learning a fair amount of German and, with the help of the camp escape committee, had some much less prisoner-like clothes. Also he had a copy of a map that had arrived in the camp in very small patchwork pieces rolled up in cigarettes. With its help, he headed south towards the border with neutral Switzerland, and he was two weeks into his journey, when early one damp morning he came across a bicycle. It had been discarded at the side of a road, with not a soul in sight.

Will was very tired of walking and eating raw potatoes and

sleeping under hedges and hiding in ditches and trudging, trudging, trudging with nothing on his feet but the remains of his football boots and blisters. He wanted the journey finished.

It was the barn and the hay bed all over again.

The owner of the bike chased after him on a better, faster one and caught up with him at his first flat tyre. He was a much less pleasant captor than the little girls had been and Will had a couple of very bad days until, once again, they took him prisoner and put him into a camp. Just as before, it was far tougher than the last, and he had to make new friends again, and wait even longer for his parcels to arrive. He gave up all hope of escaping for a third time. He didn't want to risk it; he was afraid of being shot. He wanted to get home. In his bunk at night, he walked the streets of Plymouth and he thought if he ever got there he would earn his living as a postman because he had got so fond of parcels. Even more than that, above all things, he wanted to get back and hug his mum and make it up to Ruby. The first winter that he had been a prisoner she had sent him the sherbet dab from behind the kitchen clock. The packet was faded to greyness and the sherbet was a congealed lump in one corner, but the message that came with it had read:

Peace, pax, friends.
Love from Ruby Amaryllis
Come home soon and say, What's an amaryllis, anyway?

In Will's latest prison camp, there were experts on lots of things. To help pass the time and keep the grinding hunger and boredom at bay, they used to do sports and concerts and plays and quite often they would take it in turn to give lectures. Birdwatching, War Poets, Scottish Mountains, The Ten Best Pubs in Plymouth with route maps in between them and illustrations of their signs (that was Will's). One evening, someone spoke about growing flowers, and was pleased to answer questions. That was why, years later when the war finally ended, and Will was on his way home at last, he lingered for a while in the Netherlands. The hungry Netherlands, where the winter before had been a famine, and the people had eaten grass and tulip bulbs. Although food had arrived at last, the children were still white-faced and thin, and you could trade chocolate or tinned army rations for almost anything. Will had travelled from his camp in a US army truck, and he had both chocolate and tinned beef in his pack. He went about the streets and markets with one request that he repeated over and over, and at last somebody offered what he sought. It was a swollen, bruised-looking thing, wrapped in ancient newspaper. Acquiring it bankrupted Will of both chocolate and tins, and he was sure he'd been cheated, but he took it home anyway and gave it to Ruby.

It grew long leaves and a tall green spike, and then great, glowing, ruby-red trumpets, speckled inside with gold and chocolate. It lit the room like a flame. It shone for weeks, and Will and Ruby and Violet never stopped dragging people in to admire it.

'That's an amaryllis,' Will would tell them with pride. 'It's a flower like a lily, but better.'

FORTY-ONE
Kate
Oxford, February 1946

Pax still looked like an animal raised in a scrapyard, but it was a long time since he had worn the rope collar and the leather luggage label. For six years he had owned the respectable brass tag of a dog with a home. Kate had kept the leather label, however, and now she threaded it back on to his collar. She put it there because she guessed it had come from somebody who loved him, before she had, before Rupert, in his unknown past before the war.

This night, Kate thought, Pax needed love. After the last goodbyes on the doorstep he had sunk into a shabby heap. They'd carried him in and the vet had come and said, 'Slowing down now. Not surprising with that heart, and he's fifteen years, or more, I would guess. What do you want me to do?'

'Nothing if you don't have to,' said Kate, and the vet said, no, he didn't have to, Pax was probably just slipping away in his own time. Not in pain.

They had lain him on the hearthrug, because that was his favourite place and he hadn't moved since. All the house was asleep now, except for Kate, and in the old red armchair across from the fire, Grandfather, in much the same state as Pax.

Kate was, as so often, writing. Catching the moment before it was gone.

This is now, she thought as she wrote. *Now Pax. Now Grandfather. Now the fire glow, the flames finished, the ashes whitening. Now the rain in the street.*

Too precious to be wasted.

That day family had gathered and gone. Charlie and Tod to the station together, Janey to her college, Bea and her little daughter Barley back to their Lincolnshire lambs. *Goodbye, good dog, best dog*, they had whispered at the door. Barley said, 'Kiss him better,' and stooped with a kiss, but he hadn't got better. He was deep, deep asleep, blanketed and layered and heavy with time.

'Pax,' murmured Kate, with a hand on his shoulder, and, with infinite effort, he raised very slightly one grey wispy eyebrow.

'He heard you, then,' commented Grandfather. 'Done well. Done very well.' He was sitting the night out with Kate, with his glass of whisky and the firelight and no particular thought except that the girl might need company. He'd done well too, he considered. Kept them steady. Voice of reason. Found the words for Charlie when Simon's ship was lost. Torpedoed in the North Atlantic and the boy had been bent with grief, speechless, until he had unlocked a memory.

'That night, that Christmas Eve he sang in church. Your doing, wasn't it?'

Charlie had looked up, surprised.

'I knew! Saw your face. What was it?'

'Once In,' said Charlie.

'Watched him,' Grandfather had continued. 'He had a look not often seen.' Grandfather had paused. He had no easy access to the words of happiness: radiant, glowing, luminous.

Yet he found the right one. 'Joyful.'

He and Charlie had become friends. It was Charlie who'd got him to his feet that afternoon, to make his wedding speech for Clarry and Rupert. *Charlie and Kate*, Grandfather thought. *Pick of the bunch. No brains, unfortunately.*

He looked across at the girl.

'Still writing?'

'Finished now.'

'Astonishing how you keep it up.'

It was true, Kate thought. She had kept it up. More or less. Simon had silenced her for a while, but eventually she'd picked up her pencil again. The stack of exercise books had grown. As the war went on, paper had been hard to come by, but in a way that had helped. She'd learned to ration words, to tell a happening in a few lines. Untangling Ruby's story: following the threads, she'd learned to listen.

'Dog still with us?' asked Grandfather, breaking the silence.

'Fast asleep. Nice and warm. I was thinking about Ruby.'

Grandfather snorted. 'That one. Girl who fell in love with a tree. Don't look like that! Fact. Charlie told me.'

Kate laughed.

'Asked me to dance this afternoon,' he said. 'At my age!'

'But you did. I saw you.'

'Totter. Gave it a totter. She in your book?'

'Of course. And you.'

'I'm in there?'

'Lots of times.'

'Good. I did my bit, didn't I?'

'Every single night,' said Kate. *Give me a job,* he'd said, and Vanessa had given him the blackout to manage. He'd relished it, no glimmer of light had escaped the house through all the years of the war.

'That German lad you got out the plane. What about him? In there too?'

'I wrote as much as I know, but I wish it was more.'

'Hun!'

'He wasn't.'

'How'd he end up flying a Messerschmitt, then? I was ready with that fork, you know. One bad move and I'd have been there.'

Kate kindly didn't say, 'You were stuck in a hedge,' but she did remark, 'You'd never have used it.'

'Wouldn't I? Think I'm soft?'

'Yes.'

Grandfather grunted and sank back in his chair. Pax sighed and Kate rubbed his ears. His tail lifted a fraction. *See that?* Grandfather wanted to ask, but hadn't the energy.

For an hour he slept, his breathing irregular, crackling like scrunched-up paper crackles. Shallow. When he woke Kate was half asleep herself, curled on the hearthrug, her cheek against the ancient dog. She opened her eyes to find him gazing at her.

'You'd better find out.'

'Find out?' she repeated, bewildered with sleep.

Grandfather spoke slowly, between breaths. 'The boy . . . in the plane . . . How he got there.'

'I could try.'

'Do it. Could make a real book. All the tales.'

'Perhaps.'

'Put me in. Don't forget.'

'Never.'

'Promise? Be . . . a task.'

'I'll do it. I really will. I promise.'

'Left you my money. When I'm dead.'

'Don't talk like that!'

'What there is. What I didn't . . . drink.'

'Grandfather! You're not going to die.'

'Oh, yes, I am,' he said, suddenly vigorous. 'Oh, yes. Dog will see another day, though. Look!'

Kate turned to Pax and saw his head raised, eyes now open, brightness there. Thump went his tail. Another day.

'Oh, Pax, oh, Pax,' she murmured.

'Odd choice,' said Grandfather. 'Odd . . .' he stopped, started again, 'name.'

'It's another word for . . . Grandfather . . . Grandfather?'

He smiled at her, and the years fell away from him. It was Charlie's smile, wistful, merry, endearingly kind. He said, 'Peace,' and closed his eyes.

FORTY-TWO
Erik
On the way home, June 1947

When the war ended, all over the world there were millions of people in places where they had never planned to be. It took months and often years to get them on their way back home again. It was nearly two years for Erik. He travelled by lorries and trains and ships, by America and England and France, and the nearer he got to home, the more he feared what he would find. He'd read the newspapers and heard the broadcasts, seen the sickening newsreels of the concentration camps.

His mother was back in Berlin. *For good or bad, nowhere else is home*, she'd written. She had found some rooms in a building on the outskirts of the shattered city.

Even smaller than the last, she wrote, *but there is a school for Frieda where I have cleaning work and also serve the hot meals that the Americans supply. Good soup, a whole mug each, with peas or meat in it. The children drink it thankfully and we see the difference it makes.*

If one mug of soup could make a difference, thought Erik, what had it been like before? He remembered the meals of his own childhood, the winter broths, the sausages and pancakes, apples and Christmas gingerbread, Hans's mother's homemade plum cake with whipped cream on top. Lisa would wrinkle her nose and spoon her cream on to Erik's slice.

Lisa, lost in the bombings of Berlin, but always, always when Erik thought of her, turning her defiant cartwheels in the snow.

Hans's father and mother were gone too. *They just gave up, after Lisa*, his mother had written. Frieda was well, a bright lovely girl of twelve. Uncle Karl, condemned as a traitor, had stood blindfold in front of a Nazi firing squad, having done what he could once too often.

Armer Mann, Erik's mother wrote, and he could hear her voice in the words. *Poor man.*

The journey home had seemed endless. Nights sitting upright, dozing into days of weary boredom. Snatched meals of bread and cooling, chicory-flavoured coffee. Wariness of strangers, sleeping always with your kit hugged tight in your arms. All the people hungry, all the landscapes war-broken and all of them alien. Erik lost track of time. He had written that he was on the way, but he hadn't been able to guess the day he would arrive.

So, of course, there'd been no one at the station to meet him. There were no familiar faces in the bomb-shattered streets. The address his mother had sent was hard to find, away from the centre of the city.

Yet he got there at last, pushed open the heavy door that

led from the street, and paused.

Someone had swept the stairs very clean, and as he climbed them Erik could smell cooking. Potato pancakes, the sort he had eaten as a little boy, with apple sauce or a sausage or a dollop of sour cream. Hans, if he could get it, used to like them best with cheese.

'Hans, I'm back,' said Erik.

As he climbed past each floor there were quiet, closed doors. At one he heard a baby cry, and from another there was the sound of a static-bothered radio. Then he was on the fourth flight, the last flight, and there were voices.

Familiar voices, that chattered, and then paused.

They'd heard his footsteps on the stairs.

'It's me,' called Erik, setting down his armload of packages, and then, with a catch in his throat because the silence on the other side of the door had grown so long. 'It's only me. It's Erik.'

The door was flung open and they hauled him into a room filled with light. There was a large grey cat, a table set for supper, and an album of fairy tale cigarette cards lying open on a chair. There was Frieda's screech of delight, his mother's joyful, 'Come here! Come here!' and an explosion of miniature firecracker sounds, 'Tck! Tck! Tck!'

'Kleine Oma, see, it's Erik!' shouted Frieda, prancing with excitement. 'Tante Anna, did you know? Erik, Erik, you came back!'

'Frieda!' said Erik, turning to hug thin, long-legged Frieda. 'Fraulein Trisk. Oh, Fraulein Trisk, I thought of you so often.

Wait, I'll fetch what I brought you!'

'Presents!' exclaimed Frieda, and Erik, returning with his packages, really had managed presents. Tinned meat and a bag of rice, a box of dried egg. Chocolate for Frieda, a package of coffee for his mother, and something he'd bought at a stall by the train station in Paris, and clutched to his chest all the way to Berlin.

'Oh,' said Fraulein Trisk. 'Oh,' and she looked up at Erik's mother. 'Oh,' she said to her. 'Look, a new fern, green as a forest.'

The new apartment was very small. A room with two narrow beds for Fraulein Trisk and Erik's mother. A curtained alcove for Frieda that opened from the kitchen, which was also the living room. Erik, Frieda observed, would have to sleep under the kitchen table.

'That will be no trouble,' said Erik, 'I slept on a luggage trolley in Paris.'

'No, you didn't!'

'Yes, I did. There it was, all flat and empty. There I was, in need of a bed. In England I slept in a bus.'

'All night?'

'No, but all one afternoon. I didn't mean to. I just closed my eyes for a little minute and the next thing I knew I was at the bus depot and there was a whole crowd of people looking down at me.'

'What did they say?'

'They asked, "What are you doing here?"'

'What *were* you doing there?'

'It's such a long story, Frieda. Before I was sent to Canada I had a parcel from the people who had helped me when my plane came down. The ones who were there at the time, and the surgeon who saved my arm . . .' Erik paused and laughed. 'And an old lady who lived nearby. She was a friend of theirs. She put in a big bar of yellow soap . . .'

'Useful,' said his mother, nodding. Two years after the war had ended, a bar of soap was still a thing of value in Berlin.

'Yes,' agreed Erik. 'And she wrote a message on it too. Here . . .'

From the breast pocket of his jacket Erik pulled a bundle of papers. Letters. An ancient ticket to Berlin Zoo. Battered photographs in black and white. Frieda flicked through them and said, 'No picture of me. Tante Anna and I sent you one, I remember, two Christmases ago. Both of us together. Did you lose it?'

'Sorry, Frieda. I gave it away.'

'Erik!'

'You'll not mind when I explain. Look, this is what I wanted to show you. The message from the soap.'

Erik held out a scrap of yellow soap wrapper, with careful letters in old-fashioned handwriting.

'I kept it because it was so kind,' he said. 'It made me smile. It's in English of course, but I'll translate. It says: *One fine day you come back and see us properly, young man!*'

'In Canada, I often wondered if I could really do that,' he continued, 'find the people who had helped me, I mean. Then

274

I heard that to get back to Germany I had to travel by England, so I thought perhaps I could make a detour. If I could find the hospital where they took me I hoped it would be a start. In the end it was easier than that. When I reached the city, I caught a bus and fell asleep, like I told you . . .'

'And when you woke up, there were all the people,' prompted Frieda. 'Saying "What are you doing here?"'

'Exactly. And as soon as I started to explain, one of them stepped forward and said, "You're German, aren't you?"'

'Oh, no!' said Frieda, clutching her hands to her mouth.

'I know. But it was all right. He said, "From Berlin." So I said, "Yes, from Berlin, how did you guess?" and he laughed and said, "I know someone who talks just like you."'

His mother suddenly gasped.

'And that's how I found . . .'

Erik's face gave him away, so alight was his smile.

'HANS!' shrieked Frieda.

'Hans!' said Erik's mother. 'Oh, my dear heart! Oh, Erik! Is he safe? Is he well?'

It was eight years since they'd last seen Hans, more than six since they had heard any word of him.

'Yes, yes,' said Erik. 'He's safe and well. He was badly hurt, but he got better.'

'And you met him? You spoke to him?'

'Just for an hour at the end of the day. He's based in a camp, still waiting to be repatriated. They send work teams into the city, clearing the bomb sites, and that's where I met him.'

'How did you know the way?'

'He took me. Will. The person from the bus. He was very kind.'

'And did Hans know you straight away?' asked his mother.

'Yes. I said, "Hello, Hans," and he looked at me and said, very slowly, "Erik? Erik? Well."'

Erik paused, remembering what had come next. It had been oddly awkward. He'd wanted to grab Hans, fling his arms round his shoulders like they'd done when they were boys. But instead he'd just nodded and said, 'Yes. Well, Hans.'

'They're all lost,' Hans had said blankly. 'At home. All lost.'

'No!' he'd exclaimed. 'No, Hans. Not Frieda.'

'Not Frieda?' Hans had repeated.

'Frieda is with my mother.'

'Frieda is with your mother? Safe with your mother?'

'Yes.'

'You're sure of that?'

'Yes. Yes.' Suddenly Erik had remembered, fumbled in his pocket, found the photograph they'd sent him two Christmases ago. Hans took it and stared and then he cried out to everyone around, the people he was working with, the people in the street:

'My little sister is with his mother! *Meine kleine schwester ist bei seiner mutter!*' He'd seized Erik and hugged him then, held him tight and shouted again, 'My little sister is with his mother! *Meine kleine schwester ist bei seiner mutter!*' louder each time, tears rolling down his cheeks.

'He was overjoyed to hear you were here with Tante Anna and Kleine Oma,' Erik told Frieda. 'He didn't believe it until I gave him your photograph.'

'Will he come back to Berlin?'

'Yes, as soon as he possibly can.'

'We had one letter years ago,' said Erik's mother. 'I wrote when his parents died, but we had no reply. Of course, we moved around after we left Berlin . . . He knows about his parents?'

'Yes. And Lisa.' Erik was quiet for a moment. Lisa, always arguing, always hoping. Lisa in the snow. 'Yes, he knew,' he continued. 'He had your letter. But he could find out no more. With help from the Red Cross he managed to contact our old teacher, you remember Herr Schmidt? But Herr Schmidt could give no news of any of you.'

'Poor, poor Hans,' said Erik's mother.

'Not too poor any more,' said Erik. 'Not now he has Frieda, and also . . .' Erik paused, 'and also Ruby.'

'And *who*?' asked Frieda, instantly suspicious.

'Ruby. Ruby is the girl who saw his parachute open, and went to look for him.'

'And did she help rescue you, too?'

'Yes, she and Kate together.'

'You met the girl Kate as well?' asked his mother.

'She drove down with her father when they heard I was in England. He was the doctor who fixed my shoulder.'

'Of course, of course,' said his mother. 'But first, tell us about Hans.'

'Yes. Hans comes first. Ruby never lost contact with him. Hans visits their home sometimes, since it's been allowed.'

Frieda was watching him.

'Frieda, I have to tell you something very important about Ruby. Hans said I must.'

'Why did he?'

'Because he's going to marry her.'

'MARRY HER?' shouted Frieda, and fell flat on the floor.

'Tck, tck,' said Fraulein Trisk. 'You are a very noisy girl, Frieda. How can you be so surprised at a happy ending, after all those fairy tales you read?'

'Is she nice?' demanded Frieda from the floor.

'Yes.'

'Pretty?'

'Very.'

'Does she like cats?'

'Yes.'

'How do you know?'

'She invited me to visit. Her family were very good to me. They have two cats named Sooty and Paddle.'

'English names,' said Frieda.

'Very nice cats,' said Erik.

'Oh, well,' said Frieda. 'I suppose he'd better marry her then.'

The lovely laughter of home.

'And you, Erik,' said his mother at last. 'What are your plans now?'

'We have to start again,' said Erik, stretching and running

his hands through his curly brown hair. 'We have to fix so many things.'

'The zoo?' asked Frieda. 'They say at school one day they will rebuild the zoo. Please fix the zoo, Erik. Then you can work there, and take care of all the animals, and Hans can help.'

'No, no,' said Erik, smiling down at her. 'Hans always had other plans. I was to work at the zoo, but he was going to have a coffee stall outside the gates and sell apple strudel and almond cake and hot chocolate and lemonade. We arranged it years ago.'

'Dreamers,' said his mother, lovingly.

'Tck tck, who knows?' said Fraulein Trisk. 'Some dreams come true. You were a good boy, Erik, except that time you lost those mittens. You were our little sugar rose.'

'Erik,' exclaimed Frieda, 'a little sugar rose!'

'And Hans was Dumpling Boy,' remembered Erik's mother.

'And what am I?' asked Frieda.

'You are our shining girl,' said Erik's mother, hugging her.

But for Erik, so long away, they were all shining at that moment. It was June, and the evening light was apricot-gold, streaming in through the high window. He pushed it open to look out over the city.

'Long ago, I had three small birds,' he told Frieda. 'They'd fallen from their nest, and I kept them safe in my winter hat, which was never the same again. When they were big enough they flew away. But . . . do you see?'

All over the rooftops of Berlin, the broken rooftops and the whole, there were swallows weaving sky trails.

'They're back again,' said Erik.

'Do they always come back?' asked Frieda, leaning over the windowsill to look.

'Careful,' said Erik. 'Don't fall out! Yes, always, every spring.'

FAMILY TREES

Penrose Family

This family also includes Rupert, as honorary uncle to Janey, Bea, Simon and Tod, Charlie and Kate (although he was in fact no relation at all) and, as Grandfather often gracelessly remarked, a cuckoo in the nest.

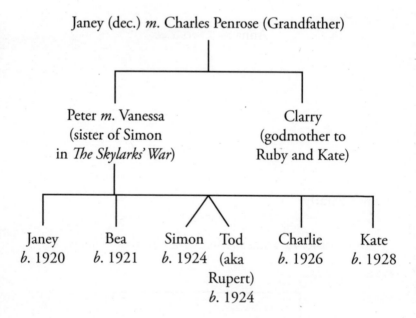

Janey (dec.) *m*. Charles Penrose (Grandfather)

Peter *m*. Vanessa (sister of Simon in *The Skylarks' War*)

Clarry (godmother to Ruby and Kate)

Janey *b*. 1920

Bea *b*. 1921

Simon *b*. 1924

Tod (aka Rupert) *b*. 1924

Charlie *b*. 1926

Kate *b*. 1928

Ruby's Family

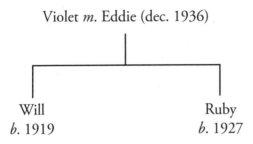

Violet *m.* Eddie (dec. 1936)

Will
b. 1919

Ruby
b. 1927

Erik's Family

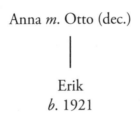

Anna *m.* Otto (dec.)

Erik
b. 1921

Hans's Family

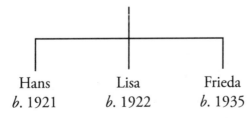

Hans's mother *m.* Hans's father (elder brother of Uncle Karl)

Hans
b. 1921

Lisa
b. 1922

Frieda
b. 1935

GLOSSARY

Words used:

French:

Je ne sais pas	I don't know
Joie de vivre	A French phrase meaning (literally) Joy of life. Which might translate as happiness in being alive.

German:

Mutti	Mummy, mum
Vati	Daddy, dad
Oma	Grandmother, Grandma
Kleine Oma	Little Grandma
Heil	Hail (a German greeting which also includes the meaning of 'good health/ blessings to you')
Heil Hitler	Compulsory Nazi greeting
Schwalben	Swallows
Kleine Schwalben	Little swallows

Luftwaffe	German airforce
Herr	Mr
Frau	Mrs
Fraulein	Miss
Reichsmark	German unit of currency between 1924 and 1948 (when if was replaced with the Deutschmark). *1 RM* was the price of a ticket to Berlin Zoo

British money:

British money was pounds, shillings, and pennies.

There were twelve pennies to a shilling, and twenty shillings to a pound.

Half a crown was a large silver coin worth two shillings and sixpence.

In 1940 a shilling would buy a loaf of bread, a pint of milk, and a Mars bar.

Rationing during the war:

Rationing was a way of making sure that everyone got a fair share of food. It began almost as soon as war was declared. Very high value things like petrol were the first to be rationed. A year or two later, petrol could not be bought at all, unless you had a good reason. A doctor, for instance, would be allowed a certain amount of petrol so that he could visit his patients.

As the war went on, more and more things were added to the list of rationed items. Foods, like meat and cheese and butter and sugar, were possible to buy, but in smaller and smaller quantities as time went on. Anything imported, such as tea or coffee, was rationed.

Schoolchildren got a hot meal at school, factories had works canteens. These things were not rationed. Nor were fish and chips! Although the portions were very small. That was partly a morale boost – the government wanted every worker to be able to have a hot meal if possible.

Rationing continued for several years after the war. This was because Europe was now in a desperate state of hunger. In Berlin, after the war, schools were set up by the US and one of the attractions to children like Frieda who went to them was their mug of warm soup in the middle of the day. It saved the lives of many children. The hope was to give them about 270 calories, and to include protein in the form of peas or beans or meat. For thousands and thousands of children, it was their main meal of the day.

Evacuee children in Britain:

Not all children were evacuated from their homes during World War II. It depended on where you lived. The country was divided into high-risk, medium-risk, and low-risk areas. In a medium-risk area, you could probably live at home. High-risk area children were sent to low-risk area places.

Plymouth, with its huge naval dockyards, was high risk, and the city suffered very badly during the war. Oxford, on the other hand, was low risk, and in fact was never bombed at all.

That is why Ruby was evacuated to live with Kate and her family.

AUTHOR'S NOTE
The World Behind the Story

Kate and Ruby, Erik and Hans, were of the generation of young people born between two wars. That is World War I (1914–1918) and World War II (1939–1945).

In the days when Kate and Ruby grew up, there were less cars in England. Money was different: pennies and shillings, half crowns and sixpences and threepenny bits. After primary age, girls went to girls' schools, and boys went to boys' schools. There were no antibiotics, so if you were like Kate, always catching things, you were probably fussed over with umbrellas and advice and extra warm vests. World War I was over, but not forgotten. What everyone wanted was for there not to be another. My own grandfather fought in World War I and he survived it, and came home, and he could just about bear it (as long as he never had to talk about it) but what he could not bear was the thought of his own two sons having to go through the same.

Probably everyone felt pretty much like that.

In Germany at this time the shock of losing World War I was still affecting every part of society. There was great poverty, and a feeling that justice had not been done. People wanted change: their national pride to be restored, and stronger leadership. Adolf Hitler promised these things, and he was the leader of the Nazi party, which became stronger and more powerful, year after year.

At first it gave people hope. There were more jobs, and less poverty. There was money for education, and industry. There were things to be proud of: a healthier population, investments in arts and science (which included Erik's beloved Berlin Zoo). But at the same time, growing just as quickly, was the terrible darkness of the persecution of the Jewish people. It is really not my story to write, because I am not Jewish, but also it's not my story to ignore, because while one part of society can say of another part, 'They are not like us and we don't want them,' no one, none of us, should forget what happened before when that was said, and what must never happen again.

ACKNOWLEDGEMENTS

There would be no books without editors, and I have the best. Thank you Sam, and the lovely publishing team at Macmillan. You have been unfailingly supportive. To Venetia, who did the editing, and who suggested I put together a set of family trees for each main character. Thank you, Karen Wojtyla at Simon & Schuster in New York, especially for loving Pax.

Thanks also to Fraser Crichton, for the most helpful copy edit I've had in 30+ years of writing.

Molly, my brilliant agent, Hans made it because of you.

British Library in St Pancras, I salute you. Your staff were magnificent before lockdown, but after that time, when I thought, 'Now I'm on my own,' I wasn't. Thank you for the shipping lists from Plymouth, and the maps of Berlin streets, and the articles discussing the historic price of rubies.

I wrote this book through grim pandemic days. I couldn't have done it without my lovely kids, working far harder than I, in hospitals and single-bedrooms-turned-into-call-centres, locked down in London and Manchester. Thank you, Jim and Bella, for keeping me going.

ABOUT THE AUTHOR

Hilary McKay won the Costa Children's Book Award for *The Skylarks' War*, the Guardian Fiction Prize for *The Exiles*, and the Smarties and the Whitbread Award for *The Exiles in Love* and *Saffy's Angel* respectively. She is also the author of *Straw Into Gold*, *A Time of Green Magic* and *The Swallows' Flight*, a companion novel to *The Skylarks' War*, among many critically-acclaimed titles. Hilary studied Botany and Zoology at the University of St Andrews, and worked as a biochemist before the draw of the pen became too strong and she decided to become a full-time writer. Hilary lives in Derbyshire with her family.

everybody
lies

everybody
lies

What the Internet
Can Tell Us About
Who We Really Are

Seth Stephens-Davidowitz

B L O O M S B U R Y
LONDON · OXFORD · NEW YORK · NEW DELHI · SYDNEY

Bloomsbury Publishing
An imprint of Bloomsbury Publishing Plc

50 Bedford Square   1385 Broadway
London   New York
WC1B 3DP   NY 10018
UK   USA

www.bloomsbury.com

BLOOMSBURY and the Diana logo are trademarks of Bloomsbury Publishing Plc

First published in 2017 in the United States by HarperCollins Publishers, New York

First published in Great Britain 2017

© Seth Stephens-Davidowitz, 2017

Designed by Suet Yee Chong

Seth Stephens-Davidowitz has asserted his right under the Copyright,
Designs and Patents Act, 1988, to be identified as Author of this work.

British Library Cataloguing-in-Publication Data
A catalogue record for this book is available from the British Library.

ISBN: HB: 978-1-4088-9471-2
       TPB: 978-1-4088-9470-5
       ePub: 978-1-4088-9469-9

2 4 6 8 10 9 7 5 3 1

Printed and bound in Great Britain by CPI Group (UK) Ltd, Croydon CR0 4YY

To find out more about our authors and books visit www.bloomsbury.com.
Here you will find extracts, author interviews, details of forthcoming
events and the option to sign up for our newsletters.

To Mom and Dad

CONTENTS

FOREWORD

Ever since philosophers speculated about a "cerebroscope," a mythical device that would display a person's thoughts on a screen, social scientists have been looking for tools to expose the workings of human nature. During my career as an experimental psychologist, different ones have gone in and out of fashion, and I've tried them all—rating scales, reaction times, pupil dilation, functional neuroimaging, even epilepsy patients with implanted electrodes who were happy to while away the hours in a language experiment while waiting to have a seizure.

Yet none of these methods provides an unobstructed view into the mind. The problem is a savage tradeoff. Human thoughts are complex propositions; unlike Woody Allen speed-reading *War and Peace,* we don't just think "It was about some Russians." But propositions in all their tangled multidimensional glory are difficult for a scientist to analyze. Sure, when people pour their hearts out, we apprehend the richness of their stream of consciousness, but monologues are not an ideal dataset for testing hypotheses. On the other hand, if we concentrate on measures that are easily quantifiable, like people's reaction time to words, or their skin response to pictures, we can do the statistics, but we've pureed the complex texture of cognition into a single number. Even the most sophisticated neuroimaging methodologies can tell us how a thought is splayed out in 3-D space, but not what the thought consists of.

As if the tradeoff between tractability and richness weren't bad enough, scientists of human nature are vexed by the Law of Small Numbers—Amos Tversky and Daniel Kahneman's name for the fallacy of thinking that the traits of a population will be reflected in any sample, no matter how small. Even the most numerate scientists have woefully defective intuitions about how many subjects one really needs in a study before one can abstract away from the random quirks and bumps and generalize to all Americans, to say nothing of *Homo sapiens*. It's all the iffier when the sample is gathered by convenience, such as by offering beer money to the sophomores in our courses.

This book is about a whole new way of studying the mind. Big Data from internet searches and other online responses are not a cerebroscope, but Seth Stephens-Davidowitz shows that they offer an unprecedented peek into people's psyches. At the privacy of their keyboards, people confess the strangest things, sometimes (as in dating sites or searches for professional advice) because they have real-life consequences, at other times precisely because they *don't* have consequences: people can unburden themselves of some wish or fear without a real person reacting in dismay or worse. Either way, the people are not just pressing a button or turning a knob, but keying in any of trillions of sequences of characters to spell out their thoughts in all their explosive, combinatorial vastness. Better still, they lay down these digital traces in a form that is easy to aggregate and analyze. They come from all walks of life. They can take part in unobtrusive experiments which vary the stimuli and tabulate the responses in real time. And they happily supply these data in gargantuan numbers.

Everybody Lies is more than a proof of concept. Time and again my preconceptions about my country and my species were turned upside-down by Stephens-Davidowitz's discoveries. Where did Donald Trump's unexpected support come from? When Ann Landers asked her readers in 1976 whether they regretted having children and was shocked to find that a majority did, was she misled by an unrepresentative, self-selected sample? Is the internet to blame for that redundantly named crisis of the late 2010s, the "filter bubble"? What triggers hate crimes? Do people seek jokes to cheer themselves up? And though I like to think that nothing can shock me, I was shocked aplenty by what the internet reveals about human sexuality—including the discovery that every month a certain number of women search for "humping stuffed animals." No experiment using reaction time or pupil dilation or functional neuroimaging could ever have turned up that fact.

Everybody will enjoy *Everybody Lies*. With unflagging curiosity and an endearing wit, Stephens-Davidowitz points to a new path for social science in the twenty-first century. With this endlessly fascinating window into human obsessions, who needs a cerebroscope?

—Steven Pinker, 2017

EVERYBODY LIES

INTRODUCTION

THE OUTLINES OF A REVOLUTION

Surely he would lose, they said.

In the 2016 Republican primaries, polling experts concluded that Donald Trump didn't stand a chance. After all, Trump had insulted a variety of minority groups. The polls and their interpreters told us few Americans approved of such outrages.

Most polling experts at the time thought that Trump would lose in the general election. Too many likely voters said they were put off by his manner and views.

But there were some clues that Trump might actually win both the primaries and the general election—on the internet.

I am an internet data expert. Every day, I track the digital trails that people leave as they make their way across the web. From the buttons or keys we click or tap, I try to understand what we really want, what we will really do, and who we really are. Let me explain how I got started on this unusual path.

The story begins—and this seems like ages ago—with the 2008 presidential election and a long-debated question in social science: How significant is racial prejudice in America?

Barack Obama was running as the first African-American presidential nominee of a major party. He won—rather easily. And the polls suggested that race was not a factor in how Americans voted. Gallup, for example, conducted numerous polls before and after Obama's first election. Their conclusion? American voters largely did not care that Barack Obama was black. Shortly after the election, two well-known professors at the University of California, Berkeley pored through other survey-based data, using more sophisticated data-mining techniques. They reached a similar conclusion.

And so, during Obama's presidency, this became the conventional wisdom in many parts of the media and in large swaths of the academy. The sources that the media and social scientists have used for eighty-plus years to understand the world told us that the overwhelming majority of Americans did not care that Obama was black when judging whether he should be their president.

This country, long soiled by slavery and Jim Crow laws, seemed finally to have stopped judging people by the color of their skin. This seemed to suggest that racism was on its last legs in America. In fact, some pundits even declared that we lived in a post-racial society.

In 2012, I was a graduate student in economics, lost in life, burnt-out in my field, and confident, even cocky, that I had a pretty good understanding of how the world worked, of what people thought and cared about in the twenty-first century. And when it came to this issue of prejudice, I allowed myself to believe, based on everything I had read in psychology and political science, that explicit racism was limited to a small percentage of Americans—the majority of them conservative Republicans, most of them living in the deep South.

Then, I found Google Trends.

Google Trends, a tool that was released with little fanfare in 2009, tells users how frequently any word or phrase has been searched in different locations at different times. It was advertised as a fun tool—perhaps enabling friends to discuss which celebrity was most popular or what fashion was suddenly hot. The earliest versions included a playful admonishment that people "wouldn't want to write your PhD dissertation" with the data, which immediately motivated me to write my dissertation with it.*

At the time, Google search data didn't seem to be a proper source of information for "serious" academic research. Unlike

---

* Google Trends has been a source of much of my data. However, since it only allows you to compare the relative frequency of different searches but does not report the absolute number of any particular search, I have usually supplemented it with Google AdWords, which reports exactly how frequently every search is made. In most cases I have also been able to sharpen the picture with the help of my own Trends-based algorithm, which I describe in my dissertation, "Essays Using Google Data," and in my *Journal of Public Economics* paper, "The Cost of Racial Animus on a Black Candidate: Evidence Using Google Search Data." The dissertation, a link to the paper, and a complete explanation of the data and code used in all the original research presented in this book are available on my website, sethsd.com.

surveys, Google search data wasn't created as a way to help us understand the human psyche. Google was invented so that people could learn about the world, not so researchers could learn about people. But it turns out the trails we leave as we seek knowledge on the internet are tremendously revealing.

In other words, people's search for information is, in itself, information. When and where they search for facts, quotes, jokes, places, persons, things, or help, it turns out, can tell us a lot more about what they really think, really desire, really fear, and really do than anyone might have guessed. This is especially true since people sometimes don't so much query Google as confide in it: "I hate my boss." "I am drunk." "My dad hit me."

The everyday act of typing a word or phrase into a compact, rectangular white box leaves a small trace of truth that, when multiplied by millions, eventually reveals profound realities. The first word I typed in Google Trends was "God." I learned that the states that make the most Google searches mentioning "God" were Alabama, Mississippi, and Arkansas—the Bible Belt. And those searches are most frequently on Sundays. None of which was surprising, but it was intriguing that search data could reveal such a clear pattern. I tried "Knicks," which it turns out is Googled most in New York City. Another no-brainer. Then I typed in my name. "We're sorry," Google Trends informed me. "There is not enough search volume" to show these results. Google Trends, I learned, will provide data only when lots of people make the same search.

But the power of Google searches is not that they can tell us that God is popular down South, the Knicks are popular in New York City, or that I'm not popular anywhere. Any survey could tell you that. The power in Google data is that people tell the giant search engine things they might not tell anyone else.

Take, for example, sex (a subject I will investigate in much greater detail later in this book). Surveys cannot be trusted to tell us the truth about our sex lives. I analyzed data from the General Social Survey, which is considered one of the most influential and authoritative sources for information on Americans' behaviors. According to that survey, when it comes to heterosexual sex, women say they have sex, on average, fifty-five times per year, using a condom 16 percent of the time. This adds up to about 1.1 billion condoms used per year. But heterosexual men say they use 1.6 billion condoms every year. Those numbers, by definition, would have to be the same. So who is telling the truth, men or women?

Neither, it turns out. According to Nielsen, the global information and measurement company that tracks consumer behavior, fewer than 600 million condoms are sold every year. So everyone is lying; the only difference is by how much.

The lying is in fact widespread. Men who have never been married claim to use on average twenty-nine condoms per year. This would add up to more than the total number of condoms sold in the United States to married and single people combined. Married people probably exaggerate how much sex they have, too. On average, married men under sixty-five tell surveys they have sex once a week. Only 1 percent say they have gone the past year without sex. Married women report having a little less sex but not much less.

Google searches give a far less lively—and, I argue, far more accurate—picture of sex during marriage. On Google, the top complaint about a marriage is not having sex. Searches for "sexless marriage" are three and a half times more common than "unhappy marriage" and eight times more common than "loveless marriage." Even unmarried couples complain somewhat frequently about not having sex. Google searches for "sexless relationship" are second only to searches for "abusive relationship." (This data, I should emphasize, is all presented anonymously. Google, of course, does not report data about any particular individual's searches.)

And Google searches presented a picture of America that was strikingly different from that post-racial utopia sketched out by the surveys. I remember when I first typed "nigger" into Google Trends. Call me naïve. But given how toxic the word is, I fully expected this to be a low-volume search. Boy, was I wrong. In the United States, the word "nigger"—or its plural, "niggers"—was included in roughly the same number of searches as the word "migraine(s)," "economist," and "Lakers." I wondered if searches for rap lyrics were skewing the results? Nope. The word used in rap songs is almost always "nigga(s)." So what was the motivation of Americans searching for "nigger"? Frequently, they were looking for jokes mocking African-Americans. In fact, 20 percent of searches with the word "nigger" also included the word "jokes." Other common searches included "stupid niggers" and "I hate niggers."

There were millions of these searches every year. A large number of Americans were, in the privacy of their own homes, making shockingly racist inquiries. The more I researched, the more disturbing the information got.

On Obama's first election night, when most of the commentary focused on praise of Obama and acknowledgment of the historic nature of his election, roughly one in every hundred Google searches that included the word "Obama" also included "kkk" or "nigger(s)." Maybe that doesn't sound so high, but think of the thousands of nonracist reasons to Google this young outsider with a charming family about to take over the world's most powerful job. On election night, searches and sign-ups for Stormfront, a white nationalist site with surprisingly high popularity in the United States, were more than ten times higher than normal. In some states, there were more searches for "nigger president" than "first black president."

There was a darkness and hatred that was hidden from the traditional sources but was quite apparent in the searches that people made.

Those searches are hard to reconcile with a society in which racism is a small factor. In 2012 I knew of Donald J. Trump mostly as a businessman and reality show performer. I had no more idea than anyone else that he would, four years later, be a serious presidential candidate. But those ugly searches are not hard to reconcile with the success of a candidate who—in his attacks on immigrants, in his angers and resentments—often played to people's worst inclinations.

The Google searches also told us that much of what we thought about the location of racism was wrong. Surveys and conventional wisdom placed modern racism predominantly in the South and mostly among Republicans. But the places with the highest racist search rates included upstate New York, western Pennsylvania, eastern Ohio, industrial Michigan and rural Illinois, along with West Virginia, southern Louisiana, and Mississippi. The true divide, Google search data suggested, was not

South versus North; it was East versus West. You don't get this sort of thing much west of the Mississippi. And racism was not limited to Republicans. In fact, racist searches were no higher in places with a high percentage of Republicans than in places with a high percentage of Democrats. Google searches, in other words, helped draw a new map of racism in the United States—and this map looked very different from what you may have guessed. Republicans in the South may be more likely to admit to racism. But plenty of Democrats in the North have similar attitudes.

Four years later, this map would prove quite significant in explaining the political success of Trump.

In 2012, I was using this map of racism I had developed using Google searches to reevaluate exactly the role that Obama's race played. The data was clear. In parts of the country with a high number of racist searches, Obama did substantially worse than John Kerry, the white Democratic presidential candidate, had four years earlier. The relationship was not explained by any other factor about these areas, including education levels, age, church attendance, or gun ownership. Racist searches did not predict poor performance for any other Democratic candidate. Only for Obama.

And the results implied a large effect. Obama lost roughly 4 percentage points nationwide just from explicit racism. This was far higher than might have been expected based on any surveys. Barack Obama, of course, was elected and reelected president, helped by some very favorable conditions for Democrats, but he had to overcome quite a bit more than anyone who was relying on traditional data sources—and that was just about everyone—had realized. There were enough racists to help win a primary or tip a general election in a year not so favorable to Democrats.

My study was initially rejected by five academic journals. Many of the peer reviewers, if you will forgive a little disgruntlement, said that it was impossible to believe that so many Americans harbored such vicious racism. This simply did not fit what people had been saying. Besides, Google searches seemed like such a bizarre dataset.

Now that we have witnessed the inauguration of President Donald J. Trump, my finding seems more plausible.

The more I have studied, the more I have learned that Google has lots of information that is missed by the polls that can be helpful in understanding—among many, many other subjects—an election.

There is information on who will actually turn out to vote. More than half of citizens who don't vote tell surveys immediately before an election that they intend to, skewing our estimation of turnout, whereas Google searches for "how to vote" or "where to vote" weeks before an election can accurately predict which parts of the country are going to have a big showing at the polls.

There might even be information on who they will vote for. Can we really predict which candidate people will vote for just based on what they search? Clearly, we can't just study which candidates are searched for most frequently. Many people search for a candidate because they love him. A similar number of people search for a candidate because they hate him. That said, Stuart Gabriel, a professor of finance at the University of California, Los Angeles, and I have found a surprising clue about which way people are planning to vote. A large percentage of election-related searches contain queries with both candidates' names. During the 2016 election between Trump and Hillary Clinton, some people searched for "Trump Clinton polls." Others looked for highlights from the "Clinton Trump debate." In fact, 12 percent of search queries with "Trump" also included the word "Clinton." More than one-quarter of search queries with "Clinton" also included the word "Trump."

We have found that these seemingly neutral searches may actually give us some clues to which candidate a person supports.

How? The order in which the candidates appear. Our research suggests that a person is significantly more likely to put the candidate they support first in a search that includes both candidates' names.

In the previous three elections, the candidate who appeared first in more searches received the most votes. More interesting, the order the candidates were searched was predictive of which way a particular state would go.

The order in which candidates are searched also seems to contain information that the polls can miss. In the 2012 election between Obama and Republican Mitt Romney, Nate Silver, the virtuoso statistician and journalist, accurately predicted the result in all fifty states. However, we found that in states that listed Romney before Obama in searches most frequently, Romney actually did better than Silver had predicted. In states that most frequently listed Obama before Romney, Obama did better than Silver had predicted.

This indicator could contain information that polls miss

because voters are either lying to themselves or uncomfortable revealing their true preferences to pollsters. Perhaps if they claimed that they were undecided in 2012, but were consistently searching for "Romney Obama polls," "Romney Obama debate," and "Romney Obama election," they were planning to vote for Romney all along.

So did Google predict Trump? Well, we still have a lot of work to do—and I'll have to be joined by lots more researchers—before we know how best to use Google data to predict election results. This is a new science, and we only have a few elections for which this data exists. I am certainly not saying we are at the point—or ever will be at the point—where we can throw out public opinion polls completely as a tool for helping us predict elections.

But there were definitely portents, at many points, on the internet that Trump might do better than the polls were predicting.

During the general election, there were clues that the electorate might be a favorable one for Trump. Black Americans told polls they would turn out in large numbers to oppose Trump. But Google searches for information on voting in heavily black areas were way down. On election day, Clinton would be hurt by low black turnout.

There were even signs that supposedly undecided voters were going Trump's way. Gabriel and I found that there were more searches for "Trump Clinton" than "Clinton Trump" in key states in the Midwest that Clinton was expected to win. Indeed, Trump owed his election to the fact that he sharply outperformed his polls there.

But the major clue, I would argue, that Trump might prove a successful candidate—in the primaries, to begin with—was all that secret racism that my Obama study had uncovered. The Google searches revealed a darkness and hatred among a meaningful number of Americans that pundits, for many years, missed. Search data revealed that we lived in a very different society from the one academics and journalists, relying on polls, thought that we lived in. It revealed a nasty, scary, and widespread rage that was waiting for a candidate to give voice to it.

People frequently lie—to themselves and to others. In 2008, Americans told surveys that they no longer cared about race. Eight years later, they elected as president Donald J. Trump, a man who retweeted a false claim that black people are responsible for the majority of murders of white Americans, defended his supporters for roughing up a Black Lives Matters protester at one of his rallies, and hesitated in repudiating support from a former leader of the Ku Klux Klan. The same hidden racism that hurt Barack Obama helped Donald Trump.

Early in the primaries, Nate Silver famously claimed that there was virtually no chance that Trump would win. As the primaries progressed and it became increasingly clear that Trump had widespread support, Silver decided to look at the data to see if he could understand what was going on. How could Trump possibly be doing so well?

Silver noticed that the areas where Trump performed best made for an odd map. Trump performed well in parts of the Northeast and industrial Midwest, as well as the South. He performed notably worse out West. Silver looked for variables to try to explain this map. Was it unemployment? Was it religion? Was it gun ownership? Was it rates of immigration? Was it opposition to Obama?

Silver found that the single factor that best correlated with Donald Trump's support in the Republican primaries was that

Racist Search Rate

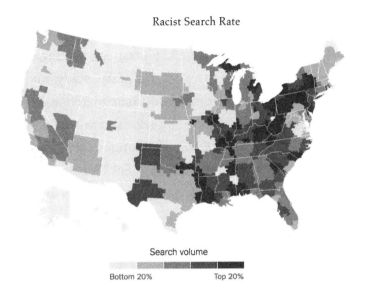

Search volume

Bottom 20%   Top 20%

Donald Trump Support in Republican Primary

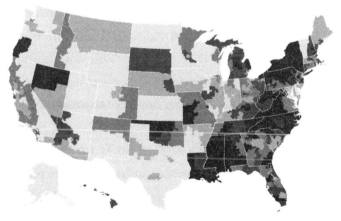

Republican voters estimated to support Mr. Trump

28%   31%   34%   37%

measure I had discovered four years earlier. Areas that supported Trump in the largest numbers were those that made the most Google searches for "nigger."

I have spent just about every day of the past four years analyzing Google data. This included a stint as a data scientist at Google, which hired me after learning about my racism research. And I continue to explore this data as an opinion writer and data journalist for the *New York Times*. The revelations have kept coming. Mental illness; human sexuality; child abuse; abortion; advertising; religion; health. Not exactly small topics, and this dataset, which didn't exist a couple of decades ago, offered surprising new perspectives on all of them. Economists and other social scientists are always hunting for new sources of data, so let me be blunt: I am now convinced that Google searches are the most important dataset ever collected on the human psyche.

This dataset, however, is not the only tool the internet has delivered for understanding our world. I soon realized there are other digital gold mines as well. I downloaded all of Wikipedia, pored through Facebook profiles, and scraped Stormfront. In addition, PornHub, one of the largest pornographic sites on the internet, gave me its complete data on the searches and video views of anonymous people around the world. In other words, I have taken a very deep dive into what is now called Big Data. Further, I have interviewed dozens of others—academics, data journalists, and entrepreneurs—who are also exploring these new realms. Many of their studies will be discussed here.

But first, a confession: I am not going to give a precise definition of what Big Data is. Why? Because it's an inherently vague concept. How big is big? Are 18,462 observations Small Data and 18,463 observations Big Data? I prefer to take an inclusive view of what qualifies: while most of the data I fiddle with is from the internet, I will discuss other sources, too. We are living through an explosion in the amount and quality of all kinds of available information. Much of the new information flows from Google and social media. Some of it is a product of digitization of information that was previously hidden away in cabinets and files. Some of it is from increased resources devoted to market research. Some of the studies discussed in this book don't use huge datasets at all but instead just employ a new and creative approach to data—approaches that are crucial in an era overflowing with information.

So why exactly is Big Data so powerful? Think of all the information that is scattered online on a given day—we have a number, in fact, for just how much information there is. On an average day in the early part of the twenty-first century, human beings generate 2.5 million trillion bytes of data.

And these bytes are clues.

A woman is bored on a Thursday afternoon. She Googles for some more "funny clean jokes." She checks her email. She signs on to Twitter. She Googles "nigger jokes."

A man is feeling blue. He Googles for "depression symptoms" and "depression stories." He plays a game of solitaire.

A woman sees the announcement of her friend getting engaged on Facebook. The woman, who is single, blocks the friend.

A man takes a break from Googling about the NFL and rap music to ask the search engine a question: "Is it normal to have dreams about kissing men?"

A woman clicks on a BuzzFeed story showing the "15 cutest cats."

A man sees the same story about cats. But on his screen it is called "15 most adorable cats." He doesn't click.

A woman Googles "Is my son a genius?"

A man Googles "how to get my daughter to lose weight."

A woman is on a vacation with her six best female friends. All her friends keep saying how much fun they're having. She sneaks off to Google "loneliness when away from husband."

A man, the previous woman's husband, is on a vacation with his six best male friends. He sneaks off to Google to type "signs your wife is cheating."

Some of this data will include information that would otherwise never be admitted to anybody. If we aggregate it all, keep it anonymous to make sure we never know about the fears, desires, and behaviors of any specific individuals, and add some data science, we start to get a new look at human beings—their behaviors, their desires, their natures. In fact, at the risk of sounding grandiose, I have come to believe that the new data increasingly available in our digital age will radically expand our understanding of humankind. The microscope showed us there is more to a drop of pond water than we think we see. The telescope showed us there is more to the night sky than we think we see. And new, digital data now shows us there is more to human society than we think we see. It may be our era's microscope or telescope—making possible important, even revolutionary insights.

There is another risk in making such declarations—not just sounding grandiose but also trendy. Many people have been making big claims about the power of Big Data. But they have been short on evidence.

This has inspired Big Data skeptics, of whom there are also many, to dismiss the search for bigger datasets. "I am not saying here that there is no information in Big Data," essayist and statistician Nassim Taleb has written. "There is plenty of information. The problem—the central issue—is that the needle comes in an increasingly larger haystack."

One of the primary goals of this book, then, is to provide the missing evidence of what can be done with Big Data—how we can find the needles, if you will, in those larger and larger haystacks. I hope to provide enough examples of Big Data offering new insights into human psychology and behavior so that you will begin to see the outlines of something truly revolutionary.

"Hold on, Seth," you might be saying right about now. "You're promising a revolution. You're waxing poetic about these big, new datasets. But thus far, you have used all of this amazing, remarkable, breathtaking, groundbreaking data to tell me basically two things: there are plenty of racists in America, and people, particularly men, exaggerate how much sex they have."

I admit sometimes the new data does just confirm the obvious. If you think these findings were obvious, wait until you get to Chapter 4, where I show you clear, unimpeachable evidence from Google searches that men have tremendous concern and insecurity around—wait for it—their penis size.

There is, I would claim, some value in proving things you may have already suspected but had otherwise little evidence for. Suspecting something is one thing. Proving it is another. But if all Big Data could do is confirm your suspicions, it would not be revolutionary. Thankfully, Big Data can do a lot more than that. Time and again, data shows me the world works in precisely the opposite way as I would have guessed. Here are some examples you might find more surprising.

You might think that a major cause of racism is economic insecurity and vulnerability. You might naturally suspect, then, that when people lose their jobs, racism increases. But, actually, neither racist searches nor membership in Stormfront rises when unemployment does.

You might think that anxiety is highest in overeducated big cities. The urban neurotic is a famous stereotype. But Google searches reflecting anxiety—such as "anxiety symptoms" or "anxiety help"—tend to be higher in places with lower levels of education, lower median incomes, and where a larger portion of the population lives in rural areas. There are higher search rates for anxiety in rural, upstate New York than New York City.

You might think that a terrorist attack that kills dozens or hundreds of people would automatically be followed by massive, widespread anxiety. Terrorism, by definition, is supposed to instill a sense of terror. I looked at Google searches reflecting anxiety. I tested how much these searches rose in a country in the days, weeks, and months following every major European or American terrorist attack since 2004. So, on average, how much did anxiety-related searches rise? They didn't. At all.

You might think that people search for jokes more often when they are sad. Many of history's greatest thinkers have claimed that we turn to humor as a release from pain. Humor has long been thought of as a way to cope with the frustrations, the pain, the inevitable disappointments of life. As Charlie Chaplin put it, "Laughter is the tonic, the relief, the surcease from pain."

However, searches for jokes are lowest on Mondays, the day when people report they are most unhappy. They are lowest on cloudy and rainy days. And they plummet after a major tragedy, such as when two bombs killed three and injured hundreds during the 2013 Boston Marathon. People are actually more likely to seek out jokes when things are going well in life than when they aren't.

Sometimes a new dataset reveals a behavior, desire, or concern that I would have never even considered. There are numerous sexual proclivities that fall into this category. For example, did you know that in India the number one search beginning "my husband wants . . ." is "my husband wants me to breastfeed him"? This comment is far more common in India than in other countries. Moreover, porn searches for depictions of women breastfeeding men are four times higher in India and Bangladesh than in any other country in the world. I certainly never would have suspected that before I saw the data.

Further, while the fact that men are obsessed with their penis size may not be too surprising, the biggest bodily insecurity for women, as expressed on Google, is surprising indeed. Based on this new data, the female equivalent of worrying about the size of your penis may be—pausing to build suspense—worrying about whether your vagina smells. Women make nearly as many searches expressing concern about their genitals as men do worrying about theirs. And the top concern women express is its odor—and how they might improve it. I certainly didn't know that before I saw the data.

Sometimes new data reveals cultural differences I had never even contemplated. One example: the very different ways that men around the world respond to their wives being pregnant. In Mexico, the top searches about "my pregnant wife" include "frases de amor para mi esposa embarazada" (words of love to my pregnant wife) and "poemas para mi esposa embarazada" (poems for my pregnant wife). In the United States, the top searches include "my wife is pregnant now what" and "my wife is pregnant what do I do."

But this book is more than a collection of odd facts or one-off studies, though there will be plenty of those. Because these methodologies are so new and are only going to get more powerful, I will lay out some ideas on how they work and what makes them groundbreaking. I will also acknowledge Big Data's limitations.

Some of the enthusiasm for the data revolution's potential has been misplaced. Most of those enamored with Big Data gush about how immense these datasets can get. This obsession with dataset size is not new. Before Google, Amazon, and Facebook, before the phrase "Big Data" existed, a conference was held in Dallas, Texas, on "Large and Complex Datasets." Jerry Friedman, a statistics professor at Stanford who was a colleague of mine when I worked at Google, recalls that 1977 conference. One distinguished statistician would get up to talk. He would explain that he had accumulated an amazing, astonishing five gigabytes of data. The next distinguished statistician would get up to talk. He would begin, "The last speaker had gigabytes. That's nothing. I've got terabytes." The emphasis of the talk, in other words, was on how much information you could accumulate, not what you hoped to do with it, or what questions you planned to answer. "I found it amusing, at the time," Friedman says, that "the thing that you were supposed to be impressed with was how large their dataset is. It still happens."

Too many data scientists today are accumulating massive sets of data and telling us very little of importance—e.g., that the Knicks are popular in New York. Too many businesses are drowning in data. They have lots of terabytes but few major insights. The size of a dataset, I believe, is frequently overrated. There is a subtle, but important, explanation for this. The bigger an effect, the fewer the number of observations necessary to see it. You only need to touch a hot stove once to realize that it's dangerous. You may need to drink coffee thousands of times to determine whether it tends to give you a headache. Which lesson is more important? Clearly, the hot stove, which, because of the intensity of its impact, shows up so quickly, with so little data.

In fact, the smartest Big Data companies are often cutting down their data. At Google, major decisions are based on only a tiny sampling of all their data. You don't always need a ton of data to find important insights. You need the right data. A major reason that Google searches are so valuable is not that there are so many of them; it is that people are so honest in them. People lie to friends, lovers, doctors, surveys, and themselves. But on Google they might share embarrassing information, about, among other things, their sexless marriages, their mental health issues, their insecurities, and their animosity toward black people.

Most important, to squeeze insights out of Big Data, you have to ask the right questions. Just as you can't point a telescope randomly at the night sky and have it discover Pluto for you, you can't download a whole bunch of data and have it discover the secrets of human nature for you. You must look in promising places—Google searches that begin "my husband wants . . ." in India, for example.

This book is going to show how Big Data is best used and explain in detail why it can be so powerful. And along the way, you'll also learn about what I and others have already discovered with it, including:

> How many men are gay?
> Does advertising work?
> Why was American Pharoah a great racehorse?
> Is the media biased?
> Are Freudian slips real?
> Who cheats on their taxes?
> Does it matter where you go to college?
> Can you beat the stock market?
> What's the best place to raise kids?
> What makes a story go viral?
> What should you talk about on a first date if you want a second?

. . . and much, much more.

But before we get to all that, we need to discuss a more basic question: why do we need data at all? And for that, I am going to introduce my grandmother.

PART I

DATA, BIG AND SMALL

1

YOUR FAULTY GUT

If you're thirty-three years old and have attended a few Thanks-givings in a row without a date, the topic of mate choice is likely to arise. And just about everybody will have an opinion.

"Seth needs a crazy girl, like him," my sister says.

"You're crazy! He needs a normal girl, to balance him out," my brother says.

"Seth's not crazy," my mother says.

"You're crazy! Of course, Seth is crazy," my father says.

All of a sudden, my shy, soft-spoken grandmother, quiet through the dinner, speaks. The loud, aggressive New York voices go silent, and all eyes focus on the small old lady with short yellow hair and still a trace of an Eastern European accent. "Seth, you need a nice girl. Not too pretty. Very smart. Good with people. Social, so you will do things. Sense of humor, because you have a good sense of humor."

Why does this old woman's advice command such

attention and respect in my family? Well, my eighty-eight-year-old grandmother has seen more than everybody else at the table. She's observed more marriages, many that worked and many that didn't. And over the decades, she has cataloged the qualities that make for successful relationships. At that Thanksgiving table, for that question, my grandmother has access to the largest number of data points. My grandmother is Big Data.

In this book, I want to demystify data science. Like it or not, data is playing an increasingly important role in all of our lives—and its role is going to get larger. Newspapers now have full sections devoted to data. Companies have teams with the exclusive task of analyzing their data. Investors give start-ups tens of millions of dollars if they can store more data. Even if you never learn how to run a regression or calculate a confidence interval, you are going to encounter a lot of data—in the pages you read, the business meetings you attend, the gossip you hear next to the watercoolers you drink from.

Many people are anxious over this development. They are intimidated by data, easily lost and confused in a world of numbers. They think that a quantitative understanding of the world is for a select few left-brained prodigies, not for them. As soon as they encounter numbers, they are ready to turn the page, end the meeting, or change the conversation.

But I have spent ten years in the data analysis business and have been fortunate to work with many of the top people in the field. And one of the most important lessons I have learned is this: Good data science is less complicated than people think. The best data science, in fact, is surprisingly intuitive.

What makes data science intuitive? At its core, data science is about spotting patterns and predicting how one variable will affect another. People do this all the time.

Just think how my grandmother gave me relationship advice. She utilized the large database of relationships that her brain has uploaded over a near century of life—in the stories she has heard from her family, her friends, her acquaintances. She limited her analysis to a sample of relationships in which the man had many qualities that I have—a sensitive temperament, a tendency to isolate himself, a sense of humor. She zeroed in on key qualities of the woman—how kind she was, how smart she was, how pretty she was. She correlated these key qualities of the woman with a key quality of the relationship— whether it was a good one. Finally, she reported her results. In other words, she spotted patterns and predicted how one variable will affect another. Grandma is a data scientist.

You are a data scientist, too. When you were a kid, you noticed that when you cried, your mom gave you attention. That is data science. When you reached adulthood, you noticed that if you complain too much, people want to hang out with you less. That is data science, too. When people hang out with you less, you noticed, you are less happy. When you are less happy, you are less friendly. When you are less friendly, people want to hang out with you even less. Data science. Data science. Data science.

Because data science is so natural, the best Big Data studies, I have found, can be understood by just about any smart person. If you can't understand a study, the problem is probably with the study, not with you.

Want proof that great data science tends to be intuitive? I recently came across a study that may be one of the most important conducted in the past few years. It is also one of the most intuitive studies I've ever seen. I want you to think not just about the importance of the study—but how natural and grandma-like it is.

The study was by a team of researchers from Columbia University and Microsoft. The team wanted to find what symptoms predict pancreatic cancer. This disease has a low five-year survival rate—only about 3 percent—but early detection can double a patient's chances.

The researchers' method? They utilized data from tens of thousands of anonymous users of Bing, Microsoft's search engine. They coded a user as having recently been given a diagnosis of pancreatic cancer based on unmistakable searches, such as "just diagnosed with pancreatic cancer" or "I was told I have pancreatic cancer, what to expect."

Next, the researchers looked at searches for health symptoms. They compared that small number of users who later reported a pancreatic cancer diagnosis with those who didn't. What symptoms, in other words, predicted that, in a few weeks or months, a user will be reporting a diagnosis?

The results were striking. Searching for back pain and then yellowing skin turned out to be a sign of pancreatic cancer; searching for just back pain alone made it unlikely someone had pancreatic cancer. Similarly, searching for indigestion and then abdominal pain was evidence of pancreatic cancer, while searching for just indigestion without abdominal pain meant a person was unlikely to have it. The researchers could identify 5 to 15 percent of cases with almost no false positives. Now, this may not sound like a great rate; but if you have pancreatic cancer, even a 10 percent chance of possibly doubling your chances of survival would feel like a windfall.

The paper detailing this study would be difficult for non-experts to fully make sense of. It includes a lot of technical jargon, such as the Kolmogorov-Smirnov test, the meaning of which, I have to admit, I had forgotten. (It's a way to determine whether a model correctly fits data.)

However, note how natural and intuitive this remarkable study is at its most fundamental level. The researchers looked at a wide array of medical cases and tried to connect symptoms to a particular illness. You know who else uses this methodology in trying to figure out whether someone has a disease? Husbands and wives, mothers and fathers, and nurses and doctors. Based on experience and knowledge, they try to connect fevers, headaches, runny noses, and stomach pains to various diseases. In other words, the Columbia and Microsoft researchers wrote a groundbreaking study by utilizing the natural, obvious methodology that everybody uses to make health diagnoses.

But wait. Let's slow down here. If the methodology of the best data science is frequently natural and intuitive, as I claim, this raises a fundamental question about the value of Big Data. If humans are naturally data scientists, if data science is intuitive, why do we need computers and statistical software? Why do we need the Kolmogorov-Smirnov test? Can't we just use our gut? Can't we do it like Grandma does, like nurses and doctors do?

This gets to an argument intensified after the release of Malcolm Gladwell's bestselling book *Blink*, which extols the magic of people's gut instincts. Gladwell tells the stories of people who, relying solely on their guts, can tell whether a statue is fake; whether a tennis player will fault before he hits the ball; how much a customer is willing to pay. The heroes in *Blink* do not run regressions; they do not calculate confidence intervals; they do not run Kolmogorov-Smirnov tests. But they generally make remarkable predictions. Many people have intuitively supported Gladwell's defense of intuition: they trust their guts and feelings. Fans of *Blink* might celebrate the wisdom of my grandmother giving relationship advice without the aid of computers. Fans of *Blink* may be less apt to celebrate my studies or the other studies profiled in this book, which use computers. If Big Data—of the computer type, rather than the grandma type—is a revolution, it has to prove that it's more powerful than our unaided intuition, which, as Gladwell has pointed out, can often be remarkable.

The Columbia and Microsoft study offers a clear example of rigorous data science and computers teaching us things our gut alone could never find. This is also one case where the size of the dataset matters. Sometimes there is insufficient experience for our unaided gut to draw upon. It is unlikely that you—or your close friends or family members—have seen enough cases of pancreatic cancer to tease out the difference between indigestion followed by abdominal pain compared to indigestion alone. Indeed, it is inevitable, as the Bing dataset gets bigger, that the researchers will pick up many more subtle patterns in the timing of symptoms—for this and other illnesses—that even doctors might miss.

Moreover, while our gut may usually give us a good general sense of how the world works, it is frequently not precise.

We need data to sharpen the picture. Consider, for example, the effects of weather on mood. You would probably guess that people are more likely to feel more gloomy on a 10-degree day than on a 70-degree day. Indeed, this is correct. But you might not guess how big an impact this temperature difference can make. I looked for correlations between an area's Google searches for depression and a wide range of factors, including economic conditions, education levels, and church attendance. Winter climate swamped all the rest. In winter months, warm climates, such as that of Honolulu, Hawaii, have 40 percent fewer depression searches than cold climates, such as that of Chicago, Illinois. Just how significant is this effect? An optimistic read of the effectiveness of antidepressants would find that the most effective drugs decrease the incidence of depression by only about 20 percent. To judge from the Google numbers, a Chicago-to-Honolulu move would be at least twice as effective as medication for your winter blues.*

Sometimes our gut, when not guided by careful computer analysis, can be dead wrong. We can get blinded by our own experiences and prejudices. Indeed, even though my grandmother is able to utilize her decades of experience to give better relationship advice than the rest of my family, she still has some dubious views on what makes a relationship last. For example, she has frequently emphasized to me the importance of having common friends. She believes that this was a key factor in her marriage's success: she spent most warm evenings

---

* Full disclosure: Shortly after I completed this study, I moved from California to New York. Using data to learn what you should do is often easy. Actually doing it is tough.

with her husband, my grandfather, in their small backyard in Queens, New York, sitting on lawn chairs and gossiping with their tight group of neighbors.

However, at the risk of throwing my own grandmother under the bus, data science suggests that Grandma's theory is wrong. A team of computer scientists recently analyzed the biggest dataset ever assembled on human relationships— Facebook. They looked at a large number of couples who were, at some point, "in a relationship." Some of these couples stayed "in a relationship." Others switched their status to "single." Having a common core group of friends, the researchers found, is a strong predictor that a relationship will *not* last. Perhaps hanging out every night with your partner and the same small group of people is not such a good thing; separate social circles may help make relationships stronger.

As you can see, our intuition alone, when we stay away from the computers and go with our gut, can sometimes amaze. But it can make big mistakes. Grandma may have fallen into one cognitive trap: we tend to exaggerate the relevance of our own experience. In the parlance of data scientists, we *weight* our data, and we give far too much weight to one particular data point: ourselves.

Grandma was so focused on her evening schmoozes with Grandpa and their friends that she did not think enough about other couples. She forgot to fully consider her brother-in-law and his wife, who chitchatted most nights with a small, consistent group of friends but fought frequently and divorced. She forgot to fully consider my parents, her daughter and son-in-law. My parents go their separate ways many nights—my dad to a jazz club or ball game with his friends, my mom to a restaurant or the theater with her friends; yet they remain happily married.

When relying on our gut, we can also be thrown off by the basic human fascination with the dramatic. We tend to overestimate the prevalence of anything that makes for a memorable story. For example, when asked in a survey, people consistently rank tornadoes as a more common cause of death than asthma. In fact, asthma causes about seventy times more deaths. Deaths by asthma don't stand out—and don't make the news. Deaths by tornadoes do.

We are often wrong, in other words, about how the world works when we rely just on what we hear or personally experience. While the methodology of good data science is often intuitive, the results are frequently counterintuitive. Data science takes a natural and intuitive human process—spotting patterns and making sense of them—and injects it with steroids, potentially showing us that the world works in a completely different way from how we thought it did. That's what happened when I studied the predictors of basketball success.

When I was a little boy, I had one dream and one dream only: I wanted to grow up to be an economist and data scientist. No. I'm just kidding. I wanted desperately to be a professional basketball player, to follow in the footsteps of my hero, Patrick Ewing, all-star center for the New York Knicks.

I sometimes suspect that inside every data scientist is a kid trying to figure out why his childhood dreams didn't come true. So it is not surprising that I recently investigated what it takes to make the NBA. The results of the investigation were surprising. In fact, they demonstrate once again how good data science can change your view of the world, and how counterintuitive the numbers can be.

The particular question I looked at is this: are you more likely to make it in the NBA if you grow up poor or middle-class?

Most people would guess the former. Conventional wisdom says that growing up in difficult circumstances, perhaps in the projects with a single, teenage mom, helps foster the drive necessary to reach the top levels of this intensely competitive sport.

This view was expressed by William Ellerbee, a high school basketball coach in Philadelphia, in an interview with *Sports Illustrated*. "Suburban kids tend to play for the fun of it," Ellerbee said. "Inner-city kids look at basketball as a matter of life or death." I, alas, was raised by married parents in the New Jersey suburbs. LeBron James, the best player of my generation, was born poor to a sixteen-year-old single mother in Akron, Ohio.

Indeed, an internet survey I conducted suggested that the majority of Americans think the same thing Coach Ellerbee and I thought: that most NBA players grow up in poverty.

Is this conventional wisdom correct?

Let's look at the data. There is no comprehensive data source on the socioeconomics of NBA players. But by being data detectives, by utilizing data from a whole bunch of sources— basketball-reference.com, ancestry.com, the U.S. Census, and others—we can figure out what family background is actually most conducive to making the NBA. This study, you will note, uses a variety of data sources, some of them bigger, some of them smaller, some of them online, and some of them offline. As exciting as some of the new digital sources are, a good data scientist is not above consulting old-fashioned sources if they can help. The best way to get the right answer to a question is to combine all available data.

The first relevant data is the birthplace of every player. For every county in the United States, I recorded how many black and white men were born in the 1980s. I then recorded how many of them reached the NBA. I compared this to a county's average household income. I also controlled for the racial demographics of a county, since—and this is a subject for a whole other book—black men are about forty times more likely than white men to reach the NBA.

The data tells us that a man has a substantially better chance of reaching the NBA if he was born in a wealthy county. A black kid born in one of the wealthiest counties in the United States, for example, is more than twice as likely to make the NBA than a black kid born in one of the poorest counties. For a white kid, the advantage of being born in one of the wealthiest counties compared to being born in one of the poorest is 60 percent.

This suggests, contrary to conventional wisdom, that poor men are actually underrepresented in the NBA. However, this data is not perfect, since many wealthy counties in the United States, such as New York County (Manhattan), also include poor neighborhoods, such as Harlem. So it's still possible that a difficult childhood helps you make the NBA. We still need more clues, more data.

So I investigated the family backgrounds of NBA players. This information was found in news stories and on social networks. This methodology was quite time-consuming, so I limited the analysis to the one hundred African-American NBA players born in the 1980s who scored the most points. Compared to the average black man in the United States, NBA superstars were about 30 percent less likely to have been born to a teenage mother or an unwed mother. In other words, the family backgrounds of the best black NBA players also suggest that a comfortable background is a big advantage for achieving success.

That said, neither the county-level birth data nor the family background of a limited sample of players gives perfect information on the childhoods of all NBA players. So I was still not entirely convinced that two-parent, middle-class families produce more NBA stars than single-parent, poor families. The more data we can throw at this question, the better.

Then I remembered one more data point that can provide telling clues to a man's background. It was suggested in a paper by two economists, Roland Fryer and Steven Levitt, that a black person's first name is an indication of his socioeconomic background. Fryer and Levitt studied birth certificates in California in the 1980s and found that, among African-Americans, poor, uneducated, and single moms tend to give their kids different names than do middle-class, educated, and married parents.

Kids from better-off backgrounds are more likely to be given common names, such as Kevin, Chris, and John. Kids from difficult homes in the projects are more likely to be given unique names, such as Knowshon, Uneek, and Breionshay. African-American kids born into poverty are nearly twice as likely to have a name that is given to no other child born in that same year.

So what about the first names of black NBA players? Do

they sound more like middle-class or poor blacks? Looking at the same time period, California-born NBA players were half as likely to have unique names as the average black male, a statistically significant difference.

Know someone who thinks the NBA is a league for kids from the ghetto? Tell him to just listen closely to the next game on the radio. Tell him to note how frequently Russell dribbles past Dwight and then tries to slip the ball past the outstretched arms of Josh and into the waiting hands of Kevin. If the NBA really were a league filled with poor black men, it would sound quite different. There would be a lot more men with names like LeBron.

Now, we have gathered three different pieces of evidence— the county of birth, the marital status of the mothers of the top scorers, and the first names of players. No source is perfect. But all three support the same story. Better socioeconomic status means a higher chance of making the NBA. The conventional wisdom, in other words, is wrong.

Among all African-Americans born in the 1980s, about 60 percent had unmarried parents. But I estimate that among African-Americans born in that decade who reached the NBA, a significant majority had married parents. In other words, the NBA is not composed primarily of men with backgrounds like that of LeBron James. There are more men like Chris Bosh, raised by two parents in Texas who cultivated his interest in electronic gadgets, or Chris Paul, the second son of middle-class parents in Lewisville, North Carolina, whose family joined him on an episode of *Family Feud* in 2011.

The goal of a data scientist is to understand the world. Once we find the counterintuitive result, we can use more data science to help us explain why the world is not as it seems. Why, for example, do middle-class men have an edge in basketball relative to poor men? There are at least two explanations.

First, because poor men tend to end up shorter. Scholars have long known that childhood health care and nutrition play a large role in adult health. This is why the average man in the developed world is now four inches taller than a century and a half ago. Data suggests that Americans from poor backgrounds, due to weaker early-life health care and nutrition, are shorter.

Data can also tell us the effect of height on reaching the NBA. You undoubtedly intuited that being tall can be of assistance to an aspiring basketball player. Just contrast the height of the typical ballplayer on the court to the typical fan in the stands. (The average NBA player is 6'7"; the average American man is 5'9".)

How much does height matter? NBA players sometimes fib a little about their height, and there is no listing of the complete height distribution of American males. But working with a rough mathematical estimate of what this distribution might look like and the NBA's own numbers, it is easy to confirm that the effects of height are enormous—maybe even more than we might have suspected. I estimate that each additional inch roughly doubles your odds of making it to the NBA. And this is true throughout the height distribution. A 5'11" man has twice the odds of reaching the NBA as a 5'10" man. A 6'11" man has twice the odds of reaching the NBA as a 6'10" man. It appears that, among men less than six feet tall, only about one in two million reach the NBA. Among those over seven feet tall, I and others have estimated, something like one in five reach the NBA.

Data, you will note, clarifies why my dream of basketball stardom was derailed. It was not because I was brought up in the suburbs. It was because I am 5'9" and white (not to mention slow). Also, I am lazy. And I have poor stamina, awful shooting form, and occasionally a panic attack when the ball gets in my hand.

A second reason that boys from tough backgrounds may struggle to make the NBA is that they sometimes lack certain social skills. Using data on thousands of schoolchildren, economists have found that middle-class, two-parent families are on average substantially better at raising kids who are trusting, disciplined, persistent, focused, and organized.

So how do poor social skills derail an otherwise promising basketball career?

Let's look at the story of Doug Wrenn, one of the most talented basketball prospects in the 1990s. His college coach, Jim Calhoun at the University of Connecticut, who has trained future NBA all-stars, claimed Wrenn jumped the highest of any man he had ever worked with. But Wrenn had a challenging upbringing. He was raised by a single mother in Blood Alley, one of the roughest neighborhoods in Seattle. In Connecticut, he consistently clashed with those around him. He would taunt players, question coaches, and wear loose-fitting clothes in violation of team rules. He also had legal troubles—he stole shoes from a store and snapped at police officers. Calhoun finally had enough and kicked him off the team.

Wrenn got a second chance at the University of

Washington. But there, too, an inability to get along with people derailed him. He fought with his coach over playing time and shot selection and was kicked off this team as well. Wrenn went undrafted by the NBA, bounced around lower leagues, moved in with his mother, and was eventually imprisoned for assault. "My career is over," Wrenn told the *Seattle Times* in 2009. "My dreams, my aspirations are over. Doug Wrenn is dead. That basketball player, that dude is dead. It's over." Wrenn had the talent not just to be an NBA player, but to be a great, even a legendary player. But he never developed the temperament to even stay on a college team. Perhaps if he'd had a stable early life, he could have been the next Michael Jordan.

Michael Jordan, of course, also had an impressive vertical leap. Plus a large ego and intense competitiveness—a personality at times that was not unlike Wrenn's. Jordan could be a difficult kid. At the age of twelve, he was kicked out of school for fighting. But he had at least one thing that Wrenn lacked: a stable, middle-class upbringing. His father was an equipment supervisor for General Electric, his mother a banker. And they helped him navigate his career.

In fact, Jordan's life is filled with stories of his family guiding him away from the traps that a great, competitive talent can fall into. After Jordan was kicked out of school, his mother responded by taking him with her to work. He was not allowed to leave the car and instead had to sit there in the parking lot reading books. After he was drafted by the Chicago Bulls, his parents and siblings took turns visiting him to make sure he avoided the temptations that come with fame and money.

Jordan's career did not end like Wrenn's, with a little-read quote in the *Seattle Times*. It ended with a speech upon induction into the Basketball Hall of Fame that was watched by millions of people. In his speech, Jordan said he tried to stay "focused on the good things about life—you know how people perceive you, how you respect them . . . how you are perceived publicly. Take a pause and think about the things that you do. And that all came from my parents."

The data tells us Jordan is absolutely right to thank his middle-class, married parents. The data tells us that in worse-off families, in worse-off communities, there are NBA-level talents who are not in the NBA. These men had the genes, had the ambition, but never developed the temperament to become basketball superstars.

And no—whatever we might intuit—being in circumstances so desperate that basketball seems "a matter of life or death" does not help. Stories like that of Doug Wrenn can help illustrate this. And data proves it.

In June 2013, LeBron James was interviewed on television after winning his second NBA championship. (He has since won a third.) "I'm LeBron James," he announced. "From Akron, Ohio. From the inner city. I am not even supposed to be here." Twitter and other social networks erupted with criticism. How could such a supremely gifted person, identified from an absurdly young age as the future of basketball, claim to be an underdog? In fact, anyone from a difficult environment, no matter his athletic prowess, has the odds stacked against him. James's accomplishments, in other words, are even more exceptional than they appear to be at first. Data proves that, too.

PART II

THE POWERS OF BIG DATA

2

WAS FREUD RIGHT?

I recently saw a person walking down a street described as a "penistrian." You caught that, right? A "penistrian" instead of a "pedestrian." I saw it in a large dataset of typos people make. A person sees someone walking and writes the word "penis." Has to mean something, right?

I recently learned of a man who dreamed of eating a banana while walking to the altar to marry his wife. I saw it in a large dataset of dreams people record on an app. A man imagines marrying a woman while eating a phallic-shaped food. That also has to mean something, right?

Was Sigmund Freud right? Since his theories first came to public attention, the most honest answer to this question would be a shrug. It was Karl Popper, the Austrian-British philosopher, who made this point clearest. Popper famously claimed that Freud's theories were not falsifiable. There was no way to test whether they were true or false.

Freud could say the person writing of a "penistrian" was revealing a possibly repressed sexual desire. The person could respond that she wasn't revealing anything; that she could have just as easily made an innocent typo, such as "pedaltrian." It would be a he-said, she-said situation. Freud could say the gentleman dreaming of eating a banana on his wedding day was secretly thinking of a penis, revealing his desire to really marry a man rather than a woman. The gentleman could say he just happened to be dreaming of a banana. He could have just as easily been dreaming of eating an apple as he walked to the altar. It would be he-said, he-said. There was no way to put Freud's theory to a real test.

Until now, that is.

Data science makes many parts of Freud falsifiable—it puts many of his famous theories to the test. Let's start with phallic symbols in dreams. Using a huge dataset of recorded dreams, we can readily note how frequently phallic-shaped objects appear. Food is a good place to focus this study. It shows up in many dreams, and many foods are shaped like phalluses—bananas, cucumbers, hot dogs, etc. We can then measure the factors that might make us dream more about certain foods than others—how frequently they are eaten, how tasty most people find them, and, yes, whether they are phallic in nature.

We can test whether two foods, both of which are equally popular, but one of which is shaped like a phallus, appear in dreams in different amounts. If phallus-shaped foods are no more likely to be dreamed about than other foods, then phallic symbols are not a significant factor in our dreams. Thanks to Big Data, this part of Freud's theory may indeed be falsifiable.

I received data from Shadow, an app that asks users to record their dreams. I coded the foods included in tens of thousands of dreams.

Overall, what makes us dream of foods? The main predictor is how frequently we consume them. The substance that is most dreamed about is water. The top twenty foods include chicken, bread, sandwiches, and rice—all notably un-Freudian.

The second predictor of how frequently a food appears in dreams is how tasty people find it. The two foods we dream about most often are the notably un-Freudian but famously tasty chocolate and pizza.

So what about phallic-shaped foods? Do they sneak into our dreams with unexpected frequency? Nope.

Bananas are the second most common fruit to appear in dreams. But they are also the second most commonly consumed fruit. So we don't need Freud to explain how often we dream about bananas. Cucumbers are the seventh most common vegetable to appear in dreams. They are the seventh most consumed vegetable. So again their shape isn't necessary to explain their presence in our minds as we sleep. Hot dogs are dreamed of far less frequently than hamburgers. This is true even controlling for the fact that people eat more burgers than dogs.

Overall, using a regression analysis (a method that allows social scientists to tease apart the impact of multiple factors) across all fruits and vegetables, I found that a food's being shaped like a phallus did not give it more likelihood of appearing in dreams than would be expected by its popularity. This theory of Freud's is falsifiable—and, at least according to my look at the data, false.

Next, consider Freudian slips. The psychologist hypothesized that we use our errors—the ways we misspeak or miswrite—to reveal our subconscious desires, frequently sexual. Can we use Big Data to test this? Here's one way: see if our errors—our slips—lean in the direction of the naughty. If our buried sexual desires sneak out in our slips, there should be a disproportionate number of errors that include words like "penis," "cock," and "sex."

This is why I studied a dataset of more than 40,000 typing errors collected by Microsoft researchers. The dataset included mistakes that people make but then immediately correct. In these tens of thousands of errors, there were plenty of individuals committing errors of a sexual sort. There was the aforementioned "penistrian." There was also someone who typed "sexurity" instead of "security" and "cocks" instead of "rocks." But there were also plenty of innocent slips. People wrote of "pindows" and "fegetables," "aftermoons" and "refriderators."

So was the number of sexual slips unusual?

To test this, I first used the Microsoft dataset to model how frequently people mistakenly switch particular letters. I calculated how often they replace a t with an s, a g with an h. I then created a computer program that made mistakes in the way that people do. We might call it Error Bot. Error Bot replaced a t with an s with the same frequency that humans in the Microsoft study did. It replaced a g with an h as often as they did. And so on. I ran the program on the same words people had gotten wrong in the Microsoft study. In other words, the bot tried to spell "pedestrian" and "rocks," "windows" and "refrigerator." But it switched an *r* with a *t* as often as people do and wrote, for example, "tocks." It switched an *r* with a *c* as often as humans do and wrote "cocks."

So what do we learn from comparing Error Bot with normally careless humans? After making a few million errors, just from misplacing letters in the ways that humans do, Error Bot had made numerous mistakes of a Freudian nature. It misspelled "seashell" as "sexshell," "lipstick" as "lipsdick," and "luckiest" as "fuckiest," along with many other similar mistakes. And—here's the key point—Error Bot, which of course does not have a subconscious, was just as likely to make errors that could be perceived as sexual as real people were. With the caveat, as we social scientists like to say, that there needs to be more research, this means that sexually oriented errors are no more likely for humans to make than can be expected by chance.

In other words, for people to make errors such as "penistrian," "sexurity," and "cocks," it is not necessary to have some connection between mistakes and the forbidden, some theory of the mind where people reveal their secret desires via their errors. These slips of the fingers can be explained entirely by the typical frequency of typos. People make lots of mistakes. And if you make enough mistakes, eventually you start saying things like "lipsdick," "fuckiest," and "penistrian." If a monkey types long enough, he will eventually write "to be or not to be." If a person types long enough, she will eventually write "penistrian."

Freud's theory that errors reveal our subconscious wants is indeed falsifiable—and, according to my analysis of the data, false.

Big Data tells us a banana is always just a banana and a "penistrian" just a misspelled "pedestrian."

So was Freud totally off-target in all his theories? Not quite. When I first got access to PornHub data, I found a revelation there that struck me as at least somewhat Freudian. In fact, this is among the most surprising things I have found yet during my data investigations: a shocking number of people visiting mainstream porn sites are looking for portrayals of incest.

Of the top hundred searches by men on PornHub, one of the most popular porn sites, sixteen are looking for incest-themed videos. Fair warning—this is going to get a little graphic: they include "brother and sister," "step mom fucks son," "mom and son," "mom fucks son," and "real brother and sister." The plurality of male incestuous searches are for scenes featuring mothers and sons. And women? Nine of the top hundred searches by women on PornHub are for incest-themed videos, and they feature similar imagery—though with the gender of any parent and child who is mentioned usually reversed. Thus the plurality of incestuous searches made by women are for scenes featuring fathers and daughters.

It's not hard to locate in this data at least a faint echo of Freud's Oedipal complex. He hypothesized a near-universal desire in childhood, which is later repressed, for sexual involvement with opposite-sex parents. If only the Viennese psychologist had lived long enough to turn his analytic skills to

PornHub data, where interest in opposite-sex parents seems to be borne out by adults—with great explicitness—and little is repressed.

Of course, PornHub data can't tell us for certain who people are fantasizing about when watching such videos. Are they actually imagining having sex with their own parents? Google searches can give some more clues that there are plenty of people with such desires.

Consider all searches of the form "I want to have sex with my . . ." The number one way to complete this search is "mom." Overall, more than three-fourths of searches of this form are incestuous. And this is not due to the particular phrasing. Searches of the form "I am attracted to . . . ," for example, are even more dominated by admissions of incestuous desires. Now I concede—at the risk of disappointing Herr Freud—that these are not particularly common searches: a few thousand people every year in the United States admitting an attraction to their mother. Someone would also have to break the news to Freud that Google searches, as will be discussed later in this book, sometimes skew toward the forbidden.

But still. There are plenty of inappropriate attractions that people have that I would have expected to have been mentioned more frequently in searches. Boss? Employee? Student? Therapist? Patient? Wife's best friend? Daughter's best friend? Wife's sister? Best friend's wife? None of these confessed desires can compete with mom. Maybe, combined with the PornHub data, that really does mean something.

And Freud's general assertion that sexuality can be shaped by childhood experiences is supported elsewhere in Google and PornHub data, which reveals that men, at least, retain an inordinate number of fantasies related to childhood. According to searches from wives about their husbands, some of the top fetishes of adult men are the desire to wear diapers and wanting to be breastfed, particularly, as discussed earlier, in India. Moreover, cartoon porn—animated explicit sex scenes featuring characters from shows popular among adolescent boys—has achieved a high degree of popularity. Or consider the occupations of women most frequently searched for in porn by men. Men who are 18–24 years old search most frequently for women who are babysitters. As do 25–64-year-old men. And men 65 years and older. And for men in every age group, teacher and cheerleader are both in the top four. Clearly, the early years of life seem to play an outsize role in men's adult fantasies.

I have not yet been able to use all this unprecedented data on adult sexuality to figure out precisely how sexual preferences form. Over the next few decades, other social scientists and I will be able to create new, falsifiable theories on adult sexuality and test them with actual data.

Already I can predict some basic themes that will undoubtedly be part of a data-based theory of adult sexuality. It is clearly not going to be the identical story to the one Freud told, with his particular, well-defined, universal stages of childhood and repression. But, based on my first look at PornHub data, I am absolutely certain the final verdict on adult sexuality will feature some key themes that Freud emphasized. Childhood will play a major role. So will mothers.

It likely would have been impossible to analyze Freud in this way ten years ago. It certainly would have been impossible eighty years ago, when Freud was still alive. So let's think through why these data sources helped. This exercise can help us understand why Big Data is so powerful.

Remember, we have said that just having mounds and mounds of data by itself doesn't automatically generate insights. Data size, by itself, is overrated. Why, then, is Big Data so powerful? Why will it create a revolution in how we see ourselves? There are, I claim, four unique powers of Big Data. This analysis of Freud provides a good illustration of them.

You may have noticed, to begin with, that we're taking pornography seriously in this discussion of Freud. And we are going to utilize data from pornography frequently in this book. Somewhat surprisingly, porn data is rarely utilized by sociologists, most of whom are comfortable relying on the traditional survey datasets they have built their careers on. But a moment's reflection shows that the widespread use of porn—and the search and views data that comes with it—is the most important development in our ability to understand human sexuality in, well . . . Actually, it's probably the most important ever. It is data that Schopenhauer, Nietzsche, Freud, and Foucault would have drooled over. This data did not exist when they were alive. It did not exist a couple decades ago. It exists now. There are many unique data sources, on a range of topics, that give us windows into areas about which we could previously just guess. *Offering up new types of data is the first power of Big Data.*

The porn data and the Google search data are not just new;

they are honest. In the pre-digital age, people hid their embarrassing thoughts from other people. In the digital age, they still hide them from other people, but not from the internet and in particular sites such as Google and PornHub, which protect their anonymity. These sites function as a sort of digital truth serum—hence our ability to uncover a widespread fascination with incest. Big Data allows us to finally see what people really want and really do, not what they say they want and say they do. *Providing honest data is the second power of Big Data.*

Because there is now so much data, there is meaningful information on even tiny slices of a population. We can compare, say, the number of people who dream of cucumbers versus those who dream of tomatoes. *Allowing us to zoom in on small subsets of people is the third power of Big Data.*

Big Data has one more impressive power—one that was not utilized in my quick study of Freud but could be in a future one: it allows us to undertake rapid, controlled experiments. This allows us to test for causality, not merely correlations. These kinds of tests are mostly used by businesses now, but they will prove a powerful tool for social scientists. *Allowing us to do many causal experiments is the fourth power of Big Data.*

Now it is time to unpack each of these powers and explore exactly why Big Data matters.

3

DATA REIMAGINED

At 6 A.M. on a particular Friday of every month, the streets of most of Manhattan will be largely desolate. The stores lining these streets will be closed, their façades covered by steel security gates, the apartments above dark and silent.

The floors of Goldman Sachs, the global investment banking institution in lower Manhattan, on the other hand, will be brightly lit, its elevators taking thousands of workers to their desks. By 7 A.M. most of these desks will be occupied.

It would not be unfair on any other day to describe this hour in this part of town as sleepy. On this Friday morning, however, there will be a buzz of energy and excitement. On this day, information that will massively impact the stock market is set to arrive.

Minutes after its release, this information will be reported by news sites. Seconds after its release, this information will be discussed, debated, and dissected, loudly, at Goldman and hundreds of other financial firms. But much of the real action in finance these days happens in milliseconds. Goldman and other financial firms paid tens of millions of dollars to get access to fiber-optic cables that reduced the time information travels from Chicago to New Jersey by just four milliseconds (from 17 to 13). Financial firms have algorithms in place to read the information and trade based on it—all in a matter of milliseconds. After this crucial information is released, the market will move in less time than it takes you to blink your eye.

So what is this crucial data that is so valuable to Goldman and numerous other financial institutions?

The monthly unemployment rate.

The rate, however—which has such a profound impact on the stock market that financial institutions have done whatever it takes to maximize the speed with which they receive, analyze, and act upon it—is from a phone survey that the Bureau of Labor Statistics conducts and the information is some three weeks—or 2 billion milliseconds—old by the time it is released.

When firms are spending millions of dollars to chip a millisecond off the flow of information, it might strike you as more than a bit strange that the government takes so long to calculate the unemployment rate.

Indeed, getting these critical numbers out sooner was one of Alan Krueger's primary agendas when he took over as President Obama's chairman of the Council of Economic Advisors in 2011. He was unsuccessful. "Either the BLS doesn't have the resources," he concluded. "Or they are stuck in twentieth-century thinking."

With the government clearly not picking up the pace anytime soon, is there a way to get at least a rough measure of the unemployment statistics at a faster rate? In this high-tech era—when nearly every click any human makes on the internet is recorded somewhere—do we really have to wait weeks to find out how many people are out of work?

One potential solution was inspired by the work of a former Google engineer, Jeremy Ginsberg. Ginsberg noticed that health data, like unemployment data, was released with a delay by the government. The Centers for Disease Control and Prevention takes one week to release influenza data, even though doctors and hospitals would benefit from having the data much sooner.

Ginsberg suspected that people sick with the flu are likely to make flu-related searches. In essence, they would report their symptoms to Google. These searches, he thought, could give a reasonably accurate measure of the current influenza rate. Indeed, searches such as "flu symptoms" and "muscle aches" have proven important indicators of how fast the flu is spreading.*

Meanwhile, Google engineers created a service, Google Correlate, that gives outside researchers the means to experiment with the same type of analyses across a wide range of fields, not just health. Researchers can take any data series that they are tracking over time and see what Google searches correlate most with that dataset.

For example, using Google Correlate, Hal Varian, chief

---

* While the initial version of Google Flu had significant flaws, researchers have recently recalibrated the model, with more success.

economist at Google, and I were able to show which searches most closely track housing prices. When housing prices are rising, Americans tend to search for such phrases as "80/20 mortgage," "new home builder," and "appreciation rate." When housing prices are falling, Americans tend to search for such phrases as "short sale process," "underwater mortgage," and "mortgage forgiveness debt relief."

So can Google searches be used as a litmus test for unemployment in the same way they can for housing prices or influenza? Can we tell, simply by what people are Googling, how many people are unemployed, and can we do so well before the government collates its survey results?

One day, I put the United States unemployment rate from 2004 through 2011 into Google Correlate.

Of the trillions of Google searches during that time, what do you think turned out to be most tightly connected to unemployment? You might imagine "unemployment office"—or something similar. That was high but not at the very top. "New jobs"? Also high but also not at the very top.

The highest during the period I searched—and these terms do shift—was "Slutload." That's right, the most frequent search was for a pornographic site. This may seem strange at first blush, but unemployed people presumably have a lot of time on their hands. Many are stuck at home, alone and bored. Another of the highly correlated searches—this one in the PG realm—is "Spider Solitaire." Again, not surprising for a group of people who presumably have a lot of time on their hands.

Now, I am not arguing, based on this one analysis, that tracking "Slutload" or "Spider Solitaire" is the best way to predict the unemployment rate. The specific diversions that unemployed people use can change over time (at one point, "Rawtube," a different porn site, was among the strongest correlations) and none of these particular terms by itself attracts anything approaching a plurality of the unemployed. But I have generally found that a mix of diversion-related searches can track the unemployment rate—and would be a part of the best model predicting it.

This example illustrates the first power of Big Data, the reimagining of what qualifies as data. Frequently, the value of Big Data is not its size; it's that it can offer you new kinds of information to study—information that had never previously been collected.

Before Google there was information available on certain leisure activities—movie ticket sales, for example—that could yield some clues as to how much time people have on their hands. But the opportunity to know how much solitaire is being played or porn is being watched is new—and powerful. In this instance this data might help us more quickly measure how the economy is doing—at least until the government learns to conduct and collate a survey more quickly.

Life on Google's campus in Mountain View, California, is very different from that in Goldman Sachs's Manhattan headquarters. At 9 A.M. Google's offices are nearly empty. If any workers are around, it is probably to eat breakfast for free—banana-blueberry pancakes, scrambled egg whites, filtered cucumber water. Some employees might be out of town: at an off-site meeting in Boulder or Las Vegas or perhaps on a free ski trip to Lake Tahoe. Around lunchtime, the sand volleyball courts and grass soccer fields will be filled. The best burrito I've ever eaten was at Google's Mexican restaurant.

How can one of the biggest and most competitive tech companies in the world seemingly be so relaxed and generous? Google harnessed Big Data in a way that no other company ever has to build an automated money stream. The company plays a crucial role in this book since Google searches are by far the dominant source of Big Data. But it is important to remember that Google's success is itself built on the collection of a new kind of data.

If you are old enough to have used the internet in the twentieth century, you might remember the various search engines that existed back then—MetaCrawler, Lycos, AltaVista, to name a few. And you might remember that these search engines were, at best, mildly reliable. Sometimes, if you were lucky, they managed to find what you wanted. Often, they would not. If you typed "Bill Clinton" into the most popular search engines in the late 1990s, the top results included a random site that just proclaimed "Bill Clinton Sucks" or a site that featured a bad Clinton joke. Hardly the most relevant information about the then president of the United States.

In 1998, Google showed up. And its search results were undeniably better those that of every one of its competitors. If you typed "Bill Clinton" into Google in 1998, you were given his website, the White House email address, and the best biographies of the man that existed on the internet. Google seemed to be magic.

What had Google's founders, Sergey Brin and Larry Page, done differently?

Other search engines located for their users the web-sites that most frequently included the phrase for which they searched. If you were looking for information on "Bill Clinton," those search engines would find, across the entire inter-net, the websites that had the most references to Bill Clinton. There were many reasons this ranking system was imperfect and one of them was that it was easy to game the system. A joke site with the text "Bill Clinton Bill Clinton Bill Clinton Bill Clinton Bill Clinton" hidden somewhere on its page would score higher than the White House's official website.*

What Brin and Page did was find a way to record a new type of information that was far more valuable than a simple count of words. Websites often would, when discussing a subject, link to the sites they thought were most helpful in understanding that subject. For example, the *New York Times*, if it mentioned Bill Clinton, might allow readers who clicked on his name to be sent to the White House's official website.

Every website creating one of these links was, in a sense, giving its opinion of the best information on Bill Clinton. Brin and Page could aggregate all these opinions on every topic. It could crowdsource the opinions of the *New York Times*, mil-lions of Listservs, hundreds of bloggers, and everyone else on the internet. If a whole slew of people thought that the most

---

* In 1998, if you searched "cars" on a popular pre-Google search en-gine, you were inundated with porn sites. These porn sites had writ-ten the word "cars" frequently in white letters on a white background to trick the search engine. They then got a few extra clicks from peo-ple who meant to buy a car but got distracted by the porn.

important link for "Bill Clinton" was his official website, this was probably the website that most people searching for "Bill Clinton" would want to see.

These kinds of links were data that other search engines didn't even consider, and they were incredibly predictive of the most useful information on a given topic. The point here is that Google didn't dominate search merely by collecting more data than everyone else. They did it by finding a *better* type of data. Fewer than two years after its launch, Google, powered by its link analysis, grew to be the internet's most popular search engine. Today, Brin and Page are together worth more than $60 billion.

As with Google, so with everyone else trying to use data to understand the world. The Big Data revolution is less about collecting more and more data. It is about collecting the right data.

But the internet isn't the only place where you can collect new data and where getting the right data can have profoundly disruptive results. This book is largely about how the data on the web can help us better understand people. The next section, however, doesn't have anything to do with web data. In fact, it doesn't have anything to do with people. But it does help illustrate the main point of this chapter: the outsize value of new, unconventional data. And the principles it teaches us are helpful in understanding the digital-based data revolution.

BODIES AS DATA

In the summer of 2013, a reddish-brown horse, of above-average size, with a black mane, sat in a small barn in upstate

New York. He was one of 152 one-year-old horses at August's Fasig-Tipton Select Yearling Sale in Saratoga Springs, and one of ten thousand one-year-old horses being auctioned off that year.

Wealthy men and women, when they shell out a lot of money on a racehorse, want the honor of choosing the horse's name. Thus the reddish-brown horse did not yet have a name and, like most horses at the auction, was instead referred to by his barn number, 85.

There was little that made No. 85 stand out at this auction. His pedigree was good but not great. His sire (father), Pioneerof [*sic*] the Nile, was a top racehorse, but other kids of Pioneerof the Nile had not had much racing success. There were also doubts based on how No. 85 looked. He had a scratch on his ankle, for example, which some buyers worried might be evidence of an injury.

The current owner of No. 85 was an Egyptian beer magnate, Ahmed Zayat, who had come to upstate New York looking to sell the horse and buy a few others.

Like almost all owners, Zayat hired a team of experts to help him choose which horses to buy. But his experts were a bit different than those used by nearly every other owner. The typical horse experts you'd see at an event like this were middle-aged men, many from Kentucky or rural Florida with little education but with a family background in the horse business. Zayat's experts, however, came from a small firm called EQB. The head of EQB was not an old-school horse man. The head of EQB, instead, was Jeff Seder, an eccentric, Philadelphia-born man with a pile of degrees from Harvard.

Zayat had worked with EQB before, so the process was

familiar. After a few days of evaluating horses, Seder's team would come back to Zayat with five or so horses they recommended buying to replace No. 85.

This time, though, was different. Seder's team came back to Zayat and told him they were unable to fulfill his request. They simply could not recommend that he buy any of the 151 other horses offered up for sale that day. Instead, they offered an unexpected and near-desperate plea. Zayat absolutely, positively could not sell horse No. 85. This horse, EQB declared, was not just the best horse in the auction; he was the best horse of the year and, quite possibly, the decade. "Sell your house," the team implored him. "Do not sell this horse."

The next day, with little fanfare, horse No. 85 was bought for $300,000 by a man calling himself Incardo Bloodstock. Bloodstock, it was later revealed, was a pseudonym used by Ahmed Zayat. In response to the pleas of Seder, Zayat had bought back his own horse, an almost unprecedented action. (The rules of the auction prevented Zayat from simply removing the horse from the auction, thus necessitating the pseudonymous transaction.) Sixty-two horses at the auction sold for a higher price than horse No. 85, with two fetching more than $1 million each.

Three months later, Zayat finally chose a name for No. 85: American Pharoah. And eighteen months later, on a 75-degree Saturday evening in the suburbs of New York City, American Pharoah became the first horse in more than three decades to win the Triple Crown.

What did Jeff Seder know about horse No. 85 that apparently nobody else knew? How did this Harvard man get so good at evaluating horses?

I first met up with Seder, who was then sixty-four, on a scorching June afternoon in Ocala, Florida, more than a year after American Pharoah's Triple Crown. The event was a week-long showcase for two-year-old horses, culminating in an auction, not dissimilar to the 2013 event where Zayat bought his own horse back.

Seder has a booming, Mel Brooks–like voice, a full head of hair, and a discernable bounce in his step. He was wearing suspenders, khakis, a black shirt with his company's logo on it, and a hearing aid.

Over the next three days, he told me his life story—and how he became so good at predicting horses. It was hardly a direct route. After graduating magna cum laude and Phi Beta Kappa from Harvard, Seder went on to get, also from Harvard, a law degree and a business degree. At age twenty-six, he was working as an analyst for Citigroup in New York City but felt unhappy and burnt-out. One day, sitting in the atrium at the firm's new offices on Lexington Avenue, he found himself studying a large mural of an open field. The painting reminded him of his love of the countryside and his love of horses. He went home and looked at himself in the mirror with his three-piece suit on. He knew then that he was not meant to be a banker and he was not meant to live in New York City. The next morning, he quit his job.

Seder moved to rural Pennsylvania and ambled through a variety of jobs in textiles and sports medicine before devoting his life full-time to his passion: predicting the success of racehorses. The numbers in horse racing are rough. Of the one thousand two-year-old horses showcased at Ocala's auction, one of the nation's most prestigious, perhaps five will end up winning a race with a significant purse. What will happen to the other 995 horses? Roughly one-third will prove too slow. Another one-third will get injured—most because their limbs can't withstand the enormous pressure of galloping at full speed. (Every year, hundreds of horses die on American race-tracks, mostly due to broken legs.) And the remaining one-third will have what you might call Bartleby syndrome. Bartleby, the scrivener in Herman Melville's extraordinary short story, stops working and answers every request his employer makes with "I would prefer not to." Many horses, early in their racing careers, apparently come to realize that they don't need to run if they don't feel like it. They may start a race running fast, but, at some point, they'll simply slow down or stop running al-together. Why run around an oval as fast as you can, especially when your hooves and hocks ache? "I would prefer not to," they decide. (I have a soft spot for Bartlebys, horse or human.)

With the odds stacked against them, how can owners pick a profitable horse? Historically, people have believed that the best way to predict whether a horse will succeed has been to analyze his or her pedigree. Being a horse expert means being able to rattle off everything anybody could possibly want to know about a horse's father, mother, grandfathers, grandmoth-ers, brothers, and sisters. Agents announce, for instance, that a big horse "came to her size legitimately" if her mother's line has lots of big horses.

There is one problem, however. While pedigree does mat-ter, it can still only explain a small part of a racing horse's suc-cess. Consider the track record of full siblings of all the horses named Horse of the Year, racing's most prestigious annual award. These horses have the best possible pedigrees—the identical family history as world-historical horses. Still, more than three-fourths do not win a major race. The traditional way of predicting horse success, the data tells us, leaves plenty of room for improvement.

It's actually not that surprising that pedigree is not that predictive. Think of humans. Imagine an NBA owner who bought his future team, as ten-year-olds, based on their pedigrees. He would have hired an agent to examine Earvin Johnson III, son of "Magic" Johnson. "He's got nice size, thus far," an agent might say. "It's legitimate size, from the Johnson line. He should have great vision, selflessness, size, and speed. He seems to be outgoing, great personality. Confident walk. Personable. This is a great bet." Unfortunately, fourteen years later, this owner would have a 6'2" (short for a pro ball player) fashion blogger for *E!* Earvin Johnson III might be of great assistance in designing the uniforms, but he would probably offer little help on the court.

Along with the fashion blogger, an NBA owner who chose a team as many owners choose horses would likely snap up Jeffrey and Marcus Jordan, both sons of Michael Jordan, and both of whom proved mediocre college players. Good luck against the Cleveland Cavaliers. They are led by LeBron James, whose mom is 5'5". Or imagine a country that elected its leaders based on their pedigrees. We'd be led by people like George W. Bush. (Sorry, couldn't resist.)

Horse agents do use other information besides pedigree. For example, they analyze the gaits of two-year-olds and examine horses visually. In Ocala, I spent hours chatting with various agents, which was long enough to determine that there was little agreement on what in fact they were looking for.

Add to these rampant contradictions and uncertainties the fact that some horse buyers have what seems like infinite funds, and you get a market with rather large inefficiencies. Ten years ago, Horse No. 153 was a two-year-old who ran faster than every other horse, looked beautiful to most agents, and had a wonderful pedigree—a descendant of Northern Dancer and Secretariat, two of the greatest racehorses of all time. An Irish billionaire and a Dubai sheik both wanted to purchase him. They got into a bidding war that quickly turned into a contest of pride. As hundreds of stunned horse men and women looked on, the bids kept getting higher and higher, until the two-year-old horse finally sold for $16 million, by far the highest price ever paid for a horse. Horse No. 153, who was given the name The Green Monkey, ran three races, earned just $10,000, and was retired.

Seder never had any interest in the traditional methods of evaluating horses. He was interested only in data. He planned to measure various attributes of racehorses and see which of them correlated with their performance. It's important to note that Seder worked out his plan half a decade before the World Wide Web was invented. But his strategy was very much based on data science. And the lessons from his story are applicable to anybody using Big Data.

For years, Seder's pursuit produced nothing but frustration. He measured the size of horses' nostrils, creating the world's first and largest dataset on horse nostril size and eventual earnings. Nostril size, he found, did not predict horse success. He gave horses EKGs to examine their hearts and cut the limbs off dead horses to measure the volume of their fast-twitch muscles. He once grabbed a shovel outside a barn to determine the size of horses' excrement, on the theory that shedding too much weight before an event can slow a horse down. None of this correlated with racing success.

Then, twelve years ago, he got his first big break. Seder decided to measure the size of the horses' internal organs. Since this was impossible with existing technology, he constructed his own portable ultrasound. The results were remarkable. He found that the size of the heart, and particularly the size of the left ventricle, was a massive predictor of a horse's success, the single most important variable. Another organ that mattered was the spleen: horses with small spleens earned virtually nothing.

Seder had a couple more hits. He digitized thousands of videos of horses galloping and found that certain gaits did correlate with racetrack success. He also discovered that some two-year-old horses wheeze after running one-eighth of a mile. Such horses sometimes sell for as much as a million dollars, but Seder's data told him that the wheezers virtually never pan out. He thus assigns an assistant to sit near the finish line and weed out the wheezers.

Of about a thousand horses at the Ocala auction, roughly ten will pass all of Seder's tests. He ignores pedigree entirely, except as it will influence the price a horse will sell for. "Pedigree tells us a horse might have a very small chance of being great," he says. "But if I can see he's great, what do I care how he got there?"

One night, Seder invited me to his room at the Hilton hotel in Ocala. In the room, he told me about his childhood, his family, and his career. He showed me pictures of his wife, daughter, and son. He told me he was one of three Jewish students in his Philadelphia high school, and that when he entered he was

4'10". (He grew in college to 5'9".) He told me about his favorite horse: Pinky Pizwaanski. Seder bought and named this horse after a gay rider. He felt that Pinky, the horse, always gave a great effort even if he wasn't the most successful.

Finally, he showed me the file that included all the data he had recorded on No. 85, the file that drove the biggest prediction of his career. Was he giving away his secret? Perhaps, but he said he didn't care. More important to him than protecting his secrets was being proven right, showing to the world that these twenty years of cracking limbs, shoveling poop, and jerry-rigging ultrasounds had been worth it.

Here's some of the data on horse No. 85:

NO. 85 (LATER AMERICAN PHAROAH) PERCENTILES AS A ONE-YEAR-OLD

	PERCENTILE
Height	56
Weight	61
Pedigree	70
Left Ventricle	*99.61*

There it was, stark and clear, the reason that Seder and his team had become so obsessed with No. 85. His left ventricle was in the 99.61st percentile!

Not only that, but all his other important organs, including the rest of his heart and spleen, were exceptionally large as well. Generally speaking, when it comes to racing, Seder had found, the bigger the left ventricle, the better. But a left ventricle as big as this can be a sign of illness if the other organs are tiny. In American Pharoah, all the key organs were bigger than average, and the left ventricle was enormous. The data screamed that No. 85 was a 1-in-100,000 or even a one-in-a-million horse.

What can data scientists learn from Seder's project?

First, and perhaps most important, if you are going to try to use new data to revolutionize a field, it is best to go into a field where old methods are lousy. The pedigree-obsessed horse agents whom Seder beat left plenty of room for improvement. So did the word-count-obsessed search engines that Google beat.

One weakness of Google's attempt to predict influenza using search data is that you can already predict influenza very well just using last week's data and a simple seasonal adjustment. There is still debate about how much search data adds to that simple, powerful model. In my opinion, Google searches have more promise measuring health conditions for which existing data is weaker and therefore something like Google STD may prove more valuable in the long haul than Google Flu.

The second lesson is that, when trying to make predictions, you needn't worry too much about why your models work. Seder could not fully explain to me why the left ventricle is so important in predicting a horse's success. Nor could he precisely account for the value of the spleen. Perhaps one day horse cardiologists and hematologists will solve these mysteries. But for now it doesn't matter. Seder is in the prediction business, not the explanation business. And, in the prediction business, you just need to know that something works, not why.

For example, Walmart uses data from sales in all their stores to know what products to shelve. Before Hurricane

Frances, a destructive storm that hit the Southeast in 2004, Walmart suspected—correctly—that people's shopping habits may change when a city is about to be pummeled by a storm. They pored through sales data from previous hurricanes to see what people might want to buy. A major answer? Strawberry Pop-Tarts. This product sells seven times faster than normal in the days leading up to a hurricane.

Based on their analysis, Walmart had trucks loaded with strawberry Pop-Tarts heading down Interstate 95 toward stores in the path of the hurricane. And indeed, these Pop-Tarts sold well.

Why Pop-Tarts? Probably because they don't require refrigeration or cooking. Why strawberry? No clue. But when hurricanes hit, people turn to strawberry Pop-Tarts apparently. So in the days before a hurricane, Walmart now regularly stocks its shelves with boxes upon boxes of strawberry Pop-Tarts. The reason for the relationship doesn't matter. But the relationship itself does. Maybe one day food scientists will figure out the association between hurricanes and toaster pastries filled with strawberry jam. But, while waiting for some such explanation, Walmart still needs to stock its shelves with strawberry Pop-Tarts when hurricanes are approaching and save the Rice Krispies treats for sunnier days.

This lesson is also clear in the story of Orley Ashenfelter. What Seder is to horses, Ashenfelter, an economist at Princeton, may be to wine.

A little over a decade ago, Ashenfelter was frustrated. He had been buying a lot of red wine from the Bordeaux region of France. Sometimes this wine was delicious, worthy of its high price. Many times, though, it was a letdown.

Why, Ashenfelter wondered, was he paying the same price for wine that turned out so differently?

One day, Ashenfelter received a tip from a journalist friend and wine connoisseur. There was indeed a way to figure out whether a wine would be good. The key, Ashenfelter's friend told him, was the weather during the growing season.

Ashenfelter's interest was piqued. He went on a quest to figure out if this was true and he could consistently purchase better wine. He downloaded thirty years of weather data on the Bordeaux region. He also collected auction prices of wines. The auctions, which occur many years after the wine was originally sold, would tell you how the wine turned out.

The result was amazing. A huge percentage of the quality of a wine could be explained simply by the weather during the growing season.

In fact, a wine's quality could be broken down to one simple formula, which we might call the First Law of Viticulture:

Price = 12.145 + 0.00117 winter rainfall + 0.0614 average growing season temperature – 0.00386 harvest rainfall.

So why does wine quality in the Bordeaux region work like this? What explains the First Law of Viticulture? There is some explanation for Ashenfelter's wine formula—heat and early irrigation are necessary for grapes to properly ripen.

But the precise details of his predictive formula go well beyond any theory and will likely never be fully understood even by experts in the field.

Why does a centimeter of winter rain add, on average, exactly 0.1 cents to the price of a fully matured bottle of red wine? Why not 0.2 cents? Why not 0.05? Nobody can answer these questions. But if there are 1,000 centimeters of additional rain in a winter, you should be willing to pay an additional $1 for a bottle of wine.

Indeed, Ashenfelter, despite not knowing exactly why his regression worked exactly as it did, used it to purchase wines. According to him, "It worked out great." The quality of the wines he drank noticeably improved.

If your goal is to predict the future—what wine will taste good, what products will sell, which horses will run fast—you do not need to worry too much about why your model works exactly as it does. Just get the numbers right. That is the second lesson of Jeff Seder's horse story.

The final lesson to be learned from Seder's successful attempt to predict a potential Triple Crown winner is that you have to be open and flexible in determining what counts as data. It is not as if the old-time horse agents were oblivious to data before Seder came along. They scrutinized race times and pedigree charts. Seder's genius was to look for data where others hadn't looked before, to consider nontraditional sources of data. For a data scientist, a fresh and original perspective can pay off.

WORDS AS DATA

One day in 2004, two young economists with an expertise in media, then Ph.D. students at Harvard, were reading about a recent court decision in Massachusetts legalizing gay marriage.

The economists, Matt Gentzkow and Jesse Shapiro, noticed

something interesting: two newspapers employed strikingly different language to report the same story. The *Washington Times*, which has a reputation for being conservative, headlined the story: "Homosexuals 'Marry' in Massachusetts." The *Washington Post*, which has a reputation for being liberal, reported that there had been a victory for "same-sex couples."

It's no surprise that different news organizations can tilt in different directions, that newspapers can cover the same story with a different focus. For years, in fact, Gentzkow and Shapiro had been pondering if they might use their economics training to help understand media bias. Why do some news organizations seem to take a more liberal view and others a more conservative one?

But Gentzkow and Shapiro didn't really have any ideas on how they might tackle this question; they couldn't figure out how they could systematically and objectively measure media subjectivity.

What Gentzkow and Shapiro found interesting, then, about the gay marriage story was not that news organizations differed in their coverage; it was *how* the newspapers' coverage differed—it came down to a distinct shift in word choice. In 2004, "homosexuals," as used by the *Washington Times*, was an old-fashioned and disparaging way to describe gay people, whereas "same-sex couples," as used by the *Washington Post*, emphasized that gay relationships were just another form of romance.

The scholars wondered whether language might be the key to understanding bias. Did liberals and conservatives consistently use different phrases? Could the words that newspapers use in stories be turned into data? What might this reveal about the American press? Could we figure out whether the press was liberal or conservative? And could we figure out why? In 2004, these weren't idle questions. The billions of words in American newspapers were no longer trapped on newsprint or microfilm. Certain websites now recorded every word included in every story for nearly every newspaper in the United States. Gentzkow and Shapiro could scrape these sites and quickly test the extent to which language could measure newspaper bias. And, by doing this, they could sharpen our understanding of how the news media works.

But, before describing what they found, let's leave for a moment the story of Gentzkow and Shapiro and their attempt to quantify the language in newspapers, and discuss how scholars, across a wide range of fields, have utilized this new type of data—words—to better understand human nature.

Language has, of course, always been a topic of interest to social scientists. However, studying language generally required the close reading of texts, and turning huge swaths of text into data wasn't feasible. Now, with computers and digitization, tabulating words across massive sets of documents is easy. Language has thus become subject to Big Data analysis. The links that Google utilized were composed of words. So are the Google searches that I study. Words feature frequently in this book. But language is so important to the Big Data revolution, it deserves its own section. In fact, it is being used so much now that there is an entire field devoted to it: "text as data."

A major development in this field is Google Ngrams. A few years ago, two young biologists, Erez Aiden and Jean-Baptiste

Michel, had their research assistants counting words one by one in old, dusty texts to try to find new insights on how certain usages of words spread. One day, Aiden and Michel heard about a new project by Google to digitize a large portion of the world's books. Almost immediately, the biologists grasped that this would be a much easier way to understand the history of language.

"We realized our methods were so hopelessly obsolete," Aiden told *Discover* magazine. "It was clear that you couldn't compete with this juggernaut of digitization." So they decided to collaborate with the search company. With the help of Google engineers, they created a service that searches through the millions of digitized books for a particular word or phrase. It then will tell researchers how frequently that word or phrase appeared in every year, from 1800 to 2010.

So what can we learn from the frequency with which words or phrases appear in books in different years? For one thing, we learn about the slow growth in popularity of sausage and the relatively recent and rapid growth in popularity of pizza.

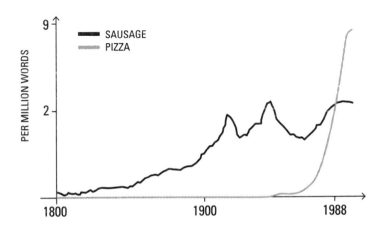

But there are lessons far more profound than that. For instance, Google Ngrams can teach us how national identity formed. One fascinating example is presented in Aiden and Michel's book, *Uncharted*.

First, a quick question. Do you think the United States is currently a united or a divided country? If you are like most people, you would say the United States is divided these days due to the high level of political polarization. You might even say the country is about as divided as it has ever been. America, after all, is now color-coded: red states are Republican; blue states are Democratic. But, in *Uncharted*, Aiden and Michel note one fascinating data point that reveals just how much more divided the United States once was. The data point is the language people use to talk about the country.

Note the words I used in the previous paragraph when I discussed how divided the country is. I wrote, "The United States *is* divided." I referred to the United States as a singular noun. This is natural; it is proper grammar and standard usage. I am sure you didn't even notice.

However, Americans didn't always speak this way. In the early days of the country, Americans referred to the United States using the plural form. For example, John Adams, in his 1799 State of the Union address, referred to "the United States in *their* treaties with his Britanic Majesty." If my book were written in 1800, I would have said, "The United States *are* divided." This little usage difference has long been a fascination for historians, since it suggests there was a point when America stopped thinking of itself as a collection of states and started thinking of itself as one nation.

So when did this happen? Historians, *Uncharted* informs us, have never been sure, as there has been no systematic way to test it. But many have long suspected the cause was the Civil War. In fact, James McPherson, former president of the American Historical Association and a Pulitzer Prize winner, noted bluntly: "The war marked a transition of the United States to a singular noun."

But it turns out McPherson was wrong. Google Ngrams gave Aiden and Michel a systematic way to check this. They could see how frequently American books used the phrase "The United States are . . ." versus "The United States is . . ." for every year in the country's history. The transformation was more gradual and didn't accelerate until well after the Civil War ended.

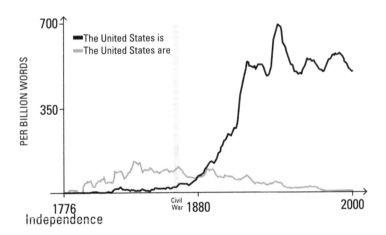

Fifteen years after the Civil War, there were still more uses of "The United States are . . ." than "The United States is . . . ," showing the country was still divided linguistically. Military victories happen quicker than changes in mindsets.

So much for how a country unites. How do a man and woman unite? Words can help here, too.

For example, we can predict whether a man and woman will go on a second date based on how they speak on the first date.

This was shown by an interdisciplinary team of Stanford and Northwestern scientists: Daniel McFarland, Dan Jurafsky, and Craig Rawlings. They studied hundreds of heterosexual speed daters and tried to determine what predicts whether they will feel a connection and want a second date.

They first used traditional data. They asked daters for their height, weight, and hobbies and tested how these factors correlated with someone reporting a spark of romantic interest. Women, on average, prefer men who are taller and share their hobbies; men, on average, prefer women who are skinnier and share their hobbies. Nothing new there.

But the scientists also collected a new type of data. They instructed the daters to take tape recorders with them. The recordings of the dates were then digitized. The scientists were thus able to code the words used, the presence of laughter, and the tone of voice. They could test both how men and women signaled they were interested and how partners earned that interest.

So what did the linguistic data tell us? First, how a man or woman conveys that he or she is interested. One of the ways a man signals that he is attracted is obvious: he laughs at a woman's jokes. Another is less obvious: when speaking, he limits the range of his pitch. There is research that suggests a monotone voice is often seen by women as masculine, which implies that men, perhaps subconsciously, exaggerate their masculinity when they like a woman.

The scientists found that a woman signals her interest by varying her pitch, speaking more softly, and taking shorter turns talking. There are also major clues about a woman's interest based on the particular words she uses. A woman is unlikely to be interested when she uses hedge words and phrases such as "probably" or "I guess."

Fellas, if a woman is hedging her statements on any topic—if she "sorta" likes her drink or "kinda" feels chilly or "probably" will have another hors d'oeuvre—you can bet that she is "sorta" "kinda" "probably" not into you.

A woman *is* likely to be interested when she talks about herself. It turns out that, for a man looking to connect, the most beautiful word you can hear from a woman's mouth may be "I": it's a sign she is feeling comfortable. A woman also is likely to be interested if she uses self-marking phrases such as "Ya know?" and "I mean." Why? The scientists noted that these phrases invite the listener's attention. They are friendly and warm and suggest a person is looking to connect, ya know what I mean?

Now, how can men and women communicate in order to get a date interested in them? The data tells us that there are plenty of ways a man can talk to raise the chances a woman likes him. Women like men who follow their lead. Perhaps not surprisingly, a woman is more likely to report a connection if a man laughs at her jokes and keeps the conversation on topics she introduces rather than constantly changing the subject to those he wants to talk about.* Women also like men who express support and sympathy. If a man says, "That's awesome!" or "That's really cool," a woman is significantly more likely to report a connection. Likewise if he uses phrases such as "That's tough" or "You must be sad."

For women, there is some bad news here, as the data seems to confirm a distasteful truth about men. Conversation plays only a small role in how they respond to women. Physical appearance trumps all else in predicting whether a man reports a connection. That said, there is one word that a woman can use to at least slightly improve the odds a man likes her and it's one we've already discussed: "I." Men are more likely to report clicking with a woman who talks about herself. And as previously noted, a woman is also more likely to report a connection after a date where she talks about herself. Thus it is a great sign, on a first date, if there is substantial discussion about the woman. The woman signals her comfort and probably appreciates that the man is not hogging the conversation. And the man likes that the woman is opening up. A second date is likely.

Finally, there is one clear indicator of trouble in a date transcript: a question mark. If there are lots of questions asked on a date, it is less likely that both the man and the woman will report a connection. This seems counterintuitive; you might

---

* One theory I am working on: Big Data just confirms everything the late Leonard Cohen ever said. For example, Leonard Cohen once gave his nephew the following advice for wooing women: "Listen well. Then listen some more. And when you think you are done listening, listen some more." That seems to be roughly similar to what these scientists found.

think that questions are a sign of interest. But not so on a first date. On a first date, most questions are signs of boredom. "What are your hobbies?" "How many brothers and sisters do you have?" These are the kinds of things people say when the conversation stalls. A great first date may include a single question at the end: "Will you go out with me again?" If this is the only question on the date, the answer is likely to be "Yes."

And men and women don't just talk differently when they're trying to woo each other. They talk differently in general.

A team of psychologists analyzed the words used in hundreds of thousands of Facebook posts. They measured how frequently every word is used by men and women. They could then declare which are the most masculine and most feminine words in the English language.

Many of these word preferences, alas, were obvious. For example, women talk about "shopping" and "my hair" much more frequently than men do. Men talk about "football" and "Xbox" much more frequently than women do. You probably didn't need a team of psychologists analyzing Big Data to tell you that.

Some of the findings, however, were more interesting. Women use the word "tomorrow" far more often than men do, perhaps because men aren't so great at thinking ahead. Adding the letter "o" to the word "so" is one of the most feminine linguistic traits. Among the words most disproportionately used by women are "soo," "sooo," "soooo," "sooooo," and "soooooo."

Maybe it was my childhood exposure to women who weren't afraid to throw the occasional f-bomb. But I always thought cursing was an equal-opportunity trait. Not so. Among the words used much more frequently by men than women are "fuck," "shit," "fucks," "bullshit," "fucking," and "fuckers."

Here are word clouds showing words used mostly by men and those used mostly by women. The larger a word appears, the more that word's use tilts toward that gender.

Males

Females

What I like about this study is the new data informs us of patterns that have long existed but we hadn't necessarily been aware of. Men and women have always spoken in different ways. But, for tens of thousands of years, this data disappeared as soon as the sound waves faded in space. Now this data is preserved on computers and can be analyzed by computers.

Or perhaps what I should have said, given my gender: "The words used to fucking disappear. Now we can take a break from watching football and playing Xbox and learn this shit. That is, if anyone gives a fuck."

It isn't just men and women who speak differently. People use different words as they age. This might even give us some clues as to how the aging process plays out. Here, from the same study, are the words most disproportionately used by people of different ages on Facebook. I call this graphic

DRINK. WORK. PRAY.

19- to 22-year-olds

23- to 29-year-olds

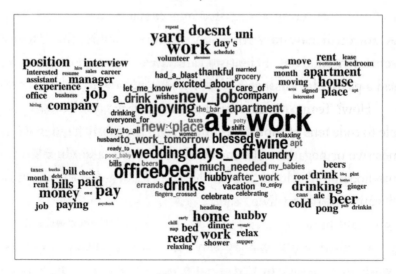

30- to 65-year-olds

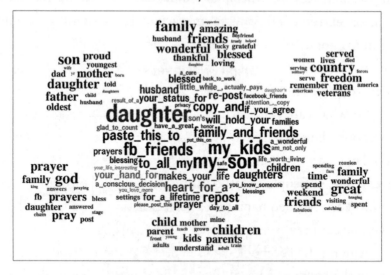

"Drink. Work. Pray." In people's teens, they're drinking. In their twenties, they are working. In their thirties and onward, they are praying.

A powerful new tool for analyzing text is something called sentiment analysis. Scientists can now estimate how happy or sad a particular passage of text is.

How? Teams of scientists have asked large numbers of people to code tens of thousands of words in the English language as positive or negative. The most positive words, according to this methodology, include "happy," "love," and "awesome." The most negative words include "sad," "death," and "depression." They thus have built an index of the mood of a huge set of words.

Using this index, they can measure the average mood of words in a passage of text. If someone writes "I am happy and in love and feeling awesome," sentiment analysis would code that as extremely happy text. If someone writes "I am sad thinking about all the world's death and depression," sentiment analysis would code that as extremely sad text. Other pieces of text would be somewhere in between.

So what can you learn when you code the mood of text? Facebook data scientists have shown one exciting possibility. They can estimate a country's Gross National Happiness every day. If people's status messages tend to be positive, the country is assumed happy for the day. If they tend to be negative, the country is assumed sad for the day.

Among the Facebook data scientists' findings: Christmas is one of the happiest days of the year. Now, I was skeptical of this analysis—and am a bit skeptical of this whole project. Generally, I think many people are secretly sad on Christmas because they are lonely or fighting with their family. More generally, I tend not to trust Facebook status updates, for reasons that I will discuss in the next chapter—namely, our propensity to lie about our lives on social media.

If you are alone and miserable on Christmas, do you really want to bother all of your friends by posting about how unhappy you are? I suspect there are many people spending a joyless Christmas who still post on Facebook about how grateful they are for their "wonderful, awesome, amazing, happy life." They then get coded as substantially raising America's Gross National Happiness. If we are going to really code Gross National Happiness, we should use more sources than just Facebook status updates.

That said, the finding that Christmas is, on balance, a joyous occasion does seem legitimately to be true. Google searches for depression and Gallup surveys also tell us that Christmas is among the happiest days of the year. And, contrary to an urban myth, suicides drop around the holidays. Even if there are some sad and lonely people on Christmas, there are many more merry ones.

These days, when people sit down to read, most of the time it is to peruse status updates on Facebook. But, once upon a time, not so long ago, human beings read stories, sometimes in books. Sentiment analysis can teach us a lot here, too.

A team of scientists, led by Andy Reagan, now at the University of California at Berkeley School of Information, downloaded the text of thousands of books and movie scripts. They could then code how happy or sad each point of the story was.

Consider, for example, the book *Harry Potter and the Deathly Hallows*. Here, from that team of scientists, is how the mood of the story changes, along with a description of key plot points.

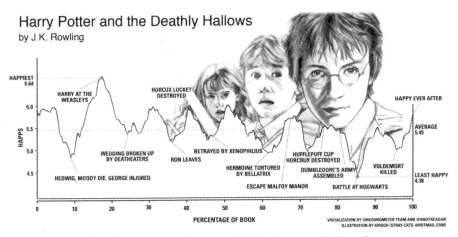

Harry Potter and the Deathly Hallows
by J.K. Rowling

Note that the many rises and falls in mood that the sentiment analysis detects correspond to key events.

Most stories have simpler structures. Take, for example, Shakespeare's tragedy *King John*. In this play, nothing goes right. King John of England is asked to renounce his throne. He is excommunicated for disobeying the pope. War breaks out. His nephew dies, perhaps by suicide. Other people die. Finally, John is poisoned by a disgruntled monk.

And here is the sentiment analysis as the play progresses.

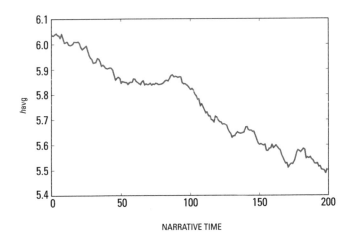

In other words, just from the words, the computer was able to detect that things go from bad to worse to worst.

Or consider the movie *127 Hours*. A basic plot summary of this movie is as follows:

> A mountaineer goes to Utah's Canyonlands National Park to hike. He befriends other hikers but then parts ways with them. Suddenly, he slips and knocks loose a boulder, which traps his hand and wrist. He attempts various escapes, but each one fails. He becomes depressed. Finally, he amputates his arm and escapes. He gets married, starts a family, and continues climbing, although now he makes sure to leave a note whenever he goes off.

And here is the sentiment analysis as the movie progresses, again by Reagan's team of scientists.

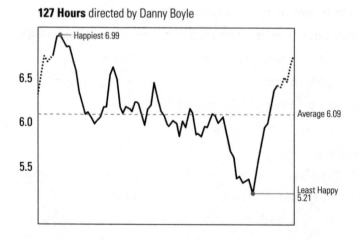

127 Hours directed by Danny Boyle

So what do we learn from the mood of thousands of these stories?

The computer scientists found that a huge percentage of stories fit into one of six relatively simple structures. They are, borrowing a chart from Reagan's team:

Rags to Riches (rise)
Riches to Rags (fall)
Man in a Hole (fall, then rise)
Icarus (rise, then fall)
Cinderella (rise, then fall, then rise)
Oedipus (fall, then rise, then fall)

There might be small twists and turns not captured by this simple scheme. For example, *127 Hours* ranks as a Man in a Hole story, even though there are moments along the way down when sentiments temporarily improve. The large, over-arching structure of most stories fits into one of the six categories. *Harry Potter and the Deathly Hallows* is an exception.

There are a lot of additional questions we might answer. For example, how has the structure of stories changed through time? Have stories gotten more complicated through the years? Do cultures differ in the types of stories they tell? What types of stories do people like most? Do different story structures appeal to men and women? What about people in different countries?

Ultimately, text as data may give us unprecedented insights into what audiences actually want, which may be different from what authors or executives think they want. Already there are some clues that point in this direction.

Consider a study by two Wharton School professors, Jonah Berger and Katherine L. Milkman, on what types of stories get shared. They tested whether positive stories or negative stories were more likely to make the *New York Times'* most-emailed list. They downloaded every *Times* article over a three-month period. Using sentiment analysis, the professors coded the mood of articles. Examples of positive stories included "Wide-Eyed New Arrivals Falling in Love with the City" and "Tony Award for Philanthropy." Stories such as "Web Rumors Tied to Korean Actress' Suicide" and "Germany: Baby Polar Bear's Feeder Dies" proved, not surprisingly, to be negative.

The professors also had information about where the story was placed. Was it on the home page? On the top right? The top left? And they had information about when the story came out. Late Tuesday night? Monday morning?

They could compare two articles—one of them positive, one of them negative—that appeared in a similar place on the *Times* site and came out at a similar time and see which one was more likely to be emailed.

So what gets shared, positive or negative articles?

Positive articles. As the authors conclude, "Content is more likely to become viral the more positive it is."

Note this would seem to contrast with the conventional journalistic wisdom that people are attracted to violent and catastrophic stories. It may be true that news media give people plenty of dark stories. There is something to the newsroom adage, "If it bleeds, it leads." The Wharton professors' study, however, suggests that people may actually want more cheery stories. It may suggest a new adage: "If it smiles, it's emailed," though that doesn't really rhyme.

So much for sad and happy text. How do you figure out what words are liberal or conservative? And what does that tell us about the modern news media? This is a bit more complicated, which brings us back to Gentzkow and Shapiro. Remember, they were the economists who saw gay marriage described different ways in two different newspapers and wondered if they could use language to uncover political bias.

The first thing these two ambitious young scholars did was examine transcripts of the *Congressional Record*. Since this record was already digitized, they could download every word used by every Democratic congressperson in 2005 and every word used by every Republican congressperson in 2005. They could then see if certain phrases were significantly more likely to be used by Democrats or Republicans.

Some were indeed. Here are a few examples in each category.

PHRASES USED FAR MORE BY DEMOCRATS	PHRASES USED FAR MORE BY REPUBLICANS
Estate tax	Death tax
Privatize social security	Reform social security
Rosa Parks	Saddam Hussein
Workers' rights	Private property rights
Poor people	Government spending

What explains these differences in language?

Sometimes Democrats and Republicans use different phrasing to describe the same concept. In 2005, Republicans tried to cut the federal inheritance tax. They tended to describe it as a "death tax" (which sounds like an imposition upon the newly deceased). Democrats described it as an "estate tax" (which sounds like a tax on the wealthy). Similarly, Republicans tried to move Social Security into individual retirement accounts. To Republicans, this was a "reform." To Democrats, this was a more dangerous-sounding "privatization."

Sometimes differences in language are a question of emphasis. Republicans and Democrats presumably both have great respect for Rosa Parks, the civil rights hero. But Democrats talked about her more frequently. Likewise, Democrats and Republicans presumably both think that Saddam Hussein, the former leader of Iraq, was an evil dictator. But Republicans repeatedly mentioned him in their attempt to justify the Iraq War. Similarly, "workers' rights" and concern for "poor people" are core principles of the Democratic Party. "Private property rights" and cutting "government spending" are core principles of Republicans.

And these differences in language use are substantial. For example, in 2005, congressional Republicans used the phrase "death tax" 365 times and "estate tax" only 46 times. For congressional Democrats, the pattern was reversed. They used the phrase "death tax" only 35 times and "estate tax" 195 times.

And if these words can tell us whether a congressperson is a Democrat or a Republican, the scholars realized, they could also tell us whether a newspaper tilts left or right. Just as Republican congresspeople might be more likely to use the phrase "death tax" to persuade people to oppose it, conservative newspapers might do the same. The relatively liberal *Washington Post* used the phrase "estate tax" 13.7 times more frequently than they used the phrase "death tax." The conservative *Wash-*

ington Times used "death tax" and "estate tax" about the same amount.

Thanks to the wonders of the internet, Gentzkow and Shapiro could analyze the language used in a large number of the nation's newspapers. The scholars utilized two websites, newslibrary.com and proquest.com, which together had digitized 433 newspapers. They then counted how frequently one thousand such politically charged phrases were used in newspapers in order to measure the papers' political slant. The most liberal newspaper, by this measure, proved to be the *Philadelphia Daily News;* the most conservative: the *Billings* (Montana) *Gazette.*

When you have the first comprehensive measure of media bias for such a wide swath of outlets, you can answer perhaps the most important question about the press: why do some publications lean left and others right?

The economists quickly homed in on one key factor: the politics of a given area. If an area is generally liberal, as Philadelphia and Detroit are, the dominant newspaper there tends to be liberal. If an area is more conservative, as are Billings and Amarillo, Texas, the dominant paper there tends to be conservative. In other words, the evidence strongly suggests that newspapers are inclined to give their readers what they want.

You might think a paper's owner would have some influence on the slant of its coverage, but as a rule, who owns a paper has less effect than we might think upon its political bias. Note what happens when the same person or company owns papers in different markets. Consider the New York Times Company. It owns what Gentzkow and Shapiro find to be the liberal-leaning *New York Times,* based in New York City, where roughly 70 percent of the population is Democratic. It also owned, at the time of the study, the conservative-leaning, by their measure, *Spartanburg Herald-Journal*, in Spartanburg, South Carolina, where roughly 70 percent of the population is Republican. There are exceptions, of course: Rupert Murdoch's News Corporation owns what just about anyone would find to be the conservative *New York Post*. But, overall, the findings suggest that the market determines newspapers' slants far more than owners do.

The study has a profound impact on how we think about the news media. Many people, particularly Marxists, have viewed American journalism as controlled by rich people or corporations with the goal of influencing the masses, perhaps to push people toward their political views. Gentzkow and Shapiro's paper suggests, however, that this is not the predominant motivation of owners. The owners of the American press, instead, are primarily giving the masses what they want so that the owners can become even richer.

Oh, and one more question—a big, controversial, and perhaps even more provocative question. Do the American news media, on average, slant left or right? Are the media on average liberal or conservative?

Gentzkow and Shapiro found that newspapers slant left. The average newspaper is more similar, in the words it uses, to a Democratic congressperson than it is to a Republican congressperson.

"Aha!" conservative readers may be ready to scream, "I told you so!" Many conservatives have long suspected newspapers have been biased to try to manipulate the masses to support left-wing viewpoints.

Not so, say the authors. In fact, the liberal bias is well calibrated to what newspaper readers want. Newspaper readership, on average, tilts a bit left. (They have data on that.) And newspapers, on average, tilt a bit left to give their readers the viewpoints they demand.

There is no grand conspiracy. There is just capitalism.

The news media, Gentzkow and Shapiro's results imply, often operate like every other industry on the planet. Just as supermarkets figure out what ice cream people want and fill their shelves with it, newspapers figure out what viewpoints people want and fill their pages with it. "It's just a business," Shapiro told me. That is what you can learn when you break down and quantify matters as convoluted as news, analysis, and opinion into their component parts: words.

PICTURES AS DATA

Traditionally, when academics or businesspeople wanted data, they conducted surveys. The data came neatly formed, drawn from numbers or checked boxes on questionnaires. This is no longer the case. The days of structured, clean, simple, survey-based data are over. In this new age, the messy traces we leave as we go through life are becoming the primary source of data.

As we've already seen, words are data. Clicks are data. Links are data. Typos are data. Bananas in dreams are data. Tone of voice is data. Wheezing is data. Heartbeats are data. Spleen size is data. Searches are, I argue, the most revelatory data.

Pictures, it turns out, are data, too.

Just as words, which were once confined to books and periodicals on dusty shelves, have now been digitized, pictures have been liberated from albums and cardboard boxes. They too have been transformed into bits and released into the cloud. And as text can give us history lessons—showing us, for example, the changing ways people have spoken—pictures can give us history lessons—showing us, for example, the changing ways people have posed.

Consider an ingenious study by a team of four computer scientists at Brown and Berkeley. They took advantage of a neat digital-era development: many high schools have scanned their historical yearbooks and made them available online. Across the internet, the researchers found 949 scanned yearbooks from American high schools spanning the years 1905–2013. This included tens of thousands of senior portraits. Using computer software, they were able to create an "average" face out of the pictures from every decade. In other words, they could figure out the average location and configuration of people's noses, eyes, lips, and hair. Here are the average faces from across the last century plus, broken down by gender:

Notice anything? Americans—and particularly women—started smiling. They went from nearly stone-faced at the start of the twentieth century to beaming by the end.

So why the change? Did Americans get happier?

Nope. Other scholars have helped answer this question. The reason is, at least to me, fascinating. When photographs were first invented, people thought of them like paintings. There was nothing else to compare them to. Thus, subjects in photos copied subjects in paintings. And since people sitting for portraits couldn't hold a smile for the many hours the painting took, they adopted a serious look. Subjects in photos adopted the same look.

What finally got them to change? Business, profit, and marketing, of course. In the mid-twentieth century, Kodak, the film and camera company, was frustrated by the limited number of pictures people were taking and devised a strategy to get them to take more. Kodak's advertising began associating photos with happiness. The goal was to get people in the habit of taking a picture whenever they wanted to show others what a good time they were having. All those smiling yearbook photos are a result of that successful campaign (as are most of the photos you see on Facebook and Instagram today).

But photos as data can tell us much more than when high school seniors began to say "cheese." Surprisingly, images may be able to tell us how the economy is doing.

Consider one provocatively titled academic paper: "Measuring Economic Growth from Outer Space." When a paper has a title like that, you can bet I'm going to read it. The authors of this paper—J. Vernon Henderson, Adam Storeygard, and David N. Weil—begin by noting that in many developing countries, existing measures of gross domestic product (GDP) are inefficient. This is because large portions of economic activity happen off the books, and the government agencies meant to measure economic output have limited resources.

The authors' rather unconventional idea? They could help measure GDP based on how much light there is in these countries at night. They got that information from photographs taken by a U.S. Air Force satellite that circles the earth fourteen times per day.

Why might light at night be a good measure of GDP? Well, in very poor parts of the world, people struggle to pay for electricity. And as a result, when economic conditions are bad, households and villages will dramatically reduce the amount of light they allow themselves at night.

Night light dropped sharply in Indonesia during the 1998 Asian financial crisis. In South Korea, night light increased 72 percent from 1992 to 2008, corresponding to a remarkably strong economic performance over this period. In North Korea, over the same time, night light actually fell, corresponding to a dismal economic performance during this time.

In 1998, in southern Madagascar, a large accumulation of rubies and sapphires was discovered. The town of Ilakaka went from little more than a truck stop to a major trading center. There was virtually no night light in Ilakaka prior to 1998. In the next five years, there was an explosion of light at night.

The authors admit their night light data is far from a perfect measure of economic output. You most definitely cannot know exactly how an economy is doing just from how much light satellites can pick up at night. The authors do not recommend using this measure at all for developed countries, such as the United States, where the existing economic data is more accurate. And to be fair, even in developing countries, they find that night light is only about as useful as the official measures. But combining both the flawed government data with the imperfect night light data gives a better estimate than either source alone could provide. You can, in other words, improve your understanding of developing economies using pictures taken from outer space.

Joseph Reisinger, a computer science Ph.D. with a soft voice, shares the night light authors' frustration with the existing datasets on the economies in developing countries. In April 2014, Reisinger notes, Nigeria updated its GDP estimate, taking into account new sectors they may have missed in previous estimates. Their estimated GDP was now 90 percent higher.

"They're the largest economy in Africa," Reisinger said, his voice slowly rising. "We don't even know the most basic thing we would want to know about that country."

He wanted to find a way to get a sharper look at economic performance. His solution is quite an example of how to reimagine what constitutes data and the value of doing so.

Reisinger founded a company, Premise, which employs a group of workers in developing countries, armed with smartphones. The employees' job? To take pictures of interesting goings-on that might have economic import.

The employees might get snapshots outside gas stations or of fruit bins in supermarkets. They take pictures of the same locations over and over again. The pictures are sent back to Premise, whose second group of employees—computer scientists—turn the photos into data. The company's analysts can code everything from the length of lines in gas stations to how many apples are available in a supermarket to the ripeness of these apples to the price listed on the apples' bin. Based on photographs of all sorts of activity, Premise can begin to put together estimates of economic output and inflation. In developing countries, long lines in gas stations are a leading indicator of economic trouble. So are unavailable or unripe apples. Premise's on-the-ground pictures of China helped them discover food inflation there in 2011 and food deflation in 2012, long before the official data came in.

Premise sells this information to banks or hedge funds and also collaborates with the World Bank.

Like many good ideas, Premise's is a gift that keeps on giving. The World Bank was recently interested in the size of the underground cigarette economy in the Philippines. In particular, they wanted to know the effects of the government's recent efforts, which included random raids, to crack down on manufacturers that produced cigarettes without paying a tax. Premise's clever idea? Take photos of cigarette boxes seen on the street. See how many of them have tax stamps, which all legitimate cigarettes do. They have found that this part of the underground economy, while large in 2015, got significantly smaller in 2016. The government's efforts worked, although seeing something usually so hidden—illegal cigarettes—required new data.

As we've seen, what constitutes data has been wildly reimagined in the digital age and a lot of insights have been found in this new information. Learning what drives media bias, what makes a good first date, and how developing economies are really doing is just the beginning.

Not incidentally, a lot of money has also been made from such new data, starting with Messrs. Brin's and Page's tens of billions. Joseph Reisinger hasn't done badly himself. Observers estimate that Premise is now making tens of millions of dollars in annual revenue. Investors recently poured $50 million into the company. This means some investors consider Premise among the most valuable enterprises in the world primarily in the business of taking and selling photos, in the same league as *Playboy*.

There is, in other words, outsize value, for scholars and entrepreneurs alike, in utilizing all the new types of data now available, in thinking broadly about what counts as data. These days, a data scientist must not limit herself to a narrow or traditional view of data. These days, photographs of supermarket lines are valuable data. The fullness of supermarket bins is data. The ripeness of apples is data. Photos from outer space are data. The curvature of lips is data. Everything is data!

And with all this new data, we can finally see through people's lies.

4

DIGITAL TRUTH SERUM

Everybody lies.

People lie about how many drinks they had on the way home. They lie about how often they go to the gym, how much those new shoes cost, whether they read that book. They call in sick when they're not. They say they'll be in touch when they won't. They say it's not about you when it is. They say they love you when they don't. They say they're happy while in the dumps. They say they like women when they really like men.

People lie to friends. They lie to bosses. They lie to kids. They lie to parents. They lie to doctors. They lie to husbands. They lie to wives. They lie to themselves.

And they damn sure lie to surveys.

Here's my brief survey for you:

Have you ever cheated on an exam? _____
Have you ever fantasized about killing someone? _____

Were you tempted to lie? Many people underreport embarrassing behaviors and thoughts on surveys. They want to look good, even though most surveys are anonymous. This is called social desirability bias.

An important paper in 1950 provided powerful evidence of how surveys can fall victim to such bias. Researchers collected data, from official sources, on the residents of Denver: what percentage of them voted, gave to charity, and owned a library card. They then surveyed the residents to see if the percentages would match. The results were, at the time, shocking. What the residents reported to the surveys was very different from the data the researchers had gathered. Even though nobody gave their names, people, in large numbers, exaggerated their voter registration status, voting behavior, and charitable giving.

	REPORTED ON SURVEY	OFFICIAL COUNT
Registered to vote	83%	69%
Voted in last presidential election	73%	61%
Voted in last mayoral election	63%	36%
Have a library card	20%	13%
Gave to a recent Community Chest charitable drive	67%	33%

Has anything changed in sixty-five years? In the age of the internet, not owning a library card is no longer embarrassing. But, while what's embarrassing or desirable may have changed, people's tendency to deceive pollsters remains strong.

A recent survey asked University of Maryland graduates

various questions about their college experience. The answers were compared to official records. People consistently gave wrong information, in ways that made them look good. Fewer than 2 percent reported that they graduated with lower than a 2.5 GPA. (In reality, about 11 percent did.) And 44 percent said they had donated to the university in the past year. (In reality, about 28 percent did.)

And it is certainly possible that lying played a role in the failure of the polls to predict Donald Trump's 2016 victory. Polls, on average, underestimated his support by about 2 percentage points. Some people may have been embarrassed to say they were planning to support him. Some may have claimed they were undecided when they were really going Trump's way all along.

Why do people misinform anonymous surveys? I asked Roger Tourangeau, a research professor emeritus at the University of Michigan and perhaps the world's foremost expert on social desirability bias. Our weakness for "white lies" is an important part of the problem, he explained. "About one-third of the time, people lie in real life," he suggests. "The habits carry over to surveys."

Then there's that odd habit we sometimes have of lying to ourselves. "There is an unwillingness to admit to yourself that, say, you were a screw-up as a student," says Tourangeau.

Lying to oneself may explain why so many people say they are above average. How big is this problem? More than 40 percent of one company's engineers said they are in the top 5 percent. More than 90 percent of college professors say they do above-average work. One-quarter of high school seniors think they are in the top 1 percent in their ability to get along with other people. If you are deluding yourself, you can't be honest in a survey.

Another factor that plays into our lying to surveys is our strong desire to make a good impression on the stranger conducting the interview, if there is someone conducting the interview, that is. As Tourangeau puts it, "A person who looks like your favorite aunt walks in. . . . Do you want to tell your favorite aunt you used marijuana last month?" * Do you want to admit that you didn't give money to your good old alma mater?

For this reason, the more impersonal the conditions, the more honest people will be. For eliciting truthful answers, internet surveys are better than phone surveys, which are better than in-person surveys. People will admit more if they are alone than if others are in the room with them.

However, on sensitive topics, every survey method will elicit substantial misreporting. Tourangeau here used a word that is often thrown around by economists: "incentive." People have no incentive to tell surveys the truth.

---

* Another reason for lying is simply to mess with surveys. This is a huge problem for any research regarding teenagers, fundamentally complicating our ability to understand this age group. Researchers originally found a correlation between a teenager's being adopted and a variety of negative behaviors, such as using drugs, drinking alcohol, and skipping school. In subsequent research, they found this correlation was entirely explained by the 19 percent of self-reported adopted teenagers who weren't actually adopted. Follow-up research has found that a meaningful percent of teenagers tell surveys they are more than seven feet tall, weigh more than four hundred pounds, or have three children. One survey found 99 percent of students who reported having an artificial limb to academic researchers were kidding.

How, therefore, can we learn what our fellow humans are really thinking and doing?

In some instances, there are official data sources we can reference to get the truth. Even if people lie about their charitable donations, for example, we can get real numbers about giving in an area from the charities themselves. But when we are trying to learn about behaviors that are not tabulated in official records or we are trying to learn what people are thinking—their true beliefs, feelings, and desires—there is no other source of information except what people may deign to tell surveys. Until now, that is.

This is the second power of Big Data: certain online sources get people to admit things they would not admit anywhere else. They serve as a digital truth serum. Think of Google searches. Remember the conditions that make people more honest. Online? Check. Alone? Check. No person administering a survey? Check.

And there's another huge advantage that Google searches have in getting people to tell the truth: incentives. If you enjoy racist jokes, you have zero incentive to share that un-PC fact with a survey. You do, however, have an incentive to search for the best new racist jokes online. If you think you may be suffering from depression, you don't have an incentive to admit this to a survey. You do have an incentive to ask Google for symptoms and potential treatments.

Even if you are lying to yourself, Google may nevertheless know the truth. A couple of days before the election, you and some of your neighbors may legitimately think you will drive to a polling place and cast ballots. But, if you and they haven't searched for any information on how to vote or where to vote, data scientists like me can figure out that turnout in your area will actually be low. Similarly, maybe you haven't admitted to yourself that you may suffer from depression, even as you're Googling about crying jags and difficulty getting out of bed. You would show up, however, in an area's depression-related searches that I analyzed earlier in this book.

Think of your own experience using Google. I am guessing you have upon occasion typed things into that search box that reveal a behavior or thought that you would hesitate to admit in polite company. In fact, the evidence is overwhelming that a large majority of Americans are telling Google some very personal things. Americans, for instance, search for "porn" more than they search for "weather." This is difficult, by the way, to reconcile with the survey data since only about 25 percent of men and 8 percent of women admit they watch pornography.

You may have also noticed a certain honesty in Google searches when looking at the way this search engine automatically tries to complete your queries. Its suggestions are based on the most common searches that other people have made. So auto-complete clues us in to what people are Googling. In fact, auto-complete can be a bit misleading. Google won't suggest certain words it deems inappropriate, such as "cock," "fuck," and "porn." This means auto-complete tells us that people's Google thoughts are less racy than they actually are. Even so, some sensitive stuff often still comes up.

If you type "Why is . . ." the first two Google auto-completes currently are "Why is the sky blue?" and "Why is there a leap day?" suggesting these are the two most common ways to complete this search. The third: "Why is my poop green?" And Google auto-complete can get disturbing. Today, if you type in "Is it normal to want to . . . ," the first suggestion is "kill." If you type in "Is it normal to want to kill . . . ," the first suggestion is "my family."

Need more evidence that Google searches can give a different picture of the world than the one we usually see? Consider searches related to regrets around the decision to have or not to have children. Before deciding, some people fear they might make the wrong choice. And, almost always, the question is whether they will regret *not having* kids. People are seven times more likely to ask Google whether they will regret not having children than whether they will regret having children.

After making their decision—either to reproduce (or adopt) or not—people sometimes confess to Google that they rue their choice. This may come as something of a shock but post-decision, the numbers are reversed. Adults with children are 3.6 times more likely to tell Google they regret their decision than are adults without children.

One caveat that should be kept in mind throughout this chapter: Google can display a bias toward unseemly thoughts, thoughts people feel they can't discuss with anyone else. Nonetheless, if we are trying to uncover hidden thoughts, Google's ability to ferret them out can be useful. And the large disparity between regrets on having versus not having kids seems to be telling us that the unseemly thought in this case is a significant one.

Let's pause for a moment to consider what it even means to make a search such as "I regret having children." Google presents itself as a source from which we can seek information directly, on topics like the weather, who won last night's game, or when the Statue of Liberty was erected. But sometimes we type our uncensored thoughts into Google, without much hope that it will be able to help us. In this case, the search window serves as a kind of confessional.

There are thousands of searches every year, for example, for "I hate cold weather," "People are annoying," and "I am sad." Of course, those thousands of Google searches for "I am sad" represent only a tiny of fraction of the hundreds of millions of people who feel sad in a given year. Searches expressing thoughts, rather than looking for information, my research has found, are only made by a small sample of everyone for whom that thought comes to mind. Similarly, my research suggests that the seven thousand searches by Americans every year for "I regret having children" represent a small sample of those who have had that thought.

Kids are obviously a huge joy for many, probably most, people. And, despite my mom's fear that "you and your stupid data analysis" are going to limit her number of grandchildren, this research has not changed my desire to have kids. But that unseemly regret is interesting—and another aspect of humanity that we tend not to see in the traditional datasets. Our culture is constantly flooding us with images of wonderful, happy families. Most people would never consider having children as something they might regret. But some do. They may admit this to no one—except Google.

THE TRUTH ABOUT SEX

How many American men are gay? This is a legendary question in sexuality research. Yet it has been among the toughest questions for social scientists to answer. Psychologists no longer believe Alfred Kinsey's famous estimate—based on surveys that oversampled prisoners and prostitutes—that 10 percent of American men are gay. Representative surveys now tell us about 2 to 3 percent are. But sexual preference has long been among the subjects upon which people have tended to lie. I think I can use Big Data to give a better answer to this question than we have ever had.

First, more on that survey data. Surveys tell us there are far more gay men in tolerant states than intolerant states. For example, according to a Gallup survey, the proportion of the population that is gay is almost twice as high in Rhode Island, the state with the highest support for gay marriage, than Mississippi, the state with the lowest support for gay marriage.

There are two likely explanations for this. First, gay men born in intolerant states may move to tolerant states. Second, gay men in intolerant states may not divulge that they are gay; they are even more likely to lie.

Some insight into explanation number one—gay mobility—can be gleaned from another Big Data source: Facebook, which allows users to list what gender they are interested in. About 2.5 percent of male Facebook users who list a gender of interest say they are interested in men; that corresponds roughly with what the surveys indicate. And Facebook too shows big differences in the gay population in states with high versus low tolerance: Facebook has the gay population more than twice as high in Rhode Island as in Mississippi.

Facebook also can provide information on how people move around. I was able to code the hometown of a sample of openly gay Facebook users. This allowed me to directly estimate how many gay men move out of intolerant states into more toler-ant parts of the country. The answer? There is clearly some mobility—from Oklahoma City to San Francisco, for example. But I estimate that men packing up their Judy Garland CDs and heading to someplace more open-minded can explain less than half of the difference in the openly gay population in tolerant versus intolerant states.*

In addition, Facebook allows us to focus in on high school students. This is a special group, because high school boys rarely get to choose where they live. If mobility explained the state-by-state differences in the openly gay population, these differences should not appear among high school users. So what does the high school data say? There are far fewer openly gay high school boys in intolerant states. Only two in one thousand male high school students in Mississippi are openly gay. So it ain't just mobility.

If a similar number of gay men are born in every state and mobility cannot fully explain why some states have so many more openly gay men, the closet must be playing a big role. Which brings us back to Google, with which so many people have proved willing to share so much.

Might there be a way to use porn searches to test how many

---

* Some may find it offensive that I associate a male preference for Judy Garland with a preference for having sex with men, even in jest. And I certainly don't mean to imply that all—or even most—gay men have a fascination with divas. But search data demonstrates that there is something to the stereotype. I estimate that a man who searches for information about Judy Garland is three times more likely to search for gay porn than straight porn. Some stereotypes, Big Data tells us, are true.

gay men there *really* are in different states? Indeed, there is. Countrywide, I estimate—using data from Google searches and Google AdWords—that about 5 percent of male porn searches are for gay-male porn. (These would include searches for such terms as "Rocket Tube," a popular gay pornographic site, as well as "gay porn.")

And how does this vary in different parts of the country? Overall, there are more gay porn searches in tolerant states compared to intolerant states. This makes sense, given that some gay men move out of intolerant places into tolerant places. But the differences are not nearly as large as the differences suggested by either surveys or Facebook. In Mississippi, I estimate that 4.8 percent of male porn searches are for gay porn, far higher than the numbers suggested by either surveys or Facebook and reasonably close to the 5.2 percent of pornography searches that are for gay porn in Rhode Island.

So how many American men are gay? This measure of pornography searches by men—roughly 5 percent are same-sex—seems a reasonable estimate of the true size of the gay population in the United States. And there is another, less straightforward way to get at this number. It requires some data science. We could utilize the relationship between tolerance and the openly gay population. Bear with me a bit here.

My preliminary research indicates that in a given state every 20 percentage points of support for gay marriage means about one and a half times as many men from that state will identify openly as gay on Facebook. Based on this, we can estimate how many men born in a hypothetically fully tolerant place—where, say, 100 percent of people supported gay marriage—would be openly gay. My estimate is about 5 percent would be, which fits the data from porn searches nicely. The closest we might have to growing up in a fully tolerant environment is high school boys in California's Bay Area. About 4 percent of them are openly gay on Facebook. That seems in line with my calculation.

I should note that I have not yet been able to come up with an estimate of same-sex attraction for women. The pornography numbers are less useful here, since far fewer women watch pornography, making the sample less representative. And of those who do, even women who are primarily attracted to men in real life seem to enjoy viewing lesbian porn. Fully 20 percent of videos watched by women on PornHub are lesbian.

Five percent of American men being gay is an estimate, of course. Some men are bisexual; some—especially when young—are not sure what they are. Obviously, you can't count this as precisely as you might the number of people who vote or attend a movie.

But one consequence of my estimate is clear: an awful lot of men in the United States, particularly in intolerant states, are still in the closet. They don't reveal their sexual preferences on Facebook. They don't admit it on surveys. And in many cases, they may even be married to women.

It turns out that wives suspect their husbands of being gay rather frequently. They demonstrate that suspicion in the surprisingly common search: "Is my husband gay?" "Gay" is 10 percent more likely to complete searches that begin "Is my husband . . ." than the second-place word, "cheating." It is eight times more common than "an alcoholic" and ten times more common than "depressed."

Most tellingly perhaps, searches questioning a husband's

sexuality are far more prevalent in the least tolerant regions. The states with the highest percentage of women asking this question are South Carolina and Louisiana. In fact, in twenty-one of the twenty-five states where this question is most frequently asked, support for gay marriage is lower than the national average.

Google and porn sites aren't the only useful data resources when it comes to men's sexuality. There is more evidence available in Big Data on what it means to live in the closet. I analyzed ads on Craigslist for males looking for "casual encounters." The percentage of these ads that are seeking casual encounters with men tends to be larger in less tolerant states. Among the states with the highest percentages are Kentucky, Louisiana, and Alabama.

And for even more of a glimpse into the closet, let's return to Google search data and get a little more granular. One of the most common searches made immediately before or after "gay porn" is "gay test." (These tests presume to tell men whether or not they are homosexual.) And searches for "gay test" are about twice as prevalent in the least tolerant states.

What does it mean to go back and forth between searching for "gay porn" and searching for "gay test"? Presumably, it suggests a fairly confused if not tortured mind. It's reasonable to suspect that some of these men are hoping to confirm that their interest in gay porn does not actually mean they're gay.

The Google search data does not allow us to see a particular user's search history over time. However, in 2006, AOL released a sample of their users' searches to academic researchers. Here are some of one anonymous user's searches over a six-day period.

Friday 03:49:55	free gay picks [*sic*]
Friday 03:59:37	locker room gay picks
Friday 04:00:14	gay picks
Friday 04:00:35	gay sex picks
Friday 05:08:23	a long gay quiz
Friday 05:10:00	a good gay test
Friday 05:25:07	gay tests for a confused man
Friday 05:26:38	gay tests
Friday 05:27:22	am i gay tests
Friday 05:29:18	gay picks
Friday 05:30:01	naked men picks
Friday 05:32:27	free nude men picks
Friday 05:38:19	hot gay sex picks
Friday 05:41:34	hot man butt sex
Wednesday 13:37:37	am i gay tests
Wednesday 13:41:20	gay tests
Wednesday 13:47:49	hot man butt sex
Wednesday 13:50:31	free gay sex vidio [*sic*]

This certainly reads like a man who is not comfortable with his sexuality. And the Google data tells us there are still many men like him. Most of them, in fact, live in states that are less tolerant of same-sex relationships.

For an even closer look at the people behind these numbers, I asked a psychiatrist in Mississippi, who specializes in helping closeted gay men, if any of his patients might want to talk to me. One man reached out. He told me he was a retired professor, in his sixties, and married to the same woman for more than forty years.

About ten years ago, overwhelmed with stress, he saw the

psychiatrist and finally acknowledged his sexuality. He has always known he was attracted to men, he says, but thought that this was universal and something that all men just hid. Shortly after beginning therapy, he had his first, and only, gay sexual encounter, with a student of his who was in his late twenties, an experience he describes as "wonderful."

He and his wife do not have sex. He says that he would feel guilty ever ending his marriage or openly dating a man. He regrets virtually every one of his major life decisions.

The retired professor and his wife will go another night without romantic love, without sex. Despite enormous progress, the persistence of intolerance will cause millions of other Americans to do the same.

You may not be shocked to learn that 5 percent of men are gay and that many remain in the closet. There have been times when most people would have been shocked. And there are still places where many people would be shocked as well.

"In Iran we don't have homosexuals like in your country," Mahmoud Ahmadinejad, then president of Iran, insisted in 2007. "In Iran we do not have this phenomenon." Likewise, Anatoly Pakhomov, mayor of Sochi, Russia, shortly before his city hosted the 2014 Winter Olympics, said of gay people, "We do not have them in our city." Yet internet behavior reveals significant interest in gay porn in Sochi and Iran.

This raises an obvious question: are there any common sexual interests in the United States today that are still considered shocking? It depends what you consider common and how easily shocked you are.

Most of the top searches on PornHub are not surprising—they include terms like "teen," "threesome," and "blowjob" for men, phrases like "passionate love making," "nipple sucking," and "man eating pussy" for women.

Leaving the mainstream, PornHub data does tell us about some fetishes that you might not have ever guessed existed. There are women who search for "anal apples" and "humping stuffed animals." There are men who search for "snot fetish" and "nude crucifixion." But these searches are rare—only about ten every month even on this huge porn site.

Another related point that becomes quite clear when reviewing PornHub data: there's someone out there for everyone. Women, not surprisingly, often search for "tall" guys, "dark" guys, and "handsome" guys. But they also sometimes search for "short" guys, "pale" guys, and "ugly" guys. There are women who search for "disabled" guys, "chubby guy with small dick," and "fat ugly old man." Men frequently search for "thin" women, women with "big tits," and women with "blonde" hair. But they also sometimes search for "fat" women, women with "tiny tits," and women with "green hair." There are men who search for "bald" women, "midget" women, and women with "no nipples." This data can be cheering for those who are not tall, dark, and handsome or thin, big-breasted, and blonde.*

---

* I think this data also has implications for one's optimal dating strategy. Clearly, one should put oneself out there, get rejected a lot, and not take rejection personally. This process will allow you, eventually, to find the mate who is most attracted to someone like you. Again, no matter what you look like, these people exist. Trust me.

What about other searches that are both common and surprising? Among the 150 most common searches by men, the most surprising for me are the incestuous ones I discussed in the chapter on Freud. Other little-discussed objects of men's desire are "shemales" (77th most common search) and "granny" (110th most common search). Overall, about 1.4 percent of men's PornHub searches are for women with penises. About 0.6 percent (0.4 percent for men under the age of thirty-four) are for the elderly. Only 1 in 24,000 PornHub searches by men are explicitly for preteens; that may have something to do with the fact that PornHub, for obvious reasons, bans all forms of child pornography and possessing it is illegal.

Among the top PornHub searches by women is a genre of pornography that, I warn you, will disturb many readers: sex featuring violence against women. Fully 25 percent of female searches for straight porn emphasize the pain and/or humiliation of the woman—"painful anal crying," "public disgrace," and "extreme brutal gangbang," for example. Five percent look for nonconsensual sex—"rape" or "forced" sex—even though these videos are banned on PornHub. And search rates for all these terms are at least twice as common among women as among men. If there is a genre of porn in which violence is perpetrated against a woman, my analysis of the data shows that it almost always appeals disproportionately to women.

Of course, when trying to come to terms with this, it is really important to remember that there is a difference between fantasy and real life. Yes, of the minority of women who visit PornHub, there is a subset who search—unsuccessfully—for rape imagery. To state the obvious, this does not mean women want to be raped in real life and it certainly doesn't make rape any less horrific a crime. What the porn data does tell us is that sometimes people have fantasies they wish they didn't have and which they may never mention to others.

Closets are not just repositories of fantasies. When it comes to sex, people keep many secrets—about how much they are having, for example.

In the introduction, I noted that Americans report using far more condoms than are sold every year. You might therefore think this means they are just saying they use condoms more often during sex than they actually do. The evidence suggests they also exaggerate how frequently they are having sex to begin with. About 11 percent of women between the ages of fifteen and forty-four say they are sexually active, not currently pregnant, and not using contraception. Even with relatively conservative assumptions about how many times they are having sex, scientists would expect 10 percent of them to become pregnant every month. But this would already be more than the total number of pregnancies in the United States (which is 1 in 113 women of childbearing age). In our sex-obsessed culture it can be hard to admit that you are just not having that much.

But if you're looking for understanding or advice, you have, once again, an incentive to tell Google. On Google, there are sixteen times more complaints about a spouse not wanting sex than about a married partner not being willing to talk. There are five and a half times more complaints about an unmarried partner not wanting sex than an unmarried partner refusing to text back.

And Google searches suggest a surprising culprit for many of these sexless relationships. There are twice as many complaints that a boyfriend won't have sex than that a girlfriend won't have sex. By far, the number one search complaint about a boyfriend is "My boyfriend won't have sex with me." (Google searches are not broken down by gender, but, since the previous analysis said that 95 percent of men are straight, we can guess that not too many "boyfriend" searches are coming from men.)

How should we interpret this? Does this really imply that boyfriends withhold sex more than girlfriends? Not necessarily. As mentioned earlier, Google searches can be biased in favor of stuff people are uptight talking about. Men may feel more comfortable telling their friends about their girlfriend's lack of sexual interest than women are telling their friends about their boyfriend's. Still, even if the Google data does not imply that boyfriends are really twice as likely to avoid sex as girlfriends, it does suggest that boyfriends avoiding sex is more common than people let on.

Google data also suggests a reason people may be avoiding sex so frequently: enormous anxiety, with much of it misplaced. Start with men's anxieties. It isn't news that men worry about how well-endowed they are, but the degree of this worry is rather profound.

Men Google more questions about their sexual organ than any other body part: more than about their lungs, liver, feet, ears, nose, throat, and brain combined. Men conduct more searches for how to make their penises bigger than how to tune a guitar, make an omelet, or change a tire. Men's top Googled concern about steroids isn't whether they may damage their health but whether taking them might diminish the size of their penis. Men's top Googled question related to how their body or mind would change as they aged was whether their penis would get smaller.

Side note: One of the more common questions for Google regarding men's genitalia is "How big is my penis?" That men turn to Google, rather than a ruler, with this question is, in my opinion, a quintessential expression of our digital era.*

Do women care about penis size? Rarely, according to Google searches. For every search women make about a partner's phallus, men make roughly 170 searches about their own. True, on the rare occasions women do express concerns about a partner's penis, it is frequently about its size, but not necessarily that it's small. More than 40 percent of complaints about a partner's penis size say that it's too big. "Pain" is the most Googled word used in searches with the phrase "___ during sex." ("Bleeding," "peeing," "crying," and "farting" round out the top five.) Yet only 1 percent of men's searches looking to change their penis size are seeking information on how to make it smaller.

Men's second-most-common sex question is how to make their sexual encounters longer. Once again, the insecurities of men do not appear to match the concerns of women. There are roughly the same number of searches asking how to make a boyfriend climax more quickly as climax more slowly. In fact, the most common concern women have related to a boyfriend's

---

* I wanted to call this book *How Big Is My Penis? What Google Searches Teach Us About Human Nature*, but my editor warned me that would be a tough sell, that people might be too embarrassed to buy a book with that title in an airport bookstore. Do you agree?

orgasm isn't about when it happened but why it isn't happening at all.

We don't often talk about body image issues when it comes to men. And while it's true that overall interest in personal appearance skews female, it's not as lopsided as stereotypes would suggest. According to my analysis of Google AdWords, which measures the websites people visit, interest in beauty and fitness is 42 percent male, weight loss is 33 percent male, and cosmetic surgery is 39 percent male. Among all searches with "how to" related to breasts, about 20 percent ask how to get rid of man breasts.

But, even if the number of men who lack confidence in their bodies is higher than most people would think, women still outpace them when it comes to insecurity about how they look. So what can this digital truth serum reveal about women's self-doubt? Every year in the United States, there are more than seven million searches looking into breast implants. Official statistics tell us that about 300,000 women go through with the procedure annually.

Women also show a great deal of insecurity about their behinds, although many women have recently flip-flopped on what it is they don't like about them.

In 2004, in some parts of the United States, the most common search regarding changing one's butt was how to make it smaller. The desire to make one's bottom bigger was overwhelmingly concentrated in areas with large black populations. Beginning in 2010, however, the desire for bigger butts grew in the rest of the United States. This interest, if not the posterior distribution itself, has tripled in four years. In 2014, there were more searches asking how to make your butt bigger than smaller in every state. These days, for every five searches looking into breast implants in the United States, there is one looking into butt implants. (Thank you, Kim Kardashian!)

Does women's growing preference for a larger bottom match men's preferences? Interestingly, yes. "Big butt porn" searches, which also used to be concentrated in black communities, have recently shot up in popularity throughout the United States.

What else do men want in a woman's body? As mentioned earlier, and as most will find blindingly obvious, men show a preference for large breasts. About 12 percent of nongeneric pornographic searches are looking for big breasts. This is nearly twenty times higher than the search volume for small-breast porn.

That said, it is not clear that this means men want women to get breast implants. About 3 percent of big-breast porn searches explicitly say they want to see natural breasts.

Google searches about one's wife and breast implants are evenly split between asking how to persuade her to get implants and perplexity as to why she wants them.

Or consider the most common search about a girlfriend's breasts: "I love my girlfriend's boobs." It is not clear what men are hoping to find from Google when making this search.

Women, like men, have questions about their genitals. In fact, they have nearly as many questions about their vaginas as men have about their penises. Women's worries about their vaginas are often health related. But at least 30 percent of their questions take up other concerns. Women want to know how to shave it, tighten it, and make it taste better. A strikingly common concern, as touched upon earlier, is how to improve its odor.

Women are most frequently concerned that their vaginas smell like fish, followed by vinegar, onions, ammonia, garlic, cheese, body odor, urine, bread, bleach, feces, sweat, metal, feet, garbage, and rotten meat.

In general, men do not make many Google searches involving a partner's genitalia. Men make roughly the same number of searches about a girlfriend's vagina as women do about a boyfriend's penis.

When men do search about a partner's vagina, it is usually to complain about what women worry about most: the odor. Mostly, men are trying to figure out how to tell a woman about a bad odor without hurting her feelings. Sometimes, however, men's questions about odor reveal their own insecurities. Men occasionally ask for ways to use the smell to detect cheating— if it smells like condoms, for example, or another man's semen.

What should we make of all this secret insecurity? There is clearly some good news here. Google gives us legitimate reasons to worry less than we do. Many of our deepest fears about how our sexual partners perceive us are unjustified. Alone, at their computers, with no incentive to lie, partners reveal themselves to be fairly nonsuperficial and forgiving. In fact, we are all so busy judging our own bodies that there is little energy left over to judge other people's.

There is also probably a connection between two of the big concerns revealed in the sexual searches on Google: lack of sex and an insecurity about one's sexual attractiveness and performance. Maybe these are related. Maybe if we worried less about sex, we'd have more of it.

What else can Google searches tell us about sex? We can do a battle of the sexes, to see who is most generous. Take all searches looking for ways to get better at performing oral sex on the opposite gender. Do men look for more tips or women? Who is more sexually generous, men or women? Women, duh. Adding up all the possibilities, I estimate the ratio is 2:1 in favor of women looking for advice on how to better perform oral sex on their partner.

And when men do look for tips on how to give oral sex, they are frequently not looking for ways of pleasing another person. Men make as many searches looking for ways to perform oral sex on themselves as they do how to give a woman an orgasm. (This is among my favorite facts in Google search data.)

THE TRUTH ABOUT HATE AND PREJUDICE

Sex and romance are hardly the only topics cloaked in shame and, therefore, not the only topics about which people keep secrets. Many people are, for good reason, inclined to keep their prejudices to themselves. I suppose you could call it progress that many people today feel they will be judged if they admit they judge other people based on their ethnicity, sexual orientation, or religion. But many Americans still do. (This is another section, I warn readers, that includes disturbing material.)

You can see this on Google, where users sometimes ask questions such as "Why are black people rude?" or "Why are Jews evil?" Below, in order, are the top five negative words used in searches about various groups.

	1.	2.	3.	4.	5.
AFRICAN AMERICANS	rude	racist	stupid	ugly	lazy
JEWS	evil	racist	ugly	cheap	greedy
MUSLIMS	evil	terrorists	bad	violent	dangerous
MEXICANS	racist	stupid	ugly	lazy	dumb
ASIANS	ugly	racist	annoying	stupid	cheap
GAYS	evil	wrong	stupid	annoying	selfish
CHRISTIANS	stupid	crazy	dumb	delusional	wrong

A few patterns among these stereotypes stand out. For example, African Americans are the only group that faces a "rude" stereotype. Nearly every group is a victim of a "stupid" stereotype; the only two that are not: Jews and Muslims. The "evil" stereotype is applied to Jews, Muslims, and gays but not black people, Mexicans, Asians, and Christians.

Muslims are the only group stereotyped as terrorists. When a Muslim American plays into this stereotype, the response can be instantaneous and vicious. Google search data can give us a minute-by-minute peek into such eruptions of hate-fueled rage.

Consider what happened shortly after the mass shooting in San Bernardino, California, on December 2, 2015. That morning, Rizwan Farook and Tashfeen Malik entered a meeting of Farook's coworkers armed with semiautomatic pistols and semiautomatic rifles and murdered fourteen people. That evening, literally minutes after the media first reported one of the shooters' Muslim-sounding name, a disturbing number

of Californians had decided what they wanted to do with
Muslims: kill them.

The top Google search in California with the word "Muslims" in it at the time was "kill Muslims." And overall, Americans searched for the phrase "kill Muslims" with about the same
frequency that they searched for "martini recipe," "migraine
symptoms," and "Cowboys roster." In the days following the
San Bernardino attack, for every American concerned with "Islamophobia," another was searching for "kill Muslims." While
hate searches were approximately 20 percent of all searches about
Muslims before the attack, more than half of all search volume
about Muslims became hateful in the hours that followed it.

And this minute-by-minute search data can tell us how
difficult it can be to calm this rage. Four days after the shooting, then-president Obama gave a prime-time address to the
country. He wanted to reassure Americans that the government could both stop terrorism and, perhaps more important,
quiet this dangerous Islamophobia.

Obama appealed to our better angels, speaking of the importance of inclusion and tolerance. The rhetoric was powerful
and moving. The *Los Angeles Times* praised Obama for "[warn-
ing] against allowing fear to cloud our judgment." The *New York
Times* called the speech both "tough" and "calming." The website
Think Progress praised it as "a necessary tool of good governance,
geared towards saving the lives of Muslim Americans." Obama's
speech, in other words, was judged a major success. But was it?

Google search data suggests otherwise. Together with Evan
Soltas, then at Princeton, I examined the data. In his speech,
the president said, "It is the responsibility of all Americans—
of every faith—to reject discrimination." But searches calling

Muslims "terrorists," "bad," "violent," and "evil" doubled during and shortly after the speech. President Obama also said, "It is our responsibility to reject religious tests on who we admit into this country." But negative searches about Syrian refugees, a mostly Muslim group then desperately looking for a safe haven, rose 60 percent, while searches asking how to help Syrian refugees dropped 35 percent. Obama asked Americans to "not forget that freedom is more powerful than fear." Yet searches for "kill Muslims" tripled during his speech. In fact, just about every negative search we could think to test regarding Muslims shot up during and after Obama's speech, and just about every positive search we could think to test declined.

In other words, Obama seemed to say all the right things. All the traditional media congratulated Obama on his healing words. But new data from the internet, offering digital truth serum, suggested that the speech actually backfired in its main goal. Instead of calming the angry mob, as everybody thought he was doing, the internet data tells us that Obama actually inflamed it. Things that we think are working can have the exact opposite effect from the one we expect. Sometimes we need internet data to correct our instinct to pat ourselves on the back.

So what should Obama have said to quell this particular form of hatred currently so virulent in America? We'll circle back to that later. Right now we're going to take a look at an age-old vein of prejudice in the United States, the form of hate that in fact stands out above the rest, the one that has been the most destructive and the topic of the research that began this book. In my work with Google search data, the single most telling fact I have found regarding hate on the internet is the popularity of the word "nigger."

Either singular or in its plural form, the word "nigger" is included in seven million American searches every year. (Again, the word used in rap songs is almost always "nigga," not "nigger," so there's no significant impact from hip-hop lyrics to account for.) Searches for "nigger jokes" are seventeen times more common than searches for "kike jokes," "gook jokes," "spic jokes," "chink jokes," and "fag jokes" combined.

When are searches for "nigger(s)"—or "nigger jokes"—most common? Whenever African-Americans are in the news. Among the periods when such searches were highest was the immediate aftermath of Hurricane Katrina, when television and newspapers showed images of desperate black people in New Orleans struggling for their survival. They also shot up during Obama's first election. And searches for "nigger jokes" rise on average about 30 percent on Martin Luther King Jr. Day.

The frightening ubiquity of this racial slur throws into doubt some current understandings of racism.

Any theory of racism has to explain a big puzzle in America. On the one hand, the overwhelming majority of black Americans think they suffer from prejudice—and they have ample evidence of discrimination in police stops, job interviews, and jury decisions. On the other hand, very few white Americans will admit to being racist.

The dominant explanation among political scientists recently has been that this is due, in large part, to widespread *implicit* prejudice. White Americans may mean well, this theory goes, but they have a subconscious bias, which influences their treatment of black Americans. Academics invented an ingenious way to test for such a bias. It is called the implicit-association test.

The tests have consistently shown that it takes most people milliseconds longer to associate black faces with positive words, such as "good," than with negative words, such as "awful." For white faces, the pattern is reversed. The extra time it takes is evidence of someone's implicit prejudice—a prejudice the person may not even be aware of.

There is, though, an alternative explanation for the discrimination that African-Americans feel and whites deny: hidden *explicit* racism. Suppose there is a reasonably widespread conscious racism of which people are very much aware but to which they won't confess—certainly not in a survey. That's what the search data seems to be saying. There is nothing implicit about searching for "nigger jokes." And it's hard to imagine that Americans are Googling the word "nigger" with the same frequency as "migraine" and "economist" without *explicit* racism having a major impact on African-Americans. Prior to the Google data, we didn't have a convincing measure of this virulent animus. Now we do. We are, therefore, in a position to see what it explains.

It explains, as discussed earlier, why Obama's vote totals in 2008 and 2012 were depressed in many regions. It also correlates with the black-white wage gap, as a team of economists recently reported. The areas that I had found make the most racist searches, in other words, underpay black people. And then there is the phenomenon of Donald Trump's candidacy. As noted in the introduction, when Nate Silver, the polling guru, looked for the geographic variable that correlated most strongly with support in the 2016 Republican primary for Trump, he found it in the map of racism I had developed. That variable was searches for "nigger(s)."

Scholars have recently put together a state-by-state measure of implicit prejudice against black people, which has enabled me to compare the effects of *explicit* racism, as measured by Google searches, and *implicit* bias. For example, I tested how much each worked against Obama in both of his presidential elections. Using regression analysis, I found that, to predict where Obama underperformed, an area's racist Google searches explained a lot. An area's performance on implicit-association tests added little.

To be provocative and to encourage more research in this area, let me put forth the following conjecture, ready to be tested by scholars across a range of fields. The primary explanation for discrimination against African Americans today is not the fact that the people who agree to participate in lab experiments make subconscious associations between negative words and black people; it is the fact that millions of white Americans continue to do things like search for "nigger jokes."

The discrimination black people regularly experience in the United States appears to be fueled more widely by explicit, if hidden, hostility. But, for other groups, subconscious prejudice may have a more fundamental impact. For example, I was able to use Google searches to find evidence of implicit prejudice against another segment of the population: young girls.

And who, might you ask, would be harboring bias against girls?

Their parents.

It's hardly surprising that parents of young children are often excited by the thought that their kids might be gifted. In fact, of all Google searches starting "Is my 2-year-old," the most common next word is "gifted." But this question is not asked equally about young boys and young girls. Parents are two and a half times more likely to ask "Is my son gifted?" than "Is my daughter gifted?" Parents show a similar bias when using other phrases related to intelligence that they may shy away from saying aloud, like, "Is my son a genius?"

Are parents picking up on legitimate differences between young girls and boys? Perhaps young boys are more likely than young girls to use big words or otherwise show objective signs of giftedness? Nope. If anything, it's the opposite. At young ages, girls have consistently been shown to have larger vocabularies and use more complex sentences. In American schools, girls are 9 percent more likely than boys to be in gifted programs. Despite all this, parents looking around the dinner table appear to see more gifted boys than girls.* In fact, on every search term related to intelligence I tested, including those indicating its absence, parents were more likely to be inquiring about their sons rather than their daughters. There are also more searches for "is my son behind" or "stupid" than comparable searches for daughters. But searches with negative words like "behind" and "stupid" are less specifically skewed toward sons than searches with positive words, such as "gifted" or "genius."

What then are parents' overriding concerns regarding their daughters? Primarily, anything related to appearance. Consider questions about a child's weight. Parents Google "Is my daughter

---

* To further test the hypothesis that parents treat kids of different genders differently, I am working on obtaining data from parenting websites. This would include a much larger number of parents than those who make these particular, specific searches.

overweight?" roughly twice as frequently as they Google "Is my son overweight?" Parents are about twice as likely to ask how to get their daughters to lose weight as they are to ask how to get their sons to do the same. Just as with giftedness, this gender bias is not grounded in reality. About 28 percent of girls are overweight, while 35 percent of boys are. Even though scales measure more overweight boys than girls, parents see—or worry about—overweight girls much more frequently than overweight boys.

Parents are also one and a half times more likely to ask whether their daughter is beautiful than whether their son is handsome. And they are nearly three times more likely to ask whether their daughter is ugly than whether their son is ugly. (How Google is expected to know whether a child is beautiful or ugly is hard to say.)

In general, parents seem more likely to use positive words in questions about sons. They are more apt to ask whether a son is "happy" and less apt to ask whether a son is "depressed."

Liberal readers may imagine that these biases are more common in conservative parts of the country, but I didn't find any evidence of that. In fact, I did not find a significant relationship between any of these biases and the political or cultural makeup of a state. Nor is there evidence that these biases have decreased since 2004, the year for which Google search data is first available. It would seem this bias against girls is more widespread and deeply ingrained than we'd care to believe.

Sexism is not the only place our stereotypes about prejudice may be off.

Vikingmaiden88 is twenty-six years old. She enjoys reading history and writing poetry. Her signature quote is from Shakespeare. I gleaned all this from her profile and posts on Stormfront.org, America's most popular online hate site. I also learned that Vikingmaiden88 has enjoyed the content on the site of the newspaper I work for, the *New York Times*. She wrote an enthusiastic post about a particular *Times* feature.

I recently analyzed tens of thousands of such Stormfront profiles, in which registered members can enter their location, birth date, interests, and other information.

Stormfront was founded in 1995 by Don Black, a former Ku Klux Klan leader. Its most popular "social groups" are "Union of National Socialists" and "Fans and Supporters of Adolf Hitler." Over the past year, according to Quantcast, roughly 200,000 to 400,000 Americans visited the site every month. A recent Southern Poverty Law Center report linked nearly one hundred murders in the past five years to registered Stormfront members.

Stormfront members are not whom I would have guessed.

They tend to be young, at least according to self-reported birth dates. The most common age at which people join the site is nineteen. And four times more nineteen-year-olds sign up than forty-year-olds. Internet and social network users lean young, but not nearly that young.

Profiles do not have a field for gender. But I looked at all the posts and complete profiles of a random sample of American users, and it turns out that you can work out the gender of most of the membership: I estimate that about 30 percent of Stormfront members are female.

The states with the most members per capita are Montana, Alaska, and Idaho. These states tend to be overwhelmingly white. Does this mean that growing up with little diversity fosters hate?

Probably not. Rather, since those states have a higher proportion of non-Jewish white people, they have more potential members for a group that attacks Jews and nonwhites. The percentage of Stormfront's target audience that joins is actually higher in areas with more minorities. This is particularly true when you look at Stormfront's members who are eighteen and younger and therefore do not themselves choose where they live.

Among this age group, California, a state with one of the largest minority populations, has a membership rate 25 percent higher than the national average.

One of the most popular social groups on the site is "In Support of Anti-Semitism." The percentage of members who join this group is positively correlated with a state's Jewish population. New York, the state with the highest Jewish population, has above-average per capita membership in this group.

In 2001, Dna88 joined Stormfront, describing himself as a "good looking, racially aware" thirty-year-old Internet developer living in "Jew York City." In the next four months, he wrote more than two hundred posts, like "Jewish Crimes Against Humanity" and "Jewish Blood Money," and directed people to a website, jewwatch.com, which claims to be a "scholarly library" on "Zionist criminality."

Stormfront members complain about minorities' speaking different languages and committing crimes. But what I found most interesting were the complaints about competition in the dating market.

A man calling himself William Lyon Mackenzie King, after a former prime minister of Canada who once suggested that

"Canada should remain a white man's country," wrote in 2003 that he struggled to "contain" his "rage" after seeing a white woman "carrying around her half black ugly mongrel niglet." In her profile, Whitepride26, a forty-one-year-old student in Los Angeles, says, "I dislike blacks, Latinos, and sometimes Asians, especially when men find them more attractive" than "a white female."

Certain political developments play a role. The day that saw the biggest single increase in membership in Stormfront's history, by far, was November 5, 2008, the day after Barack Obama was elected president. There was, however, no increased interest in Stormfront during Donald Trump's candidacy and only a small rise immediately after he won. Trump rode a wave of white nationalism. There is no evidence here that he created a wave of white nationalism.

Obama's election led to a surge in the white nationalist movement. Trump's election seems to be a response to that.

One thing that does not seem to matter: economics. There was no relationship between monthly membership registration and a state's unemployment rate. States disproportionately affected by the Great Recession saw no comparative increase in Google searches for Stormfront.

But perhaps what was most interesting—and surprising— were some of the topics of conversation Stormfront members have. They are similar to those my friends and I talk about. Maybe it was my own naïveté, but I would have imagined white nationalists inhabiting a different universe from that of my friends and me. Instead they have long threads praising *Game of Thrones* and discussing the comparative merits of on-line dating sites, like PlentyOfFish and OkCupid.

And the key fact that shows that Stormfront users are inhabiting similar universes as people like me and my friends: the popularity of the *New York Times* among Stormfront users. It isn't just VikingMaiden88 hanging around the *Times* site. The site is popular among many of its members. In fact, when you compare Stormfront users to people who visit the Yahoo News site, it turns out that the Stormfront crowd is twice as likely to visit nytimes.com.

Members of a hate site perusing the oh-so-liberal nytimes .com? How could this possibly be? If a substantial number of Stormfront members get their news from nytimes.com, it means our conventional wisdom about white nationalists is wrong. It also means our conventional wisdom about how the internet works is wrong.

THE TRUTH ABOUT THE INTERNET

The internet, most everybody agrees, is driving Americans apart, causing most people to hole up in sites geared toward people like them. Here's how Cass Sunstein of Harvard Law School described the situation: "Our communications market is rapidly moving [toward a situation where] people restrict themselves to their own points of view—liberals watching and reading mostly or only liberals; moderates, moderates; conservatives, conservatives; Neo-Nazis, Neo-Nazis."

This view makes sense. After all, the internet gives us a virtually unlimited number of options from which we can consume the news. I can read whatever I want. You can read whatever you want. VikingMaiden88 can read whatever she wants. And people, if left to their own devices, tend to seek out viewpoints that confirm what they believe. Thus, surely, the internet must be creating extreme political segregation.

There is one problem with this standard view. The data tells us that it is simply not true.

The evidence against this piece of conventional wisdom comes from a 2011 study by Matt Gentzkow and Jesse Shapiro, two economists whose work we discussed earlier.

Gentzkow and Shapiro collected data on the browsing behavior of a large sample of Americans. Their dataset also included the ideology—self-reported—of their subjects: whether people considered themselves more liberal or conservative. They used this data to measure the political segregation on the internet.

How? They performed an interesting thought experiment.

Suppose you randomly sampled two Americans who happen to both be visiting the same news website. What is the probability one of them will be liberal and the other conservative? How frequently, in other words, do liberals and conservatives "meet" on news sites?

To think about this further, suppose liberals and conservatives on the internet never got their online news from the same place. In other words, liberals exclusively visited liberal websites, conservatives exclusively conservative ones. If this were the case, the chances that two Americans on a given news site have opposing political views would be 0 percent. The internet would be perfectly *segregated*. Liberals and conservatives would never mix.

Suppose, in contrast, that liberals and conservatives did not differ at all in how they got their news. In other words, a liberal and a conservative were equally likely to visit any particular news site. If this were the case, the chances that two Americans on a given news website have opposing political views would be roughly 50 percent. The internet would be perfectly *desegregated*. Liberals and conservatives would perfectly mix.

So what does the data tell us? In the United States, according to Gentzkow and Shapiro, the chances that two people visiting the same news site have different political views is about 45 percent. In other words, the internet is far closer to perfect desegregation than perfect segregation. Liberals and conservatives are "meeting" each other on the web all the time.

What really puts the lack of segregation on the internet in perspective is comparing it to segregation in other parts of our lives. Gentzkow and Shapiro could repeat their analysis for various offline interactions. What are the chances that two family members have different political views? Two neighbors? Two colleagues? Two friends?

Using data from the General Social Survey, Gentzkow and Shapiro found that all these numbers were lower than the chances that two people on the same news website have different politics.

PROBABILITY THAT SOMEONE YOU MEET HAS OPPOSING POLITICAL VIEWS

On a News Website	45.2%
Coworker	41.6%
Offline Neighbor	40.3
Family Member	37%
Friend	34.7%

In other words, you are more likely to come across someone with opposing views online than you are offline.

Why isn't the internet more segregated? There are two factors that limit political segregation on the internet.

First, somewhat surprisingly, the internet news industry is dominated by a few massive sites. We usually think of the internet as appealing to the fringes. Indeed, there are sites for everybody, no matter your viewpoints. There are landing spots for pro-gun and anti-gun crusaders, cigar rights and dollar coin activists, anarchists and white nationalists. But these sites together account for a small fraction of the internet's news traffic. In fact, in 2009, four sites—Yahoo News, AOL News, msnbc.com, and cnn.com—collected more than half of news views. Yahoo News remains the most popular news site among Americans, with close to 90 million unique monthly visitors— or some 600 times Stormfront's audience. Mass media sites like Yahoo News appeal to a broad, politically diverse audience.

The second reason the internet isn't all that segregated is that many people with strong political opinions visit sites of the opposite viewpoint, if only to get angry and argue. Political junkies do not limit themselves only to sites geared toward them. Someone who visits thinkprogress.org and moveon.org— two extremely liberal sites—is more likely than the average internet user to visit foxnews.com, a right-leaning site. Someone who visits rushlimbaugh.com or glennbeck.com—two extremely conservative sites—is more likely than the average internet user to visit nytimes.com, a more liberal site.

Gentzkow and Shapiro's study was based on data from 2004–09, relatively early in the history of the internet. Might the internet have grown more compartmentalized since then?

Have social media and, in particular, Facebook altered their conclusion? Clearly, if our friends tend to share our political views, the rise of social media should mean a rise of echo chambers. Right?

Again, the story is not so simple. While it is true that people's friends on Facebook are more likely than not to share their political views, a team of data scientists—Eytan Bakshy, Solomon Messing, and Lada Adamic—have found that a surprising amount of the information people get on Facebook comes from people with opposing views.

How can this be? Don't our friends tend to share our political views? Indeed, they do. But there is one crucial reason that Facebook may lead to a more diverse political discussion than offline socializing. People, on average, have substantially more friends on Facebook than they do offline. And these weak ties facilitated by Facebook are more likely to be people with opposite political views.

In other words, Facebook exposes us to weak social connections—the high school acquaintance, the crazy third cousin, the friend of the friend of the friend you sort of, kind of, maybe know. These are people you might never go bowling with or to a barbecue with. You might not invite them over to a dinner party. But you do Facebook friend them. And you do see their links to articles with views you might have never otherwise considered.

In sum, the internet actually brings people of different political views together. The average liberal may spend her morning with her liberal husband and liberal kids; her afternoon with her liberal coworkers; her commute surrounded by liberal bumper stickers; her evening with her liberal yoga classmates.

When she comes home and peruses a few conservative comments on cnn.com or gets a Facebook link from her Republican high school acquaintance, this may be her highest conservative exposure of the day.

I probably never encounter white nationalists in my favorite coffee shop in Brooklyn. But VikingMaiden88 and I both frequent the *New York Times* site.

THE TRUTH ABOUT CHILD ABUSE AND ABORTION

The internet can give us insights into not just disturbing attitudes but also disturbing behaviors. Indeed, Google data may be effective at alerting us to crises that are missed by all the usual sources. People, after all, turn to Google when they are in trouble.

Consider child abuse during the Great Recession.

When this major economic downturn started in late 2007, many experts were naturally worried about the effect it might have on children. After all, many parents would be stressed and depressed, and these are major risk factors for maltreatment. Child abuse might skyrocket.

Then the official data came in, and it seemed that the worry was unfounded. Child protective service agencies reported that they were getting fewer cases of abuse. Further, these drops were largest in states that were hardest hit by the recession. "The doom-and-gloom predictions haven't come true," Richard Gelles, a child welfare expert at the University of Pennsylvania, told the Associated Press in 2011. Yes, as counterintuitive as it may have seemed, child abuse seemed to have plummeted during the recession.

But did child abuse really drop with so many adults out of work and extremely distressed? I had trouble believing this. So I turned to Google data.

It turns out, some kids make some tragic, and heart-wrenching, searches on Google—such as "my mom beat me" or "my dad hit me." And these searches present a different—and agonizing—picture of what happened during this time. The number of searches like this shot up during the Great Recession, closely tracking the unemployment rate.

Here's what I think happened: it was the reporting of child abuse cases that declined, not the child abuse itself. After all, it is estimated that only a small percentage of child abuse cases are reported to authorities anyway. And during a recession, many of the people who tend to report child abuse cases (teachers and police officers, for example) and handle cases (child protective service workers) are more likely to be overworked or out of work.

There were many stories during the economic downturn of people trying to report potential cases facing long wait times and giving up.

Indeed, there is more evidence, this time not from Google, that child abuse actually rose during the recession. When a child dies due to abuse or neglect it has to be reported. Such deaths, although rare, did rise in states that were hardest hit by the recession.

And there is some evidence from Google that more people were suspecting abuse in hard-hit areas. Controlling for pre-recession rates and national trends, states that had comparatively suffered the most had increased search rates for child abuse and neglect. For every percentage point increase in the unemployment rate, there was an associated 3 percent increase in the search rate for "child abuse" or "child neglect." Presumably, most of these people never successfully reported the abuse, as these states had the biggest drops in the reporting.

Searches by suffering kids increase. The rate of child deaths spike. Searches by people suspecting abuse go up in hard-hit states. But reporting of cases goes down. A recession seems to cause more kids to tell Google that their parents are hitting or beating them and more people to suspect that they see abuse. But the overworked agencies are able to handle fewer cases.

I think it's safe to say that the Great Recession did make child abuse worse, although the traditional measures did not show it.

Anytime I suspect people may be suffering off the books now, I turn to Google data. One of the potential benefits of this new data, and knowing how to interpret it, is the possibility of helping vulnerable people who might otherwise go overlooked by authorities.

So when the Supreme Court was recently looking into the effects of laws making it more difficult to get an abortion, I turned to the query data. I suspected women affected by this legislation might look into off-the-books ways to terminate a pregnancy. They did. And these searches were highest in states that had passed laws restricting abortions.

The search data here is both useful and troubling.

In 2015, in the United States, there were more than 700,000 Google searches looking into self-induced abortions. By comparison, there were some 3.4 million searches for abortion clinics that year. This suggests that a significant percentage of women considering an abortion have contemplated doing it themselves.

Women searched, about 160,000 times, for ways of getting abortion pills through unofficial channels—"buy abortion pills online" and "free abortion pills." They asked Google about abortion by herbs like parsley or by vitamin C. There were some 4,000 searches looking for directions on coat hanger abortions, including about 1,300 for the exact phrase "how to do a coat hanger abortion." There were also a few hundred looking into abortion through bleaching one's uterus and punching one's stomach.

What drives interest in self-induced abortion? The geography and timing of the Google searches point to a likely culprit: when it's hard to get an official abortion, women look into off-the-books approaches.

Search rates for self-induced abortion were fairly steady from 2004 through 2007. They began to rise in late 2008, coinciding with the financial crisis and the recession that followed. They took a big leap in 2011, jumping 40 percent. The Guttmacher Institute, a reproductive rights organization, singles out 2011 as the beginning of the country's recent crackdown on abortion; ninety-two state provisions that restrict access to abortion were enacted. Looking by comparison at Canada, which has not seen a crackdown on reproductive rights, there was no comparable increase in searches for self-induced abortions during this time.

The state with the highest rate of Google searches for self-induced abortions is Mississippi, a state with roughly three million people and, now, just one abortion clinic. Eight of the ten states with the highest search rates for self-induced abortions are considered by the Guttmacher Institute to be hostile or very hostile to abortion. None of the ten states with the lowest search rates for self-induced abortion are in either category.

Of course, we cannot know from Google searches how many women successfully give themselves abortions, but evidence suggests that a significant number may. One way to illuminate this is to compare abortion and birth data.

In 2011, the last year with complete state-level abortion data, women living in states with few abortion clinics had many fewer legal abortions.

Compare the ten states with the most abortion clinics per capita (a list that includes New York and California) to the ten states with the fewest abortion clinics per capita (a list that includes Mississippi and Oklahoma). Women living in states with the fewest abortion clinics had 54 percent fewer legal abortions—a difference of eleven abortions for every thousand women between the ages of fifteen and forty-four. Women living in states with the fewest abortion clinics also had more live births. However, the difference was not enough to make up for the lower number of abortions. There were six more live births for every thousand women of childbearing age.

In other words, there appear to have been some missing pregnancies in parts of the country where it was hardest to get an abortion. The official sources don't tell us what happened to those five missing births for each thousand women in states where it is hard to get an abortion.

Google provides some pretty good clues.

We can't blindly trust government data. The government may tell us that child abuse or abortion has fallen and politicians may celebrate this achievement. But the results we think we're seeing may be an artifact of flaws in the methods of data collection. The truth may be different—and, sometimes, far darker.

THE TRUTH ABOUT YOUR FACEBOOK FRIENDS

This book is about Big Data, in general. But this chapter has mostly emphasized Google searches, which I have argued reveal a hidden world very different from the one we think we see. So are other Big Data sources digital truth serum, as well? The fact is, many Big Data sources, such as Facebook, are often the opposite of digital truth serum.

On social media, as in surveys, you have no incentive to tell the truth. On social media, much more so than in surveys, you have a large incentive to make yourself look good. Your online presence is not anonymous, after all. You are courting an audience and telling your friends, family members, colleagues, acquaintances, and strangers who you are.

To see how biased data pulled from social media can be, consider the relative popularity of the *Atlantic,* a respected, highbrow monthly magazine, versus the *National Enquirer,* a gossipy, often-sensational magazine. Both publications have similar average circulations, selling a few hundred thousand copies. (The *National Enquirer* is a weekly, so it actually sells more total copies.) There are also a comparable number of Google searches for each magazine.

However, on Facebook, roughly 1.5 million people either

like the *Atlantic* or discuss articles from the *Atlantic* on their profiles. Only about 50,000 like the *Enquirer* or discuss its contents.

ATLANTIC VS. NATIONAL ENQUIRER POPULARITY COMPARED BY DIFFERENT SOURCES

Circulation	Roughly 1 *Atlantic* for every 1 *National Enquirer*
Google Searches	1 *Atlantic* for every 1 *National Enquirer*
Facebook Likes	27 *Atlantic* for every 1 *National Enquirer*

For assessing magazine popularity, circulation data is the ground truth. Google data comes close to matching it. And Facebook data is overwhelmingly biased against the trashy tabloid, making it the worst data for determining what people really like.

And as with reading preferences, so with life. On Facebook, we show our cultivated selves, not our true selves. I use Facebook data in this book, in fact in this chapter, but always with this caveat in mind.

To gain a better understanding of what social media misses, let's return to pornography for a moment. First, we need to address the common belief that the internet is dominated by smut. This isn't true. The majority of content on the internet is nonpornographic. For instance, of the top ten most visited websites, not one is pornographic. So the popularity of porn, while enormous, should not be overstated.

Yet, that said, taking a close look at how we like and share pornography makes it clear that Facebook, Instagram, and

Twitter only provide a limited window into what's truly popular on the internet. There are large subsets of the web that operate with massive popularity but little social presence.

The most popular video of all time, as of this writing, is
Psy's "Gangnam Style," a goofy pop music video that satirizes
trendy Koreans. It's been viewed about 2.3 billion times on
YouTube alone since its debut in 2012. And its popularity is
clear no matter what site you are on. It's been shared across different social media platforms tens of millions of times.

The most popular pornographic video of all time may be
"Great Body, Great Sex, Great Blowjob." It's been viewed more
than 80 million times. In other words, for every thirty views
of "Gangnam Style," there has been about at least one view of
"Great Body, Great Sex, Great Blowjob." If social media gave
us an accurate view of the videos people watched, "Great Body,
Great Sex, Great Blowjob" should be posted millions of times.
But this video has been shared on social media only a few
dozen times and always by porn stars, not by average users.
People clearly do not feel the need to advertise their interest in
this video to their friends.

Facebook is digital brag-to-my-friends-about-how-good-
my-life-is serum. In Facebook world, the average adult seems
to be happily married, vacationing in the Caribbean, and perusing the *Atlantic*. In the real world, a lot of people are angry, on
supermarket checkout lines, peeking at the *National Enquirer*,
ignoring the phone calls from their spouse, whom they haven't
slept with in years. In Facebook world, family life seems perfect. In the real world, family life is messy. It can occasionally
be so messy that a small number of people even regret having
children. In Facebook world, it seems every young adult is at

a cool party Saturday night. In the real world, most are home alone, binge-watching shows on Netflix. In Facebook world, a girlfriend posts twenty-six happy pictures from her getaway with her boyfriend. In the real world, immediately after posting this, she Googles "my boyfriend won't have sex with me." And, perhaps at the same time, the boyfriend watches "Great Body, Great Sex, Great Blowjob."

DIGITAL TRUTH	DIGITAL LIES
• Searches	• Social media posts
• Views	• Social media likes
• Clicks	• Dating profiles
• Swipes	

THE TRUTH ABOUT YOUR CUSTOMERS

In the early morning of September 5, 2006, Facebook introduced a major update to its home page. The early versions of Facebook had only allowed users to click on profiles of their friends to learn what they were doing. The website, considered a big success, had at the time 9.4 million users.

But after months of hard work, engineers had created something they called "News Feed," which would provide users with updates on the activities of all their friends.

Users immediately reported that they hated News Feed. Ben Parr, a Northwestern undergraduate, created "Students Against Facebook news feed." He said that "news feed is just too creepy, too stalker-esque, and a feature that has to go." Within a few days, the group had 700,000 members echoing

Parr's sentiment. One University of Michigan junior told the *Michigan Daily,* "I'm really creeped out by the new Facebook. It makes me feel like a stalker."

David Kirkpatrick tells this story in his authorized account of the website's history, *The Facebook Effect: The Inside Story of the Company That Is Connecting the World.* He dubs the introduction of News Feed "the biggest crisis Facebook has ever faced." But Kirkpatrick reports that when he interviewed Mark Zuckerberg, cofounder and head of the rapidly growing company, the CEO was unfazed.

The reason? Zuckerberg had access to digital truth serum: numbers on people's clicks and visits to Facebook. As Kirkpatrick writes:

> Zuckerberg in fact knew that people liked the News Feed, no matter what they were saying in the groups. He had the data to prove it. People were spending more time on Facebook, on average, than before News Feed launched. And they were doing more there—dramatically more. In August, users viewed 12 billion pages on the service. But by October, with News Feed under way, they viewed 22 billion.

And that was not all the evidence at Zuckerberg's disposal. Even the viral popularity of the anti–News Feed group was evidence of the power of News Feed. The group was able to grow so rapidly precisely because so many people had heard that their friends had joined—and they learned this through their News Feed.

In other words, while people were joining in a big public

uproar over how unhappy they were about seeing all the details of their friends' lives on Facebook, they were coming back to Facebook to see all the details of their friends' lives. News Feed stayed. Facebook now has more than one billion daily active users.

In his book *Zero to One*, Peter Thiel, an early investor in Facebook, says that great businesses are built on secrets, either secrets about nature or secrets about people. Jeff Seder, as discussed in Chapter 3, found the natural secret that left ventricle size predicted horse performance. Google found the natural secret of how powerful the information in links can be.

Thiel defines "secrets about people" as "things that people don't know about themselves or things they hide because they don't want others to know." These kinds of businesses, in other words, are built on people's lies.

You could argue that all of Facebook is founded on an unpleasant secret about people that Zuckerberg learned while at Harvard. Zuckerberg, early in his sophomore year, created a website for his fellow students called Facemash. Modeled on a site called "Am I Hot or Not?," Facemash would present pictures of two Harvard students and then have other students judge who was better looking.

The sophomore's site was greeted with outrage. The *Harvard Crimson*, in an editorial, accused young Zuckerberg of "catering to the worst side" of people. Hispanic and African-American groups accused him of sexism and racism. Yet, before Harvard administrators shut down Zuckerberg's internet access—just a few hours after the site was founded—450 people had viewed the site and voted 22,000 times on different images. Zuckerberg had learned an important secret: people can claim they're furious, they can decry something as distasteful, and yet they'll still click.

And he learned one more thing: for all their professions of seriousness, responsibility, and respect for others' privacy, people, even Harvard students, had a great interest in evaluating people's looks. The views and votes told him that. And later—since Facemash proved too controversial—he took this knowledge of just how interested people could be in superficial facts about others they sort of knew and harnessed it into the most successful company of his generation.

Netflix learned a similar lesson early on in its life cycle: don't trust what people tell you; trust what they do.

Originally, the company allowed users to create a queue of movies they wanted to watch in the future but didn't have time for at the moment. This way, when they had more time, Netflix could remind them of those movies.

However, Netflix noticed something odd in the data. Users were filling their queues with plenty of movies. But days later, when they were reminded of the movies on the queue, they rarely clicked.

What was the problem? Ask users what movies they plan to watch in a few days, and they will fill the queue with aspirational, highbrow films, such as black-and-white World War II documentaries or serious foreign films. A few days later, however, they will want to watch the same movies they usually want to watch: lowbrow comedies or romance films. People were consistently lying to themselves.

Faced with this disparity, Netflix stopped asking people to tell them what they wanted to see in the future and started building a model based on millions of clicks and views from similar customers. The company began greeting its users with suggested lists of films based not on what they claimed to like but on what the data said they were likely to view. The result: customers visited Netflix more frequently and watched more movies.

"The algorithms know you better than you know yourself," says Xavier Amatriain, a former data scientist at Netflix.

THE OUTSIZE VALUE OF IGNORING WHAT PEOPLE TELL YOU

WHAT PEOPLE SAY	REALITY	IPSO FACTO ...
They don't want to stalk their friends.	There is little in this world they want more than to keep up with and judge their friends.	Mark Zuckerberg, cofounder of Facebook, is worth $55.2 billion.
They don't want to buy products that are produced in sweatshops.	They will buy nice, "reasonably priced" products.	Phil Knight, cofounder of Nike, is worth $25.4 billion.
They want to listen to news in the morning.	They want to hear about midgets having sex with porn stars in the morning.	Howard Stern is worth $500 million.
They have no interest in reading about bondage, dominance, and sadomasochism.	They want to read about BDSM between a young college graduate and a business magnate.	*50 Shades of Gray* has sold 125 million copies.
They want politicians to outline their policy positions.	They want politicians to spare them the details but seem tough and self-assured.	Donald Trump

CAN WE HANDLE THE TRUTH?

You may find parts of this chapter depressing. Digital truth serum has revealed an abiding interest in judging people based on their looks; the continued existence of millions of closeted gay men; a meaningful percentage of women fantasizing about rape; widespread animus against African-Americans; a hidden child abuse and self-induced abortion crisis; and an outbreak of violent Islamophobic rage that only got worse when the president appealed for tolerance. Not exactly cheery stuff. Often, after I give a talk on my research, people come up to me and say, "Seth, it's all very interesting. But it's *so* depressing."

I can't pretend there isn't a darkness in some of this data. If people consistently tell us what they think we want to hear, we will generally be told things that are more comforting than the truth. Digital truth serum, on average, will show us that the world is worse than we have thought.

Do we need to know this? Learning about Google searches, porn data, and who clicks on what might not make you think, "This is great. We can understand who we really are." You might instead think, "This is horrible. We can understand who we really are."

But the truth helps—and not just for Mark Zuckerberg or others looking to attract clicks or customers. There are at least three ways that this knowledge can improve our lives.

First, there can be comfort in knowing that you are not alone in your insecurities and embarrassing behavior. It can be nice to know others are insecure about their bodies. It is probably nice for many people—particularly those who aren't having much sex—to know the whole world isn't fornicating like rabbits. And it may be valuable for a high school boy in Mississippi with a crush on the quarterback to know that, despite the low numbers of openly gay men around him, plenty of others feel the same kinds of attraction.

There's another area—one I haven't yet discussed—where Google searches can help show you are not alone. When you were young, a teacher may have told you that, if you have a question, you should raise your hand and ask it because if you're confused, others are, too. If you were anything like me, you ignored your teacher's advice and sat there silently, afraid to open your mouth. Your questions were too dumb, you thought; everyone else's were more profound. The anonymous, aggregate Google data can tell us once and for all how right our teachers were. Plenty of basic, sub-profound questions lurk in other minds, too.

Consider the top questions Americans had during Obama's 2014 State of the Union speech. (See the color photo at end of the book.)

YOU'RE NOT THE ONLY ONE WONDERING: TOP GOOGLED QUESTIONS DURING THE STATE OF THE UNION

How old is Obama?

Who is sitting next to Biden?

Why is Boehner wearing a green tie?

Why is Boehner orange?

Now, you might read these questions and think they speak poorly of our democracy. To be more concerned about the color of someone's tie or his skin tone instead of the content of the president's speech doesn't reflect well on us. To not know who

John Boehner, then the Speaker of the House of Representatives, is also doesn't say much for our political engagement.

I prefer instead to think of such questions as demonstrating the wisdom of our teachers. These are the types of questions people usually don't raise, because they sound too silly. But lots of people have them—and Google them.

In fact, I think Big Data can give a twenty-first-century update to a famous self-help quote: "Never compare your insides to everyone else's outsides."

A Big Data update may be: "Never compare your Google searches to everyone else's social media posts."

Compare, for example, the way that people describe their husbands on public social media and in anonymous searches.

TOP WAYS PEOPLE DESCRIBE THEIR HUSBANDS

SOCIAL MEDIA POSTS	SEARCHES
the best	gay
my best friend	a jerk
amazing	amazing
the greatest	annoying
so cute	mean

Since we see other people's social media posts but not their searches, we tend to exaggerate how many women consistently think their husbands are "the best," "the greatest," and "so cute." * We tend to minimize how many women think their

---

* I analyzed Twitter data. I thank Emma Pierson for help downloading this. I did not include descriptors of what one's husband is doing right now, which are prevalent on social media but wouldn't really make

husbands are "a jerk," "annoying," and "mean." By analyzing anonymous and aggregate data, we may all understand that we're not the only ones who find marriage, and life, difficult. We may learn to stop comparing our searches to everyone else's social media posts.

The second benefit of digital truth serum is that it alerts us to people who are suffering. The Human Rights Campaign has asked me to work with them in helping educate men in certain states about the possibility of coming out of the closet. They are looking to use the anonymous and aggregate Google search data to help them decide where best to target their resources. Similarly, child protective service agencies have contacted me to learn in what parts of the country there may be far more child abuse than they are recording.

One surprising topic I was also contacted about: vaginal odors. When I first wrote about this in the *New York Times*, of all places, I did so in an ironic tone. The section made me, and others, chuckle.

However, when I later explored some of the message boards that come up when someone makes these searches they included numerous posts from young girls convinced that their lives were ruined due to anxiety about vaginal odor. It's no joke. Sex ed experts have contacted me, asking how they can best incorporate some of the internet data to reduce the paranoia among young girls.

---

sense on search. Even these descriptions tilt toward the favorable. The top ways to describe what a husband is doing right now on social media are "working" and "cooking."

While I feel a bit out of my depth on all these matters, they are serious, and I believe data science can help.

The final—and, I think, most powerful—value in this digital truth serum is indeed its ability to lead us from problems to solutions. With more understanding, we might find ways to reduce the world's supply of nasty attitudes.

Let's return to Obama's speech about Islamophobia. Recall that every time Obama argued that people should respect Muslims more, the very people he was trying to reach became more enraged.

Google searches, however, reveal that there was one line that did trigger the type of response then-president Obama might have wanted. He said, "Muslim Americans are our friends and our neighbors, our co-workers, our sports heroes and, yes, they are our men and women in uniform, who are willing to die in defense of our country."

After this line, for the first time in more than a year, the top Googled noun after "Muslim" was not "terrorists," "extremists," or "refugees." It was "athletes," followed by "soldiers." And, in fact, "athletes" kept the top spot for a full day afterward.

When we lecture angry people, the search data implies that their fury can grow. But subtly provoking people's curiosity, giving new information, and offering new images of the group that is stoking their rage may turn their thoughts in different, more positive directions.

Two months after that original speech, Obama gave another televised speech on Islamophobia, this time at a mosque. Perhaps someone in the president's office had read Soltas's and my *Times* column, which discussed what had worked and what didn't. For the content of this speech was noticeably different.

Obama spent little time insisting on the value of tolerance. Instead, he focused overwhelmingly on provoking people's curiosity and changing their perceptions of Muslim Americans. Many of the slaves from Africa were Muslim, Obama told us; Thomas Jefferson and John Adams had their own copies of the Koran; the first mosque on U.S. soil was in North Dakota; a Muslim American designed skyscrapers in Chicago. Obama again spoke of Muslim athletes and armed service members but also talked of Muslim police officers and firefighters, teachers and doctors.

And my analysis of the Google searches suggests this speech was more successful than the previous one. Many of the hateful, rageful searches against Muslims dropped in the hours after the president's address.

There are other potential ways to use search data to learn what causes, or reduces, hate. For example, we might look at how racist searches change after a black quarterback is drafted in a city or how sexist searches change after a woman is elected to office. We might see how racism responds to community policing or how sexism responds to new sexual harassment laws.

Learning of our subconscious prejudices can also be useful. For example, we might all make an extra effort to delight in little girls' minds and show less concern with their appearance. Google search data and other wellsprings of truth on the internet give us an unprecedented look into the darkest corners of the human psyche. This is at times, I admit, difficult to face. But it can also be empowering. We can use the data to fight the darkness. Collecting rich data on the world's problems is the first step toward fixing them.

5

ZOOMING IN

My brother, Noah, is four years younger than I. Most people, upon first meeting us, find us eerily similar. We both talk too loudly, are balding in the same way, and have great difficulty keeping our apartments tidy.

But there are differences: I count pennies. Noah buys the best. I love Leonard Cohen and Bob Dylan. For Noah, it's Cake and Beck.

Perhaps the most notable difference between us is our attitude toward baseball. I am obsessed with baseball and, in particular, my love of the New York Mets has always been a core part of my identity. Noah finds baseball impossibly boring, and his hatred of the sport has long been a core part of his identity.*

---

* Full disclosure: When I was fact-checking this book, Noah denied that his hatred of America's pastime is a key part of his personality. He does admit to hating baseball, but he believes his kindness, love of

Seth Stephens-Davidowitz
Baseball-o-Phile

Noah Stephens-Davidowitz
Baseball-o-Phobe

How can two guys with such similar genes, raised by the same parents, in the same town, have such opposite feelings about baseball? What determines the adults we become? More fundamentally, what's *wrong* with Noah? There's a growing field within developmental psychology that mines massive adult databases and correlates them with key childhood events. It can help us tackle this and related questions. We might call this increasing use of Big Data to answer psychological questions Big Psych.

To see how this works, let's consider a study I conducted on how childhood experiences influence which baseball team you support—or whether you support any team at all. For this study, I used Facebook data on "likes" of baseball teams. (In the

---

children, and intelligence are the core elements of his personality—and that his attitudes about baseball would not even make the top ten. However, I concluded that it's sometimes hard to see one's own identity objectively and, as an outside observer, I am able to see that hating baseball is indeed fundamental to who Noah is, whether he's able to recognize it or not. So I left it in.

previous chapter I noted that Facebook data can be deeply misleading on sensitive topics. With this study, I am assuming that nobody, not even a Phillies fan, is embarrassed to acknowledge a rooting interest in a particular team on Facebook.)

To begin with, I downloaded the number of males of every age who "like" each of New York's two baseball teams. Here are the percent that are Mets fans, by year of birth.

PERCENT OF MALE NEW YORK BASEBALL FANS WHO
LIKE THE METS, BY YEAR OF BIRTH

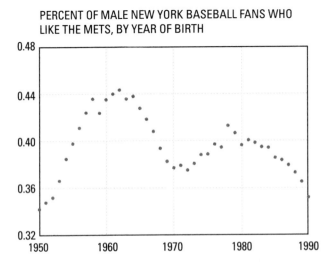

The higher the point, the more Mets fans. The popularity of the team rises and falls then rises and falls again, with the Mets being very popular among those born in 1962 and 1978. I'm guessing baseball fans might have an idea as to what's going on here. The Mets have won just two World Series: in 1969 and 1986. These men were roughly seven to eight years old when the Mets won. Thus a huge predictor of Mets fandom, for boys at least, is whether the Mets won a World Series when they were around the age seven or eight.

In fact, we can extend this analysis. I downloaded information on Facebook showing how many fans of every age "like" every one of a comprehensive selection of Major League Baseball teams.

I found that there are also an unusually high number of male Baltimore Orioles fans born in 1962 and male Pittsburgh Pirates fans born in 1963. Those men were eight-year-old boys when these teams were champions. Indeed, calculating the age of peak fandom for all the teams I studied, then figuring out how old these fans would have been, gave me this chart:

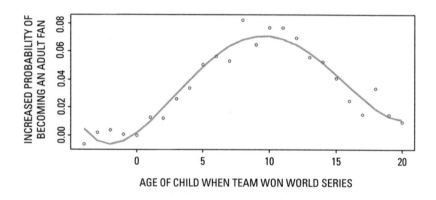

AGE OF CHILD WHEN TEAM WON WORLD SERIES

Once again we see that the most important year in a man's life, for the purposes of cementing his favorite baseball team as an adult, is when he is more or less eight years old. Overall, five to fifteen is the key period to win over a boy. Winning when a man is nineteen or twenty is about one-eighth as important in determining who he will root for as winning when he is eight. By then, he will already either love a team for life or he won't.

You might be asking, what about women baseball fans? The patterns are much less sharp, but the peak age appears to be twenty-two years old.

This is my favorite study. It relates to two of my most beloved topics: baseball and the sources of my adult discontent. I was firmly hooked in 1986 and have been suffering along—rooting for the Mets—ever since. Noah had the good sense to be born four years later and was spared this pain.

Now, baseball is not the most important topic in the world, or so my Ph.D. advisors repeatedly told me. But this methodology might help us tackle similar questions, including how people develop their political preferences, sexual proclivities, musical taste, and financial habits. (I would be particularly interested on the origins of my brother's wacky ideas on the latter two subjects.) My prediction is that we will find that many of our adult behaviors and interests, even those that we consider fundamental to who we are, can be explained by the arbitrary facts of when we were born and what was going on in certain key years while we were young.

Indeed, some work has already been done on the origin of political preferences. Yair Ghitza, chief scientist at Catalist, a data analysis company, and Andrew Gelman, a political scientist and statistician at Columbia University, tried to test the conventional idea that most people start out liberal and become increasingly conservative as they age. This is the view expressed in a famous quote often attributed to Winston Churchill: "Any man who is under 30, and is not a liberal, has no heart; and any man who is over 30, and is not a conservative, has no brains."

Ghitza and Gelman pored through sixty years of survey data, taking advantage of more than 300,000 observations on voting preferences. They found, contrary to Churchill's claim, that teenagers sometimes tilt liberal and sometimes tilt conservative. As do the middle-aged and the elderly.

These researchers discovered that political views actually

form in a way not dissimilar to the way our sports team preferences do. There is a crucial period that imprints on people for life. Between the key ages of fourteen and twenty-four, numerous Americans will form their views based on the popularity of the current president. A popular Republican or unpopular Democrat will influence many young adults to become Republicans. An unpopular Republican or popular Democrat puts this impressionable group in the Democratic column.

And these views, in these key years, will, on average, last a lifetime.

To see how this works, compare Americans born in 1941 and those born a decade later.

Those in the first group came of age during the presidency of Dwight D. Eisenhower, a popular Republican. In the early 1960s, despite being under thirty, this generation strongly tilted toward the Republican Party. And members of this generation have consistently tilted Republican as they have aged.

Americans born ten years later—baby boomers—came of age during the presidencies of John F. Kennedy, an extremely popular Democrat; Lyndon B. Johnson, an initially popular Democrat; and Richard M. Nixon, a Republican who eventually resigned in disgrace. Members of this generation have tilted liberal their entire lives.

With all this data, the researchers were able to determine the single most important year for developing political views: age eighteen.

And they found that these imprint effects are substantial. Their model estimates that the Eisenhower experience resulted in about a 10 percentage point lifetime boost for Republicans among Americans born in 1941. The Kennedy, Johnson, and Nixon experience gave Democrats a 7 percentage point advantage among Americans born in 1952.

I've made it clear that I am skeptical of survey data, but I am impressed with the large number of responses examined here. In fact, this study could not have been done with one small survey. The researchers needed the hundreds of thousands of observations, aggregated from many surveys, to see how preferences change as people age.

Data size was also crucial for my baseball study. I needed to zoom in not only on fans of each team but on people of every age. Millions of observations are required to do this and Facebook and other digital sources routinely offer such numbers.

This is where the bigness of Big Data really comes into play. You need a lot of pixels in a photo in order to be able to zoom in with clarity on one small portion of it. Similarly, you need a lot of observations in a dataset in order to be able to zoom in with clarity on one small subset of that data—for example, how popular the Mets are among men born in 1978. A small survey of a couple of thousand people won't have a large enough sample of such men.

This is the third power of Big Data: Big Data allows us to meaningfully zoom in on small segments of a dataset to gain new insights on who we are. And we can zoom in on other dimensions besides age. If we have enough data, we can see how people in particular towns and cities behave. And we can see how people carry on hour-by-hour or even minute-by-minute.

In this chapter, human behavior gets its close-up.

WHAT'S REALLY GOING ON IN OUR COUNTIES, CITIES, AND TOWNS?

In hindsight it's surprising. But when Raj Chetty, then a professor at Harvard, and a small research team first got a hold of a rather large dataset—all Americans' tax records since 1996—they were not certain anything would come of it. The IRS had handed over the data because they thought the researchers might be able to use it to help clarify the effects of tax policy.

The initial attempts Chetty and his team made to use this Big Data led, in fact, to numerous dead ends. Their investigations of the consequences of state and federal tax policies reached mostly the same conclusions everybody else had just by using surveys. Perhaps Chetty's answers, using the hundreds of millions of IRS data points, were a bit more precise. But getting the same answers as everybody else, with a little more precision, is not a major social science accomplishment. It is not the type of work that top journals are eager to publish.

Plus, organizing and analyzing all the IRS data was time-consuming. Chetty and his team—drowning in data—were taking more time than everybody else to find the same answers as everybody else.

It was beginning to look like the Big Data skeptics were right. You didn't need data for hundreds of millions of Americans to understand tax policy; a survey of ten thousand people was plenty. Chetty and his team were understandably discouraged.

And then, finally, the researchers realized their mistake. "Big Data is not just about doing the same thing you would have done with surveys except with more data," Chetty explains. They were asking little data questions of the massive collection of data they had been handed. "Big Data really should allow you to use completely different designs than what you would have with a survey," Chetty adds. "You can, for example, zoom in on geographies."

In other words, with data on hundreds of millions of people, Chetty and his team could spot patterns among cities, towns, and neighborhoods, large and small.

As a graduate student at Harvard, I was in a seminar room when Chetty presented his initial results using the tax records of every American. Social scientists refer in their work to observations—how many data points they have. If a social scientist is working with a survey of eight hundred people, he would say, "We have eight hundred observations." If he is working with a laboratory experiment with seventy people, he would say, "We have seventy observations."

"We have one-point-two billion observations," Chetty said, straight-faced. The audience giggled nervously.

Chetty and his coauthors began, in that seminar room and then in a series of papers, to give us important new insights into how America works.

Consider this question: is America a land of opportunity? Do you have a shot, if your parents are not rich, to become rich yourself?

The traditional way to answer this question is to look at a representative sample of Americans and compare this to similar data from other countries.

Here is the data for a variety of countries on equality of opportunity. The question asked: what is the chance that a person with parents in the bottom 20 percent of the income distribution reaches the top 20 percent of the income distribution?

CHANCES A PERSON WITH POOR PARENTS WILL BECOME RICH (SELECTED COUNTRIES)

United States	7.5
United Kingdom	9.0
Denmark	11.7
Canada	13.5

As you can see, America does *not* score well.

But this simple analysis misses the real story. Chetty's team zoomed in on geography. They found the odds differ a huge amount depending on where in the United States you were born.

CHANCES A PERSON WITH POOR PARENTS WILL BECOME RICH (SELECTED PARTS OF THE UNITED STATES)

San Jose, CA	12.9
Washington, DC	10.5
United States Average	*7.5*
Chicago, IL	6.5
Charlotte, NC	4.4

In some parts of the United States, the chance of a poor kid succeeding is as high as in any developed country in the world. In other parts of the United States, the chance of a poor kid succeeding is lower than in any developed country in the world.

These patterns would never be seen in a small survey, which might only include a few people in Charlotte and San Jose, and which therefore would prevent you from zooming in like this.

In fact, Chetty's team could zoom in even further. Because they had so much data—data on every single American—they could even zoom in on the small groups of people who moved from city to city to see how that might have affected their prospects: those who moved from New York City to Los Angeles, Milwaukee to Atlanta, San Jose to Charlotte. This allowed them to test for causation, not just correlation (a distinction I'll discuss in the next chapter). And, yes, moving to the right city in one's formative years made a significant difference.

So is America a "land of opportunity"?

The answer is neither yes nor no. The answer is: some parts are, and some parts aren't.

As the authors write, "The U.S. is better described as a collection of societies, some of which are 'lands of opportunity' with high rates of mobility across generations, and others in which few children escape poverty."

So what is it about parts of the United States where there is high income mobility? What makes some places better at equaling the playing field, of allowing a poor kid to have a pretty good life? Areas that spend more on education provide a better chance to poor kids. Places with more religious people and lower crime do better. Places with more black people do worse. Interestingly, this has an effect on not just the black kids but on the white kids living there as well. Places with lots of single mothers do worse. This effect too holds not just for kids of single mothers but for kids of married parents living in places with lots of single mothers. Some of these results suggest that a poor kid's peers matter. If his friends have a difficult background and little opportunity, he may struggle more to escape poverty.

The data tells us that some parts of America are better at giving kids a chance to escape poverty. So what places are best at giving people a chance to escape the grim reaper?

We like to think of death as the great equalizer. Nobody, after all, can avoid it. Not the pauper nor the king, the homeless man nor Mark Zuckerberg. Everybody dies.

But if the wealthy can't avoid death, data tells us that they can now delay it. American women in the top 1 percent of income live, on average, ten years longer than American women in the bottom 1 percent of income. For men, the gap is fifteen years.

How do these patterns vary in different parts of the United States? Does your life expectancy vary based on where you live? Is this variation different for rich and poor people? Again, by zooming in on geography, Raj Chetty's team found the answers.

Interestingly, for the wealthiest Americans, life expectancy is hardly affected by where they live. If you have excesses of money, you can expect to make it roughly eighty-nine years as a woman and about eighty-seven years as a man. Rich people everywhere tend to develop healthier habits—on average, they exercise more, eat better, smoke less, and are less likely to suffer from obesity. Rich people can afford the treadmill, the organic avocados, the yoga classes. And they can buy these things in any corner of the United States.

For the poor, the story is different. For the poorest Americans, life expectancy varies tremendously depending on where they live. In fact, living in the right place can add five years to a poor person's life expectancy.

So why do some places seem to allow the impoverished to live so much longer? What attributes do cities where poor people live the longest share?

Here are four attributes of a city—three of them do not correlate with poor people's life expectancy, and one of them does. See if you can guess which one matters.

WHAT MAKES POOR PEOPLE IN A CITY LIVE MUCH LONGER?

The city has a high level of religiosity.

The city has low levels of pollution.

The city has a higher percentage of residents covered by health insurance.

A lot of rich people live in the city.

The first three—religion, environment, and health insurance—do not correlate with longer life spans for the poor. The variable that does matter, according to Chetty and the others who worked on this study? How many rich people live in a city. More rich people in a city means the poor there live longer. Poor people in New York City, for example, live a lot longer than poor people in Detroit.

Why is the presence of rich people such a powerful predictor of poor people's life expectancy? One hypothesis—and this is speculative—was put forth by David Cutler, one of the authors of the study and one of my advisors. Contagious behavior may be driving some of this.

There is a large amount of research showing that habits are contagious. So poor people living near rich people may pick up a lot of their habits. Some of these habits—say, pretentious vocabulary—aren't likely to affect one's health. Others—working out—will definitely have a positive impact. Indeed, poor people living near rich people exercise more, smoke less, and are less likely to suffer from obesity.

My personal favorite study by Raj Chetty's team, which had access to that massive collection of IRS data, was their inquiry into why some people cheat on their taxes while others do not. Explaining this study is a bit more complicated.

The key is knowing that there is an easy way for self-employed people with one child to maximize the money they receive from the government. If you report that you had taxable income of exactly $9,000 in a given year, the government will write you a check for $1,377—that amount represents the Earned Income Tax Credit, a grant to supplement the earnings of the working poor, minus your payroll taxes. Report any more than that, and your payroll taxes will go up. Report any less than that, and the Earned Income Tax Credit drops. A taxable income of $9,000 is the sweet spot.

And, wouldn't you know it, $9,000 is the most common taxable income reported by self-employed people with one child.

Did these Americans adjust their work schedules to make sure they earned the perfect income? Nope. When these workers were randomly audited—a very rare occurrence—it was almost always found that they made nowhere near $9,000—they earned either substantially less or substantially more.

In other words, they cheated on their taxes by pretending they made the amount that would give them the fattest check from the government.

So how typical was this type of tax fraud and who among the self-employed with one child was most likely to commit it? It turns out, Chetty and colleagues reported, that there were huge differences across the United States in how common this type of cheating was. In Miami, among people in this category, an astonishing 30 percent reported they made $9,000. In Philadelphia, just 2 percent did.

What predicts who is going to cheat? What is it about places that have the greater number of cheaters and those that have lower numbers? We can correlate rates of cheating with other city-level demographics and it turns out that there are two strong predictors: a high concentration of people in the area qualifying for the Earned Income Tax Credit and a high concentration of tax professionals in the neighborhood.

What do these factors indicate? Chetty and the authors had an explanation. The key motivator for cheating on your taxes in this manner was information.

Most self-employed one-kid taxpayers simply did not know that the magic number for getting a big fat check from the government was $9,000. But living near others who might—either their neighbors or tax assisters—dramatically increased the odds that they would learn about it.

In fact, Chetty's team found even more evidence that knowledge drove this kind of cheating. When Americans moved from an area where this variety of tax fraud was low to an area where it was high, they learned and adopted the trick. Through time, cheating spread from region to region throughout the United States. Like a virus, cheating on taxes is contagious.

Now stop for a moment and think about how revealing this study is. It demonstrated that, when it comes to figuring out who will cheat on their taxes, the key isn't determining who is honest and who is dishonest. It is determining who knows how to cheat and who doesn't.

So when someone tells you they would never cheat on their taxes, there's a pretty good chance that they are—you guessed it—lying. Chetty's research suggests that many would if they knew how.

If you want to cheat on your taxes (and I am *not* recommending this), you should live near tax professionals or live near tax cheaters who can show you the way. If you want to have kids who are world-famous, where should you live? This ability to zoom in on data and get really granular can help answer this question, too.

I was curious where the most successful Americans come from, so one day I decided to download Wikipedia. (You can do that sort of thing nowadays.)

With a little coding, I had a dataset of more than 150,000 Americans deemed by Wikipedia's editors to be notable enough to warrant an entry. The dataset included county of birth, date of birth, occupation, and gender. I merged it with county-level birth data gathered by the National Center for Health Statistics. For every county in the United States, I calculated the odds of making it into Wikipedia if you were born there.

Is being profiled in Wikipedia a meaningful marker of notable achievement? There are certainly limitations. Wikipedia's editors skew young and male, which may bias the sample. And some types of notability are not particularly worthy. Ted Bundy, for example, rates a Wikipedia entry because he killed dozens of young women. That said, I was able to remove criminals without affecting the results much.

I limited the study to baby boomers (those born between 1946 and 1964) because they have had nearly a full lifetime to become notable. Roughly one in 2,058 American-born baby boomers were deemed notable enough to warrant a Wikipedia entry. About 30 percent made it through achievements in art or entertainment, 29 percent through sports, 9 percent via politics, and 3 percent in academia or science.

The first striking fact I noticed in the data was the enormous geographic variation in the likelihood of becoming a big success, at least on Wikipedia's terms. Your chances of achieving notability were highly dependent on where you were born.

Roughly one in 1,209 baby boomers born in California reached Wikipedia. Only one in 4,496 baby boomers born in West Virginia did. Zoom in by county and the results become more telling. Roughly one in 748 baby boomers born in Suffolk County, Massachusetts, where Boston is located, made it to Wikipedia. In some other counties, the success rate was twenty times lower.

Why do some parts of the country appear to be so much

better at churning out America's movers and shakers? I closely examined the top counties. It turns out that nearly all of them fit into one of two categories.

First, and this surprised me, many of these counties contained a sizable college town. Just about every time I saw the name of a county that I had not heard of near the top of the list, like Washtenaw, Michigan, I found out that it was dominated by a classic college town, in this case Ann Arbor. The counties graced by Madison, Wisconsin; Athens, Georgia; Columbia, Missouri; Berkeley, California; Chapel Hill, North Carolina; Gainesville, Florida; Lexington, Kentucky; and Ithaca, New York, are all in the top 3 percent.

Why is this? Some of it is may well be due to the gene pool: sons and daughters of professors and graduate students tend to be smart (a trait that, in the game of big success, can be mighty useful). And, indeed, having more college graduates in an area is a strong predictor of the success of the people born there.

But there is most likely something more going on: early exposure to innovation. One of the fields where college towns are most successful in producing top dogs is music. A kid in a college town will be exposed to unique concerts, unusual radio stations, and even independent record stores. And this isn't limited to the arts. College towns also incubate more than their expected share of notable businesspeople. Maybe early exposure to cutting-edge art and ideas helps them, too.

The success of college towns does not just cross regions. It crosses race. African-Americans were noticeably underrepresented on Wikipedia in nonathletic fields, especially business and science. This undoubtedly has a lot to do with discrimination. But one small county, where the 1950 population was

84 percent black, produced notable baby boomers at a rate near those of the highest counties.

Of fewer than 13,000 boomers born in Macon County, Alabama, fifteen made it to Wikipedia—or one in 852. Every single one of them is black. Fourteen of them were from the town of Tuskegee, home of Tuskegee University, a historically black college founded by Booker T. Washington. The list included judges, writers, and scientists. In fact, a black child born in Tuskegee had the same probability of becoming a notable in a field outside of sports as a white child born in some of the highest-scoring, majority-white college towns.

The second attribute most likely to make a county's natives successful was the presence in that county of a big city. Being born in San Francisco County, Los Angeles County, or New York City all offered among the highest probabilities of making it to Wikipedia. (I grouped New York City's five counties together because many Wikipedia entries did not specify a borough of birth.)

Urban areas tend to be well supplied with models of success. To see the value of being near successful practitioners of a craft when young, compare New York City, Boston, and Los Angeles. Among the three, New York City produces notable journalists at the highest rate; Boston produces notable scientists at the highest rate; and Los Angeles produces notable actors at the highest rate. Remember, we are talking about people who were born there, not people who moved there. And this holds true even after subtracting people with notable parents in that field.

Suburban counties, unless they contained major college towns, performed far worse than their urban counterparts.

My parents, like many boomers, moved away from crowded sidewalks to tree-shaded streets—in this case from Manhattan to Bergen County, New Jersey—to raise their three children. This was potentially a mistake, at least from the perspective of having notable children. A child born in New York City is 80 percent more likely to make it into Wikipedia than a kid born in Bergen County. These are just correlations, but they do suggest that growing up near big ideas is better than growing up with a big backyard.

The stark effects identified here might be even stronger if I had better data on places lived throughout childhood, since many people grow up in different counties than the one where they were born.

The success of college towns and big cities is striking when you just look at the data. But I also delved more deeply to undertake a more sophisticated empirical analysis.

Doing so showed that there was another variable that was a strong predictor of a person's securing an entry in Wikipedia: the proportion of immigrants in your county of birth. The greater the percentage of foreign-born residents in an area, the higher the proportion of children born there who go on to notable success. (Take that, Donald Trump!) If two places have similar urban and college populations, the one with more immigrants will produce more prominent Americans. What explains this?

A lot of it seems to be directly attributable to the children of immigrants. I did an exhaustive search of the biographies of the hundred most famous white baby boomers, according to the Massachusetts Institute of Technology's Pantheon project, which is also working with Wikipedia data. Most of these were entertainers. At least thirteen had foreign-born mothers, including Oliver Stone, Sandra Bullock, and Julianne Moore. This rate is more than three times higher than the national average during this period. (Many had fathers who were immigrants, including Steve Jobs and John Belushi, but this data was more difficult to compare to national averages, since information on fathers is not always included on birth certificates.)

What about variables that don't impact success? One that I found more than a little surprising was how much money a state spends on education. In states with similar percentages of its residents living in urban areas, education spending did not correlate with rates of producing notable writers, artists, or business leaders.

It is interesting to compare my Wikipedia study to one of Chetty's team's studies discussed earlier. Recall that Chetty's team was trying to figure out what areas are good at allowing people to reach the upper middle class. My study was trying to figure out what areas are good at allowing people to reach fame. The results are strikingly different.

Spending a lot on education helps kids reach the upper middle class. It does little to help them become a notable writer, artist, or business leader. Many of these huge successes hated school. Some dropped out.

New York City, Chetty's team found, is not a particularly good place to raise a child if you want to ensure he reaches the upper middle class. It is a great place, my study found, if you want to give him a chance at fame.

When you look at the factors that drive success, the large variation between counties begins to make sense. Many counties combine all the main ingredients for success. Return, again, to Boston. With numerous universities, it is stewing in innovative ideas. It is an urban area with many extremely accomplished people offering youngsters examples of how to make it. And it draws plenty of immigrants, whose children are driven to apply these lessons.

What if an area has none of these qualities? Is it destined to produce fewer superstars? Not necessarily. There is another path: extreme specialization. Roseau County, Minnesota, a small rural county with few foreigners and no major universities, is a good example. Roughly 1 in 740 people born here made it into Wikipedia. Their secret? All nine were professional hockey players, no doubt helped by the county's world-class youth and high school hockey programs.

So is the point here—assuming you're not so interested in raising a hockey star—to move to Boston or Tuskegee if you want to give your future children the utmost advantage? It can't hurt. But there are larger lessons here. Usually, economists and sociologists focus on how to avoid bad outcomes, such as poverty and crime. Yet the goal of a great society is not only to leave fewer people behind; it is to help as many people as possible to really stand out. Perhaps this effort to zoom in on the places where hundreds of thousands of the most famous Americans were born can give us some initial strategies: encouraging immigration, subsidizing universities, and supporting the arts, among them.

Usually, I study the United States. So when I think of zooming in by geography, I think of zooming in on our cities and towns—of looking at places like Macon County, Alabama, and Roseau County, Minnesota. But another huge—and still growing—advantage of data from the internet is that it is easy to collect data from around the world. We can then see how countries differ. And data scientists get an opportunity to tip-toe into anthropology.

One somewhat random topic I recently explored: how does pregnancy play out in different countries around the world? I examined Google searches by pregnant women. The first thing I found was a striking similarity in the physical symptoms about which women complain.

I tested how often various symptoms were searched in combination with the word "pregnant." For example, how often is "pregnant" searched in conjunction with "nausea," "back pain," or "constipation"? Canada's symptoms were very close to those in the United States. Symptoms in countries like Britain, Australia, and India were all roughly similar, too.

Pregnant women around the world apparently also crave the same things. In the United States, the top Google search in this category is "craving ice during pregnancy." The next four are salt, sweets, fruit, and spicy food. In Australia, those cravings don't differ all that much: the list features salt, sweets, chocolate, ice, and fruit. What about India? A similar story: spicy food, sweets, chocolate, salt, and ice cream. In fact, the top five are very similar in all of the countries I looked at.

Preliminary evidence suggests that no part of the world has stumbled upon a diet or environment that drastically changes the physical experience of pregnancy.

But the thoughts that surround pregnancy most definitely do differ.

Start with questions about what pregnant women can

safely do. The top questions in the United States: can pregnant women "eat shrimp," "drink wine," "drink coffee," or "take Tylenol"?

When it comes to such concerns, other countries don't have much in common with the United States or one another. Whether pregnant women can "drink wine" is not among the top ten questions in Canada, Australia, or Britain. Australia's concerns are mostly related to eating dairy products while pregnant, particularly cream cheese. In Nigeria, where 30 percent of the population uses the internet, the top question is whether pregnant women can drink cold water.

Are these worries legitimate? It depends. There is strong evidence that pregnant women are at an increased risk of listeria from unpasteurized cheese. Links have been established between drinking too much alcohol and negative outcomes for the child. In some parts of the world, it is believed that drinking cold water can give your baby pneumonia; I don't know of any medical support for this.

The huge differences in questions posed around the world are most likely caused by the overwhelming flood of information coming from disparate sources in each country: legitimate scientific studies, so-so scientific studies, old wives' tales, and neighborhood chatter. It is difficult for women to know what to focus on—or what to Google.

We can see another clear difference when we look at the top searches for "how to ___ during pregnancy?" In the United States, Australia, and Canada, the top search is "how to prevent stretch marks during pregnancy." But in Ghana, India, and Nigeria, preventing stretch marks is not even in the top five. These countries tend to be more concerned with how to have sex or how to sleep.

TOP FIVE SEARCHES (IN ORDER) FOR "HOW TO ___ DURING PREGNANCY"

UNITED STATES	INDIA	AUSTRALIA	BRITAIN	NIGERIA	SOUTH AFRICA
prevent stretch marks	sleep	prevent stretch marks	lose weight	have sex	have sex
lose weight	do sex	lose weight	prevent stretch marks	lose weight	lose weight
have sex	have sex	avoid stretch marks	avoid stretch marks	make love	prevent stretch marks
avoid stretch marks	sex	sleep	sleep	stay healthy	sleep
stay fit	take care	have sex	have sex	stop vomiting	stop vomiting

TOP FIVE SEARCHES BEGINNING WITH "CAN PREGNANT WOMEN ___?"

UNITED STATES	eat shrimp	drink wine	drink coffee	take Tylenol	eat sushi
BRITAIN	eat prawns	eat smoked salmon	eat cheesecake	eat mozzarella	eat mayonnaise
AUSTRALIA	eat cream cheese	eat prawns	eat bacon	eat sour cream	eat feta cheese

(continued on next page)

NIGERIA	drink cold water	drink wine	drink coffee	have sex	take moringa (edible plant)
SINGAPORE	drink green tea	eat ice cream	eat durian	drink coffee	eat pineapple
SPAIN	eat pâté	eat jamón	take paracetamol (pain relief)	eat tuna	sunbathe
GERMANY	fly	eat salami	go in sauna	eat honey	eat mozzarella
BRAZIL	dye their hair	take Dipirona (pain relief)	take paracetamol	ride a bike	fly

There is undoubtedly more to learn from zooming in on aspects of health and culture in different corners of the world. But my preliminary analysis suggests that Big Data will tell us that humans are even less powerful than we realized when it comes to transcending our biology. Yet we come up with remarkably different interpretations of what it all means.

HOW WE FILL OUR MINUTES AND HOURS

"The adventures of a young man whose principal interests are rape, ultra-violence, and Beethoven."

That was how Stanley Kubrick's controversial *A Clockwork Orange* was advertised. In the movie, the fictional young protagonist, Alex DeLarge, committed shocking acts of violence with chilling detachment. In one of the film's most notorious scenes, he raped a woman while belting out "Singin' in the Rain."

Almost immediately, there were reports of copycat incidents. Indeed, a group of men raped a seventeen-year-old girl while singing the same song. The movie was shut down in many European countries, and some of the more shocking scenes were removed for a version shown in America.

There are, in fact, many examples of real life imitating art, with men seemingly hypnotized by what they had just seen on-screen. A showing of the gang movie *Colors* was followed by a violent shooting. A showing of the gang movie *New Jack City* was followed by riots.

Perhaps most disturbing, four days after the release of *The Money Train,* men used lighter fluid to ignite a subway toll booth, almost perfectly mimicking a scene in the film. The only difference between the fictional and real-world arson: In the movie, the operator escaped. In real life, he burned to death.

There is also some evidence from psychological experiments that subjects exposed to a violent film will report more anger and hostility, even if they don't precisely imitate one of the scenes.

In other words, anecdotes and experiments suggest violent movies can incite violent behavior. But how big an effect do they really have? Are we talking about one or two murders every decade or hundreds of murders every year? Anecdotes and experiments can't answer this.

To see if Big Data could, two economists, Gordon Dahl

and Stefano DellaVigna, merged together three Big Datasets for the years 1995 to 2004: FBI hourly crime data, box-office numbers, and a measure of the violence in every movie from kids-in-mind.com.

The information they were using was complete—every movie and every crime committed in every hour in cities throughout the United States. This would prove important.

Key to their study was the fact that on some weekends, the most popular movie was a violent one—*Hannibal* or *Dawn of the Dead,* for example—while on other weekends, the most popular movie was nonviolent, such as *Runaway Bride* or *Toy Story.*

The economists could see exactly how many murders, rapes, and assaults were committed on weekends when a prominent violent movie was released and compare that to the number of murders, rapes, and assaults there were on weekends when a prominent peaceful movie was released.

So what did they find? When a violent movie was shown, did crime rise, as some experiments suggest? Or did it stay the same?

On weekends with a popular violent movie, the economists found, crime dropped.

You read that right. On weekends with a popular violent movie, when millions of Americans were exposed to images of men killing other men, crime dropped—significantly.

When you get a result this strange and unexpected, your first thought is that you've done something wrong. Each author carefully went over the coding. No mistakes. Your second thought is that there is some other variable that will explain these results. They checked if time of year affected the results.

It didn't. They collected data on weather, thinking perhaps somehow this was driving the relationship. It wasn't.

"We checked all our assumptions, everything we were doing," Dahl told me. "We couldn't find anything wrong."

Despite the anecdotes, despite the lab evidence, and as bizarre as it seemed, showing a violent movie somehow caused a big drop in crime. How could this possibly be?

The key to figuring it out for Dahl and DellaVigna was utilizing their Big Data to zoom in closer. Survey data traditionally provided information that was annual or at best perhaps monthly. If we are really lucky, we might get data for a weekend. By comparison, as we've increasingly been using comprehensive datasets, rather than small-sample surveys, we have been able to home in by the hour and even the minute. This has allowed us to learn a lot more about human behavior.

Sometimes fluctuations over time are amusing, if not earth-shattering. EPCOR, a utility company in Edmonton, Canada, reported minute-by-minute water consumption data during the 2010 Olympic gold medal hockey match between the United States and Canada, which an estimated 80 percent of Canadians watched. The data tells us that shortly after each period ended, water consumption shot up. Toilets across Edmonton were clearly flushing.

Google searches can also be broken down by the minute, revealing some interesting patterns in the process. For example, searches for "unblocked games" soar at 8 A.M. on weekdays and stay high through 3 P.M., no doubt in response to schools' attempts to block access to mobile games on school property without banning students' cell phones.

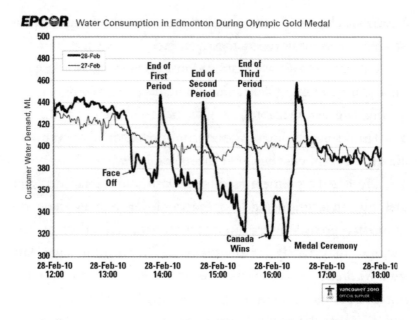

EPC⊕R Water Consumption in Edmonton During Olympic Gold Medal

Search rates for "weather," "prayer," and "news" peak before 5:30 A.M., evidence that most people wake up far earlier than I do. Search rates for "suicide" peak at 12:36 A.M. and are at the lowest levels around 9 A.M., evidence that most people are far less miserable in the morning than I am.

The data shows that the hours between 2 and 4 A.M. are prime time for big questions: What is the meaning of consciousness? Does free will exist? Is there life on other planets? The popularity of these questions late at night may be a result, in part, of cannabis use. Search rates for "how to roll a joint" peak between 1 and 2 A.M.

And in their large dataset, Dahl and DellaVigna could look at how crime changed by the hour on those movies weekends. They found that the drop in crime when popular violent movies were shown—relative to other weekends—began in the early evening.

Crime was lower, in other words, before the violent scenes even started, when theatergoers may have just been walking in.

Can you guess why? Think, first, about who is likely to choose to attend a violent movie. It's young men—particularly young, aggressive men.

Think, next, about where crimes tend to be committed. Rarely in a movie theater. There have been exceptions, most notably a 2012 premeditated shooting in a Colorado theater. But, by and large, men go to theaters unarmed and sit, silently.

Offer young, aggressive men the chance to see *Hannibal,* and they will go to the movies. Offer young, aggressive men *Runaway Bride* as their option, and they will take a pass and instead go out, perhaps to a bar, club, or a pool hall, where the incidence of violent crime is higher.

Violent movies keep potentially violent people off the streets.

Puzzle solved. Right? Not quite yet. There was one more strange thing in the data. The effects started right when the movies started showing; however, they did not stop after the movie ended and the theater closed. On evenings where violent movies were showing, crime was lower well into the night, from midnight to 6 A.M.

Even if crime was lower while the young men were in the movie theater, shouldn't it rise after they left and were no longer preoccupied? They had just watched a violent movie, which experiments say makes people more angry and aggressive.

Can you think of any explanations for why crime still dropped after the movie ended? After much thought, the authors, who were crime experts, had another "Aha" moment.

They knew that alcohol is a major contributor to crime. The authors had sat in enough movie theaters to know that virtually no theaters in the United States serve liquor. Indeed, the authors found that alcohol-related crimes plummeted in late-night hours after violent movies.

Of course, Dahl and DellaVigna's results were limited. They could not, for instance, test the months-out, lasting effects—to see how long the drop in crime might last. And it's still possible that consistent exposure to violent movies ultimately leads to more violence. However, their study does put the immediate impact of violent movies, which has been the main theme in these experiments, into perspective. Perhaps a violent movie does influence some people and make them unusually angry and aggressive. However, do you know what undeniably influences people in a violent direction? Hanging out with other potentially violent men and drinking.*

---

* This story shows how things that seem bad may be good if they prevent something worse. Ed McCaffrey, a Stanford-educated former wide receiver, uses this argument to justify letting all four of his sons play football: "These guys have energy. And, so, if they're not playing football, they're skateboarding, they're climbing trees, they're playing tag in the backyard, they're doing paintball. I mean, they're not going to sit there and do nothing. And, so, the way I look at it is, hey, at least there's rules within the sport of football. . . . My kids have been to the emergency room for falling off decks, getting in bike crashes, skateboarding, falling out of trees. I mean, you name it . . . Yea, it's a violent collision sport. But, also, my guys just have the personality, where, at least they're not squirrel-jumping off mountains and doing crazy stuff like that. So, it's organized aggression, I guess." McCaffrey's argument, made in an interview on *The Herd with Colin Cowherd*, is one I had never heard before. After reading the Dahl/DellaVigna paper, I take the argument seriously. An

This makes sense now. But it didn't make sense before Dahl and DellaVigna began analyzing piles of data.

One more important point that becomes clear when we zoom in: the world is complicated. Actions we take today can have distant effects, most of them unintended. Ideas spread— sometimes slowly; other times exponentially, like viruses. People respond in unpredictable ways to incentives.

These connections and relationships, these surges and swells, cannot be traced with tiny surveys or traditional data methods. The world, quite simply, is too complex and too rich for little data.

OUR DOPPELGANGERS

In June 2009, David "Big Papi" Ortiz looked like he was done. During the previous half decade, Boston had fallen in love with their Dominican-born slugger with the friendly smile and gapped teeth.

He had made five consecutive All-Star games, won an MVP Award, and helped end Boston's eighty-six-year championship drought. But in the 2008 season, at the age of thirty-two, his numbers fell off. His batting average had dropped 68 points, his on-base percentage 76 points, his slugging percentage 114 points. And at the start of the 2009 season, Ortiz's numbers were dropping further.

Here's how Bill Simmons, a sportswriter and passion-

---

advantage of huge real-world datasets, rather than laboratory data, is that they can pick up these kinds of effects.

ate Boston Red Sox fan, described what was happening in the early months of the 2009 season: "It's clear that David Ortiz no longer excels at baseball. . . . Beefy sluggers are like porn stars, wrestlers, NBA centers and trophy wives: When it goes, it goes." Great sports fans trust their eyes, and Simmons's eyes told him Ortiz was finished. In fact, Simmons predicted he would be benched or released shortly.

Was Ortiz really finished? If you're the Boston general manager, in 2009, do you cut him? More generally, how can we predict how a baseball player will perform in the future? Even more generally, how can we use Big Data to predict what people will do in the future?

A theory that will get you far in data science is this: look at what sabermetricians (those who have used data to study baseball) have done and expect it to spread out to other areas of data science. Baseball was among the first fields with comprehensive datasets on just about everything, and an army of smart people willing to devote their lives to making sense of that data. Now, just about every field is there or getting there. Baseball comes first; every other field follows. Sabermetrics eats the world.

The simplest way to predict a baseball player's future is to assume he will continue performing as he currently is. If a player has struggled for the past 1.5 years, you might guess that he will struggle for the next 1.5 years.

By this methodology, Boston should have cut David Ortiz.

However, there might be more relevant information. In the 1980s, Bill James, who most consider the founder of sabermetrics, emphasized the importance of age. Baseball players, James found, peaked early—at around the age of twenty-seven.

Teams tended to ignore just how much players decline as they age. They overpaid for aging players.

By this more advanced methodology, Boston should definitely have cut David Ortiz.

But this age adjustment might miss something. Not all players follow the same path through life. Some players might peak at twenty-three, others at thirty-two. Short players may age differently from tall players, fat players from skinny players. Baseball statisticians found that there were types of players, each following a different aging path. This story was even worse for Ortiz: "beefy sluggers" indeed do, on average, peak early and collapse shortly past thirty.

If Boston considered his recent past, his age, and his size, they should, without a doubt, have cut David Ortiz.

Then, in 2003, statistician Nate Silver introduced a new model, which he called PECOTA, to predict player performance. It proved to be the best—and, also, the coolest. Silver searched for players' doppelgangers. Here's how it works. Build a database of every Major League Baseball player ever, more than 18,000 men. And include everything you know about those players: their height, age, and position; their home runs, batting average, walks, and strikeouts for each year of their careers. Now, find the twenty ballplayers who look most similar to Ortiz right up until that point in his career—those who played like he did when he was 24, 25, 26, 27, 28, 29, 30, 31, 32, and 33. In other words, find his doppelgangers. Then see how Ortiz's doppelgangers' careers progressed.

A doppelganger search is another example of zooming in. It zooms in on the small subset of people most similar to a given person. And, as with all zooming in, it gets better the more data you have. It turns out, Ortiz's doppelgangers gave a very different prediction for Ortiz's future. Ortiz's doppelgangers included Jorge Posada and Jim Thome. These players started their careers a bit slow; had amazing bursts in their late twenties, with world-class power; and then struggled in their early thirties.

Silver then predicted how Ortiz would do based on how these doppelgangers ended up doing. And here's what he found: they regained their power. For trophy wives, Simmons may be right: when it goes, it goes. But for Ortiz's doppelgangers, when it went, it came back.

The doppelganger search, the best methodology ever used to predict baseball player performance, said Boston should be patient with Ortiz. And Boston indeed was patient with their aging slugger. In 2010, Ortiz's average rose to .270. He hit 32 home runs and made the All-Star team. This began a string of four consecutive All-Star games for Ortiz. In 2013, batting in his traditional third spot in the lineup, at the age of thirty-seven, Ortiz batted .688 as Boston defeated St. Louis, 4 games to 2, in the World Series. Ortiz was voted World Series MVP.*

As soon as I finished reading Nate Silver's approach to predicting the trajectory of ballplayers, I immediately began thinking about whether I might have a doppelganger, too.

---

* You can probably tell by this part of the book I tend to be cynical about good stories. I wanted one feel-good story in here, so I am leaving my cynicism to a footnote. I suspect PECOTA just found out that Ortiz was a steroid user who stopped using steroids and would start using them again. From the standpoint of prediction, it is actually pretty cool if PECOTA was able to detect that—but it makes it a less moving story.

Doppelganger searches are promising in many fields, not just athletics. Could I find the person who shares the most interests with me? Maybe if I found the person most similar to me, we could hang out. Maybe he would know some restaurants we would like. Maybe he could introduce me to things I had no idea I might have an affinity for.

A doppelganger search zooms in on individuals and even on the traits of individuals. And, as with all zooming in, it gets sharper the more data you have. Suppose I searched for my doppelganger in a dataset of ten or so people. I might find someone who shared my interest in books. Suppose I searched for my doppelganger in a dataset of a thousand or so people. I might find someone who had a thing for popular physics books. But suppose I searched for my doppelganger in a dataset of hundreds of millions of people. Then I might be able to find someone who was really, truly similar to me.

One day, I went doppelganger hunting on social media. Using the entire corpus of Twitter profiles, I looked for the people on the planet who have the most common interests with me.

You can certainly tell a lot about my interests from whom I follow on my Twitter account. Overall, I follow some 250 people, showing my passions for sports, politics, comedy, science, and morose Jewish folksingers.

So is there anybody out there in the universe who follows all 250 of these accounts, my Twitter twin? Of course not. Doppelgangers aren't identical to us, only similar. Nor is there anybody who follows 200 of the accounts I follow. Or even 150.

However, I did eventually find an account that followed an

amazing 100 of the accounts I follow: Country Music Radio Today. Huh? It turns out, Country Music Radio Today was a bot (it no longer exists) that followed 750,000 Twitter profiles in the hope that they would follow back.

I have an ex-girlfriend who I suspect would get a kick out of this result. She once told me I was more like a robot than a human being.

All joking aside, my initial finding that my doppelganger was a bot that followed 750,000 random accounts does make an important point about doppelganger searches. For a doppelganger search to be truly accurate, you don't want to find someone who merely likes the same things you like. You also want to find someone who dislikes the things you dislike.

My interests are apparent not just from the accounts I follow but from those I choose not to follow. I am interested in sports, politics, comedy, and science but not food, fashion, or theater. My follows show that I like Bernie Sanders but not Elizabeth Warren, Sarah Silverman but not Amy Schumer, the *New Yorker* but not the *Atlantic*, my friends Noah Popp, Emily Sands, and Josh Gottlieb but not my friend Sam Asher. (Sorry, Sam. But your Twitter feed is a snooze.)

Of all 200 million people on Twitter, who has the most similar profile to me? It turns out my doppelganger is *Vox* writer Dylan Matthews. This was kind of a letdown, for the purposes of improving my media consumption, as I already follow Matthews on Twitter and Facebook and compulsively read his *Vox* posts. So learning he was my doppelganger hasn't really changed my life. But it's still pretty cool to know the person most similar to you in the world, especially if it's someone you admire. And when I finish this book and stop being a hermit, maybe Matthews and I can hang out and discuss the writings of James Surowiecki.

The Ortiz doppelganger search was neat for baseball fans. And my doppelganger search was entertaining, at least to me. But what else can these searches reveal? For one thing, doppelganger searches have been used by many of the biggest internet companies to dramatically improve their offerings and user experience. Amazon uses something like a doppelganger search to suggest what books you might like. They see what people similar to you select and base their recommendations on that.

Pandora does the same in picking what songs you might want to listen to. And this is how Netflix figures out the movies you might like. The impact has been so profound that when Amazon engineer Greg Linden originally introduced doppelganger searches to predict readers' book preferences, the improvement in recommendations was so good that Amazon founder Jeff Bezos got to his knees and shouted, "I'm not worthy!" to Linden.

But what is really interesting about doppelganger searches, considering their power, is not how they're commonly being used now. It is how frequently they are not used. There are major areas of life that could be vastly improved by the kind of personalization these searches allow. Take our health, for instance.

Isaac Kohane, a computer scientist and medical researcher at Harvard, is trying to bring this principle to medicine. He wants to organize and collect all of our health information so that instead of using a one-size-fits-all approach, doctors can find patients just like you. Then they can employ more personalized, more focused diagnoses and treatments.

Kohane considers this a natural extension for the medical field and not even a particularly radical one. "What is a diagnosis?" Kohane asks. "A diagnosis really is a statement that you share properties with previously studied populations. When I diagnose you with a heart attack, God forbid, I say you have a pathophysiology that I learned from other people means you have had a heart attack."

A diagnosis is, in essence, a primitive kind of doppelganger search. The problem is that the datasets doctors use to make their diagnoses are small. These days a diagnosis is based on a doctor's experience with the population of patients he or she has treated and perhaps supplemented by academic papers from small populations that other researchers have encountered. As we've seen, though, for a doppelganger search to really get good, it would have to include many more cases.

Here is a field where some Big Data could really help. So what's taking so long? Why isn't it already widely used? The problem lies with data collection. Most medical reports still exist on paper, buried in files, and for those that are computerized, they're often locked up in incompatible formats. We often have better data, Kohane notes, on baseball than on health. But simple measures would go a long way. Kohane talks repeatedly of "low-hanging fruit." He believes, for instance, that merely creating a complete dataset of children's height and weight charts and any diseases they might have would be revolutionary for pediatrics. Each child's growth path then could be compared to every other child's growth path. A computer could find children who were on a similar trajectory and automatically flag any troubling patterns. It might detect a child's height leveling off prematurely, which in certain scenarios would likely point to one of two possible causes: hypothyroidism or a brain tumor.

Early diagnosis in both cases would be a huge boon. "These are rare birds," according to Kohane, "one-in-ten-thousand kind of events. Children, by and large, are healthy. I think we could diagnose them earlier, at least a year earlier. One hundred percent, we could."

James Heywood is an entrepreneur who has a different approach to deal with difficulties linking medical data. He created a website, PatientsLikeMe.com, where individuals can report their own information—their conditions, treatments, and side effects. He's already had a lot of success charting the varying courses diseases can take and how they compare to our common understanding of them.

His goal is to recruit enough people, covering enough conditions, so that people can find their health doppelganger. Heywood hopes that you can find people of your age and gender, with your history, reporting symptoms similar to yours—and see what has worked for them. That would be a very different kind of medicine, indeed.

DATA STORIES

In many ways the act of zooming in is more valuable to me than the particular findings of a particular study, because it offers a new way of seeing and talking about life.

When people learn that I am a data scientist and a writer, they sometimes will share some fact or survey with me. I often find this data boring—static and lifeless. It has no story to tell.

Likewise, friends have tried to get me to join them in reading novels and biographies. But these hold little interest for me as well. I always find myself asking, "Would that happen in other situations? What's the more general principle?" Their stories feel small and unrepresentative.

What I have tried to present in this book is something that, for me, is like nothing else. It is based on data and numbers; it is illustrative and far-reaching. And yet the data is so rich that you can visualize the people underneath it. When we zoom in on every minute of Edmonton's water consumption, I *see* the people getting up from their couch at the end of the period. When we zoom in on people moving from Philadelphia to Miami and starting to cheat on their taxes, I *see* these people talking to their neighbors in their apartment complex and learning about the tax trick. When we zoom in on baseball fans of every age, I *see* my own childhood and my brother's childhood and millions of adult men still crying over a team that won them over when they were eight years old.

At the risk of once again sounding grandiose, I think the economists and data scientists featured in this book are creating not only a new tool but a new genre. What I have tried to present in this chapter, and much of this book, is data so big and so rich, allowing us to zoom in so close that, without limiting ourselves to any particular, unrepresentative human being, we can still tell complex and evocative stories.

6

ALL THE WORLD'S A LAB

February 27, 2000, started as an ordinary day on Google's Mountain View campus. The sun was shining, the bikers were pedaling, the masseuses were massaging, the employees were hydrating with cucumber water. And then, on this ordinary day, a few Google engineers had an idea that unlocked the secret that today drives much of the internet. The engineers found the best way to get you clicking, coming back, and staying on their sites.

Before describing what they did, we need to talk about correlation versus causality, a huge issue in data analysis—and one that we have not yet adequately addressed.

The media bombard us with correlation-based studies seemingly every day. For example, we have been told that those of us who drink a moderate amount of alcohol tend to be in better health. That is a correlation.

Does this mean drinking a moderate amount will improve

one's health—a causation? Perhaps not. It could be that good health causes people to drink a moderate amount. Social scientists call this reverse causation. Or it could be that there is an independent factor that causes both moderate drinking and good health. Perhaps spending a lot of time with friends leads to both moderate alcohol consumption and good health. Social scientists call this omitted-variable bias.

How, then, can we more accurately establish causality? The gold standard is a randomized, controlled experiment. Here's how it works. You randomly divide people into two groups. One, the treatment group, is asked to do or take something. The other, the control group, is not. You then see how each group responds. The difference in the outcomes between the two groups is your causal effect.

For example, to test whether moderate drinking causes good health, you might randomly pick some people to drink one glass of wine per day for a year, randomly choose others to drink no alcohol for a year, and then compare the reported health of both groups. Since people were randomly assigned to the two groups, there is no reason to expect one group would have better initial health or have socialized more. You can trust that the effects of the wine are causal. Randomized, controlled experiments are the most trusted evidence in any field. If a pill can pass a randomized, controlled experiment, it can be dispensed to the general populace. If it cannot pass this test, it won't make it onto pharmacy shelves.

Randomized experiments have increasingly been used in the social sciences as well. Esther Duflo, a French economist at MIT, has led the campaign for greater use of experiments in developmental economics, a field that tries to figure out the best ways to help the poorest people in the world. Consider Duflo's study, with colleagues, of how to improve education in rural India, where more than half of middle school students cannot read a simple sentence. One potential reason students struggle so much is that teachers don't show up consistently. On a given day in some schools in rural India, more than 40 percent of teachers are absent.

Duflo's test? She and her colleagues randomly divided schools into two groups. In one (the treatment group), in addition to their base pay, teachers were paid a small amount— 50 rupees, or about $1.15—for every day they showed up to work. In the other, no extra payment for attendance was given. The results were remarkable. When teachers were paid, teacher absenteeism dropped in half. Student test performance also improved substantially, with the biggest effects on young girls. By the end of the experiment, girls in schools where teachers were paid to come to class were 7 percentage points more likely to be able to write.

According to a *New Yorker* article, when Bill Gates learned of Duflo's work, he was so impressed he told her, "We *need* to fund you."

THE ABCS OF A/B TESTING

So randomized experiments are the gold standard for proving causality, and their use has spread through the social sciences. Which brings us back to Google's offices on February 27, 2000. What did Google do on that day that revolutionized the internet?

On that day, a few engineers decided to perform an experiment on Google's site. They randomly divided users into two groups. The treatment group was shown twenty links on the search results pages. The control group was shown the usual ten. The engineers then compared the satisfaction of the two groups based on how frequently they returned to Google.

This is a revolution? It doesn't seem so revolutionary. I already noted that randomized experiments have been used by pharmaceutical companies and social scientists. How can copying them be such a big deal?

The key point—and this was quickly realized by the Google engineers—is that experiments in the digital world have a huge advantage relative to experiments in the offline world. As convincing as offline randomized experiments can be, they are also resource-intensive. For Duflo's study, schools had to be contacted, funding had to be arranged, some teachers had to be paid, and all students had to be tested. Offline experiments can cost thousands or hundreds of thousands of dollars and take months or years to conduct.

In the digital world, randomized experiments can be cheap and fast. You don't need to recruit and pay participants. Instead, you can write a line of code to randomly assign them to a group. You don't need users to fill out surveys. Instead, you can measure mouse movements and clicks. You don't need to hand-code and analyze the responses. You can build a program to automatically do that for you. You don't have to contact anybody. You don't even have to tell users they are part of an experiment.

This is the fourth power of Big Data: it makes randomized experiments, which can find truly causal effects, much, much easier to conduct—anytime, more or less anywhere, as long as you're online. In the era of Big Data all the world's a lab.

This insight quickly spread through Google and then the rest of Silicon Valley, where randomized controlled experiments have been renamed "A/B testing." In 2011, Google engineers ran seven thousand A/B tests. And this number is only rising.

If Google wants to know how to get more people to click on ads on their sites, they may try two shades of blue in ads—one shade for Group A, another for Group B. Google can then compare click rates. Of course, the ease of such testing can lead to overuse. Some employees felt that because testing was so effortless, Google was overexperimenting. In 2009, one frustrated designer quit after Google went through forty-one marginally different shades of blue in A/B testing. But this designer's stand in favor of art over obsessive market research has done little to stop the spread of the methodology.

Facebook now runs a thousand A/B tests per day, which means that a small number of engineers at Facebook start more randomized, controlled experiments in a given day than the entire pharmaceutical industry starts in a year.

A/B testing has spread beyond the biggest tech firms. A former Google employee, Dan Siroker, brought this methodology to Barack Obama's first presidential campaign, which A/B-tested home page designs, email pitches, and donation forms. Then Siroker started a new company, Optimizely, which allows organizations to perform rapid A/B testing. In 2012,

Optimizely was used by Obama as well as his opponent, Mitt Romney, to maximize sign-ups, volunteers, and donations. It's also used by companies as diverse as Netflix, TaskRabbit, and *New York* magazine.

To see how valuable testing can be, consider how Obama used it to get more people engaged with his campaign. Obama's home page initially included a picture of the candidate and a button below the picture that invited people to "Sign Up."

Was this the best way to greet people? With the help of Siroker, Obama's team could test whether a different picture and button might get more people to actually sign up. Would more people click if the home page instead featured a picture of Obama with a more solemn face? Would more people click if the button instead said "Join Now"? Obama's team showed users different combinations of pictures and buttons and measured how many of them clicked the button. See if you can predict the winning picture and winning button.

Pictures Tested

Buttons Tested

The winner was the picture of Obama's family and the button "Learn More." And the victory was huge. By using that combination, Obama's campaign team estimated it got 40 per-

Winning Combination

cent more people to sign up, netting the campaign roughly $60 million in additional funding.

There is another great benefit to the fact that all this gold-standard testing can be done so cheap and easy: it further frees us from our reliance upon our intuition, which, as noted in Chapter 1, has its limitations. A fundamental reason for A/B testing's importance is that people are unpredictable. Our intuition often fails to predict how they will respond.

Was your intuition correct on Obama's optimal website?

Here are some more tests for your intuition. The *Boston Globe* A/B-tests headlines to figure out which ones get the most people to click on a story. Try to guess the winners from these pairs:

ONE OF THESE HEADLINES WAS WAY BETTER THAN THE OTHER IN GETTING CLICKS.

	HEADLINE A	HEADLINE B
1.	Can the SnotBot drone save the whales?	Can this drone help save the whales?
2.	Of course "deflated balls" is a top search term in Massachusetts	This top Mass. Google search term is pretty embarrassing
3.	Hookup contest at heart of St. Paul rape trial	No charges in prep school sex scandal
4.	Woman makes bank off rare baseball card	Woman makes $179,000 off rare baseball card
5.	MBTA projects annual operating deficit will double by 2020	Get ready: the MBTA's deficit is about to double
6.	How Massachusetts helped win you the right to birth control access	How Boston University helped end "crimes against chastity"
7.	When the first subway opened in Boston	Cartoons from when the first subway opened in Boston
8.	Victim and family in prep-school rape trial blame toxic culture	Victim and family in prep-school rape trial releases statement
9.	Guy in "Free Brady" hat is only one able to foil Miley Cyrus prank	Pats fan gets an eyeful for recognizing an undercover Miley Cyrus

Finished your guesses? The answers are in bold below.

	HEADLINE A	HEADLINE B	WINNER?
1.	**Can the SnotBot drone save the whales?**	Can this drone help save the whales?	53% more clicks for A
2.	Of course "deflated balls" is a top search term in Massachusetts	**This top Mass. Google search term is pretty embarrassing**	986% more clicks for B

(continued on next page)

	HEADLINE A	HEADLINE B	WINNER?
3.	Hookup contest at heart of St. Paul rape trial	**No charges in prep school sex scandal**	108% more clicks for B
4.	**Woman makes bank off rare baseball card**	Woman makes $179,000 off rare baseball card	38% more clicks for A
5.	MBTA projects annual operating deficit will double by 2020	**Get ready: the MBTA's deficit is about to double**	62% more clicks for B
6.	How Massachusetts helped win you the right to birth control access	**How Boston University helped end "crimes against chastity"**	188% more clicks for B
7.	**When the first subway opened in Boston**	Cartoons from when the first subway opened in Boston	33% more clicks for A
8.	Victim and family in prep-school rape trial blame toxic culture	**Victim and family in prep-school rape trial releases statement**	76% more clicks for B
9.	Guy in "Free Brady" hat is only one able to foil Miley Cyrus prank	**Pats fan gets an eyeful for recognizing an undercover Miley Cyrus**	67% more clicks for B

I predict you got more than half right, perhaps by considering what you would click on. But you probably did not guess all of these correctly.

Why? What did you miss? What insights into human behavior did you lack? What lessons can you learn from your mistakes?

We usually ask questions such as these after making bad predictions.

But look how difficult it is to draw general conclusions from the *Globe* headlines. In the first headline test, changing a single word, "this" to "SnotBot," led to a big win. This might suggest more details win. But in the second headline, "deflated balls," the detailed term, loses. In the fourth headline, "makes bank" beats the number $179,000. This might suggest slang terms win. But the slang term "hookup contest" loses in the third headline.

The lesson of A/B testing, to a large degree, is to be wary of general lessons. Clark Benson is the CEO of ranker.com, a news and entertainment site that relies heavily on A/B testing to choose headlines and site design. "At the end of the day, you can't assume anything," Benson says. "Test literally everything."

Testing fills in gaps in our understanding of human nature. These gaps will always exist. If we knew, based on our life experience, what the answer would be, testing would not be of value. But we don't, so it is.

Another reason A/B testing is so important is that seemingly small changes can have big effects. As Benson puts it, "I'm constantly amazed with minor, minor factors having outsized value in testing."

In December 2012, Google changed its advertisements. They added a rightward-pointing arrow surrounded by a square.

Notice how bizarre this arrow is. It points rightward to absolutely nothing. In fact, when these arrows first appeared, many Google customers were critical. Why were they adding meaningless arrows to the ad, they wondered?

Well, Google is protective of its business secrets, so they don't say exactly how valuable the arrows were. But they did say that these arrows had won in A/B testing. The reason Google added them is that they got a lot more people to click. And this minor, seemingly meaningless change made Google and their ad partners oodles of money.

So how can you find these small tweaks that produce outsize profits? You have to test lots of things, even many that seem trivial. In fact, Google's users have noted numerous times that ads have been changed a tiny bit only to return to their previous form. They have unwittingly become members of treatment groups in A/B tests—but at the cost only of seeing these slight variations.

Centering Experiment (Didn't Work)

Best Selling iPad 2 Case
The ZAGGmate™ - Tough Aluminum Case
with build in Bluetooth Keyboard
www.zagg.com

Green Star Experiment (Didn't Work)

Foster's Hollywood Restaurant **Reviews**, Madrid, Spain …
www.tripadvisor.co.uk > … > Madrid > Madrid Restaurants ⏷ TripAdvisor ⏷
★ ★ ★ ⯪ ★ Rating: 3 - 118 reviews
Foster's Hollywood, Madrid: See 118 unbiased **reviews** of **Foster's Hollywood**, rated 3 of 5 on TripAdvisor and ranked #3647 of 6489 restaurants in Madrid

New Font Experiment (Didn't Work)

Live Stock Market News
Free Charts, News and Tips from UTVi Experts. Visit us Today!
UTVi.com/Stocks

ALL THE WORLD'S A LAB   **219**

The above variations never made it to the masses. They lost. But they were part of the process of picking winners. The road to a clickable arrow is paved with ugly stars, faulty positionings, and gimmicky fonts.

It may be fun to guess what makes people click. And if you are a Democrat, it might be nice to know that testing got Obama more money. But there is a dark side to A/B testing.

In his excellent book *Irresistible*, Adam Alter writes about the rise of behavioral addictions in contemporary society. Many people are finding aspects of the internet increasingly difficult to turn off.

My favorite dataset, Google searches, can give us some clues as to what people find most addictive. According to Google, most addictions remain the ones people have struggled with for many decades—drugs, sex, and alcohol, for example. But the internet is starting to make its presence felt on the list—with "porn" and "Facebook" now among the top ten reported addictions.

TOP ADDICTIONS REPORTED TO GOOGLE, 2016

Drugs	Alcohol	Gambling
Sex	Sugar	Facebook
Porn	Love	

A/B testing may be playing a role in making the internet so darn addictive.

Tristan Harris, a "design ethicist," was quoted in *Irresistible* explaining why people have such a hard time resisting certain sites on the internet: "There are a thousand people on the other side of the screen whose job it is to break down the self-regulation you have."

And these people are using A/B testing.

Through testing, Facebook may figure out that making a particular button a particular color gets people to come back to their site more often. So they change the button to that color. Then they may figure out that a particular font gets people to come back to their site more often. So they change the text to that font. Then they may figure out that emailing people at a certain time gets them coming back to their site more often. So they email people at that time.

Pretty soon, Facebook becomes a site optimized to maximize how much time people spend on Facebook. In other words, find enough winners of A/B tests and you have an addictive site. It is the type of feedback that cigarette companies never had.

A/B testing is increasingly a tool of the gaming industry. As Alter discusses, World of Warcraft A/B-tests various versions of its game. One mission might ask you to kill someone. Another might ask you to save something. Game designers can give different samples of players' different missions and then see which ones keep more people playing. They might find, for example, that the mission that asked you to save a person got people to return 30 percent more often. If they test many, many missions, they start finding more and more winners. These 30 percent wins add up, until they have a game that keeps many adult men holed up in their parents' basement.

If you are a little disturbed by this, I am with you. And we will talk a bit more about the ethical implications of this and other aspects of Big Data near the end of this book. But for better or worse, experimentation is now a crucial tool in the data scientists' tool kit. And there is another form of experimentation sitting in that tool kit. It has been used to ask a variety of questions, including whether TV ads really work.

NATURE'S CRUEL—BUT ENLIGHTENING—EXPERIMENTS

It's January 22, 2012, and the New England Patriots are playing the Baltimore Ravens in the AFC Championship game.

There's a minute left in the game. The Ravens are down, but they've got the ball. The next sixty seconds will determine which team will play in the Super Bowl. The next sixty seconds will help seal players' legacies. And the last minute of this game will do something that, for an economist, is far more profound: the last sixty seconds will help finally tell us, once and for all, Do advertisements work?

The notion that ads improve sales is obviously crucial to our economy. But it is maddeningly hard to prove. In fact, this is a textbook example of exactly how difficult it is to distinguish between correlation and causation.

There's no doubt that products that advertise the most also have the highest sales. Twentieth Century Fox spent $150 million marketing the movie *Avatar*, which became the highest-grossing film of all time. But how much of the $2.7 billion in *Avatar* ticket sales was due to the heavy marketing? Part of the reason 20th Century Fox spent so much money on promotion was presumably that they knew they had a desirable product.

Firms believe they know how effective their ads are. Economists are skeptical they really do. University of Chicago economics professor Steven Levitt, while collaborating with an electronics company, was underwhelmed when the firm tried to convince him they knew how much their ads worked. How, Levitt wondered, could they be so confident?

The company explained that, every year, in the days preceding Father's Day, they ramp up their TV ad spending. Sure enough, every year, before Father's Day, they have the highest sales. Uh, maybe that's just because a lot of kids buy electronics for their dads, particularly for Father's Day gifts, regardless of advertising.

"They got the causality completely backwards," says Levitt in a lecture. At least they might have. We don't know. "It's a really hard problem," Levitt adds.

As important as this problem is to solve, firms are reluctant to conduct rigorous experiments. Levitt tried to convince the electronics company to perform a randomized, controlled experiment to precisely learn how effective their TV ads were. Since A/B testing isn't possible on television yet, this would require seeing what happens without advertising in some areas.

Here's how the firm responded: "Are you crazy? We can't not advertise in twenty markets. The CEO would kill us." That ended Levitt's collaboration with the company.

Which brings us back to this Patriots-Ravens game. How can the results of a football game help us determine the causal effects of advertising? Well, it can't tell us the effects of a particular ad campaign from a particular company. But it can give evidence on the average effects of advertisements from many large campaigns.

It turns out, there is a hidden advertising experiment in games like this. Here's how it works. By the time these championship games are played, companies have purchased, and produced, their Super Bowl advertisements. When businesses decide which ads to run, they don't know which teams will play in the game.

But the results of the playoffs will have a huge impact on who actually watches the Super Bowl. The two teams that ultimately qualify will bring with them an enormous amount of viewers. If New England, which plays near Boston, wins, far more people in Boston will watch the Super Bowl than folks in Baltimore. And vice versa.

To the firms, it is the equivalent of a coin flip to determine whether tens of thousands of extra people in Baltimore or Boston will be exposed to their advertisement, a flip that will happen after their spots are purchased and produced.

Now, back to the field, where Jim Nantz on CBS is announcing the final results of this experiment.

> Here comes Billy Cundiff, to tie this game, and, in all likelihood, send it to overtime. The last two years, sixteen of sixteen on field goals. Thirty-two yards to tie it. And the kick. Look out! Look out! It's no good. . . . And the Patriots take the knee and will now take the journey to Indianapolis. They're heading to Super Bowl Forty-Six.

Two weeks later, Super Bowl XLVI would score a 60.3 audience share in Boston and a 50.2 share in Baltimore. Sixty

thousand more people in Boston would watch the 2012 advertisements.

The next year, the same two teams would meet for the AFC
Championship. This time, Baltimore would win. The extra ad
exposures for the 2013 Super Bowl advertisements would be
seen in Baltimore.

	2012 SUPER BOWL RATINGS (BOSTON PLAYS)	2013 SUPER BOWL RATINGS (BALTIMORE PLAYS)
Boston	56.7	48.0
Baltimore	47.9	59.6

Hal Varian, chief economist at Google; Michael D. Smith,
economist at Carnegie Mellon; and I used these two games and
all the other Super Bowls from 2004 to 2013 to test whether—
and, if so, how much—Super Bowl ads work. Specifically we
looked at whether when a company advertises a movie in the
Super Bowl, they see a big jump in ticket sales in the cities that
had higher viewership for the game.

They indeed do. People in cities of teams that qualify for
the Super Bowl attend movies that were advertised during the
Super Bowl at a significantly higher rate than do those in cities of teams that just missed qualifying. More people in those
cities saw the ad. More people in those cities decided to go to
the film.

One alternative explanation might be that having a team
in the Super Bowl makes you more likely to go see movies.
However, we tested a group of movies that had similar budgets
and were released at similar times but that did not advertise in

the Super Bowl. There was no increased attendance in the cities of the Super Bowl teams.

Okay, as you might have guessed, advertisements work. This isn't too surprising.

But it's not just that they work. The ads were incredibly effective. In fact, when we first saw the results, we double- and triple- and quadruple-checked them to make sure they were right—because the returns were so large. The average movie in our sample paid about $3 million for a Super Bowl ad slot. They got $8.3 million in increased ticket sales, a 2.8-to-1 return on their investment.

This result was confirmed by two other economists, Wesley R. Hartmann and Daniel Klapper, who independently and earlier came up with a similar idea. These economists studied beer and soft drink ads run during the Super Bowl, while also utilizing the increased ad exposures in the cities of teams that qualify. They found a 2.5-to-1 return on investment. As expensive as these Super Bowl ads are, our results and theirs suggest they are so effective in upping demand that companies are actually dramatically underpaying for them.

And what does all of this mean for our friends back at the electronics company Levitt had worked with? It's possible that Super Bowl ads are more cost-effective than other forms of advertising. But at the very least our study does suggest that all that Father's Day advertising is probably a good idea.

One virtue of the Super Bowl experiment is that it wasn't necessary to intentionally assign anyone to treatment or control groups. It happened based on the lucky bounces in a football game. It happened, in other words, naturally. Why is that an advantage? Because nonnatural, randomly controlled experiments, while super-powerful and easier to do in the digital age, still are not always possible.

Sometimes we can't get our act together in time. Sometimes, as with that electronics company that didn't want to run an experiment on its ad campaign, we are too invested in the answer to test it.

Sometimes experiments are impossible. Suppose you are interested in how a country responds to losing a leader. Does it go to war? Does its economy stop functioning? Does nothing much change? Obviously, we can't just kill a significant number of presidents and prime ministers and see what happens. That would be not only impossible but immoral. Universities have built up, over many decades, institutional review boards (IRBs) that determine if a proposed experiment is ethical.

So if we want to know causal effects in a certain scenario and it is unethical or otherwise unfeasible to do an experiment, what can we do? We can utilize what economists—defining nature broadly enough to include football games—call natural experiments.

For better or worse (okay, clearly worse), there is a huge random component to life. Nobody knows for sure what or who is in charge of the universe. But one thing is clear: whoever is running the show—the laws of quantum mechanics, God, a pimply kid in his underwear simulating the universe on his computer—they, She, or he is *not* going through IRB approval.

Nature experiments on us all the time. Two people get

shot. One bullet stops just short of a vital organ. The other doesn't. These bad breaks are what make life unfair. But, if it is any consolation, the bad breaks do make life a little easier for economists to study. Economists use the arbitrariness of life to test for causal effects.

Of forty-three American presidents, sixteen have been victims of serious assassination attempts, and four have been killed. The reasons that some lived were essentially random.

Compare John F. Kennedy and Ronald Reagan. Both men had bullets headed directly for their most vulnerable body parts. JFK's bullet exploded his brain, killing him shortly afterward. Reagan's bullet stopped centimeters short of his heart, allowing doctors to save his life. Reagan lived, while JFK died, with no rhyme or reason—just luck.

These attempts on leaders' lives and the arbitrariness with which they live or die is something that happens throughout the world. Compare Akhmad Kadyrov, of Chechyna, and Adolf Hitler, of Germany. Both men have been inches away from a fully functioning bomb. Kadyrov died. Hitler had changed his schedule, wound up leaving the booby-trapped room a few minutes early to catch a train, and thus survived.

And we can use nature's cold randomness—killing Kennedy but not Reagan—to see what happens, on average, when a country's leader is assassinated. Two economists, Benjamin F. Jones and Benjamin A. Olken, did just that. The control group here is any country in the years immediately after a near-miss assassination—for example, the United States in the mid-1980s. The treatment group is any country in the years immediately after a completed assassination—for example, the United States in the mid-1960s.

What, then, is the effect of having your leader murdered? Jones and Olken found that successful assassinations dramatically alter world history, taking countries on radically different paths. A new leader causes previously peaceful countries to go to war and previously warring countries to achieve peace. A new leader causes economically booming countries to start busting and economically busting countries to start booming.

In fact, the results of this assassination-based natural experiment overthrew a few decades of conventional wisdom on how countries function. Many economists previously leaned toward the view that leaders largely were impotent figureheads pushed around by external forces. Not so, according to Jones and Olken's analysis of nature's experiment.

Many would not consider this examination of assassination attempts on world leaders an example of Big Data. The number of assassinated or almost assassinated leaders in the study was certainly small—as was the number of wars that did or did not result. The economic datasets necessary to characterize the trajectory of an economy were large but for the most part predate digitalization.

Nonetheless, such natural experiments—though now used almost exclusively by economists—are powerful and will take on increasing importance in an era with more, better, and larger datasets. This is a tool that data scientists will not long forgo.

And yes, as should be clear by now, economists are playing a major role in the development of data science. At least I'd like to think so, since that was my training.

Where else can we find natural experiments—in other words, situations where the random course of events places people in treatment and control groups?

The clearest example is a lottery, which is why economists love them—not playing them, which we find irrational, but studying them. If a Ping-Pong ball with a three on it rises to the top, Mr. Jones will be rich. If it's a ball with a six instead, Mr. Johnson will be.

To test the causal effects of monetary windfalls, economists compare those who win lotteries to those who buy tickets but lose. These studies have generally found that winning the lottery does not make you happy in the short run but does in the long run.*

Economists can also utilize the randomness of lotteries to see how one's life changes when a neighbor gets rich. The data shows that your neighbor winning the lottery can have an impact on your own life. If your neighbor wins the lottery, for example, you are more likely to buy an expensive car, such as a BMW. Why? Almost certainly, economists maintain, the cause is jealousy after your richer neighbor purchased his own expensive car. Chalk it up to human nature. If Mr. Johnson sees Mr. Jones driving a brand-new BMW, Mr. Johnson wants one, too.

Unfortunately, Mr. Johnson often can't afford this BMW, which is why economists found that neighbors of lottery winners are significantly more likely to go bankrupt. Keeping up with the Joneses, in this instance, is impossible.

---

* A famous 1978 paper that claimed that winning the lottery does not make you happy has largely been debunked.

But natural experiments don't have to be explicitly random, like lotteries. Once you start looking for randomness, you see it everywhere—and can use it to understand how our world works.

Doctors are part of a natural experiment. Every once in a while, the government, for essentially arbitrary reasons, changes the formula it uses to reimburse physicians for Medicare patients. Doctors in some counties see their fees for certain procedures rise. Doctors in other counties see their fees drop.

Two economists—Jeffrey Clemens and Joshua Gottlieb, a former classmate of mine—tested the effects of this arbitrary change. Do doctors always give patients the same care, the care they deem most necessary? Or are they driven by financial incentives?

The data clearly shows that doctors can be motivated by monetary incentives. In counties with higher reimbursements, some doctors order substantially more of the better-reimbursed procedures—more cataract surgeries, colonoscopies, and MRIs, for example.

And then, the big question: do their patients fare better after getting all this extra care? Clemens and Gottlieb reported only "small health impacts." The authors found no statistically significant impact on mortality. Give stronger financial incentives to doctors to order certain procedures, this natural experiment suggests, and some will order more procedures that don't make much difference for patients' health and don't seem to prolong their lives.

Natural experiments can help answer life-or-death questions. They can also help with questions that, to some young people, feel like life-or-death.

Stuyvesant High School (known as "Stuy") is housed in a ten-floor, $150 million tan, brick building overlooking the Hudson River, a few blocks from the World Trade Center, in lower Manhattan. Stuy is, in a word, impressive. It offers fifty-five Advanced Placement (AP) classes, seven languages, and electives in Jewish history, science fiction, and Asian-American literature. Roughly one-quarter of its graduates are accepted to an Ivy League or similarly prestigious college. Stuyvesant trained Harvard physics professor Lisa Randall, Obama strategist David Axelrod, Academy Award–winning actor Tim Robbins, and novelist Gary Shteyngart. Its commencement speakers have included Bill Clinton, Kofi Annan, and Conan O'Brien.

The only thing more remarkable than Stuyvesant's offerings and graduates is its cost: zero dollars. It is a public high school and probably the country's best. Indeed, a recent study used 27 million reviews by 300,000 students and parents to rank every public high school in the United States. Stuy ranked number one. It is no wonder, then, that ambitious, middle-class New York parents and their equally ambitious progeny can become obsessed with Stuy's brand.

For Ahmed Yilmaz,* the son of an insurance agent and teacher in Queens, Stuy was "*the* high school."

"Working-class and immigrant families see Stuy as a way out," Yilmaz explains. "If your kid goes to Stuy, he is going to go to a legit, top-twenty university. The family will be okay."

So how can you get into Stuyvesant High School? You

---

* I have changed his name and a few details.

have to live in one of the five boroughs of New York City and score above a certain number on the admission exam. That's it. No recommendations, no essay, no legacy admission, no affirmative action. One day, one test, one score. If your number is above a certain threshold, you're in.

Each November, approximately 27,000 New York youngsters sit for the admission exam. The competition is brutal. Fewer than 5 percent of those who take the test get into Stuy.

Yilmaz explains that his mother had "worked her ass off" and put what little money she had into his preparation for the test. After months spending every weekday afternoon and full weekends preparing, Yilmaz was confident he would get into Stuy. He still remembers the day he received the envelope with the results. He missed by two questions.

I asked him what it felt like. "What does it feel like," he responded, "to have your world fall apart when you're in middle school?"

His consolation prize was hardly shabby—Bronx Science, another exclusive and highly ranked public school. But it was not Stuy. And Yilmaz felt Bronx Science was more a specialty school meant for technical people. Four years later, he was rejected from Princeton. He attended Tufts and has shuffled through a few careers. Today he is a reasonably successful employee at a tech company, although he says his job is "mind-numbing" and not as well compensated as he'd like.

More than a decade later, Yilmaz admits that he sometimes wonders how life would have played out had he gone to Stuy. "Everything would be different," he says. "Literally, everyone I know would be different." He wonders if Stuyvesant High School would have led him to higher SAT scores, a university like Princeton or Harvard (both of which he considers significantly better than Tufts), and perhaps more lucrative or fulfilling employment.

It can be anything from entertaining to self-torture for human beings to play out hypotheticals. What would my life be like if I made the move on that girl or that boy? If I took that job? If I went to that school? But these what-ifs seem unanswerable. Life is not a video game. You can't replay it under different scenarios until you get the results you want.

Milan Kundera, the Czech-born writer, has a pithy quote about this in his novel *The Unbearable Lightness of Being:* "Human life occurs only once, and the reason we cannot determine which of our decisions are good and which bad is that in a given situation we can make only one decision; we are not granted a second, third or fourth life in which to compare various decisions."

Yilmaz will never experience a life in which he somehow managed to score two points higher on that test.

But perhaps there's a way we can gain some insight on how different his life may or may not have been by doing a study of large numbers of Stuyvesant High School students.

The blunt, naïve methodology would be to compare all the students who went to Stuyvesant and all those who did not. We could analyze how they performed on AP tests and SATs—and what colleges they were accepted into. If we did this, we would find that students who went to Stuyvesant score much higher on standardized tests and get accepted to substantially better universities. But as we've seen already in this chapter, this kind of evidence, by itself, is not convincing. Maybe the reason Stuyvesant students perform so much better is that Stuy attracts much better students in the first place. Correlation here does not prove causation.

To test the *causal* effects of Stuyvesant High School, we need to compare two groups that are almost identical: one that got the Stuy treatment and one that did not. We need a natural experiment. But where can we find it?

The answer: students, like Yilmaz, who scored very, very close to the cutoff necessary to attend Stuyvesant.* Students who just missed the cutoff are the control group; students who just made the cut are the treatment group.

There is little reason to suspect students on either side of the cutoff differ much in talent or drive. What, after all, causes a person to score just a point or two higher on a test than another? Maybe the lower-scoring one slept ten minutes too little or ate a less nutritious breakfast. Maybe the higher-scoring one had remembered a particularly difficult word on the test from a conversation she had with her grandmother three years earlier.

In fact, this category of natural experiments—utilizing sharp numerical cutoffs—is so powerful that it has its own name among economists: regression discontinuity. Anytime there is a precise number that divides people into two different groups—a discontinuity—economists can compare—or regress—the outcomes of people very, very close to the cutoff.

---

* In looking for people like Yilmaz who scored near the cutoff, I was blown away by the number of people—in their twenties through their fifties—who remember this test-taking experience from their early teens and speak about missing a cutoff in dramatic terms. This includes former congressman and New York City mayoral candidate Anthony Weiner, who says he missed Stuy by a single point. "They didn't want me," he told me, in a phone interview.

Two economists, M. Keith Chen and Jesse Shapiro, took advantage of a sharp cutoff used by federal prisons to test the effects of rough prison conditions on future crime. Federal inmates in the United States are given a score, based on the nature of their crime and their criminal history. The score determines the conditions of their prison stay. Those with a high enough score will go to a high-security correctional facility, which means less contact with other people, less freedom of movement, and likely more violence from guards or other inmates.

Again, it would not be fair to compare the entire universe of prisoners who went to high-security prisons to the entire universe of prisoners who went to low-security prisons. High-security prisons will include more murderers and rapists, low-security prisons more drug offenders and petty thieves.

But those right above or right below the sharp numerical threshold had virtually identical criminal histories and backgrounds. This one measly point, however, meant a very different prison experience.

The result? The economists found that prisoners assigned to harsher conditions were more likely to commit additional crimes once they left. The tough prison conditions, rather than deterring them from crime, hardened them and made them more violent once they returned to the outside world.

So what did such a "regression discontinuity" show for Stuyvesant High School? A team of economists from MIT and Duke—Atila Abdulkadiroğlu, Joshua Angrist, and Parag Pathak—performed the study. They compared the outcomes of New York pupils on both sides of the cutoff. In other words, these economists looked at hundreds of students who, like

Yilmaz, *missed* Stuyvesant by a question or two. They compared them to hundreds of students who had a better test day and *made* Stuy by a question or two. Their measures of success were AP scores, SAT scores, and the rankings of the colleges they eventually attended.

Their stunning results were made clear by the title they gave the paper: "Elite Illusion." The effects of Stuyvesant High School? Nil. Nada. Zero. Bupkus. Students on either side of the cutoff ended up with indistinguishable AP scores and indistinguishable SAT scores and attended indistinguishably prestigious universities.

The entire reason that Stuy students achieve more in life than non-Stuy students, the researchers concluded, is that better students attend Stuyvesant in the first place. Stuy does not *cause* you to perform better on AP tests, do better on your SATs, or end up at a better college.

"The intense competition for exam school seats," the economists wrote, "does not appear to be justified by improved learning for a broad set of students."

Why might it not matter which school you go to? Some more stories can help get at the answer. Consider two more students, Sarah Kaufmann and Jessica Eng, two young New Yorkers who both dreamed from an early age of going to Stuy. Kaufmann's score was just on the cutoff; she made it by one question. "I don't think anything could be that exciting again," Kaufmann recalls. Eng's score was just below the cutoff; she missed by one question. Kaufmann went to her dream school, Stuy. Eng did not.

So how did their lives end up? Both have since had successful, and rewarding, careers—as do most people who score in the top 5 percent of all New Yorkers on tests. Eng, ironically, enjoyed her high school experience more. Bronx Science, where she attended, was the only high school with a Holocaust museum. Eng discovered she loved curation and studied anthropology at Cornell.

Kaufmann felt a little lost in Stuy, where students were heavily focused on grades and she felt there was too much emphasis on testing, not on teaching. She called her experience "definitely a mixed bag." But it was a learning experience. She realized, for college, she would only apply to liberal arts schools, which had more emphasis on teaching. She got accepted to her dream school, Wesleyan University. There she found a passion for helping others, and she is now a public interest lawyer.

People adapt to their experience, and people who are going to be successful find advantages in any situation. The factors that make you successful are your talent and your drive. They are not who gives your commencement speech or other advantages that the biggest name-brand schools offer.

This is only one study, and it is probably weakened by the fact that most of the students who just missed the Stuyvesant cutoff ended up at another fine school. But there is growing evidence that, while going to a good school is important, there is little gained from going to the greatest possible school.

Take college. Does it matter if you go to one of the best universities in the world, such as Harvard, or a solid school such as Penn State?

Once again, there is a clear correlation between the ranking of one's school and how much money people make. Ten years into their careers, the average graduate of Harvard makes $123,000. The average graduate of Penn State makes $87,800.

But this correlation does not imply causation.

Two economists, Stacy Dale and Alan B. Krueger, thought of an ingenious way to test the causal role of elite universities on the future earning potential of their graduates. They had a large dataset that tracked a whole host of information on high school students, including where they applied to college, where they were accepted to college, where they attended college, their family background, and their income as adults.

To get a treatment and control group, Dale and Krueger compared students with similar backgrounds who were accepted by the same schools but chose different ones. Some students who got into Harvard attended Penn State—perhaps to be nearer to a girlfriend or boyfriend or because there was a professor they wanted to study under. These students, in other words, were just as talented, according to admissions committees, as those who went to Harvard. But they had different educational experiences.

So when two students, from similar backgrounds, both got into Harvard but one chose Penn State, what happened? The researchers' results were just as stunning as those on Stuyvesant High School. Those students ended up with more or less the same incomes in their careers. If future salary is the measure, similar students accepted to similarly prestigious schools who choose to attend different schools end up in about the same place.

Our newspapers are peppered with articles about hugely successful people who attended Ivy League schools: people like Microsoft founder Bill Gates and Facebook founders Mark Zuckerberg and Dustin Moskovitz, all of whom attended Harvard. (Granted, they all dropped out, raising additional questions about the value of an Ivy League education.)

There are also stories of people who were talented enough to get accepted to an Ivy League school, chose to attend a less prestigious school, and had extremely successful lives: people like Warren Buffett, who started at the Wharton School at the University of Pennsylvania, an Ivy League business school, but transferred to the University of Nebraska–Lincoln because it was cheaper, he hated Philadelphia, and he thought the Wharton classes were boring. The data suggests, earnings-wise at least, that choosing to attend a less prestigious school is a fine decision, for Buffett and others.

This book is called *Everybody Lies*. By this, I mostly mean that people lie—to friends, to surveys, and to themselves—to make themselves look better.

But the world also lies to us by presenting us with faulty, misleading data. The world shows us a huge number of successful Harvard graduates but fewer successful Penn State graduates, and we assume that there is a huge advantage to going to Harvard.

By cleverly making sense of nature's experiments, we can correctly make sense of the world's data—to find what's really useful and what is not.

Natural experiments relate to the previous chapter, as well. They often require zooming in—on the treatment and control groups: the cities in the Super Bowl experiment, the counties in the Medicare pricing experiment, the students close to the cutoff in the Stuyvesant experiment. And zooming in, as discussed in the previous chapter, often requires large, comprehensive datasets—of the type that are increasingly available as the world is digitized. Since we don't know when nature will choose to run her experiments, we can't set up a small survey to measure the results. We need a lot of existing data to learn from these interventions. We need Big Data.

There is one more important point to make about the experiments—either our own or those of nature—detailed in this chapter. Much of this book has focused on understanding the world—how much racism cost Obama, how many men are really gay, how insecure men and women are about their bodies. But these controlled or natural experiments have a more practical bent. They aim to improve our decision making, to help us learn interventions that work and those that do not.

Companies can learn how to get more customers. The government can learn how to use reimbursement to best motivate doctors. Students can learn what schools will prove most valuable. These experiments demonstrate the potential of Big Data to replace guesses, conventional wisdom, and shoddy correlations with what actually works—*causally.*

PART III

BIG DATA: HANDLE WITH CARE

7

BIG DATA, BIG SCHMATA? WHAT IT CANNOT DO

"**S**eth, Lawrence Summers would like to meet with you," the email said, somewhat cryptically. It was from one of my Ph.D. advisers, Lawrence Katz. Katz didn't tell me why Summers was interested in my work, though I later found out Katz had known all along.

I sat in the waiting room outside Summers's office. After some delay, the former Treasury secretary of the United States, former president of Harvard, and winner of some of the biggest awards in economics, summoned me inside.

Summers began the meeting by reading my paper on racism's effect on Obama, which his secretary had printed for him. Summers is a speed reader. As he reads, he occasionally sticks his tongue out and to the right, while his eyes rapidly shift left and right and down the page. Summers reading a social science paper reminds me of a great pianist performing a sonata. He is so focused he seems to lose track of all else. In fewer than five minutes, he had completed my thirty-page paper.

"You say that Google searches for 'nigger' suggest racism," Summers said. "That seems plausible. They predict where Obama gets less support than Kerry. That is interesting. Can we really think of Obama and Kerry as the same?"

"They were ranked as having similar ideologies by political scientists," I responded. "Also, there is no correlation between racism and changes in House voting. The result stays strong even when we add controls for demographics, church attendance, and gun ownership." This is how we economists talk. I had grown animated.

Summers paused and stared at me. He briefly turned to the TV in his office, which was tuned to CNBC, then stared at me again, then looked at the TV, then back at me. "Okay, I like this paper," Summers said. "What else are you working on?"

The next sixty minutes may have been the most intellectually exhilarating of my life. Summers and I talked about interest rates and inflation, policing and crime, business and charity. There is a reason so many people who meet Summers are enthralled. I have been fortunate to speak with some incredibly smart people in my life; Summers struck me as the smartest. He is obsessed with ideas, more than all else, which seems to be what often gets him in trouble. He had to resign his presidency at Harvard after suggesting the possibility that part of the reason for the shortage of women in the sciences might be that men have more variation in their IQs. If he finds an idea interesting, Summers tends to say it, even if it offends some ears.

It was now a half hour past the scheduled end time for our meeting. The conversation was intoxicating, but I still had no idea why I was there, nor when I was supposed to leave, nor how I would know when I was supposed to leave. I got the feeling, by this point, that Summers himself may have forgotten why he had set up this meeting.

And then he asked the million-dollar—or perhaps billion-dollar—question. "You think you can predict the stock market with this data?"

Aha. Here at last was the reason Summers had summoned me to his office.

Summers is hardly the first person to ask me this particular question. My father has generally been supportive of my unconventional research interests. But one time he did broach the subject. "Racism, child abuse, abortion," he said. "Can't you make any money off this expertise of yours?" Friends and other family members have raised the subject, as well. So have coworkers and strangers on the internet. Everyone seems to want to know whether I can use Google searches—or other Big Data—to pick stocks. Now it was the former Treasury secretary of the United States. This was more serious.

So *can* new Big Data sources successfully predict which ways stocks are headed? The short answer is no.

In the previous chapters we discussed the four powers of Big Data. This chapter is all about Big Data's limitations—both what we cannot do with it and, on occasion, what we ought not do with it. And one place to start is by telling the story of the failed attempt by Summers and myself to beat the markets.

In Chapter 3, we noted that new data is most likely to yield big returns when the existing research in a given field is weak. It is an unfortunate truth about the world that you will have a much easier time getting new insights about racism, child abuse, or abortion than you will getting a new, profitable insight into how a business is performing. That's because massive resources are already devoted to looking for even the slightest edge in measuring business performance. The competition in finance is fierce. That was already a strike against us.

Summers, who is not someone known for effusing about other people's intelligence, was certain the hedge funds were already way ahead of us. I was quite taken during our conversation by how much respect he had for them and how many of my suggestions he was convinced they'd beaten us to. I proudly shared with him an algorithm I had devised that allowed me to obtain more complete Google Trends data. He said it was clever. When I asked him if Renaissance, a quantitative hedge fund, would have figured out that algorithm, he chuckled and said, "Yeah, of course they would have figured that out."

The difficulty of keeping up with the hedge funds wasn't the only fundamental problem that Summers and I ran up against in using new, big datasets to beat the markets.

THE CURSE OF DIMENSIONALITY

Suppose your strategy for predicting the stock market is to find a lucky coin—but one that will be found through careful testing. Here's your methodology: You label one thousand coins—1 to 1,000. Every morning, for two years, you flip each coin, record whether it came up heads or tails, and then note whether the Standard & Poor's Index went up or down that day. You pore through all your data. And voilà! You've found something. It turns out that 70.3 percent of the time Coin 391 came up heads the S&P Index rose. The relationship is statistically significant, highly so. You have found your lucky coin!

Just flip Coin 391 every morning and buy stocks whenever it comes up heads. Your days of Target T-shirts and ramen noodle dinners are over. Coin 391 is your ticket to the good life!

Or not.

You have become another victim of one of the most diabolical aspects of "the curse of dimensionality." It can strike whenever you have lots of variables (or "dimensions")—in this case, one thousand coins—chasing not that many observations—in this case, 504 trading days over those two years. One of those dimensions—Coin 391, in this case—is likely to get lucky. Decrease the number of variables—flip only one hundred coins—and it will become much less likely that one of them will get lucky. Increase the number of observations—try to predict the behavior of the S&P Index for twenty years—and coins will struggle to keep up.

The curse of dimensionality is a major issue with Big Data, since newer datasets frequently give us exponentially more variables than traditional data sources—every search term, every category of tweet, etc. Many people who claim to predict the market utilizing some Big Data source have merely been entrapped by the curse. All they've really done is find the equivalent of Coin 391.

Take, for example, a team of computer scientists from Indiana University and Manchester University who claimed they could predict which way the markets would go based on what people were tweeting. They built an algorithm to code the world's day-to-day moods based on tweets. They used techniques similar to the sentiment analysis discussed in

Chapter 3. However, they coded not just one mood but many moods—happiness, anger, kindness, and more. They found that a preponderance of tweets suggesting calmness, such as "I feel calm," predicts that the Dow Jones Industrial Average is likely to rise six days later. A hedge fund was founded to exploit their findings.

What's the problem here?

The fundamental problem is that they tested too many things. And if you test enough things, just by random chance, one of them will be statistically significant. They tested many emotions. And they tested each emotion one day before, two days before, three days before, and up to seven days before the stock market behavior that they were trying to predict. And all these variables were used to try to explain just a few months of Dow Jones ups and downs.

Calmness six days earlier was not a legitimate predictor of the stock market. Calmness six days earlier was the Big Data equivalent of our hypothetical Coin 391. The tweet-based hedge fund was shut down one month after starting due to lackluster returns.

Hedge funds trying to time the markets with tweets are not the only ones battling the curse of dimensionality. So are the numerous scientists who have tried to find the genetic keys to who we are.

Thanks to the Human Genome Project, it is now possible to collect and analyze the complete DNA of people. The potential of this project seemed enormous.

Maybe we could find the gene that causes schizophrenia. Maybe we could discover the gene that causes Alzheimer's and Parkinson's and ALS. Maybe we could find the gene that causes—gulp—intelligence. Is there one gene that can add a whole bunch of IQ points? Is there one gene that makes a genius?

In 1998, Robert Plomin, a prominent behavioral geneticist, claimed to have found the answer. He received a dataset that included the DNA and IQs of hundreds of students. He compared the DNA of "geniuses"—those with IQs of 160 or higher—to the DNA of those with average IQs.

He found a striking difference in the DNA of these two groups. It was located in one small corner of chromosome 6, an obscure but powerful gene that was used in the metabolism of the brain. One version of this gene, named IGF2r, was twice as common in geniuses.

"First Gene to Be Linked with High Intelligence Is Reported Found," headlined the *New York Times*.

You may think of the many ethical questions Plomin's finding raised. Should parents be allowed to screen their kids for IGF2r? Should they be allowed to abort a baby with the low-IQ variant? Should we genetically modify people to give them a high IQ? Does IGF2r correlate with race? Do we want to know the answer to that question? Should research on the genetics of IQ continue?

Before bioethicists had to tackle any of these thorny questions, there was a more basic question for geneticists, including Plomin himself. Was the result accurate? Was it really true that IGF2r could predict IQ? Was it really true that geniuses were twice as likely to carry a certain variant of this gene?

Nope. A few years after his original study, Plomin got access to another sample of people that also included their DNA and IQ scores. This time, IGF2r did not correlate with IQ. Plomin—and this is a sign of a good scientist—retracted his claim.

This, in fact, has been a general pattern in the research into genetics and IQ. First, scientists report that they have found a genetic variant that predicts IQ. Then scientists get new data and discover their original assertion was wrong.

For example, in a recent paper, a team of scientists, led by Christopher Chabris, examined twelve prominent claims about genetic variants associated with IQ. They examined data from ten thousand people. They could not reproduce the correlation for any of the twelve.

What's the issue with all of these claims? The curse of dimensionality. The human genome, scientists now know, differs in millions of ways. There are, quite simply, too many genes to test.

If you test enough tweets to see if they correlate with the stock market, you will find one that correlates just by chance. If you test enough genetic variants to see if they correlate with IQ, you will find one that correlates just by chance.

How can you overcome the curse of dimensionality? You have to have some humility about your work and not fall in love with your results. You have to put these results through additional tests. For example, before you bet your life savings on Coin 391, you would want to see how it does over the next couple of years. Social scientists call this an "out-of-sample" test. And the more variables you try, the more humble you have to be. The more variables you try, the tougher the out-of-sample test has to be. It is also crucial to keep track of every test you attempt. Then you can know exactly how likely it is you are falling victim to the curse and how skeptical you should be of your results. Which brings us back to Larry Summers and me. Here's how we tried to beat the markets.

Summers's first idea was to use searches to predict future sales of key products, such as iPhones, that might shed light on the future performance of the stock of a company, such as Apple. There was indeed a correlation between searches for "iPhones" and iPhones sales. When people are Googling a lot for "iPhones," you can bet a lot of phones are being sold. However, this information was already incorporated into the Apple stock price. Clearly, when there were lots of Google searches for "iPhones," hedge funds had also figured out that it would be a big seller, regardless of whether they used the search data or some other source.

Summers's next idea was to predict future investment in developing countries. If a large number of investors were going to be pouring money into countries such as Brazil or Mexico in the near future, then stocks for companies in these countries would surely rise. Perhaps we could predict a rise in investment with key Google searches—such as "invest in Mexico" or "investment opportunities in Brazil." This proved a dead end. The problem? The searches were too rare. Instead of revealing meaningful patterns, this search data jumped all over the place.

We tried searches for individual stocks. Perhaps if people were searching for "GOOG," this meant they were about to buy Google. These searches seemed to predict that the stocks would be traded a lot. But they did not predict whether the stocks would rise or fall. One major limitation is that these searches did not tell us whether someone was interested in buying or selling the stock.

One day, I excitedly showed Summers a new idea I had: past searches for "buy gold" seemed to correlate with future increases in the price of gold. Summers told me I should test it going forward to see if it remained accurate. It stopped working, perhaps because some hedge fund had found the same relationship.

In the end, over a few months, we didn't find anything useful in our tests. Undoubtedly, if we had looked for a correlation with market performance in each of the billions of Google search terms, we would have found one that worked, however weakly. But it likely would have just been our own Coin 391.

THE OVEREMPHASIS ON WHAT IS MEASURABLE

In March 2012, Zoë Chance, a marketing professor at Yale, received a small white pedometer in her office mailbox in downtown New Haven, Connecticut. She aimed to study how this device, which measures the steps you take during the day and gives you points as a result, can inspire you to exercise more.

What happened next, as she recounted in a TEDx talk, was a Big Data nightmare. Chance became so obsessed and addicted to increasing her numbers that she began walking everywhere, from the kitchen to the living room, to the dining room, to the basement, in her office. She walked early in the morning, late at night, at nearly all hours of the day—twenty thousand steps in a given twenty-four hour period. She checked her pedometer hundreds of times per day, and much that remained of her human communication was with other pedometer users online, discussing strategies to improve scores. She remembers putting the pedometer on her three-year-old daughter when her daughter was walking, because she was so obsessed with getting the number higher.

Chance became so obsessed with maximizing this number that she lost all perspective. She forgot the reason someone would want to get the number higher—exercising, not having her daughter walk a few steps. Nor did she complete any academic research about the pedometer. She finally got rid of the device after falling late one night, exhausted, while trying to get in more steps. Though she is a data-driven researcher by profession, the experience affected her profoundly. "It makes me skeptical of whether having access to additional data is always a good thing," Chance says.

This is an extreme story. But it points to a potential problem with people using data to make decisions. Numbers can be seductive. We can grow fixated with them, and in so doing we can lose sight of more important considerations. Zoë Chance lost sight, more or less, of the rest of her life.

Even less obsessive infatuations with numbers can have drawbacks. Consider the twenty-first-century emphasis on testing in American schools—and judging teachers based on how their students score. While the desire for more objective measures of what happens in classrooms is legitimate, there are many things that go on there that can't readily be captured in numbers. Moreover, all of that testing pressured many teachers to teach to the tests—and worse. A small number, as was proven in a paper by Brian Jacob and Steven Levitt, cheated outright in administering those tests.

The problem is this: the things we can measure are often not exactly what we care about. We can measure how students do on multiple-choice questions. We can't easily measure critical thinking, curiosity, or personal development. Just trying to increase a single, easy-to-measure number—test scores or the number of steps taken in a day—doesn't always help achieve what we are really trying to accomplish.

In its efforts to improve its site, Facebook runs into this danger as well. The company has tons of data on how people use the site. It's easy to see whether a particular News Feed story was liked, clicked on, commented on, or shared. But, according to Alex Peysakhovich, a Facebook data scientist with whom I have written about these matters, not one of these is a perfect proxy for more important questions: What was the experience of using the site like? Did the story connect the user with her friends? Did it inform her about the world? Did it make her laugh?

Or consider baseball's data revolution in the 1990s. Many teams began using increasingly intricate statistics—rather than relying on old-fashioned human scouts—to make decisions. It was easy to measure offense and pitching but not fielding, so some organizations ended up underestimating the importance of defense. In fact, in his book *The Signal and the Noise*, Nate Silver estimates that the Oakland A's, a data-driven organization profiled in *Moneyball*, were giving up eight to ten wins per year in the mid-nineties because of their lousy defense.

The solution is not always more Big Data. A special sauce is often necessary to help Big Data work best: the judgment of humans and small surveys, what we might call small data. In an interview with Silver, Billy Beane, the A's then general manager and the main character in *Moneyball*, said that he actually had begun increasing his scouting budget.

To fill in the gaps in its giant data pool, Facebook too has to take an old-fashioned approach: asking people what they think. Every day as they load their News Feed, hundreds of Facebook users are presented with questions about the stories they see there. Facebook's automatically collected datasets (likes, clicks, comments) are supplemented, in other words, by smaller data ("Do you want to see this post in your News Feed?" "Why?"). Yes, even a spectacularly successful Big Data organization like Facebook sometimes makes use of the source of information much disparaged in this book: a small survey.

Indeed, because of this need for small data as a supplement to its mainstay—massive collections of clicks, likes, and posts—Facebook's data teams look different than you might guess. Facebook employs social psychologists, anthropologists, and sociologists precisely to find what the numbers miss.

Some educators, too, are becoming more alert to blind spots in Big Data. There is a growing national effort to supplement mass testing with small data. Student surveys have proliferated. So have parent surveys and teacher observations, where other experienced educators watch a teacher during a lesson.

"School districts realize they shouldn't be focusing solely on test scores," says Thomas Kane, a professor of education at Harvard. A three-year study by the Bill & Melinda Gates Foundation bears out the value in education of both big and small data. The authors analyzed whether test-score-based models, student surveys, or teacher observations were best at measuring which teachers most improved student learning. When they put the three measures together into a composite score, they got the best results. "Each measure adds something of value," the report concluded.

In fact, it was just as I was learning that many Big Data operations use small data to fill in the holes that I showed up in Ocala, Florida, to meet Jeff Seder. Remember, he was the Harvard-educated horse guru who used lessons learned from a huge dataset to predict the success of American Pharoah.

After sharing all the computer files and math with me, Seder admitted that he had another weapon: Patty Murray.

Murray, like Seder, has high intelligence and elite credentials—a degree from Bryn Mawr. She also left New York City for rural life. "I like horses more than humans," Murray admits. But Murray is a bit more traditional in her approaches to evaluating horses. She, like many horse agents, personally examines horses, seeing how they walk, checking for scars and bruises, and interrogating their owners.

Murray then collaborates with Seder as they pick the final horses they want to recommend. Murray sniffs out problems with the horses, problems that Seder's data, despite being the most innovative and important dataset ever collected on horses, still misses.

I am predicting a revolution based on the revelations of Big Data. But this does not mean we can just throw data at any question. And Big Data does not eliminate the need for all the other ways humans have developed over the millennia to understand the world. They complement each other.

8

MO DATA, MO PROBLEMS? WHAT WE SHOULDN'T DO

S ometimes, the power of Big Data is so impressive it's scary. It raises ethical questions.

THE DANGER OF EMPOWERED CORPORATIONS

Recently, three economists—Oded Netzer and Alain Lemaire, both of Columbia, and Michal Herzenstein of the University of Delaware—looked for ways to predict the likelihood of whether a borrower would pay back a loan. The scholars utilized data from Prosper, a peer-to-peer lending site. Potential borrowers write a brief description of why they need a loan and why they are likely to make good on it, and potential lenders decide whether to provide them the money. Overall, about 13 percent of borrowers defaulted on their loan.

It turns out the language that potential borrowers use is a strong predictor of their probability of paying back. And it is an important indicator even if you control for other relevant information lenders were able to obtain about those potential borrowers, including credit ratings and income.

Listed below are ten phrases the researchers found that are commonly used when applying for a loan. Five of them positively correlate with paying back the loan. Five of them negatively correlate with paying back the loan. In other words, five tend to be used by people you can trust, five by people you cannot. See if you can guess which are which.

God	lower interest rate	after-tax
promise	will pay	hospital
debt-free	graduate	
minimum payment	thank you	

You might think—or at least hope—that a polite, openly religious person who gives his word would be among the most likely to pay back a loan. But in fact this is not the case. This type of person, the data shows, is less likely than average to make good on their debt.

Here are the phrases grouped by the likelihood of paying back.

**TERMS USED IN LOAN APPLICATIONS BY PEOPLE
MOST LIKELY TO PAY BACK**

debt-free	after-tax	graduate
lower interest rate	minimum payment	

TERMS USED IN LOAN APPLICATIONS BY PEOPLE MOST LIKELY TO DEFAULT

God	will pay	hospital
promise	thank you	

Before we discuss the ethical implications of this study, let's think through, with the help of the study's authors, what it reveals about people. What should we make of the words in the different categories?

First, let's consider the language that suggests someone is more likely to make their loan payments. Phrases such as "lower interest rate" or "after-tax" indicate a certain level of financial sophistication on the borrower's part, so it's perhaps not surprising they correlate with someone more likely to pay their loan back. In addition, if he or she talks about positive achievements such as being a college "graduate" and being "debt-free," he or she is also likely to pay their loans.

Now let's consider language that suggests someone is unlikely to pay their loans. Generally, if someone tells you he will pay you back, he will not pay you back. The more assertive the promise, the more likely he will break it. If someone writes "I promise I will pay back, so help me God," he is among the least likely to pay you back. Appealing to your mercy—explaining that he needs the money because he has a relative in the "hospital"—also means he is unlikely to pay you back. In fact, mentioning any family member—a husband, wife, son, daughter, mother, or father—is a sign someone will not be paying back. Another word that indicates default is "explain," meaning if people are trying to explain why they are going to be able to pay back a loan, they likely won't.

The authors did not have a theory for why thanking people is evidence of likely default.

In sum, according to these researchers, giving a detailed plan of how he can make his payments and mentioning commitments he has kept in the past are evidence someone will pay back a loan. Making promises and appealing to your mercy is a clear sign someone will go into default. Regardless of the reasons—or what it tells us about human nature that making promises is a sure sign someone will, in actuality, not do something—the scholars found the test was an extremely valuable piece of information in predicting default. Someone who mentions God was 2.2 times more likely to default. This was among the single highest indicators that someone would not pay back.

But the authors also believe their study raises ethical questions. While this was just an academic study, some companies do report that they utilize online data in approving loans. Is this acceptable? Do we want to live in a world in which companies use the words we write to predict whether we will pay back a loan? It is, at a minimum, creepy—and, quite possibly, scary.

A consumer looking for a loan in the near future might have to worry about not merely her financial history but also her online activity. And she may be judged on factors that seem absurd—whether she uses the phrase "Thank you" or invokes "God," for example. Further, what about a woman who legitimately needs to help her sister in a hospital and will most certainly pay back her loan afterward? It seems awful to punish her because, on average, people claiming to need help for medical bills have often been proven to be lying. A world functioning this way starts to look awfully dystopian.

This is the ethical question: Do corporations have the right to judge our fitness for their services based on abstract but statistically predictive criteria not directly related to those services?

Leaving behind the world of finance, let's look at the larger implications on, for example, hiring practices. Employers are increasingly scouring social media when considering job candidates. That may not raise ethical questions if they're looking for evidence of bad-mouthing previous employers or revealing previous employers' secrets. There may even be some justification for refusing to hire someone whose Facebook or Instagram posts suggest excessive alcohol use. But what if they find a seemingly harmless indicator that correlates with something they care about?

Researchers at Cambridge University and Microsoft gave fifty-eight thousand U.S. Facebook users a variety of tests about their personality and intelligence. They found that Facebook likes are frequently correlated with IQ, extraversion, and conscientiousness. For example, people who like Mozart, thunderstorms, and curly fries on Facebook tend to have higher IQs. People who like Harley-Davidson motorcycles, the country music group Lady Antebellum, or the page "I Love Being a Mom" tend to have lower IQs. Some of these correlations may be due to the curse of dimensionality. If you test enough things, some will randomly correlate. But some interests may legitimately correlate with IQ.

Nonetheless, it would seem unfair if a smart person who happens to like Harleys couldn't get a job commensurate with his skills because he was, without realizing it, signaling low intelligence.

In fairness, this is not an entirely new problem. People have long been judged by factors not directly related to job performance—the firmness of their handshakes, the neatness of their dress. But a danger of the data revolution is that, as more of our life is quantified, these proxy judgments can get more esoteric yet more intrusive. Better prediction can lead to subtler and more nefarious discrimination.

Better data can also lead to another form of discrimination, what economists call price discrimination. Businesses are often trying to figure out what price they should charge for goods or services. Ideally they want to charge customers the maximum they are willing to pay. This way, they will extract the maximum possible profit.

Most businesses usually end up picking one price that everyone pays. But sometimes they are aware that the members of a certain group will, on average, pay more. This is why movie theaters charge more to middle-aged customers—at the height of their earning power—than to students or senior citizens and why airlines often charge more to last-minute purchasers. They price discriminate.

Big Data may allow businesses to get substantially better at learning what customers are willing to pay—and thus gouging certain groups of people. Optimal Decisions Group was a pioneer in using data science to predict how much consumers are willing to pay for insurance. How did they do it? They used a methodology that we have previously discussed in this book. They found prior customers most similar to those currently looking to buy insurance—and saw how high a premium they were willing to take on. In other words, they ran a doppelganger search. A doppelganger search is entertaining if it helps us predict whether a baseball player will return to his former greatness. A doppelganger search is great if it helps us cure someone's disease. But if a doppelganger search helps a corporation extract every last penny from you? That's not so cool. My spendthrift brother would have a right to complain if he got charged more online than tightwad me.

Gambling is one area in which the ability to zoom in on customers is potentially dangerous. Big casinos are using something like a doppelganger search to better understand their consumers. Their goal? To extract the maximum possible profit—to make sure more of your money goes into their coffers.

Here's how it works. Every gambler, casinos believe, has a "pain point." This is the amount of losses that will sufficiently frighten her so that she leaves your casino for an extended period of time. Suppose, for example, that Helen's "pain point" is $3,000. This means if she loses $3,000, you've lost a customer, perhaps for weeks or months. If Helen loses $2,999, she won't be happy. Who, after all, likes to lose money? But she won't be so demoralized that she won't come back tomorrow night.

Imagine for a moment that you are managing a casino. And imagine that Helen has shown up to play the slot machines. What is the optimal outcome? Clearly, you want Helen to get as close as possible to her "pain point" without crossing it. You want her to lose $2,999, enough that you make big profits but not so much that she won't come back to play again soon.

How can you do this? Well, there are ways to get Helen to stop playing once she has lost a certain amount. You can offer her free meals, for example. Make the offer enticing enough, and she will leave the slots for the food.

But there's one big challenge with this approach. How do you know Helen's "pain point"? The problem is, people have different "pain points." For Helen, it's $3,000. For John, it might be $2,000. For Ben, it might be $26,000. If you convince Helen to stop gambling when she lost $2,000, you left profits on the table. If you wait too long—after she has lost $3,000— you have lost her for a while. Further, Helen might not want to tell you her pain point. She may not even know what it is herself.

So what do you do? If you have made it this far in the book, you can probably guess the answer. You utilize data science. You learn everything you can about a number of your customers—their age, gender, zip code, and gambling behavior. And, from that gambling behavior—their winnings, losings, comings, and goings—you estimate their "pain point."

You gather all the information you know about Helen and find gamblers who are similar to her—her doppelgangers, more or less. Then you figure out how much pain they can withstand. It's probably the same amount as Helen. Indeed, this is what the casino Harrah's does, utilizing a Big Data warehouse firm, Terabyte, to assist them.

Scott Gnau, general manager of Terabyte, explains, in the excellent book *Super Crunchers*, what casino managers do when they see a regular customer nearing their pain point: "They come out and say, 'I see you're having a rough day. I know you like our steakhouse. Here, I'd like you to take your wife to dinner on us right now.'"

This might seem the height of generosity: a free steak dinner. But really it's self-serving. The casino is just trying to get customers to quit before they lose so much that they'll leave for an extended period of time. In other words, management is us-ing sophisticated data analysis to try to extract as much money from customers, over the long term, as it can.

We have a right to fear that better and better use of online data will give casinos, insurance companies, lenders, and other corporate entities too much power over us.

On the other hand, Big Data has also been enabling con-sumers to score some blows against businesses that overcharge them or deliver shoddy products.

One important weapon is sites, such as Yelp, that publish reviews of restaurants and other services. A recent study by economist Michael Luca, of Harvard, has shown the extent to which businesses are at the mercy of Yelp reviews. Comparing those reviews to sales data in the state of Washington, he found that one fewer star on Yelp will make a restaurant's revenues drop 5 to 9 percent.

Consumers are also aided in their struggles with business by comparison shopping sites—like Kayak and Booking.com. As discussed in *Freakonomics*, when an internet site began re-porting the prices different companies were charging for term life insurance, these prices fell dramatically. If an insurance company was overcharging, customers would know it and use someone else. The total savings to consumers? One billion dol-lars per year.

Data on the internet, in other words, can tell businesses which customers to avoid and which they can exploit. It can also tell customers the businesses they should avoid and who is trying to exploit them. Big Data to date has helped both sides in the struggle between consumers and corporations. We have to make sure it remains a fair fight.

THE DANGER OF EMPOWERED GOVERNMENTS

When her ex-boyfriend showed up at a birthday party, Adriana Donato knew he was upset. She knew that he was mad. She knew that he had struggled with depression. As he invited her for a drive, there was one thing Donato, a twenty-year-old zoology student, did not know. She did not know her ex-boyfriend, twenty-two-year-old James Stoneham, had spent the previous three weeks searching for information on how to murder somebody and about murder law, mixed in with the occasional search about Donato.

If she had known this, presumably she would not have gotten in the car. Presumably, she would not have been stabbed to death that evening.

In the movie *Minority Report,* psychics collaborate with police departments to stop crimes before they happen. Should Big Data be made available to police departments to stop crimes before they happen? Should Donato have at least been warned about her ex-boyfriend's foreboding searches? Should the police have interrogated Stoneham?

First, it must be acknowledged that there is growing evidence that Google searches related to criminal activity do correlate with criminal activity. Christine Ma-Kellams, Flora Or, Ji Hyun Baek, and Ichiro Kawachi have shown that Google searches related to suicide correlate strongly with state-level suicide rates. In addition, Evan Soltas and I have shown that weekly Islamophobic searches—such as "I hate Muslims" or "kill Muslims"—correlate with anti-Muslim hate crimes that week. If more people are making searches saying they want to do something, more people are going to do that thing.

So what should we do with this information? One simple, fairly uncontroversial idea: we can utilize the area-level data to allocate resources. If a city has a huge rise in suicide-related searches, we can up the suicide awareness in this city. The city government or nonprofits might run commercials explaining where people can get help, for example. Similarly, if a city has a huge rise in searches for "kill Muslims," police departments might be wise to change how they patrol the streets. They might dispatch more officers to protect the local mosque, for example.

But one step we should be very reluctant to take: going after individuals before any crime has been committed. This seems, to begin with, an invasion of privacy. There is a large ethical leap from the government having the search data of thousands or hundreds of thousands of people to the police department having the search data of an individual. There is a large ethical leap from protecting a local mosque to ransacking someone's house. There is a large ethical leap from advertising suicide prevention to locking someone up in a mental hospital against his will.

The reason to be extremely cautious using individual-level data, however, goes beyond even ethics. There is a data reason as well. It is a large leap for data science to go from trying to predict the actions of a city to trying to predict the actions of an individual.

Let's return to suicide for a moment. Every month, there are about 3.5 million Google searches in the United States related to suicide, with the majority of them suggesting suicidal ideation—searches such as "suicidal," "commit suicide," and "how to suicide." In other words, every month, there is more than one search related to suicide for every one hundred Americans. This brings to mind a quote from the philosopher Friedrich Nietzsche: "The thought of suicide is a great consolation: by means of it one gets through many a dark night." Google search data shows how true that is, how common the thought of suicide is. However, every month, there are fewer than four thousand suicides in the United States. Suicidal ideation is incredibly common. Suicide is not. So it wouldn't make a lot of sense for cops to be showing up at the door of everyone who has ever made some online noise about wanting to blow their brains out—if for no other reason than that the police wouldn't have time for anything else.

Or consider those incredibly vicious Islamophobic searches. In 2015, there were roughly 12,000 searches in the United States for "kill Muslims." There were 12 murders of Muslims reported as hate crimes. Clearly, the vast majority of people who make this terrifying search do not go through with the corresponding act.

There is some math that explains the difference between predicting the behavior of an individual and predicting the behavior in a city. Here's a simple thought experiment. Suppose there are one million people in a city and one mosque. Suppose, if someone does not search for "kill Muslims," there is only a 1-in-100,000,000 chance that he will attack a mosque. Suppose if someone does search for "kill Muslims," this chance rises sharply, to 1 in 10,000. Suppose Islamophobia has skyrocketed and searches for "kill Muslims" have risen from 100 to 1,000.

In this situation, math shows that the chances of a mosque being attacked has risen about fivefold, from about 2 percent to 10 percent. But the chances of an individual who searched for "kill Muslims" actually attacking a mosque remains only 1 in 10,000.

The proper response in this situation is not to jail all the people who searched for "kill Muslims." Nor is it to visit their houses. There is a tiny chance that any one of these people in particular will commit a crime. The proper response, however, would be to protect that mosque, which now has a 10 percent chance of being attacked.

Clearly, many horrific searches never lead to horrible actions.

That said, it is at least theoretically possible that there are some classes of searches that suggest a reasonably high probability of a horrible follow-through. It is at least theoretically possible, for example, that data scientists could in the future build a model that could have found that Stoneham's searches related to Donato were significant cause for concern.

In 2014, there were about 6,000 searches for the exact phrase "how to kill your girlfriend" and 400 murders of girlfriends. If all of these murderers had made this exact search beforehand, that would mean 1 in 15 people who searched "how to kill your girlfriend" went through with it. Of course, many, probably most, people who murdered their girlfriends did not make this exact search. This would mean the true probability that this particular search led to murder is lower, probably a lot lower.

But if data scientists could build a model that showed that the threat against a particular individual was, say, 1 in 100, we might want to do something with that information. At the least, the person under threat might have the right to be informed that there is a 1-in-100 chance she will be murdered by a particular person.

Overall, however, we have to be very cautious using search data to predict crimes at an individual level. The data clearly tells us that there are many, many horrifying searches that rarely lead to horrible actions. And there has been, as of yet, no proof that the government can predict a particular horrible action, with high probability, just from examining these searches. So we have to be really cautious about allowing the government to intervene at the individual level based on search data. This is not just for ethical or legal reasons. It's also, at least for now, for data science reasons.

CONCLUSION

HOW MANY PEOPLE FINISH BOOKS?

After signing my book contract, I had a clear vision of how the book should be structured. Near the start, you may recall, I described a scene at my family's Thanksgiving table. My family members debated my sanity and tried to figure out why I, at thirty-three, couldn't seem to find the right girl.

The conclusion to this book, then, practically wrote itself. I would meet and marry the girl. Better still, I would use Big Data to meet the right girl. Perhaps I could weave in tidbits from the courting process throughout. Then the story would all come together in the conclusion, which would describe my wedding day and double as a love letter to my new wife.

Unfortunately, life didn't match my vision. Locking myself in my apartment and avoiding the world while writing a book probably didn't help my romantic life. And I, alas, still need to find a wife. More important, I needed a new conclusion.

I pored over many of my favorite books in trying to find what makes a great conclusion. The best conclusions, I concluded, bring to the surface an important point that has been there all along, hovering just beneath the surface. For this book, that big point is this: social science is becoming a real science. And this new, real science is poised to improve our lives.

In the beginning of Part II, I discussed Karl Popper's critique of Sigmund Freud. Popper, I noted, didn't think that Freud's wacky vision of the world was scientific. But I didn't mention something about Popper's critique. It was actually far broader than just an attack on Freud. Popper didn't think *any* social scientist was particularly scientific. Popper was simply unimpressed with the rigor of what these so-called scientists were doing.

What motivated Popper's crusade? When he interacted with the best intellectuals of his day—the best physicists, the best historians, the best psychologists—Popper noted a striking difference. When the physicists talked, Popper believed in what they were doing. Sure, they sometimes made mistakes. Sure, they sometimes were fooled by their subconscious biases. But physicists were engaged in a process that was clearly finding deep truths about the world, culminating in Einstein's Theory of Relativity. When the world's most famous social scientists talked, in contrast, Popper thought he was listening to a bunch of gobbledygook.

Popper is hardly the only person to have made this distinction. Just about everybody agrees that physicists, biologists, and chemists are real scientists. They utilize rigorous experiments to find how the physical world works. In contrast, many people think that economists, sociologists, and psychologists are soft scientists who throw around meaningless jargon so they can get tenure.

To the extent this was ever true, the Big Data revolution has changed that. If Karl Popper were alive today and attended a presentation by Raj Chetty, Jesse Shapiro, Esther Duflo, or (humor me) myself, I strongly suspect he would not have the same reaction he had back then. To be honest, he might be more likely to question whether today's great string theorists are truly scientific or just engaging in self-indulgent mental gymnastics.

If a violent movie comes to a city, does crime go up or down? If more people are exposed to an ad, do more people use the product? If a baseball team wins when a boy is twenty, will he be more likely to root for them when he's forty? These are all clear questions with clear yes-or-no answers. And in the mountains of honest data, we can find them.

This is the stuff of science, not pseudoscience.

This does not mean the social science revolution will come in the form of simple, timeless laws.

Marvin Minsky, the late MIT scientist and one of the first to study the possibility of artificial intelligence, suggested that psychology got off track by trying to copy physics. Physics had success finding simple laws that held in all times and all places.

Human brains, Minsky suggested, may not be subject to such laws. The brain, instead, is likely a complex system of hacks—one part correcting mistakes in other parts. The economy and political system may be similarly complex.

For this reason, the social science revolution is unlikely to come in the form of neat formulas, such as $E = MC^2$. In fact, if someone is claiming a social science revolution based on a neat formula, you should be skeptical.

The revolution, instead, will come piecemeal, study by study, finding by finding. Slowly, we will get a better understanding of the complex systems of the human mind and society.

A proper conclusion sums up, but it also points the way to more things to come.

For this book, that's easy. The datasets I have discussed herein are revolutionary, but they have barely been explored. There is so much more to be learned. Frankly, the overwhelming majority of academics have ignored the data explosion caused by the digital age. The world's most famous sex researchers stick with the tried and true. They ask a few hundred subjects about their desires; they don't ask sites like PornHub for their data. The world's most famous linguists analyze individual texts; they largely ignore the patterns revealed in billions of books. The methodologies taught to graduate students in psychology, political science, and sociology have been, for the most part, untouched by the digital revolution. The broad, mostly unexplored terrain opened by the data explosion has been left to a small number of forward-thinking professors, rebellious grad students, and hobbyists.

That will change.

For every idea I have talked about in this book, there are a hundred ideas just as important ready to be tackled. The research discussed here is the tip of the tip of the iceberg, a scratch on the scratch of the surface.

So what else is coming?

For one, a radical expansion of the methodology that was used in one of the most successful public health studies of all time. In the mid-nineteenth century, John Snow, a British physician, was interested in what was causing a cholera outbreak in London.

His ingenious idea: he mapped every cholera case in the city. When he did this, he found the disease was largely clustered around one particular water pump. This suggested the disease spread through germ-infested water, disproving the then-conventional idea that it spread through bad air.

Big Data—and the zooming in that it allows—makes this type of study easy. For any disease, we can explore Google search data or other digital health data. We can find if there are any tiny pockets of the world where prevalence of this disease is unusually high or unusually low. Then we can see what these places have in common. Is there something in the air? The water? The social norms?

We can do this for migraines. We can do this for kidney stones. We can do this for anxiety and depression and Alzheimer's and pancreatic cancer and high blood pressure and back pain and constipation and nosebleeds. We can do this for everything. The analysis that Snow did once, we might be able to do four hundred times (something as of this writing I am already starting to work on).

We might call this—taking a simple method and utilizing Big Data to perform an analysis several hundred times in a short period of time—science at scale. Yes, the social and behavioral sciences are most definitely going to scale. Zooming in on health conditions will help these sciences scale. Another thing that will help them scale: A/B testing. We discussed A/B testing in the context of businesses getting users to click on headlines and ads—and this has been the predominant use of the methodology. But A/B testing can be used to uncover things more fundamental—and socially valuable—than an arrow that gets people to click on an ad.

Benjamin F. Jones is an economist at Northwestern who is trying to use A/B testing to better help kids learn. He has helped create a platform, EDU STAR, which allows for schools to randomly test different lesson plans.

Many companies are in the education software business. With EDU STAR, students log in to a computer and are randomly exposed to different lesson plans. Then they take short tests to see how well they learned the material. Schools, in other words, learn what software works best for helping students grasp material.

Already, like all great A/B testing platforms, EDU STAR is yielding surprising results. One lesson plan that many educators were very excited about included software that utilized games to help teach students fractions. Certainly, if you turned math into a game, students would have more fun, learn more, and do better on tests. Right? Wrong. Students who were taught fractions via a game tested worse than those who learned fractions in a more standard way.

Getting kids to learn more is an exciting, and socially beneficial, use of the testing that Silicon Valley pioneered to get people to click on more ads. So is getting people to sleep more.

The average American gets 6.7 hours of sleep every night. Most Americans want to sleep more. But 11 P.M. rolls around, and *SportsCenter* is on or YouTube is calling. So shut-eye waits. Jawbone, a wearable-device company with hundreds of thousands of customers, performs thousands of tests to try to find interventions that help get their users to do what they want to do: go to bed earlier.

Jawbone scored a huge win using a two-pronged goal. First, ask customers to commit to a not-that-ambitious goal. Send them a message like this: "It looks like you haven't been sleeping much in the last 3 days. Why don't you aim to get to bed by 11:30 tonight? We know you normally get up at 8 A.M." Then the users will have an option to click on "I'm in."

Second, when 10:30 comes, Jawbone will send another message: "We decided you'd aim to sleep at 11:30. It's 10:30 now. Why not start now?"

Jawbone found this strategy led to twenty-three minutes of extra sleep. They didn't get customers to actually get to bed at 10:30, but they did get them to bed earlier.

Of course, every part of this strategy had to be optimized through lots of experimentation. Start the original goal too early—ask users to commit to going to bed by 11 P.M.—and few will play along. Ask users to go to bed by midnight and little will be gained.

Jawbone used A/B testing to find the sleep equivalent of Google's right-pointing arrow. But instead of getting a few more clicks for Google's ad partners, it yields a few more minutes of rest for exhausted Americans.

In fact, the whole field of psychology might utilize the tools of Silicon Valley to dramatically improve their research. I'm eagerly anticipating the first psychology paper that, instead of detailing a couple of experiments done with a few undergrads, shows the results of a thousand rapid A/B tests.

The days of academics devoting months to recruiting a small number of undergrads to perform a single test will come to an end. Instead, academics will utilize digital data to test a few hundred or a few thousand ideas in just a few seconds. We'll be able to learn a lot more in a lot less time.

Text as data is going to teach us a lot more. How do ideas spread? How do new words form? How do words disappear? How do jokes form? Why are certain words funny and others not? How do dialects develop? I bet, within twenty years, we will have profound insights on all these questions.

I think we might consider utilizing kids' online behavior—appropriately anonymized—as a supplement to traditional tests to see how they are learning and developing. How is their spelling? Are they showing signs of dyslexia? Are they developing mature, intellectual interests? Do they have friends? There are clues to all these questions in the thousands of keystrokes every child makes every day.

And there is another, not-trivial area, where plenty more insights are coming.

In the song "Shattered," by the Rolling Stones, Mick Jagger describes all that makes New York City, the Big Apple, so magical. Laughter. Joy. Loneliness. Rats. Bedbugs. Pride. Greed. People dressed in paper bags. But Jagger devotes the most words for what makes the city truly special: "sex and sex and sex and sex."

As with the Big Apple, so with Big Data. Thanks to the

digital revolution, insights are coming in health. Sleep. Learning. Psychology. Language. Plus, sex and sex and sex and sex.

One question I am currently exploring: how many dimensions of sexuality are there? We usually think of someone as gay or straight. But sexuality is clearly more complex than that. Among gay people and straight people, people have types—some men like "blondes," others "brunettes," for instance. Might these preferences be as strong as the preferences for gender? Another question I am looking into: where do sexual preferences come from? Just as we can figure out the key years that determine baseball fandom or political views, we can now find the key years that determine adult sexual preferences. To learn these answers, you will have to buy my next book, tentatively titled *Everybody (Still) Lies*.

The existence of porn—and the data that comes with it—is a revolutionary development in the science of human sexuality.

It took time for the natural sciences to begin changing our lives—to create penicillin, satellites, and computers. It may take time before Big Data leads the social and behavioral sciences to important advances in the way we love, learn, and live. But I believe such advances are coming. I hope you see at least the outlines of such developments from this book. I hope, in fact, that some of you reading this book help create such advances.

To properly write a conclusion, an author should think about why he wrote the book in the first place. What goal is he trying to achieve?

I think the largest reason I wrote this book is as a result of one of the most formative experiences of my life. You see, a little more than a decade ago, the book *Freakonomics* came out. The surprise bestseller described the research of Steven Levitt, an award-winning economist at the University of Chicago mentioned frequently in this book. Levitt was a "rogue economist" who seemed to be able to use data to answer any question his quirky mind could think to ask: Do sumo wrestlers cheat? Do contestants on game shows discriminate? Do real estate agents get you the same deals they get for themselves?

I was just out of college, having majored in philosophy, with little idea what I wanted to do with my life. After reading *Freakonomics*, I knew. I wanted to do what Steven Levitt did. I wanted to pore through mountains of data to find out how the world *really* worked. I would follow him, I decided, and get a Ph.D. in economics.

So much has changed in the intervening twelve years. A couple of Levitt's studies were found to have coding errors. Levitt said some politically incorrect things about global warming. *Freakonomics* has gone out of favor in intellectual circles.

But I think, a few mistakes aside, the years have been kind to the larger point Levitt was trying to make. Levitt was telling us that a combination of curiosity, creativity, and data could dramatically improve our understanding of the world. There were stories hidden in data that were ready to be told and this has been proven right over and over again.

And I hope this book might have the same effect on others that *Freakonomics* had on me. I hope there is some young person reading this right now who is a bit confused on what she wants to do with her life. If you have a bit of statistical skill, an abundance of creativity, and curiosity, enter the data analysis business.

This book, in fact, and if I can be so bold, may be seen as next-level *Freakonomics*. A major difference between the studies discussed in *Freakonomics* and those discussed in this book is the ambition. In the 1990s, when Levitt made his name, there wasn't that much data available. Levitt prided himself on going after quirky questions, where data did exist. He largely ignored big questions where the data did not exist. Today, however, with so much data available on just about every topic, it makes sense to go after big, profound questions that get to the core of what it means to be a human being.

The future of data analysis is bright. The next Kinsey, I strongly suspect, will be a data scientist. The next Foucault will be a data scientist. The next Freud will be a data scientist. The next Marx will be a data scientist. The next Salk might very well be a data scientist.

Anyway, those were my attempts to do some of the things that a proper conclusion does. But great conclusions, I came to realize, do a lot more. So much more. A great conclusion must be ironic. It must be moving. A great conclusion must be profound and playful. It must be deep, humorous, and sad. A great conclusion must, in one sentence or two, make a point that sums up everything that has come before, everything that is coming. It must do so with a unique, novel point—a twist. A great book must end on a smart, funny, provocative bang.

Now might be a good time to talk a bit about my writing

process. I am not a particularly verbose writer. This book is only about seventy-five thousand words, which is a bit short for a topic as rich as this one.

But what I lack in breadth, I make up in obsessiveness. I spent five months on, and wrote forty-seven drafts of, my first *New York Times* sex column, which was two thousand words. Some chapters in this book took sixty drafts. I can spend hours finding the right word for a sentence in a footnote.

I lived much of my past year as a hermit. Just me and my computer. I lived in the hippest part of New York City and went out approximately never. This is, in my opinion, my magnum opus, the best idea I will have in my life. And I was willing to sacrifice whatever it took to make it right. I wanted to be able to defend every word in this book. My phone is filled with emails I forgot to respond to, e-vites I never opened, Bumble messages I ignored.*

After thirteen months of hard work, I was finally able to send in a near-complete draft. One part, however, was missing: the conclusion.

---

* Since everybody lies, you should question much of this story. Maybe I'm not an obsessive worker. Maybe I didn't work extraordinarily hard on this book. Maybe I, like lots of people, can exaggerate just how much I work. Maybe my thirteen months of "hard work" included full months in which I did no work at all. Maybe I didn't live as a hermit. Maybe, if you checked my Facebook profile, you'd see pictures of me out with friends during this supposed hermit period. Or maybe I was a hermit, but it was not self-imposed. Maybe I spent many nights alone, unable to work, hoping in vain that someone would contact me. Maybe nobody e-vites me to anything. Maybe nobody messages me on Bumble. Everybody lies. Every narrator is unreliable.

I explained to my editor, Denise, that it could take another few months. I told her six months was my most likely guess. The conclusion is, in my opinion, the most important part of the book. And I was only beginning to learn what makes a great conclusion. Needless to say, Denise was not pleased.

Then, one day, a friend of mine emailed me a study by Jordan Ellenberg. Ellenberg, a mathematician at the University of Wisconsin, was curious about how many people actually finish books. He thought of an ingenious way to test it using Big Data. Amazon reports how many people quote various lines in books. Ellenberg realized he could compare how frequently quotes were highlighted at the beginning of the book versus the end of the book. This would give a rough guide to readers' propensity to make it to the end. By his measure, more than 90 percent of readers finished Donna Tartt's novel *The Goldfinch*. In contrast, only about 7 percent made it through Nobel Prize economist Daniel Kahneman's magnum opus, *Thinking, Fast and Slow*. Fewer than 3 percent, this rough methodology estimated, made it to the end of economist Thomas Piketty's much discussed and praised *Capital in the 21st Century*. In other words, people tend not to finish treatises by economists.

One of the points of this book is we have to follow the Big Data *wherever* it leads and act accordingly. I may hope that most readers are going to hang on my every word and try to detect patterns linking the final pages to what happened earlier. But, no matter how hard I work on polishing my prose, most people are going to read the first fifty pages, get a few points, and move on with their lives.

Thus, I conclude this book in the only appropriate way: by following the data, what people actually do, not what they say. I am going to get a beer with some friends and stop working on this damn conclusion. Too few of you, Big Data tells me, are still reading.

ACKNOWLEDGMENTS

This book was a team effort.

These ideas were developed while I was a student at Harvard, a data scientist at Google, and a writer for the *New York Times*.

Hal Varian, with whom I worked at Google, has been a major influence on the ideas of this book. As best I can tell, Hal is perpetually twenty years ahead of his time. His book *Information Rules*, written with Carl Shapiro, basically predicted the future. And his paper "Predicting the Present," with Hyunyoung Choi, largely started the Big Data revolution in the social sciences that is described in this book. He is also an amazing and kind mentor, as so many who have worked under him can attest. A classic Hal move is to do most of the work on a paper you are coauthoring with him and then insist that your name goes before his. Hal's combination of genius and generosity is something I have rarely encountered.

My writing and ideas developed under Aaron Retica, who has been my editor for every single *New York Times* column. Aaron is a polymath. He somehow knows everything about music, history, sports, politics, sociology, economics, and God only knows what else. He is responsible for a huge amount of what is good about the *Times* columns that have my name on them. Other players on the team for these columns include Bill

Marsh, whose graphics continue to blow me away, Kevin Mc-
Carthy, and Gita Daneshjoo. This book includes passages from
these columns, reprinted with permission.

Steven Pinker, who kindly agreed to write the foreword,
has long been a hero of mine. He has set the bar for a modern
book on social science—an engaging exploration of the funda-
mentals of human nature, making sense of the best research
from a range of disciplines. That bar is one I will be struggling
to reach my entire life.

My dissertation, from which this book has grown, was
written under my brilliant and patient advisers Alberto Ale-
sina, David Cutler, Ed Glaeser, and Lawrence Katz.

Denise Oswald is an amazing editor. If you want to know
how good her editing is, compare this final draft to my first
draft—actually, you can't do that because I am not going to
ever show anyone else that embarrassing first draft. I also
thank the rest of the team at HarperCollins, including Michael
Barrs, Lynn Grady, Lauren Janiec, Shelby Meizlik, and Amber
Oliver.

Eric Lupfer, my agent, saw potential in this project from
the beginning, was instrumental in forming the proposal, and
helped carry it through.

For superb fact-checking, I thank Melvis Acosta.

Other people from whom I learned a lot in my profes-
sional and academic life include Susan Athey, Shlomo Ben-
artzi, Jason Bordoff, Danielle Bowers, David Broockman, Bo
Cowgill, Steven Delpome, John Donohue, Bill Gale, Claudia
Goldin, Suzanne Greenberg, Shane Greenstein, Steve Grove,
Mike Hoyt, David Laibson, A.J. Magnuson, Dana Maloney,
Jeffrey Oldham, Peter Orszag, David Reiley, Jonathan Rosen-

berg, Michael Schwarz, Steve Scott, Rich Shavelson, Michael D. Smith, Lawrence Summers, Jon Vaver, Michael Wiggins, and Qing Wu.

I thank Tim Requarth and NeuWrite for helping me develop my writing.

For help in interpreting studies, I thank Christopher Chabris, Raj Chetty, Matt Gentzkow, Solomon Messing, and Jesse Shapiro.

I asked Emma Pierson and Katia Sobolski if they might give advice on a chapter in my book. They decided, for reasons I do not understand, to offer to read the entire book—and give wise counsel on every paragraph.

My mother, Esther Davidowitz, read the entire book on multiple occasions and helped dramatically improve it. She also taught me, by example, that I should follow my curiosity, no matter where it led. When I was interviewing for an academic job, a professor grilled me: "What does your mother think of this work you do?" The idea was that my mom might be embarrassed that I was researching sex and other taboo topics. But I always knew she was proud of me for following my curiosity, wherever it led.

Many people read sections and offered helpful comments. I thank Eduardo Acevedo, Coren Apicella, Sam Asher, David Cutler, Stephen Dubner, Christopher Glazek, Jessica Goldberg, Lauren Goldman, Amanda Gordon, Jacob Leshno, Alex Peysakhovich, Noah Popp, Ramon Roullard, Greg Sobolski, Evan Soltas, Noah Stephens-Davidowitz, Lauren Stephens-Davidowitz, and Jean Yang. Actually, Jean was basically my best friend while I wrote this, so I thank her for that, too.

For help in collecting data, I thank Brett Goldenberg, James

Rogers, and Mike Williams at MindGeek and Rob McQuown and Sam Miller at Baseball Prospectus.

I am grateful for financial support from the Alfred Sloan Foundation.

At one point, while writing this book, I was deeply stuck, lost, and close to abandoning the project. I then went to the country with my dad, Mitchell Stephens. Over the course of a week, Dad put me back together. He took me for walks in which we discussed love, death, success, happiness, and writing—and then sat me down so we could go over every sentence of the book. I could not have finished this book without him.

All remaining errors are, of course, my own.

NOTES

INTRODUCTION

2 *American voters largely did not care that Barack Obama:* Katie Fretland, "Gallup: Race Not Important to Voters," The Swamp, *Chicago Tribune,* June 2008.

2 *Berkeley pored through:* Alexandre Mas and Enrico Moretti, "Racial Bias in the 2008 Presidential Election," *American Economic Review* 99, no. 2 (2009).

2 *post-racial society:* On the November 12, 2009, episode of his show, Lou Dobbs said we lived in a "post-partisan, post-racial society." On the January 27, 2010, episode of his show, Chris Matthews said that President Obama was "post-racial by all appearances." For other examples, see Michael C. Dawson and Lawrence D. Bobo, "One Year Later and the Myth of a Post-Racial Society," *Du Bois Review: Social Science Research on Race* 6, no. 2 (2009).

5 *I analyzed data from the General Social Survey:* Details on all these calculations can be found on my website, sethsd.com, in the csv labeled "Sex Data." Data from the General Social Survey can be found at http://gss.norc.org/.

5 *fewer than 600 million condoms:* Data provided to the author.

7 *searches and sign-ups for Stormfront:* Author's analysis of Google Trends data. I also scraped data on all members of Stormfront, as discussed in Seth Stephens-Davidowitz, "The Data of Hate," *New York Times,* July 13, 2014, SR4. The relevant data can be downloaded at sethsd.com, in the data section headlined "Stormfront."

7 *more searches for "nigger president" than "first black president":* Author's analysis of Google Trends data. The states for which this is true include Kentucky, Louisiana, Arizona, and North Carolina.

9 *rejected by five academic journals:* The paper was eventually

published as Seth Stephens-Davidowitz, "The Cost of Racial Animus on a Black Candidate: Evidence Using Google Search Data," *Journal of Public Economics* 118 (2014). More details about the research can be found there. In addition, the data can be found at my website, sethsd.com, in the data section headlined "Racism."

13 *single factor that best correlated:* "Strongest correlate I've found for Trump support is Google searches for the n-word. Others have reported this too" (February 28, 2016, tweet). See also Nate Cohn, "Donald Trump's Strongest Supporters: A New Kind of Democrat," *New York Times*, December 31, 2015, A3.

13 This shows the percent of Google searches that include the word "nigger(s)." Note that, because the measure is as a percent of Google searches, it is not arbitrarily higher in places with large populations or places that make a lot of searches. Note also that some of the differences in this map and the map for Trump support have obvious explanations. Trump lost popularity in Texas and Arkansas because they were the home states of two of his opponents, Ted Cruz and Mike Huckabee.

13 This is survey data from Civis Analytics from December 2015. Actual voting data is less useful here, since it is highly influenced by when the primary took place and the voting format. The maps are reprinted with permission from the *New York Times*.

15 *2.5 million trillion bytes of data:* "Bringing Big Data to the Enterprise," IBM, https://www-01.ibm.com/software/data/bigdata/what-is-big-data.html.

17 *needle comes in an increasingly larger haystack:* Nassim M. Taleb, "Beware the Big Errors of 'Big Data,'" *Wired*, February 8, 2013, http://www.wired.com/2013/02/big-data-means-big-errors-people.

18 *neither racist searches nor membership in Stormfront:* I examined how internet racism changed in parts of the country with high and low exposure to the Great Recession. I looked at both Google search rates for "nigger(s)" and Stormfront membership. The relevant data can be downloaded at sethsd.com, in the data sections headlined "Racial Animus" and "Stormfront."

18 *But Google searches reflecting anxiety:* Seth Stephens-Davidowitz, "Fifty States of Anxiety," *New York Times*, August 7, 2016,

SR2. Note, while the Google searches do give much bigger samples, this pattern is consistent with evidence from surveys. See, for example, William C. Reeves et al., "Mental Illness Surveillance Among Adults in the United States," *Morbidity and Mortality Weekly Report Supplement* 60, no. 3 (2011).

18 *search for jokes:* This is discussed in Seth Stephens-Davidowitz, "Why Are You Laughing?" *New York Times*, May 15, 2016, SR9. The relevant data can be downloaded at sethsd.com, in the data section headlined "Jokes."

19 *"my husband wants me to breastfeed him":* This is discussed in Seth Stephens-Davidowitz, "What Do Pregnant Women Want?" *New York Times*, May 17, 2014, SR6.

19 *porn searches for depictions of women breastfeeding men:* Author's analysis of PornHub data.

19 *Women make nearly as many:* This is discussed in Seth Stephens-Davidowitz, "Searching for Sex," *New York Times*, January 25, 2015, SR1.

20 *"poemas para mi esposa embarazada":* Stephens-Davidowitz, "What Do Pregnant Women Want?"

21 *Friedman says:* I interviewed Jerry Friedman by phone on October 27, 2015.

21 *sampling of all their data:* Hal R. Varian, "Big Data: New Tricks for Econometrics," *Journal of Economic Perspectives* 28, no. 2 (2014).

CHAPTER 1: YOUR FAULTY GUT

26 *The best data science, in fact, is surprisingly intuitive:* I am speaking about the corner of data analysis I know about—data science that tries to explain and predict human behavior. I am not speaking of artificial intelligence that tries to, say, drive a car. These methodologies, while they do utilize tools discovered from the human brain, are less easy to understand.

28 *what symptoms predict pancreatic cancer:* John Paparrizos, Ryan W. White, and Eric Horvitz, "Screening for Pancreatic Adenocarcinoma Using Signals from Web Search Logs: Feasibility Study and Results," *Journal of Oncology Practice* (2016).

31 *Winter climate swamped all the rest:* This research is discussed in

Seth Stephens-Davidowitz, "Dr. Google Will See You Now," *New York Times*, August 11, 2013, SR12.

32 *biggest dataset ever assembled on human relationships:* Lars Backstrom and Jon Kleinberg, "Romantic Partnerships and the Dispersion of Social Ties: A Network Analysis of Relationship Status on Facebook," in *Proceedings of the 17th ACM Conference on Computer Supported Cooperative Work & Social Computing* (2014).

33 *people consistently rank:* Daniel Kahneman, *Thinking, Fast and Slow* (New York: Farrar, Straus and Giroux, 2011).

33 *asthma causes about seventy times more deaths:* Between 1979 and 2010, on average, 55.81 Americans died from tornados and 4216.53 Americans died from asthma. See Annual U.S. Killer Tornado Statistics, National Weather Service, http://www.spc.noaa.gov/climo/torn/fatalmap.php and Trends in Asthma Morbidity and Mortality, American Lung Association, Epidemiology and Statistics Unit.

33 *Patrick Ewing:* My favorite Ewing videos are "Patrick Ewing's Top 10 Career Plays," YouTube video, posted September 18, 2015, https://www.youtube.com/watch?v=Y29gMuYymv8; and "Patrick Ewing Knicks Tribute," YouTube video, posted May 12, 2006, https://www.youtube.com/watch?v=8T2l5Emzu-I.

34 *"basketball as a matter of life or death":* S. L. Price, "Whatever Happened to the White Athlete?" *Sports Illustrated*, December 8, 1997.

34 *an internet survey:* This was a Google Consumer Survey I conducted on October 22, 2013. I asked, "Where would you guess that the majority of NBA players were born?" The two choices were "poor neighborhoods" and "middle-class neighborhoods"; 59.7 percent of respondents picked "poor neighborhoods."

36 *a black person's first name is an indication of his socioeconomic background:* Roland G. Fryer Jr. and Steven D. Levitt, "The Causes and Consequences of Distinctively Black Names," *Quarterly Journal of Economics* 119, no. 3 (2004).

37 *Among all African-Americans born in the 1980s:* Centers for Disease Control and Prevention, "Health, United States, 2009," Table 9, Nonmarital Childbearing, by Detailed Race and Hispanic Origin

of Mother, and Maternal Age: United States, Selected Years 1970–2006.

37 *Chris Bosh . . . Chris Paul:* "Not Just a Typical Jock: Miami Heat Forward Chris Bosh's Interests Go Well Beyond Basketball," Palm BeachPost.com, February 15, 2011, http://www.palmbeachpost .com/news/sports/basketball/not-just-a-typical-jock-miami-heat -forward-chris-b/nLp7Z/; Dave Walker, "Chris Paul's Family to Compete on 'Family Feud,' nola.com, October 31, 2011, http:// www.nola.com/tv/index.ssf/2011/10/chris_pauls_family_to_com pete.html.

38 *four inches taller:* "Why Are We Getting Taller as a Species?" *Scientific American,* http://www.scientificamerican.com/article/why -are-we-getting-taller/. Interestingly, Americans have stopped getting taller. Amanda Onion, "Why Have Americans Stopped Growing Taller?" ABC News, July 3, 2016, http://abcnews.go.com /Technology/story?id=98438&page=1. I have argued that one of the reasons there has been a huge increase in foreign-born NBA players is that other countries are catching up to the United States in height. The number of American-born seven-footers in the NBA increased sixteenfold from 1946 to 1980 as Americans grew. It has since leveled off, as Americans have stopped growing. Meanwhile, the number of seven-footers from other countries has risen substantially. The biggest increase in international players, I found, has been extremely tall men from countries, such as Turkey, Spain, and Greece, where there have been noticeable increases in childhood health and adult height in recent years.

38 *Americans from poor backgrounds:* Carmen R. Isasi et al., "Association of Childhood Economic Hardship with Adult Height and Adult Adiposity among Hispanics/Latinos: The HCHS/SOL Socio-Cultural Ancillary Study," *PloS One* 11, no. 2 (2016); Jane E. Miller and Sanders Korenman, "Poverty and Children's Nutritional Status in the United States," *American Journal of Epidemiology* 140, no. 3 (1994); Harry J. Holzer, Diane Whitmore Schanzenbach, Greg J. Duncan, and Jens Ludwig, "The Economic Costs of Childhood Poverty in the United States," *Journal of Children and Poverty* 14, no. 1 (2008).

38 *the average American man is 5'9":* Cheryl D. Fryar, Qiuping Gu, and Cynthia L. Ogden, "Anthropometric Reference Data for Children and Adults: United States, 2007–2010," *Vital and Health Statistics Series* 11, no. 252 (2012).

39 *something like one in five reach the NBA:* Pablo S. Torre, "Larger Than Real Life," *Sports Illustrated,* July 4, 2011.

39 *middle-class, two-parent families:* Tim Kautz, James J. Heckman, Ron Diris, Bas Ter Weel, and Lex Borghans, "Fostering and Measuring Skills: Improving Cognitive and Non-Cognitive Skills to Promote Lifetime Success," National Bureau of Economic Research Working Paper 20749, 2014.

39 *Wrenn jumped the highest:* Desmond Conner, "For Wrenn, Sky's the Limit," *Hartford Courant,* October 21, 1999.

39 *But Wrenn:* Doug Wrenn's story is told in Percy Allen, "Former Washington and O'Dea Star Doug Wrenn Finds Tough Times," *Seattle Times,* March 29, 2009.

40 *"Doug Wrenn is dead":* Ibid.

40 *Jordan could be a difficult kid:* Melissa Isaacson, "Portrait of a Legend," ESPN.com, September 9, 2009, http://www.espn.com/chicago /columns/story?id=4457017&columnist=isaacson_melissa. A good Jordan biography is Roland Lazenby, *Michael Jordan: The Life* (Boston: Back Bay Books, 2015).

40 *His father was:* Barry Jacobs, "High-Flying Michael Jordan Has North Carolina Cruising Toward Another NCAA Title," *People,* March 19, 1984.

40 *Jordan's life is filled with stories of his family guiding him:* Isaacson, "Portrait of a Legend."

41 *speech upon induction into the Basketball Hall of Fame:* Michael Jordan's Basketball Hall of Fame Enshrinement Speech, YouTube video, posted February 21, 2012, https://www.youtube.com/watch ?v=XLzBMGXfK4c. The most interesting aspect of Jordan's speech is not that he is so effusive about his parents; it is that he still feels the need to point out slights from early in his career. Perhaps a lifelong obsession with slights is necessary to become the greatest basketball player of all time.

41 *LeBron James was interviewed:* "I'm LeBron James from Akron,

Ohio," YouTube video, posted June 20, 2013, https://www.youtube
.com/watch?v=XceMbPVAggk.

CHAPTER 2: WAS FREUD RIGHT?

47 *a food's being shaped like a phallus:* I coded foods as being shaped
as a phallus if they were significantly more long than wide and
generally round. I counted cucumbers, corn, carrots, eggplant,
squash, and bananas. The data and code can be found at sethsd.com.

48 *errors collected by Microsoft researchers:* The dataset can be
downloaded at https://www.microsoft.com/en-us/download/de
tails.aspx?id=52418. The researchers asked users of Amazon Me-
chanical Turk to describe images. They analyzed the keystroke logs
and noted any time someone corrected a word. More details can
be found in Yukino Baba and Hisami Suzuki, "How Are Spelling
Errors Generated and Corrected? A Study of Corrected and Un-
corrected Spelling Errors Using Keystroke Logs," Proceedings of
the Fiftieth Annual Meeting of the Association for Computational
Linguistics, 2012. The data, code, and a further description of this
research can be found at sethsd.com.

51 *Consider all searches of the form "I want to have sex with my":*
The full data—warning: graphic—is as follows:

"I WANT TO HAVE SEX WITH . . ."

	MONTHLY GOOGLE SEARCHES WITH THIS EXACT PHRASE
my mom	720
my son	590
my sister	590
my cousin	480
my dad	480
my boyfriend	480
my brother	320
my daughter	260
my friend	170
my girlfriend	140

52 *cartoon porn:* For example, *"porn"* is one of the most common words included in Google searches for various extremely popular animated programs, as seen below.

CARTOONS, MEET PORN
(MOST COMMON GOOGLE SEARCHES FOR VARIOUS CARTOONS)

family guy porn	watch the simpsons	**futurama porn**	scooby doo games
family guy episodes	**the simpsons porn**	futurama leela	scooby doo movie
family guy free	the simpsons online	futurama episodes	**scooby doo porn**
watch family guy	the simpsons movie	futurama online	scooby doo velma

52 *babysitters:* Based on author's calculations, these are the most popular female occupations in porn searches by men, broken down by the age of men:

OCCUPATIONS OF WOMEN IN MALE PORN SEARCHES, BY AGE OF MEN

	18-24	25-64	65+
1.	Babysitter	Babysitter	Babysitter
2.	Teacher	Yoga Instructor	Cheerleader
3.	Yoga Instructor	Teacher	Doctor
4.	Cheerleader	Cheerleader	Teacher
5.	Doctor	Real Estate Agent	Real Estate Agent
6.	Prostitute	Doctor	Nurse
7.	Real Estate Agent	Prostitute	Yoga Instructor
8.	Nurse	Secretary	Secretary
9.	Secretary	Nurse	Prostitute

CHAPTER 3: DATA REIMAGINED

56 *algorithms in place:* Matthew Leising, "HFT Treasury Trading Hurts Market When News Is Released," Bloomberg Markets,

December 16, 2014; Nathaniel Popper, "The Robots Are Coming for Wall Street," *New York Times Magazine*, February 28, 2016, MM56; Richard Finger, "High Frequency Trading: Is It a Dark Force Against Ordinary Human Traders and Investors?" *Forbes*, September 30, 2013, http://www.forbes.com/sites/richardfinger /2013/09/30/high-frequency-trading-is-it-a-dark-force-against -ordinary-human-traders-and-investors/#50875fc751a6.

56 *Alan Krueger:* I interviewed Alan Krueger by phone on May 8, 2015.

57 *important indicators of how fast the flu:* The initial paper was Jeremy Ginsberg, Matthew H. Mohebbi, Rajan S. Patel, Lynnette Brammer, Mark S. Smolinski, and Larry Brilliant, "Detecting Influenza Epidemics Using Search Engine Query Data," *Nature* 457, no. 7232 (2009). The flaws in the original model were discussed in David Lazer, Ryan Kennedy, Gary King, and Alessandro Vespignani, "The Parable of Google Flu: Traps in Big Data Analysis," *Science* 343, no. 6176 (2014). A corrected model is presented in Shihao Yang, Mauricio Santillana, and S. C. Kou, "Accurate Estimation of Influenza Epidemics Using Google Search Data Via ARGO," *Proceedings of the National Academy of Sciences* 112, no. 47 (2015).

58 *which searches most closely track housing prices:* Seth Stephens-Davidowitz and Hal Varian, "A Hands-on Guide to Google Data," mimeo, 2015. Also see Marcelle Chauvet, Stuart Gabriel, and Chandler Lutz, "Mortgage Default Risk: New Evidence from Internet Search Queries," *Journal of Urban Economics* 96 (2016).

60 *Bill Clinton:* Sergey Brin and Larry Page, "The Anatomy of a Large-Scale Hypertextual Web Search Engine," Seventh International World-Wide Web Conference, April 14–18, 1998, Brisbane, Australia.

61 *porn sites:* John Battelle, *The Search: How Google and Its Rivals Rewrote the Rules of Business and Transformed Our Culture* (New York: Penguin, 2005).

61 *crowdsource the opinions:* A good discussion of this can be found in Steven Levy, *In the Plex: How Google Thinks, Works, and Shapes Our Lives* (New York: Simon & Schuster, 2011).

64 *"Sell your house":* This quote was also included in Joe Drape,

"Ahmed Zayat's Journey: Bankruptcy and Big Bets," *New York Times*, June 5, 2015, A1. However, the article incorrectly attributes the quote to Seder. It was actually made by another member of his team.

65 *I first met up with Seder:* I interviewed Jeff Seder and Patty Murray in Ocala, Florida, from June 12, 2015, through June 14, 2015.

66 *Roughly one-third:* The reasons racehorses fail are rough estimates by Jeff Seder, based on his years in the business.

66 *hundreds of horses die:* Supplemental Tables of Equine Injury Database Statistics for Thoroughbreds, http://jockeyclub.com/pdfs/eid_7_year_tables.pdf.

66 *mostly due to broken legs:* "Postmortem Examination Program," California Animal Health and Food Laboratory System, 2013.

67 *Still, more than three-fourths do not win a major race:* Avalyn Hunter, "A Case for Full Siblings," *Bloodhorse*, April 18, 2014, http://www.bloodhorse.com/horse-racing/articles/115014/a-case-for-full-siblings.

67 *Earvin Johnson III:* Melody Chiu, "E. J. Johnson Loses 50 Lbs. Since Undergoing Gastric Sleeve Surgery," *People*, October 1, 2014.

67 *LeBron James, whose mom is 5'5":* Eli Saslow, "Lost Stories of LeBron, Part 1," ESPN.com, October 17, 2013, http://www.espn.com/nba/story/_/id/9825052/how-lebron-james-life-changed-fourth-grade-espn-magazine.

68 *The Green Monkey:* See Sherry Ross, "16 Million Dollar Baby," New York *Daily News*, March 12, 2006, and Jay Privman, "The Green Monkey, Who Sold for $16M, Retired," ESPN.com, February 12, 2008, http://www.espn.com/sports/horse/news/story?id=3242341. A video of the auction is available at "$16 Million Horse," YouTube video, posted November 1, 2008, https://www.youtube.com/watch?v=EyggMC85Zsg.

71 *weakness of Google's attempt to predict influenza:* Sharad Goel, Jake M. Hofman, Sébastien Lahaie, David M. Pennock, and Duncan J. Watts, "Predicting Consumer Behavior with Web Search," *Proceedings of the National Academy of Sciences* 107, no. 41 (2010).

72 *Strawberry Pop-Tarts:* Constance L. Hays, "What Wal-Mart Knows About Customers' Habits," *New York Times,* November 14, 2004.

74 *"It worked out great":* I interviewed Orley Ashenfelter by phone on October 27, 2016.

80 *studied hundreds of heterosexual speed daters:* Daniel A. McFarland, Dan Jurafsky, and Craig Rawlings, "Making the Connection: Social Bonding in Courtship Situations," *American Journal of Sociology* 118, no. 6 (2013).

82 *Leonard Cohen once gave his nephew the following advice for wooing women:* Jonathan Greenberg, "What I Learned From My Wise Uncle Leonard Cohen," *Huffington Post,* November 11, 2016.

83 *the words used in hundreds of thousands of Facebook:* H. Andrew Schwartz et al., "Personality, Gender, and Age in the Language of Social Media: The Open-Vocabulary Approach," *PloS One* 8, no. 9 (2013). The paper also breaks down the ways people speak based on how they score on personality tests. Here is what they found:

88 *text of thousands of books and movie scripts:* Andrew J. Reagan, Lewis Mitchell, Dilan Kiley, Christopher M. Danforth, and Peter Sheridan Dodds, "The Emotional Arcs of Stories Are Dominated by Six Basic Shapes," *EPJ Data Science* 5, no. 1 (2016).

91 *what types of stories get shared:* Jonah Berger and Katherine L. Milkman, "What Makes Online Content Viral?" *Journal of Marketing Research* 49, no. 2 (2012).

95 *why do some publications lean left:* This research is all fleshed out in Matthew Gentzkow and Jesse M. Shapiro, "What Drives Media Slant? Evidence from U.S. Daily Newspapers," *Econometrica* 78, no. 1 (2010). Although they were merely Ph.D. students when this project started, Gentzkow and Shapiro are now star economists. Gentzkow, now a professor at Stanford, won the 2014 John Bates Clark Medal, given to the top economist under the age of forty. Shapiro, now a professor at Brown, is an editor of the prestigious *Journal of Political Economy.* Their joint paper on media slant is among the most cited papers for each.

96 *Rupert Murdoch:* Murdoch's ownership of the conservative *New York Post* could be explained by the fact that New York is so big, it can support newspapers of multiple viewpoints. However, it seems pretty clear the *Post* consistently loses money. See, for example, Joe Pompeo, "How Much Does the 'New York Post' Actually Lose?" *Politico,* August 30, 2013, http://www.politico.com/media/story/2013/08/how-much-does-the-new-york-post-actually-lose-001176.

97 *Shapiro told me:* I interviewed Matt Gentzkow and Jesse Shapiro on August 16, 2015, at the Royal Sonesta Boston.

98 *scanned yearbooks from American high schools:* Kate Rakelly, Sarah Sachs, Brian Yin, and Alexei A. Efros, "A Century of Portraits: A Visual Historical Record of American High School Yearbooks," paper presented at International Conference on Computer Vision, 2015. The photos are reprinted with permission from the authors.

99 *subjects in photos copied subjects in paintings:* See, for example, Christina Kotchemidova, "Why We Say 'Cheese': Producing the Smile in Snapshot Photography," *Critical Studies in Media Communication* 22, no. 1 (2005).

100 *measure GDP based on how much light there is in these countries at night:* J. Vernon Henderson, Adam Storeygard, and David N. Weil, "Measuring Economic Growth from Outer Space," *American Economic Review* 102, no. 2 (2012).

101 *estimated GDP was now 90 percent higher:* Kathleen Caulderwood, "Nigerian GDP Jumps 89% as Economists Add in Telecoms, Nollywood," *IBTimes*, April 7, 2014, http://www.ibtimes.com /nigerian-gdp-jumps-89-economists-add-telecoms-nollywood -1568219.

101 *Reisinger said:* I interviewed Joe Reisinger by phone on June 10, 2015.

103 *$50 million:* Leena Rao, "SpaceX and Tesla Backer Just Invested $50 Million in This Startup," *Fortune,* September 24, 2015.

CHAPTER 4: DIGITAL TRUTH SERUM

106 *important paper in 1950:* Hugh J. Parry and Helen M. Crossley, "Validity of Responses to Survey Questions," *Public Opinion Quarterly* 14, 1 (1950).

106 *survey asked University of Maryland graduates:* Frauke Kreuter, Stanley Presser, and Roger Tourangeau, "Social Desirability Bias in CATI, IVR, and Web Surveys," *Public Opinion Quarterly* 72(5), 2008.

107 *failure of the polls:* For an article arguing that lying might be a problem in trying to predict support for Trump, see Thomas B. Edsall, "How Many People Support Trump but Don't Want to Admit It?" *New York Times,* May 15, 2016, SR2. But for an argument that this was not a large factor, see Andrew Gelman, "Explanations for That Shocking 2% Shift," *Statistical Modeling, Causal Inference, and Social Science,* November 9, 2016, http://andrewgelman .com/2016/11/09/explanations-shocking-2-shift/.

107 *says Tourangeau:* I interviewed Roger Tourangeau by phone on May 5, 2015.

107 *so many people say they are above average:* This is discussed in Adam Grant, *Originals: How Non-Conformists Move the World* (New York: Viking, 2016). The original source is David Dunning, Chip Heath, and Jerry M. Suls, "Flawed Self-Assessment: Impli-

cations for Health, Education, and the Workplace," *Psychological Science in the Public Interest* 5 (2004).

108 *mess with surveys:* Anya Kamenetz, " 'Mischievous Responders' Confound Research on Teens," *nprED,* May 22, 2014, http://www .npr.org/sections/ed/2014/05/22/313166161/mischievous-respond ers-confound-research-on-teens. The original research this article discusses is Joseph P. Robinson-Cimpian, "Inaccurate Estimation of Disparities Due to Mischievous Responders," *Educational Researcher* 43, no. 4 (2014).

110 *search for "porn" more than they search for "weather":* https:// www.google.com/trends/explore?date=all&geo=US&q=porn,weat her.

110 *admit they watch pornography:* Amanda Hess, "How Many Women Are Not Admitting to Pew That They Watch Porn?" *Slate,* October 11, 2013, http://www.slate.com/blogs/xx_factor /2013/10/11/pew_online_viewing_study_percentage_of_women _who_watch_online_porn_is_growing.html.

110 *"cock," "fuck," and "porn":* Nicholas Diakopoulus, "Sex, Violence, and Autocomplete Algorithms," *Slate,* August 2, 2013, http:// www.slate.com/articles/technology/future_tense/2013/08/words _banned_from_bing_and_google_s_autocomplete_algorithms .html.

111 *3.6 times more likely to tell Google they regret:* I estimate, including various phrasings, there are about 1,730 American Google searches every month explicitly saying they regret having children. There are only about 50 expressing a regret not having children. There are about 15.9 million Americans over the age of forty-five who have no children. There are about 152 million Americans who have children. This means, among the eligible population, people with children are about 3.6 times as likely to express a regret on Google than people without children. Obviously, as mentioned in the text but worth emphasizing again, these confessionals to Google are only made by a small, select number of people—presumably those feeling a strong enough regret that they momentarily forget that Google cannot help them here.

113 *highest support for gay marriage:* These estimates are from Nate

Silver, "How Opinion on Same-Sex Marriage Is Changing, and What It Means," FiveThirtyEight, March 26, 2013, http://fivethirty eight.blogs.nytimes.com/2013/03/26/how-opinion-on-same-sex -marriage-is-changing-and-what-it-means/?_r=0.

113 *About 2.5 percent of male Facebook users who list a gender of interest say they are interested in men:* Author's analysis of Facebook ads data. I do not include Facebook users who list "men and women." My analysis suggests a non-trivial percent of users who say they are interested in men and women interpret the question as interest in friendship rather than romantic interest.

115 *about 5 percent of male porn searches are for gay-male porn:* As discussed, Google Trends does not break down searches by gender. Google AdWords breaks down page views for various categories by gender. However, this data is far less precise. To estimate the searches by gender, I first use the search data to get a statewide estimate of the percent of gay porn searches by state. I then normalize this data by the Google AdWords gender data. Another way to get gender-specific data is using PornHub data. However, PornHub could be a highly selected sample, since many gay people might instead use sites focused only on gay porn. PornHub suggests that gay porn use among men is lower than Google searches would suggest. However, it confirms that there is not a strong relationship between tolerance toward homosexuality and male gay porn use. All this data and further notes are available on my website, at sethsd.com, in the section "Sex."

116 *4 percent of them are openly gay on Facebook:* Author's calculation of Facebook ads data: On February 8, 2017, roughly 300 male high school students in San Francisco-Oakland-San Jose media market on Facebook said they were interested in men. Roughly, 7,800 said they were interested in women.

119 *"In Iran we don't have homosexuals":* " 'We Don't Have Any Gays in Iran,' Iranian President Tells Ivy League Audience," Daily Mail.com, September 25, 2007, http://www.dailymail.co.uk/news /article-483746/We-dont-gays-Iran-Iranian-president-tells-Ivy -League-audience.html.

119 *"We do not have them in our city":* Brett Logiurato, "Sochi Mayor

Claims There Are No Gay People in the City," *Sports Illustrated,* January 27, 2014.

119 *internet behavior reveals significant interest in gay porn in Sochi and Iran:* According to Google AdWords, there are tens of thousands of searches every year for "гей порно" (gay porn). The percent of porn searches for gay porn is roughly similar in Sochi as in the United States. Google AdWords does not include data for Iran. PornHub also does not report data for Iran. However, PornMD studied their search data and reported that five of the top ten search terms in Iran were for gay porn. This included "daddy love" and "hotel businessman" and is reported in Joseph Patrick McCormick, "Survey Reveals Searches for Gay Porn Are Top in Countries Banning Homosexuality," *PinkNews,* http://www.pinknews .co.uk/2013/03/13/survey-reveals-searches-for-gay-porn-are-top -in-countries-banning-homosexuality/. According to Google Trends, about 2 percent of porn searches in Iran are for gay porn, which is lower than in the United States but still suggests widespread interest.

122 *When it comes to sex:* Stephens-Davidowitz, "Searching for Sex." Data for this section can be found on my website, sethsd.com, in the section "Sex."

122 *11 percent of women:* Current Contraceptive Status Among Women Aged 15–44: United States, 2011–2013, Centers for Disease Control and Prevention, http://www.cdc.gov/nchs/data/data briefs/db173_table.pdf#1.

122 *10 percent of them to become pregnant every month:* David Spiegelhalter, "Sex: What Are the Chances?" BBC News, March 15, 2012, http://www.bbc.com/future/story/20120313-sex-in-the-city-or -elsewhere.

122 *1 in 113 women of childbearing age:* There are roughly 6.6 million pregnancies every year and there are 62 million women between ages 15 and 44.

128 *performing oral sex on the opposite gender:* As mentioned, I do not know the gender of a Google searcher. I am assuming that the overwhelming majority of searches looking how to perform cunnilingus are by men and that the overwhelming majority of searches

looking how to perform fellatio are by women. This is both because the large majority of people are straight and because there might be less of a need to learn how to please a same-sex partner.

128 *top five negative words:* Author's analysis of Google AdWords data.

130 *kill them:* Evan Soltas and Seth Stephens-Davidowitz, "The Rise of Hate Search," *New York Times*, December 13, 2015, SR1. Data and more details can be found on my website, sethsd.com, in the section "Islamophobia."

132 *seventeen times more common:* Author's analysis of Google Trends data.

132 *Martin Luther King Jr. Day:* Author's analysis of Google Trends data.

133 *correlates with the black-white wage gap:* Ashwin Rode and Anand J. Shukla, "Prejudicial Attitudes and Labor Market Outcomes," mimeo, 2013.

134 *Their parents:* Seth Stephens-Davidowitz, "Google, Tell Me. Is My Son a Genius?" *New York Times*, January 19, 2014, SR6. The data for exact searches can be found using Google AdWords. Estimates can also be found with Google Trends, by comparing searches with the words "gifted" and "son" versus "gifted" and "daughter." Compare, for example, https://www.google.com/trends/explore?date=all&geo=US&q=gifted%20son,gifted%20daughter and https://www.google.com/trends/explore?date=all&geo=US&q=overweight%20son,overweight%20daughter. One exception to the general pattern that there are more questions about sons' brains and daughters' bodies is there are more searches for "fat son" than "fat daughter." This seems to be related to the popularity of incest porn discussed earlier. Roughly 20 percent of searches with the words "fat" and "son" also include the word "porn."

135 *girls are 9 percent more likely than boys to be in gifted programs:* "Gender Equity in Education: A Data Snapshot," Office for Civil Rights, U.S. Department of Education, June 2012, http://www2.ed.gov/about/offices/list/ocr/docs/gender-equity-in-education.pdf.

136 *About 28 percent of girls are overweight, while 35 percent of boys are:* Data Resource Center for Child and Adolescent Health,

http://www.childhealthdata.org/browse/survey/results?q=2415
&g=455&a=3879&r=1.

137 *Stormfront profiles:* Stephens-Davidowitz, "The Data of Hate."
The relevant data can be downloaded at sethsd.com, in the data
section headlined "Stormfront."

139 *Stormfront during Donald Trump's candidacy:* Google search interest in Stormfront was similar in October 2016 to the levels it
was during October 2015. This is in stark contrast to the situation
during Obama's first election. In October 2008, search interest in
Stormfront had risen almost 60 percent compared to the previous
October. On the day after Obama was elected, Google searches for
Stormfront had risen roughly tenfold. On the day after Trump was
elected, Stormfront searches rose about two-point-five-fold. This
was roughly equivalent to the rise the day after George W. Bush
was elected in 2004 and may largely reflect news interest among
political junkies.

141 *political segregation on the internet:* Matthew Gentzkow and
Jesse M. Shapiro, "Ideological Segregation Online and Offline,"
Quarterly Journal of Economics 126, no. 4 (2011).

144 *friends on Facebook:* Eytan Bakshy, Solomon Messing, and Lada
A. Adamic, "Exposure to Ideologically Diverse News and Opinion on Facebook," *Science* 348, no. 6239 (2015). They found that,
among the 9 percent of active Facebook users who declare their
ideology, about 23 percent of their friends who also declare an ideology have the opposite ideology and 28.5 percent of the news they
see on Facebook is from the opposite ideology. These numbers are
not directly comparable with other numbers on segregation because they only include the small sample of Facebook users who
declare their ideology. Presumably, these users are much more
likely to be politically active and associate with other politically
active users with the same ideology. If this is correct, the diversity
among all users will be much greater.

144 *one crucial reason that Facebook:* Another factor that makes social
media surprisingly diverse is that it gives a big bonus to extremely
popular and widely shared articles, no matter their political slant.
See Solomon Messing and Sean Westwood, "Selective Exposure

in the Age of Social Media: Endorsements Trump Partisan Source Affiliation When Selecting News Online," 2014.

144 *more friends on Facebook than they do offline:* See Ben Quinn, "Social Network Users Have Twice as Many Friends Online as in Real Life," *Guardian*, May 8, 2011. This article discusses a 2011 study by the Cystic Fibrosis Trust, which found that the average social network user has 121 online friends compared with 55 physical friends. According to a 2014 Pew Research study, the average Facebook user had more than 300 friends. See Aaron Smith, "6 New Facts About Facebook," February 3, 2014, http://www.pewre search.org/fact-tank/2014/02/03/6-new-facts-about-facebook/.

144 *weak ties:* Eytan Bakshy, Itamar Rosenn, Cameron Marlow, and Lada Adamic, "The Role of Social Networks in Information Diffusion," *Proceedings of the 21st International Conference on World Wide Web*, 2012.

145 *"doom-and-gloom predictions haven't come true":* "Study: Child Abuse on Decline in U.S.," Associated Press, December 12, 2011.

146 *did child abuse really drop:* See Seth Stephens-Davidowitz, "How Googling Unmasks Child Abuse," *New York Times*, July 14, 2013, SR5, and Seth Stephens-Davidowitz, "Unreported Victims of an Economic Downturn," mimeo, 2013.

146 *facing long wait times and giving up:* "Stopping Child Abuse: It Begins With You," *The Arizona Republic*, March 26, 2016.

147 *off-the-books ways to terminate a pregnancy:* Seth Stephens-Davidowitz, "The Return of the D.I.Y. Abortion," *New York Times*, March 6, 2016, SR2. Data and more details can be found on my website, sethsd.com, in the section "Self-Induced Abortion."

150 *similar average circulations:* Alliance for Audited Media, Consumer Magazines, http://abcas3.auditedmedia.com/ecirc/magtitle search.asp.

151 *On Facebook:* Author's calculations, on October 4, 2016, using Facebook's Ads Manager.

151 *top ten most visited websites:* "List of Most Popular Websites," Wikipedia. According to Alexa, which tracks browsing behavior, as of September 4, 2016, the most popular porn site was XVideos, and this was the 57th-most-popular website. According to SimilarWeb,

as of September 4, 2016, the most popular porn site was XVideos, and this was the 17th-most-popular website. The top ten, according to Alexa, are Google, YouTube, Facebook, Baidu, Yahoo!, Amazon, Wikipedia, Tencent QQ, Google India, and Twitter.

153 *In the early morning of September 5, 2006:* This story is from David Kirkpatrick, *The Facebook Effect: The Inside Story of the Company That Is Connecting the World* (New York: Simon & Schuster, 2010).

155 *great businesses are built on secrets:* Peter Thiel and Blake Masters, *Zero to One: Notes on Startups, or How to Build the Future* (New York: The Crown Publishing Group, 2014).

157 *says Xavier Amatriain:* I interviewed Xavier Amatriain by phone on May 5, 2015.

159 *top questions Americans had during Obama's 2014:* Author's analysis of Google Trends data.

162 *this time at a mosque:* "The President Speaks at the Islamic Society of Baltimore," YouTube video, posted February 3, 2016, https://www.youtube.com/watch?v=LRRVdVqAjdw.

163 *hateful, rageful searches against Muslims dropped in the hours after the president's address:* Author's analysis of Google Trends data. Searches for "kill Muslims" were lower than the comparable period a week before. In addition, searches that included "Muslims" and one of the top five negative words about this group were lower.

CHAPTER 5: ZOOMING IN

166 *how childhood experiences influence which baseball team you support:* Seth Stephens-Davidowitz, "They Hook You When You're Young," *New York Times*, April 20, 2014, SR5. Data and code for this study can be found on my website, sethsd.com, in the section "Baseball."

170 *the single most important year:* Yair Ghitza and Andrew Gelman, "The Great Society, Reagan's Revolution, and Generations of Presidential Voting," unpublished manuscript.

173 *Chetty explains:* I interviewed Raj Chetty by phone on July 30, 2015.

176 *escape the grim reaper:* Raj Chetty et al., "The Association Be-

tween Income and Life Expectancy in the United States, 2001–2014," *JAMA* 315, no. 16 (2016).

178 *Contagious behavior may be driving some of this:* Julia Belluz, "Income Inequality Is Chipping Away at Americans' Life Expectancy," vox.com, April 11, 2016.

178 *why some people cheat on their taxes:* Raj Chetty, John Friedman, and Emmanuel Saez, "Using Differences in Knowledge Across Neighborhoods to Uncover the Impacts of the EITC on Earnings," *American Economic Review* 103, no. 7 (2013).

180 *I decided to download Wikipedia:* This is from Seth Stephens-Davidowitz, "The Geography of Fame," *New York Times*, March 23, 2014, SR6. Data can be found on my website, sethsd.com, in the section "Wikipedia Birth Rate, by County." For help downloading and coding county of birth of every Wikipedia entrant, I thank Noah Stephens-Davidowitz.

183 *a big city:* For more evidence on the value of cities, see Ed Glaeser, *Triumph of the City* (New York: Penguin, 2011). (Glaeser was my advisor in graduate school.)

191 *many examples of real life imitating art:* David Levinson, ed., *Encyclopedia of Crime and Punishment* (Thousand Oaks, CA: SAGE, 2002).

191 *subjects exposed to a violent film will report more anger and hostility:* Craig Anderson et al., "The Influence of Media Violence on Youth," *Psychological Science in the Public Interest* 4 (2003).

192 *On weekends with a popular violent movie:* Gordon Dahl and Stefano DellaVigna, "Does Movie Violence Increase Violent Crime?" *Quarterly Journal of Economics* 124, no. 2 (2009).

195 *Google searches can also be broken down by the minute:* Seth Stephens-Davidowitz, "Days of Our Digital Lives," *New York Times*, July 5, 2015, SR4.

196 *alcohol is a major contributor to crime:* Anna Richardson and Tracey Budd, "Young Adults, Alcohol, Crime and Disorder," *Criminal Behaviour and Mental Health* 13, no. 1 (2003); Richard A. Scribner, David P. MacKinnon, and James H. Dwyer, "The Risk of Assaultive Violence and Alcohol Availability in Los Angeles County," *American Journal of Public Health* 85, no. 3 (1995);

Dennis M. Gorman, Paul W. Speer, Paul J. Gruenewald, and Erich W. Labouvie, "Spatial Dynamics of Alcohol Availability, Neighborhood Structure and Violent Crime," *Journal of Studies on Alcohol* 62, no. 5 (2001); Tony H. Grubesic, William Alex Pridemore, Dominique A. Williams, and Loni Philip-Tabb, "Alcohol Outlet Density and Violence: The Role of Risky Retailers and Alcohol-Related Expenditures," *Alcohol and Alcoholism* 48, no. 5 (2013).

196 *letting all four of his sons play football:* "Ed McCaffrey Knew Christian McCaffrey Would Be Good from the Start—'The Herd,'" YouTube video, posted December 3, 2015, https://www.youtube.com/watch?v=boHMmp7DpX0.

197 *analyzing piles of data:* Researchers have found more from utilizing this crime data broken down into small time increments. One example? Domestic violence complaints rise immediately after a city's football team loses a game it was expected to win. See David Card and Gordon B. Dahl, "Family Violence and Football: The Effect of Unexpected Emotional Cues on Violent Behavior," *Quarterly Journal of Economics* 126, no. 1 (2011).

197 *Here's how Bill Simmons:* Bill Simmons, "It's Hard to Say Goodbye to David Ortiz," ESPN.com, June 2, 2009, http://www.espn.com/espnmag/story?id=4223584.

198 *how can we predict how a baseball player will perform in the future:* This is discussed in Nate Silver, *The Signal and the Noise: Why So Many Predictions Fail—But Some Don't* (New York: Penguin, 2012).

199 *"beefy sluggers" indeed do, on average, peak early:* Ryan Campbell, "How Will Prince Fielder Age?" October 28, 2011, http://www.fangraphs.com/blogs/how-will-prince-fielder-age/.

199 *Ortiz's doppelgangers':* This data was kindly provided to me by Rob McQuown of Baseball Prospectus.

204 *Kohane asks:* I interviewed Isaac Kohane by phone on June 15, 2015.

205 *James Heywood is an entrepreneur:* I interviewed James Heywood by phone on August 17, 2015.

CHAPTER 6: ALL THE WORLD'S A LAB

207 *February 27, 2000:* This story is discussed, among other places, in Brian Christian, "The A/B Test: Inside the Technology That's Changing the Rules of Business," *Wired*, April 25, 2012, http://www.wired.com/2012/04/ff_abtesting/.

209 *When teachers were paid, teacher absenteeism dropped:* Esther Duflo, Rema Hanna, and Stephen P. Ryan, "Incentives Work: Getting Teachers to Come to School," *American Economic Review* 102, no. 4 (2012).

209 *when Bill Gates learned of Duflo's work:* Ian Parker, "The Poverty Lab," *New Yorker*, May 17, 2010.

211 *Google engineers ran seven thousand A/B tests:* Christian, "The A/B Test."

211 *forty-one marginally different shades of blue:* Douglas Bowman, "Goodbye, Google," stopdesign, March 20, 2009, http://stopdesign.com/archive/2009/03/20/goodbye-google.html.

211 *Facebook now runs:* Eytan Bakshy, "Big Experiments: Big Data's Friend for Making Decisions," April 3, 2014, https://www.facebook.com/notes/facebook-data-science/big-experiments-big-datas-friend-for-making-decisions/10152160441298859/. Sources for information on pharmaceutical studies can be found at "How many clinical trials are started each year?" Quora post, https://www.quora.com/How-many-clinical-trials-are-started-each-year.

211 *Optimizely:* I interviewed Dan Siroker by phone on April 29, 2015.

214 *netting the campaign roughly $60 million:* Dan Siroker, "How Obama Raised $60 Million by Running a Simple Experiment," Optimizely blog, November 29, 2010, https://blog.optimizely.com/2010/11/29/how-obama-raised-60-million-by-running-a-simple-experiment/.

214 *The* Boston Globe *A/B-tests headlines:* The *Boston Globe* A/B tests and results were provided to the author. Some details about the *Globe*'s testing can be found at "The Boston Globe: Discovering and Optimizing a Value Proposition for Content," Marketing Sherpa Video Archive, https://www.marketingsherpa.com/video/boston-globe-optimization-summit2. This includes a recorded

conversation between Peter Doucette of the *Globe* and Pamela Markey at MECLABS.

217 *Benson says:* I interviewed Clark Benson by phone on July 23, 2015.

217 *added a rightward-pointing arrow surrounded by a square:* "Enhancing Text Ads on the Google Display Network," Inside AdSense, December 3, 2012, https://adsense.googleblog.com/2012/12/enhancing-text-ads-on-google-display.html.

218 *Google customers were critical:* See, for example, "Large arrows appearing in google ads—please remove," DoubleClick Publisher Help Forum, https://productforums.google.com/forum/#!topic/dfp/p_TRMqWUF9s.

219 *the rise of behavioral addictions in contemporary society:* Adam Alter, *Irresistible: The Rise of Addictive Technology and the Business of Keeping Us Hooked* (New York: Penguin, 2017).

219 *Top addictions reported to Google:* Author's analysis of Google Trends data.

222 *says Levitt in a lecture:* This is discussed in a video currently featured on the Freakonomics page of the Harry Walker Speakers Bureau, http://www.harrywalker.com/speakers/authors-of-freakonomics/.

225 *beer and soft drink ads run during the Super Bowl:* Wesley R. Hartmann and Daniel Klapper, "Super Bowl Ads," unpublished manuscript, 2014.

226 *a pimply kid in his underwear:* For the strong case that we likely are living in a computer simulation, see Nick Bostrom, "Are We Living in a Computer Simulation?" *Philosophical Quarterly* 53, no. 211 (2003).

227 *Of forty-three American presidents:* Los Angeles Times staff, "U.S. Presidential Assassinations and Attempts," *Los Angeles Times*, January 22, 2012, http://timelines.latimes.com/us-presidential-assassinations-and-attempts/.

227 *Compare John F. Kennedy and Ronald Reagan:* Benjamin F. Jones and Benjamin A. Olken, "Do Assassins Really Change History?" *New York Times*, April 12, 2015, SR12.

227 *Kadyrov died:* A disturbing video of the attack can be seen at "Pa-

rade surprise (Chechnya 2004)," YouTube video, posted March 31, 2009, https://www.youtube.com/watch?v=fHWhs5QkfuY.

227 *Hitler had changed his schedule:* This story is also discussed in Jones and Olken, "Do Assassins Really Change History?"

228 *the effect of having your leader murdered:* Benjamin F. Jones and Benjamin A. Olken, "Hit or Miss? The Effect of Assassinations on Institutions and War," *American Economic Journal: Macroeconomics* 1, no. 2 (2009).

229 *winning the lottery does not:* This point is made in John Tierney, "How to Win the Lottery (Happily)," *New York Times*, May 27, 2014, D5. Tierney's piece discusses the following studies: Bénédicte Apouey and Andrew E. Clark, "Winning Big but Feeling No Better? The Effect of Lottery Prizes on Physical and Mental Health," *Health Economics* 24, no. 5 (2015); Jonathan Gardner and Andrew J. Oswald, "Money and Mental Wellbeing: A Longitudinal Study of Medium-Sized Lottery Wins," *Journal of Health Economics* 26, no. 1 (2007); and Anna Hedenus, "At the End of the Rainbow: Post-Winning Life Among Swedish Lottery Winners," unpublished manuscript, 2011. Tierney's piece also points out that the famous 1978 study—Philip Brickman, Dan Coates, and Ronnie Janoff-Bulman, "Lottery Winners and Accident Victims: Is Happiness Relative?" *Journal of Personality and Social Psychology* 36, no. 8 (1978)—which found that winning the lottery does not make you happy was based on a tiny sample.

229 *your neighbor winning the lottery:* See Peter Kuhn, Peter Kooreman, Adriaan Soetevent, and Arie Kapteyn, "The Effects of Lottery Prizes on Winners and Their Neighbors: Evidence from the Dutch Postcode Lottery," *American Economic Review* 101, no. 5 (2011), and Sumit Agarwal, Vyacheslav Mikhed, and Barry Scholnick, "Does Inequality Cause Financial Distress? Evidence from Lottery Winners and Neighboring Bankruptcies," working paper, 2016.

229 *neighbors of lottery winners:* Agarwal, Mikhed, and Scholnick, "Does Inequality Cause Financial Distress?"

230 *doctors can be motivated by monetary incentives:* Jeffrey Clemens and Joshua D. Gottlieb, "Do Physicians' Financial Incentives Affect Medical Treatment and Patient Health?" *American Eco-*

nomic Review 104, no. 4 (2014). Note that these results do not mean that doctors are evil. In fact, the results might be more troubling if the extra procedures doctors ordered when they were paid more to order them actually saved lives. If this were the case, it would mean that doctors needed to be paid enough to order lifesaving treatments. Clemens and Gottlieb's results suggest, instead, that doctors will order lifesaving treatments no matter how much money they are given to order them. For procedures that don't help all that much, doctors must be paid enough to order them. Another way to say this: doctors don't pay too much attention to monetary incentives for life-threatening stuff; they pay a ton of attention to monetary incentives for unimportant stuff.

231 *$150 million:* Robert D. McFadden and Eben Shapiro, "Finally, a Face to Fit Stuyvesant: A High School of High Achievers Gets a High-Priced Home," *New York Times,* September 8, 1992.

231 *It offers:* Course offerings are available on Stuy's website, http://stuy.enschool.org/index.jsp.

231 *one-quarter of its graduates are accepted:* Anna Bahr, "When the College Admissions Battle Starts at Age 3," *New York Times,* July 29, 2014, http://www.nytimes.com/2014/07/30/upshot/when-the-college-admissions-battle-starts-at-age-3.html.

231 *Stuyvesant trained:* Sewell Chan, "The Obama Team's New York Ties," *New York Times,* November 25, 2008; Evan T. R. Rosenman, "Class of 1984: Lisa Randall," *Harvard Crimson,* June 2, 2009; "Gary Shteyngart on Stuyvesant High School: My New York," YouTube video, posted August 4, 2010, https://www.youtube.com/watch?v=NQ_phGkC-Tk; Candace Amos, "30 Stars Who Attended NYC Public Schools," New York *Daily News,* May 29, 2015.

231 *Its commencement speakers have included:* Carl Campanile, "Kids Stuy High Over Bubba: He'll Address Ground Zero School's Graduation," *New York Post,* March 22, 2002; United Nations Press Release, "Stuyvesant High School's 'Multicultural Tapestry' Eloquent Response to Hatred, Says Secretary-General in Graduation Address," June 23, 2004; "Conan O'Brien's Speech at Stuyvesant's Class of 2006 Graduation in Lincoln Center," YouTube video, posted May 6, 2012, https://www.youtube.com/watch?v=zAMkUE9Oxnc.

231 *Stuy ranked number one:* See https://k12.niche.com/rankings /public-high-schools/best-overall/.

232 *Fewer than 5 percent:* Pamela Wheaton, "8th-Graders Get High School Admissions Results," *Insideschools,* March 4, 2016, http:// insideschools.org/blog/item/1001064-8th-graders-get-high -school-admissions-results.

235 *prisoners assigned to harsher conditions:* M. Keith Chen and Jesse M. Shapiro, "Do Harsher Prison Conditions Reduce Recidivism? A Discontinuity-Based Approach," *American Law and Economics Review* 9, no. 1 (2007).

236 *The effects of Stuyvesant High School?* Atila Abdulkadiroğlu, Joshua Angrist, and Parag Pathak, "The Elite Illusion: Achievement Effects at Boston and New York Exam Schools," *Econometrica* 82, no. 1 (2014). The same null result was independently found by Will Dobbie and Roland G. Fryer Jr., "The Impact of Attending a School with High-Achieving Peers: Evidence from the New York City Exam Schools," *American Economic Journal: Applied Economics* 6, no. 3 (2014).

238 *average graduate of Harvard makes:* See http://www.payscale .com/college-salary-report/bachelors.

238 *similar students accepted to similarly prestigious schools who choose to attend different schools end up in about the same place:* Stacy Berg Dale and Alan B. Krueger, "Estimating the Payoff to Attending a More Selective College: An Application of Selection on Observables and Unobservables," *Quarterly Journal of Economics* 117, no. 4 (2002).

239 *Warren Buffett:* Alice Schroeder, *The Snowball: Warren Buffett and the Business of Life* (New York: Bantam, 2008).

CHAPTER 7: BIG DATA, BIG SCHMATA? WHAT IT CANNOT DO

247 *claimed they could predict which way:* Johan Bollen, Huina Mao, and Xiaojun Zeng, "Twitter Mood Predicts the Stock Market," *Journal of Computational Science* 2, no. 1 (2011).

248 *The tweet-based hedge fund was shut down:* James Mackintosh, "Hedge Fund That Traded Based on Social Media Signals Didn't Work Out," *Financial Times,* May 25, 2012.

250 *could not reproduce the correlation:* Christopher F. Chabris et al., "Most Reported Genetic Associations with General Intelligence Are Probably False Positives," *Psychological Science* (2012).

252 *Zoë Chance:* This story is discussed in TEDx Talks, "How to Make a Behavior Addictive: Zoë Chance at TEDx Mill River," YouTube video, posted May 14, 2013, https://www.youtube.com /watch?v=AHfiKav9fcQ. Some details of the story, such as the color of the pedometer, were fleshed out in interviews. I interviewed Chance by phone on April 20, 2015, and by email on July 11, 2016, and September 8, 2016.

253 *Numbers can be seductive:* This section is from Alex Peysakhovich and Seth Stephens-Davidowitz, "How Not to Drown in Numbers," *New York Times*, May 3, 2015, SR6.

254 *cheated outright in administering those tests:* Brian A. Jacob and Steven D. Levitt, "Rotten Apples: An Investigation of the Prevalence and Predictors of Teacher Cheating," *Quarterly Journal of Economics* 118, no. 3 (2003).

255 *says Thomas Kane:* I interviewed Thomas Kane by phone on April 22, 2015.

256 *"Each measure adds something of value":* Bill and Melinda Gates Foundation, "Ensuring Fair and Reliable Measures of Effective Teaching," http://k12education.gatesfoundation.org/wp-content/up loads/2015/05/MET_Ensuring_Fair_and_Reliable_Measures_Prac titioner_Brief.pdf.

CHAPTER 8: MO DATA, MO PROBLEMS?
WHAT WE SHOULDN'T DO

257 *Recently, three economists:* Oded Netzer, Alain Lemaire, and Michal Herzenstein, "When Words Sweat: Identifying Signals for Loan Default in the Text of Loan Applications," 2016.

258 *about 13 percent of borrowers:* Peter Renton, "Another Analysis of Default Rates at Lending Club and Prosper," October 25, 2012, http://www.lendacademy.com/lending-club-prosper-default -rates/.

261 *Facebook likes are frequently correlated:* Michal Kosinski, David Stillwell, and Thore Graepel, "Private Traits and Attributes Are

Predictable from Digital Records of Human Behavior," *PNAS* 110, no. 15 (2013).

265 *businesses are at the mercy of Yelp reviews:* Michael Luca, "Reviews, Reputation, and Revenue: The Case of Yelp," unpublished manuscript, 2011.

266 *Google searches related to suicide:* Christine Ma-Kellams, Flora Or, Ji Hyun Baek, and Ichiro Kawachi, "Rethinking Suicide Surveillance: Google Search Data and Self-Reported Suicidality Differentially Estimate Completed Suicide Risk," *Clinical Psychological Science* 4, no. 3 (2016).

267 *3.5 million Google searches:* This uses a methodology discussed on my website in the notes on self-induced abortion. I compare searches in the Google category "suicide" to searches for "how to tie a tie." There were 6.6 million Google searches for "how to tie a tie" in 2015. There were 6.5 times more searches in the category suicide. 6.5*6.6/12 » 3.5.

268 *12 murders of Muslims reported as hate crimes:* Bridge Initiative Team, "When Islamophobia Turns Violent: The 2016 U.S. Presidential Election," May 2, 2016, available at http://bridge.georgetown .edu/when-islamophobia-turns-violent-the-2016-u-s-presidential -elections/.

CONCLUSION

272 *What motivated Popper's crusade?:* Karl Popper, *Conjectures and Refutations* (London: Routledge & Kegan Paul, 1963).

275 *mapped every cholera case in the city:* Simon Rogers, "John Snow's Data Journalism: The Cholera Map That Changed the World," *Guardian*, March 15, 2013.

276 *Benjamin F. Jones:* I interviewed Benjamin Jones by phone on June 1, 2015. This work is also discussed in Aaron Chatterji and Benjamin Jones, "Harnessing Technology to Improve K–12 Education," Hamilton Project Discussion Paper, 2012.

283 *people tend not to finish treatises by economists:* Jordan Ellenberg, "The Summer's Most Unread Book Is . . . ," *Wall Street Journal*, July 3, 2014.

INDEX